THE WORLD'S CLASSICS

THE YELLOW WALL-PAPER
AND OTHER STORIES

CHARLOTTE PERKINS GILMAN, America's leading early twentieth-century feminist intellectual, was born Charlotte Anna Perkins, 3 July 1860. She was related to the famous Beecher family on her father's side, although he deserted Charlotte and her mother soon after her birth. Her childhood was marked by genteel poverty, frequent moves, and her mother's withholding of physical affection and her disapproval of Gilman's imaginative life. She had three important female friendships—with Martha Luther, then with Grace Channing, and Adeline Knapp, a San Francisco journalist. Her marriage in 1884 to the artist Walter Stetson was plagued by the depression she suffered periodically for the rest of her life. Her marriage over, she left Providence, Rhode Island, for Pasadena, California in 1888 with her daughter and Grace Channing. In California between 1890 and 1895 she began her lifetime career as a reform writer and lecturer on women, economics, and ethics. *Women and Economics* (1898) made her internationally famous. Her marriage in 1900 to Houghton Gilman, a younger cousin and cultivated lawyer, thrived until his death in 1934. Between 1900 and 1915 she was in great demand as a public lecturer, and as owner and author of her own monthly magazine, the *Forerunner* (1909–16), she wrote non-fiction, a story for each issue, and several serialized novels. In 1935 she took her own life: she had incurable cancer and carried out her plan to end her life as she had lived it, on her own terms.

ROBERT SHULMAN is Professor of English and American Studies at the University of Washington. He is the author of *Social Criticism and Nineteenth-Century American Fictions* and numerous articles on nineteenth- and twentieth-century American literature and political culture.

THE WORLD'S CLASSICS

CHARLOTTE PERKINS GILMAN

The Yellow Wall-Paper and Other Stories

Edited with an Introduction by
ROBERT SHULMAN

Oxford   New York

OXFORD UNIVERSITY PRESS

1995

Oxford University Press, Walton Street, Oxford OX2 6DP

Oxford New York
Athens Auckland Bangkok Bombay
Calcutta Cape Town Dar es Salaam Delhi
Florence Hong Kong Istanbul Karachi
Kuala Lumpur Madras Madrid Melbourne
Mexico City Nairobi Paris Singapore
Taipei Tokyo Toronto

and associated companies in
Berlin Ibadan

Oxford is a trade mark of Oxford University Press

British Library Cataloguing in Publication Data
Data available

Library of Congress Cataloging in Publication Data
Gilman, Charlotte Perkins, 1860–1935.
The yellow wall-paper, and other stories / edited with an
introduction by Robert Shulman.
p. cm.— (The world's classics)
Includes bibliographical references.
1. Women—United States—Fiction. I. Shulman, Robert, 1930–
II. Title. III. Series.
PS1744.G57A6 1995   813'.4—dc20   94-47081
ISBN 0-19-282449-X (paperback)

1 3 5 7 9 10 8 6 4 2

Typeset by Best-set Typesetter Ltd., Hong Kong
Printed in Great Britain by
BPC Paperbacks Ltd.
Aylesbury, Bucks

CONTENTS

INTRODUCTION

CHARLOTTE PERKINS GILMAN—then Charlotte Perkins Stetson—wrote 'The Yellow Wall-Paper' in 1890. More than a century later the story continues to challenge and disturb readers. In tapping into and transforming her deepest feelings about the sources of her own depression and brush with insanity, Gilman illuminates the situation of many middle-class women then and now. The specific details have changed—unlike the narrator of 'The Yellow Wall-Paper', women, for example, are no longer confined to the house. Women are now free to work and 'congenial work', the narrator believes, 'with excitement and change, would do me good', would help cure a sickness her physician husband refuses to recognize as real. But if the details have changed, 'the pattern' has turned out to be remarkably persistent and it is 'the pattern' the narrator reacts against. Literally the pattern of the wallpaper, metaphorically 'the pattern' comes to suggest the configuration of values and practices that govern the relation between men and women, husbands and wives, male physicians and female patients, which is to say that 'the pattern' involves the socially acceptable power relations of a world controlled by men. This pattern may have changed less than the particulars of Gilman's narrative.

As even this brief account indicates, in 'The Yellow Wall-Paper' Gilman probes conflicts and contradictions in a suggestive way that has compelled readers, first at the time of its original publication in the *New England Magazine* in 1892, a little later in booklet form in 1899, again in William Dean Howells's *The Great Modern American Stories* in 1920, and, after a long period of neglect, in multiple reprints following its rediscovery in the 1973 Feminist Press edition. The earliest readers may or may not have understood Gilman's profound questioning of conventional gender relations and the situation of middle-class women clinically depressed by what they experienced as irreconcilable conflicts between their desire for freedom and their acceptance of the values of 'true womanhood'. Horace E. Scudder, the editor of the influential *Atlantic Monthly*, rejected

'The Yellow Wall-Paper' because, as he said in his accompanying note, 'I could not forgive myself if I made others as miserable as I have made myself'![1] As one of the gate-keepers of the late Victorian period, Scudder may well have seen what Gilman was up to and refused to publish because he disapproved.

Two other contemporary readers, one sympathetic, one negative, focused on 'The Yellow Wall-Paper' as a story of 'mental disease' (*Living*, 120). Gilman herself reinforced this emphasis in her 1913 essay, 'Why I Wrote "The Yellow Wallpaper?"'[2] She wanted, she said, to show 'the error of his ways' to the prominent American neurologist, S. Weir Mitchell, so that he would change his famous rest cure for 'neurasthenic' and 'hysterical' women. In 'The Yellow Wall-Paper' John is a doctor as well as the husband of a young wife he is treating for a 'nervous condition'. Because as both husband and doctor his values and control are central to 'the pattern' the narrator finds increasingly unbearable, it is too limiting to see the story simply or even primarily as an exposure of Mitchell. This important physician had nonetheless treated Gilman in 1887 and his rest cure is undermined in the story.

In 'The Yellow Wall-Paper' Gilman shows that the narrator, as opposed to John and S. Weir Mitchell, has ideas of her own about the curative value for her of work, change, and lively company. The narrator's prescription for a cure makes better sense than 'the phosphates or phosphites—whichever it is—and tonics', the rigid schedule, the constant feeding, the raw meat, the compulsory rest, and the prohibition against intellectual and social stimulation that John, following Mitchell, prescribes and enforces. Underlying the Mitchell rest cure is the assumption that women are intellectually inferior to men, that the source of their 'neurasthenia' or 'hysteria' ('slight hysteria', in the narrator's case) is the overuse of their minds, and that even though a physical, neurological cause was posited but could never be located, physical treatment—air, rest, massage, feeding, and then moderate exercise—was prescribed to effect a cure. Total

---

[1] Charlotte Perkins Gilman, *The Living of Charlotte Perkins Gilman: An Autobiography*, intro. Ann J. Lane (Madison: University of Wisconsin Press, 1935, 1990), 119. Subsequent references will be in parentheses in the text.

[2] Gilman, see Appendix B, p. 331 of this book.

dependence on the will and authority of the male physician was basic, hence the isolation and the prohibition against lively company.

Mitchell avoided some of the more draconian practices such as 'leeching, cauterization, and "normal" ovariotomy–procedures that were also used to treat women with nervous ailments'.[3] Although Mitchell had a devoted following and became wealthy and internationally renowned, his rest cure did not work for intellectually active women like Gilman, Jane Addams, Alice James, Virginia Woolf, and two of Gilman's Beecher aunts. It did not work for William Dean Howells's daughter, Winifred, whose autopsy revealed, not a problem with the will, self-control, or the mind, but an organic problem Mitchell's theories prevented him from seeing.

Unlike Gilman, who is challenging the authority, assumptions, and practices of a major representative of the emerging culture of professional medicine, the narrator of 'The Yellow Wall-Paper' keeps her ideas of a cure to herself. Except in her private journal, she defers to John as husband and physician. Through ironic indirection, Gilman powerfully uses the narrator's insights, acquiescence, and covert rebellion to undercut the authority John embodies in both these roles, which also engage the basic issue of late nineteenth-century assumptions about men and women.

S. Weir Mitchell, then, is only part of the context for 'The Yellow Wall-Paper'. This story and the most powerful of Gilman's subsequent intellectual works are grounded emotionally in her struggles throughout the 1880s. These conflicts themselves are inseparable from the strains Gilman experienced as a member of a national culture and the Beecher family tradition that significantly influenced that culture. A key figure is Walter Stetson, a young artist from a financially poor branch of the Stetson hat family. When Stetson proposed to her seventeen days after they met on 12 January 1882 and the two fell in love, Gilman—then Charlotte Anna Perkins—was committed to improving the world and making a name for herself. She was, after

[3] Ellen L. Bassuk, 'The Rest Cure: Repetition or Resolution of Victorian Women's Conflicts?', in *The Female Body in Western Culture*, ed. Susan Rubin Suléiman (Cambridge: Harvard University Press, 1985), 139.

all, a Beecher whose great aunts were Harriet Beecher Stowe, Catherine Beecher, and Isabel Beecher, three of the most influential American reformers of the nineteenth century. Gilman was 21, in vibrant health, and she knew that marriage was at odds with her ambitions. 'I cannot marry,' she wrote Stetson after he proposed, 'although I am fitted to enjoy all that marriage can give to the utmost. Were I to marry, my thoughts, my acts, my whole life would be centered in husband and children. To do the work that I have planned I must be free.'[4]

She admired Stetson, she was strongly attracted to him sexually, and for two years she struggled to reconcile her commitment to herself and the world with her susceptibility to the demands of conventions she both accepted and rebelled against. After Stetson experienced an emotional setback, on 20 May 1883 she finally agreed to marry him but insisted on a year's delay. Even before her marriage she was suffering from depression, although before meeting Stetson she had been in excellent health and she continued to be an accomplished gymnast.

Before and continuing into their marriage, Gilman tried to undergo a secular, women's version of the Protestant conversion experience, a process that contributed significantly to the agony of her emotional state. The pressure of Stetson's fervently held religious views and his admiration and desire for her reinforced her feelings for him and her own sense of what was right and proper for women. Like one of her great grandfather Lyman Beecher's Calvinist communicants, she tried to convince herself to be subservient, to become as a little child, to tame her will, and to defer to Stetson. 'She is very gentle and tenderly careful now,' Stetson wrote in his diary for 16 March 1883, two months before their engagement. 'She is like an affectionate child that wants to be taken in arms and fondled—so confiding and desirous of being near me she is. One sees little just now of the daring and independent manner of the Charlotte that I first knew. . . . She has tamed her effort to doing things for me and that has had a strange effect on her. It has made her more like what is best in other women—more thoughtful, bland, gracious, humble, dependent' (_Endure_, 140).

---

[4] Mary Armfield Hill, ed., _Endure: The Diaries of Charles Walter Stetson_ (Philadelphia: Temple University Press, 1985), 32. Subsequent references will be cited in parentheses in the text.

Gilman agreed but also perceptively observed that 'I have lost *power*. I do not feel myself so strong a person as I was before. I seem to have taken a lower seat, to have become less in some way, to have shrunk' (*Endure*, 149). Her will none the less continually reasserted itself. 'She had one of those spasms of wanting to make a name for herself in the world by doing good work,' Stetson wrote on 22 March 1883, 'wanting to have people know her as Charlotte Perkins, not the wife of me. She drew back with her old time feeling of independence from the prospect of sinking herself in our community' (*Endure*, 144). For Stetson these 'relapses' seem 'almost like a form of insanity. It is all her old ambitious "freedom"-loving nature rising in rebellion against the "weakness" of tenderness and love' (*Endure*, 246).

In the process, Gilman suffered rounds of debilitating depression before and after her marriage, and before and after the birth of her daughter, whom she named after Catherine Beecher. Six months before the wedding Stetson observed in his diary that 'she was very very sad'. In imagery reminiscent of 'The Yellow Wall-Paper' Gilman, he goes on, revealed her state of mind in 'a picture of a wan creature who had traversed a desert and came, worn out, to an insurmountable wall which extended around the earth. It was powerful,' Stetson realized, 'albeit the doing of it was not so artistic as might be. It *was* powerful. If she keeps on like that she will do great things. I know it was a literal transcript of her mind' (*Endure*, 244). Also several months before her marriage, Gilman published an equally powerful revelation of her state of mind, the poem, 'In Duty Bound', an anatomy of the imprisonment she feared marriage would entail. A month before her engagement she wrote in her diary for 15 April 1883, 'write four sheets to Walter. Read a little Rossetti. Cry a good deal.'[5] Uncontrollable crying recurs periodically for the next several years.

From Stetson's point of view six months into the marriage, 'she is more sensitive and easily fatigued both physically & mentally & at times despondent, especially when she has fears that all that dreamed of life of great usefulness, may be past or beyond her reach' (*Endure*, 264). Married less than a year, in her diary

---

[5] Charlotte Perkins Gilman Collection, Arthur and Elizabeth Schlesinger Library, Radcliffe College.

she gives details about housework, reading, darning hose and begins her 27 January 1885 entry, 'do not feel well. Sleep between 11 & 12.' For 28 January, 'not well yet. Manage after a two hours sleep to do my usual housework, but hardly.' For 29 January: 'worse'. For 30 January, 'much better this morning. Wash dishes during the day and cook some rice for supper. Worse in afternoon and evening, but not so bad as yesterday. . . . Bad night, lame all over.' On 7 September 1886, 'Walter slept with baby.' On 8 September: 'feel miserably.' On 9 September, 'feel better. . . . read again in the evening.' On the 11th—'feel dismal,' although a four mile row on the river 'did me good.' By the 13th, 'a fairly good day. But always the pain underneath.'[6]

Although Stetson helped during the long stretches when Gilman was incapacitated and although he loved her, Stetson also basically accepted the conventional divisions: he was to be in his studio painting and trying to make a living for his family; she was to support him emotionally and care for the house and child. Gilman, however, was in her own right a skilful artist trained at the Rhode Island School of Design. And she continued to have intense intellectual ambitions that conflicted with the demands and expectations of a conventional marriage. Further complicating her situation, Stetson criticized her for being too demonstrably ardent, a tendency she then controlled.

Both Stetson and Gilman were thoughtful, high-minded, conscientious people. Stetson's view of what was right and proper carried the authority of his personal presence and the weight of conventional, religiously and socially sanctioned opinion. On her side, day after day Gilman experienced the deepest conflicts, since she accepted and reacted against what she and others expected of her. In part she was living through a central, unresolved contradiction in the Beecher tradition. Her great aunts were the prime formulators of the ideology of domesticity and 'the true woman', self-sacrificing and devoted to home, husband, and children. But for Stowe and Catherine Beecher, the domestic ideology also empowered women by giving them a sphere of moral authority and physical control within the home.

[6] Charlotte Perkins Gilman Collection.

In their writing and personal lives, moreover, they embodied the values of intellectual achievement and fierce independence. In some of the most influential works of nineteenth-century American culture—in Stowe's *Uncle Tom's Cabin* (1852), Catherine Beecher's *A Treatise on Domestic Economy* (1842), and Stowe and Beecher's *The American Woman's Home* (1869)—they actively engaged the dilemmas of the middle-class American woman. They responded to their situation creatively and productively. Responding to what they experienced as irreconcilable conflicts, they also suffered periods of clinical depression. Working within the same cultural and family tradition, Gilman produced major work and she, too, suffered from severe depression, though with declining frequency during the later years of her life.

Reinforcing these conflicts, her immediate family experience was with a father who deserted his family soon after she was born and with a mother who none the less pined for her absent husband, withheld physical affection from her daughter, and was critical of her daughter's inner, imaginative life. Far from the home as a stable refuge, moreover, she spent her childhood on the move in the homes of relatives for whom she was a poor relation or in rented homes sporadically supported by an absent father. At every point her immediate experience contradicted the domestic ideology, which for women privileged self-sacrificing devotion to home, husband, and child. At the same time that she rebelled, however, Gilman was also susceptible to the values of devotion to husband and child. She was simultaneously compelled by the Beecher commitment to independence and intellectual achievement, embodied in her great aunts and father.

During her worst period of agonized depression in the middle 1880s, as her condition became increasingly serious Gilman accepted an invitation from her friend Grace Channing to spend a winter in Pasadena. To an extent she acted like her father. She left her husband behind, placed her daughter with her mother, and began to feel better almost as soon as the train left. When she returned, so did her bouts of depression. At a later stage, she consulted S. Weir Mitchell. His concluding advice was 'to live as domestic a life as possible, to have but two hours' intellectual life a day, and never to touch pen, brush or pencil again, as long as I lived'.[7] Gilman rejected his warnings against intellectual activity. In the months before seeing Mitchell in April 1887, she had begun to deal with her situation by trying to change some of its sources. She became intensely involved in suffrage activity and 'the woman's question'. After she left Stetson in 1888, she probed the sources even more deeply in 'The Yellow Wall-Paper'.

Because Stetson's point of view is available in his diaries, a drama as compelling as any in the nineteenth century emerges from the interplay between him and Gilman, whose diaries and letters also survive. Stetson comments in detail on Gilman's condition, includes letters from her with his own analysis, and, in *Endure*, the editor, Mary Hill, has also included Grace Channing's later commentary (Grace Channing became Stetson's second wife). Both Stetson and Gilman are active correspondents and diarists, so that the conflicts are powerfully, eloquently articulated. Gilman transformed her version into 'The Yellow Wall-Paper', *Women and Economics* (1898), and the short stories of the 1890s and of the *Forerunner* years (1909–16), or rather, she drew actively on her experience and went on to create a powerful critique of and alternatives to 'the pattern' she knew from the inside. In particular, it is worth stressing that her depression precedes the birth of her child. The narrator of 'The Yellow Wall-Paper' is not identical with Gilman but she has transformed her own condition into the 'nervous condition' in the story, so that the narrator's initial and deepening sickness is much more profound than the postpartum depression critics sometimes mention.

Gilman's biography as it emerges from and illuminates late nineteenth-century American culture and the Beecher family tradition contributes to but hardly exhausts the meaning of 'The Yellow Wall-Paper'. Critics of 'The Yellow Wall-Paper' from William Dean Howells in 1919 to Gilman's 1990 biographer, Ann J. Lane, have seen it as a horror story, to cite another important perspective. For Lane the complex feminist implications of 'The Yellow Wall-Paper' simply supplement its 'power as a story of horror'.[8] For Howells, who wants to recognize 'the

[7] Gilman, see Appendix B, p. 331 of this book.
[8] Ann J. Lane, *To 'Herland' and Beyond: The Life and Work of Charlotte Perkins Gilman* (New York: Pantheon Books, 1990), 130.

supreme awfulness' of the story, the 'awfulness' is unspecified.[9] 'Horror' and 'awfulness' imply the Gothic tradition Gilman uses to help her stylize and generalize her personal experience. At the outset the narrator of 'The Yellow Wall-Paper' hopes that the secluded mansion they have rented for the summer will prove to be 'haunted', a hope that is disturbingly fulfilled as the narrator thinks she sees a figure gradually emerge from behind the wall-paper. The haunted castle, the imprisoned wife, and especially the exploration of the ordinarily repressed all characterize the Gothic tale.

In Poe's influential version—in her autobiography Gilman associates 'The Yellow Wall-Paper' with Poe—the house becomes a symbol of the divided, diseased mind, as in 'The Fall of the House of Usher' and the rigidly segmented rooms and self-enclosed castle of 'The Masque of the Red Death'. Gilman retains Poe's allegory or near allegory—'the pattern' of the wall-paper and its influence on the narrator and her projected alter ego, for example, gradually come to suggest the control and power the narrator hates but finds herself unable to resist directly. Gilman similarly retains Poe's concern with and insights into the workings of the divided, compartmentalized mind and the process leading to madness. For Poe and Gilman, moreover, aesthetics are central. Roderick Usher and the prince of 'The Masque of the Red Death', for example, are both imaginative men whose Taste and imagination lead to the mental disintegration Poe fears. Gilman reverses the emphasis: in opposition to John, her narrator values the imagination and values the aesthetic coherence she cannot find in the contradictions of the conventional pattern, which is to say that she exhausts herself trying to find the meaning she longs for in the patterns of the conventional order. Another difference with Poe, then, is that Gilman adds the crucial dimension of feminist anger and sensitivity to dilemmas experienced by many middle-class women. In this basic respect her story is an achievement not only of the Gothic in general but also of the female Gothic in particular.

In the 1790s Ann Radcliffe established the conventions of this popular genre. A century later, as Eugenia C. Delamotte perceptively observes, 'Gilman both exploits and explores the conven-

[9] Quoted in Lane, *'Herland'*, 146.

tions of the genre from a feminist perspective.' Gilman, that is, gives an independent 're-visioning' of her predecessors' insight that Gothic fear is a mask for anger, that the imprisoned woman is both vulnerable and seeking communion with the repressed Other Woman, 'that woman's "separate sphere" is a house of horrors', and, as Delamotte concludes, 'that the "mysteries" heroines try so desperately to decipher while immured in Gothic space are only a disguise for the real mystery, woman herself'.[10]

The complexities, ambivalence, and depth of Gilman's feminist probing of the female Gothic bear on her version of another American cultural tradition, that of the divided self. In Melville's 'Bartleby, the Scrivener: A Tale of Wall Street' (1853), Hawthorne's 'My Kinsman, Major Molineux' (1832), Bellamy's *Looking Backward* (1888), and James's 'The Jolly Corner' (1909), for example, typically the divisions within and between selves result from the pressures of the market society. These works focus on maimed alter egos, fierce doubles, and severe inner divisions that mirror the Wall Street offices and the involvement in the acquisitive process of success in cut-throat America. In all of these works and the country they emerge from and illuminate, the energies of the market society drive and divide the inhabitants of the masculine sphere of power.

In 'The Yellow Wall-Paper' these market society energies, values, and practices are in the background. The narrator is writing what is in effect a Gothic tale but she is denied a public, professional outlet for her work. She values 'congenial work', presumably that of professional author, and she criticizes the profession of perfect housekeeper, represented by John's conventional sister, Jennie. John's power and control, his rigid practicality and contempt for 'fantasy', his combination of love and condescension, his—and to an extent the narrator's—assumption that he is entitled to pursue his career outside and she is to remain at home—all indicate the pervasiveness of the underlying division between the masculine sphere of work and power and the feminine sphere of domesticity. This gender division, an important component of the late nineteenth-century market so-

---

[10] Eugenia C. Delamotte, 'Male and Female Mysteries in "The Yellow Wall-paper"', *Legacy*, 5 (Spring 1988), 3, 5, 11.

ciety, is foregrounded in 'The Yellow Wall-Paper' much more prominently than in the typical American work probing the fierce alter egos and divided selves of the dominant tradition.

For Charlotte Perkins Gilman—or Charlotte Anna Perkins—the divided self took the form of a contest 'to satisfy the demands of two opposing natures in myself', as she wrote her intimate friend Martha Luther in one of a series of letters in July 1881.[11] In contrast to Martha, who had met the man she was to marry a year later, to explain why she herself is 'glad not to marry', Gilman identified one of these sides as 'the mother side', the other 'as a self, you know, not merely . . . a woman, or that useful animal a wife and mother'. The mother-wife-woman side is related to marriage and 'inexpressible instincts'. The self—'individual strength and development of personal power of character'—is related to achievement, to working 'for mankind', and 'will I think make up, and more than make up in usefulness and effect, for the other happiness that part of me would so enjoy' (24 July 1881, 54–5). In choosing to reject marriage for a life devoted to mankind, Gilman believed—prematurely, as it turned out—that she had at last resolved 'the long tiresome effort to satisfy the demands of two opposing natures in myself, and all I've done now is suppress the weaker one once and for all', so that the mother-woman side is also for Gilman the 'weaker' side (30 July 1881, 56). A writer who sees herself as divided or compartmentalized and who gives gender traits to each side might understandably imagine the narrator and her 'creeping' but defiant alter ego in 'The Yellow Wall-Paper'. In expressing her feelings for Grace Channing, Gilman wrote in December 1890 'it is awful to be a man inside and not able to marry the woman you love! When Martha married it cracked my heart a good deal—your loss will finish it.'[12] Gilman, however, does not explore this sexual division in 'The Yellow Wall-Paper' or in any of her works.

For Gilman, other personal sources of the cultural tendency to divide or discipline the self go back to her childhood. Always

[11] Juliet A. Langley, '"Audacious Fancies": A Collection of Letters from Charlotte Perkins Gilman to Martha Luther', *Trivia*, 6 (1985), 56 (30 July 1881). Subsequent references will be cited by date and page in parentheses in the text.
[12] Quoted in Lane, *'Herland'*, 130.

imaginative, she had a vital inner life filled with stories about 'a Prince and Princess of magic powers, who went about the world collecting unhappy children and taking them to a guarded Paradise in the South Seas' (*Living*, 23). As she recognized when she included this account in her autobiography, Gilman's imaginative life was a refuge against difficult family circumstances. When her mother learned that Gilman was making up stories, she pressured her to stop, on the questionable grounds that imaginative activity was a threat to sanity. At 13 Gilman promised she would give up the 'inner fortress' of her fantasy life until she reached 21. The result was a disciplined compartmentalizing of the self that leaves its mark on the characterization of the narrator, the alter ego, and the role of the imagination in 'The Yellow Wall-Paper', just as it illuminates Gilman's depression and perhaps her avoidance of imaginative and emotional depths in her subsequent fiction.

In the title of the story in the *New England Magazine*, the wallpaper the narrator makes into a symbol of her situation is spelled 'wall-paper'. This spelling emphasizes two elements, the wall or barrier, finally the bars and prison; and the paper, the surface on which is printed 'the pattern', the visual text the narrator interprets or onto which she projects her feelings about the conventional values and practices which control her life. Focusing on the wallpaper as text and on writing and textuality as concerns was the contribution of a series of important essays written on 'The Yellow Wall-Paper' during the decade after Elaine Hedges and the Feminist Press made 'The Yellow Wall-Paper' available for contemporary readers in 1973. Another persistent interest in Gilman criticism is her biography, a revealing approach as long as we recognize that in 'The Yellow Wall-Paper' the narrator and her text are not identical with the Charlotte Perkins Gilman (or Charlotte Perkins Stetson) who created them. The wallpaper itself, for example, is Gilman's invention, not part of her breakdown. In even more basic ways the narrator, action, and imagery of the story are independent of Gilman, who puts them to complex uses.

For all its depth 'The Yellow Wall-Paper' is accessible, it responds to close analysis, and it invites and rewards active interpretation. 'The Yellow Wall-Paper' has opened up to critics sensitive to the issues of textuality as well as to Freudian and Lacanian psychology. It has been illuminated as transformed autobiography, as female Gothic, and, in multiple ways as critique of gender relations. As a result, we now have a sense of Gilman's craft, intuition, and understanding, of her success in showing that each stage of her narrator's covert rebellion and gradual descent into madness is precipitated by the control, excessive oversight, and essential neglect of representatives of a conventional order the narrator cannot stand or overtly stand against. Recent critics have rightly stressed the tensions and ambiguities, particularly at the end and in the merging of narrator and alter ego, all of which defy the definitiveness of closure. To what extent is the narrator's madness a triumph, to what extent a painful, qualified liberation revealing her continuing resistance and ties to the pattern she can neither stand or completely escape? To what extent and on what grounds is the narrator a reliable narrator? Far from exhausting the implications of the story, the varying approaches to it remind us that 'The Yellow Wall-Paper' is open to interpretation, particularly to the interpretation of readers who are enjoying Gilman for the first time.

'The Yellow Wall-Paper' is so compelling that as readers go on to her other short stories they may feel disappointed, since except for 'The Giant Wistaria' and 'The Rocking Chair', both in the Gothic mode, Gilman's subsequent stories lack the emotional depth and suggestive power of the work generally and deservedly accepted as the masterpiece of her fiction. Since Gilman's stories have a genuine interest of their own, different from that of 'The Yellow Wall-Paper' but authentic and rewarding, it would be a shame to simply pass over them. They, too, deserve and respond to our attention. Readers now have a chance to read a large, representative selection of a body of fiction that has previously been available—or, more properly, unavailable—only in hard-to-find magazines. Of particular interest are the generally overlooked stories she wrote at the same time as and shortly after 'The Yellow Wall-Paper', between 1890 and 1895.

Speaking of her first collection of poems, *In This Our World* (1893), Gilman said, 'I don't call it a book of poems. I call it a tool box. It was written to drive nails with.'[13] She is also noted for her assessment of 'The Yellow Wall-Paper', 'that it was no more "literature" than my other stuff, being written "with a purpose". In my judgment', Gilman concluded in her autobiography 'it is a pretty poor thing to write, to talk, without a purpose' (*Living*, 121). The opposition between 'literature' and writing 'with a purpose', however, does not necessarily hold. In her practice of engaged literature, Gilman in particular drew on her study of writers as diverse as Henry James and Louisa May Alcott, Mark Twain and Mary E. Wilkins, Edgar Allan Poe and Edward Bellamy, George Eliot and Nathaniel Hawthorne.

She published these studies during an extraordinary five months in 1894–5, at the end of her stay in California. During this period Gilman and two friends lived together and wrote and edited a weekly journal, the *Impress*, in her words a publication 'for men and women of wide aims and views'. As part of her contribution Gilman wrote a series of 'imitations', each weekly story in the manner of a different unnamed writer. They were not parodies but serious attempts to catch the essence of writers like Henry James and George Eliot but also revealing of Gilman's thematic concerns and stylistic insights. Prizes were awarded to the reader who identified the writer. Gilman also followed up with a revealing 'Story Study', an analysis of the writer's underlying qualities. This remarkable group of stories and commentaries takes us into Gilman's workshop and shows us a writer sensitive to the nuances of style and creatively engaged with the art of fiction. Gilman's 'nails' and 'tool box' did not emerge from a vacuum.

In 1890 at exactly the same time that in 'The Yellow Wall-Paper' she was working herself back to sanity by probing the full implications of her own marriage, ambivalence, and 'cure', Gilman was giving inspiring lectures to the clubs formed to promote Edward Bellamy's Nationalist movement. In 1889 or early 1890 Gilman read Bellamy's *Looking Backward* (1888). Bellamy lucidly criticized the inequities of robber-baron capitalism and as a solution proposed a co-operative society modelled

[13] Quoted in Mary A. Hill, *Charlotte Perkins Gilman: The Making of a Radical Feminist 1860–1896* (Philadelphia: Temple University Press, 1980), 214.

on a rational, centrally-organized industrial army. In Bellamy's new society women were freed of household drudgery and instead performed useful outside work, the routine of cooking and cleaning replaced by such innovations as communal kitchens. *Looking Backward* strongly appealed to middle-class women appalled at the misery of the industrial poor and the ravages of labor-management warfare and inspired by the liberating prospects Bellamy brought to life. Bellamy's novel had an immediate impact—as a nineteenth-century cultural force it rivaled *Uncle Tom's Cabin* in sales and influence. People organized thousands of Nationalist Clubs to implement Bellamy's ideas. In California in the early 1890s Gilman began her lifetime career as lecturer and reformer in the talks she gave to these clubs on such topics as 'Human Nature' (1890), 'The Labor Movement' (1892), and 'The Ethics of Woman's Work' (1894).[14]

In her lectures Gilman brought into the open the changes and the new values she implied in 'The Yellow Wall-Paper'. She was also developing ideas about a fully human life based on meaningful work and about the basic role of women and conscious change as integral to human evolution. These ideas came to their most compelling expression in *Women and Economics* (1898), the book that made Gilman internationally famous. If Bellamy gave Gilman her initial impetus and audience, in 'Our Better Halves' (1888) and *Dynamic Sociology* (1883), Lester Ward gave her a core idea, that women, not men, were the central force of human evolution. In her non-fiction Gilman used the scientific prestige of Darwinian evolutionary thought—or rather, of reform Darwinism—to place her criticism of the treatment and prospects of women in a sweeping universal context.

For Gilman and her contemporaries this vantage point was persuasive and gave her intellectual credibility but her evolutionary reconstruction has not worn well. Gilman is more compelling in imagining an alternative society in utopias like *Herland* (1915) and *Moving the Mountain* (1911) than she is in creating a fictional evolutionary past in works like *Women and Economics* and *The Man-Made World* (1911), although in other respects

[14] Larry Ceplair, ed., *Charlotte Perkins Gilman: A Nonfiction Reader* (New York: Columbia University Press, 1991), 25–83.

these books are still vital. Her universal approach, however, obscures cultural differences and highlights the extent to which for her, contemporary white, middle-class America equates with the human race at its best and worst. Gilman would have been receptive to both the concepts of culture and of ideology. She could easily have used these intellectual formulations to expose the practices which in her evolutionary account made women into vestiges of a primitive stage which civilization had moved beyond in most areas of modern life. The concepts of culture or ideology might also have helped Gilman avoid her slippery use of 'race', sometimes to mean 'human race', sometimes national-ities or skin colour, and often uncritically to privilege white America.

In her short fiction the evolutionary apparatus is absent but her fictional world is none the less white and middle class. Ex-cept on occasion as racially stereotyped servants, as in 'In Two Houses', African Americans are absent and so is the ethnic diver-sity that was transforming America. Because in her short stories Gilman is not concerned with evolution, however, she concen-trates on her strengths. Particularly in her *Forerunner* stories, she poses, explores, and offers workable solutions to a range of women's problems. Instead of relying on formulas or abstrac-tions, Gilman has a gift for particularizing and humanizing issues. Her stories have general implications but because they often emerge from the immediate circumstances of Gilman's life, at best they have an uncontrived authenticity. They may have 'a purpose' but the purpose usually emerges from the inside and is not externally or mechanically imposed. As in 'The Un-expected' (1890), written at about the same time as 'The Yellow Wall-Paper', Gilman also deals jokingly with personal conflicts that she handles tragically in 'The Yellow Wall-Paper' or, as in 'Dr Clair's Place' (1915), she works out alternatives to the Mitchell rest cure and 'The Yellow Wall-Paper' situation. The differences with 'The Yellow Wall-Paper' give some of the later stories their interest.

In California between 'The Yellow Wall-Paper' in 1890 and the *Impress* 'imitations' and 'An Unnatural Mother' in 1894–5, Gilman wrote a significant and still neglected body of short fiction. Even when they have a realistic setting, these and her later stories are often fables or parables. In the satiric fable 'An Extinct Angel' (1891), Gilman disposes of the dominant nineteenth-century view of the angelic 'true woman'. As her own conflicts about and within marriage indicate and as the narrator of 'The Yellow Wall-Paper' confirms, 'the true woman' syndrome was still influential—and in ways we prefer to downplay, perhaps still is. Gilman skillfully exposes the cult of self-sacrifice, cheerful devotion to husband and child, and immersion in a domesticity whose dirty work she unmasks, as she does the devotion to purity, which for Gilman prevents women, 'the angels, from learning anything about our gross human wisdom'.

In a female Gothic variation on these themes, in 'The Giant Wistaria' (1891) Gilman sets up an interplay between a contemporary frame-tale and a Colonial story of a stigmatized illegitimate birth. 'The Giant Wistaria' is alive with suggestive implications about unjust patriarchal dogmatism, rebellious and fatally suppressed female sexuality, and the return into the present of what has been culturally repressed in the past. The relation of the frame-tale and its characters to the original story also hints that it would be a mistake for us, another century later, to deny the power of the ancient attitudes and practices Gilman has Jack and Jenny expose.

'Dark', a key word in 'The Giant Wistaria', is matched by 'darkness', the concluding word in 'Through This' (1893). The two stories none the less differ in tone, language, and genre. They illustrate the extent to which, particularly during the early 1890s, Gilman was experimenting with fictional approaches. In 'Through This' a young middle-class wife and mother gives a first-person narrative of her day, beginning with the promising move from 'darkness' through the emerging colours to 'sunshine' and 'a new day'. As the mundane details accumulate, however, she becomes progressively more distracted and dejected. For white, middle-class women Gilman succeeds in giving an unpolemical, feminist version of Marx on 'The Working Day'. At the end she reverses the order of the words that open the story: 'warm gold—pale yellow—clear pink—soft lavender—dull blue—dim gray—darkness'. The simplicity and finality make a powerful statement—or understatement—a reminder that for all her commitment to 'a purpose', Gilman repeatedly involves the reader rather than dotting every ideological 'i'.

In her short stories of the early 1890s Gilman experiments with and enters into different points of view. In 'That Rare Jewel' (1890), for example, she looks at late Victorian courtship rituals from both the young man and young woman's viewpoint. In 'Circumstances Alter Cases' (1890), she continues to probe the dilemmas of expectations about making and breaking engagements. By setting up and then reversing a case told from the man's point of view, Gilman ingeniously exposes the double standard. The underlying emotional power, however, emerges in the letters and diaries related to her troubled relation to Walter Stetson rather than in fictional versions like 'Circumstances Alter Cases' or 'That Rare Jewel'.

After the experiments of her *Impress* stories, just before she left California Gilman published 'An Unnatural Mother' (1895). The story was important to her: she published a shortened version in the *Forerunner* in 1913 and a full version just before she closed the *Forerunner* in 1916. Gilman had been pilloried in the Hearst press for divorcing Walter Stetson and later sending her daughter to live with him and his new wife, Grace Channing. 'An Unnatural Mother' is a response to the scandal; an indictment of provincial, traditional biases about medicine, sexual innocence, and childrearing; an affirmation of Gilman's belief in freedom; and an expression of her ambivalence about what she had done.

In the seven California years between 1888 and 1895 Gilman transformed her personal depression and her immediate experiences into a powerful probing of the conflicts American women experienced in achieving their full humanity. She had endured a 'dreadful' summer in 1887 after returning from the Mitchell rest cure. By August 1887 she decided to end her marriage and Grace Channing sustained her during the year it took to work out the finances and other arrangements. In October 1888 Gilman returned to California with her daughter Katherine and Grace Channing. Seeking a reconciliation, Walter Stetson unexpectedly came to Pasadena in December 1888. He stayed for a year, became close to Grace Channing, and at last accepted that the marriage was over. Gilman's satisfaction was qualified, however, because she herself lost her friend, who became engaged to and later married Stetson when their divorce was official in 1894. After Channing went East to be with him, Gilman wrote her on 3 December 1890, 'It is awful to be a man inside and not able to marry the woman you love!. . . . I want you—I love you—*I* need you *myself!*'[15] Earlier, between the ages of 17 and 21, before she married Walter Stetson she had a deep love relation with Martha Lane. In 1891 she met Adeline Knapp, a writer for the San Francisco *Call*, and loved her intensely 'that way', as she later wrote her husband-to-be, Houghton Gilman.[16] The relation with Knapp broke up in 1894. In *Disorderley Conduct* Carol Smith-Rosenburg supplies an illuminating context for these classic instances of nineteenth-century women's friendships. Among the silences in Gilman's subsequent work are the inner divisions, the complex sexuality, and the joy and anguish she knew with Martha Luther, Grace Channing, and Adeline Knapp. Her unwillingness to explore her own sexual division and its related joy and pain helps account for the choice of subject matter and absence of emotional depth in her fiction after 'The Yellow Wall-Paper'.

During her seven years in California Gilman continued to suffer periods of almost paralysing depression. But she also worked productively, raised and temporarily gave up her daughter, ran boarding-houses, cared for and buried her mother, divorced Walter Stetson, and experienced the love and loss of Grace Channing and Adeline Knapp. In the public world during her California years Gilman became an increasingly well-known women's organizer and effective reform lecturer. She developed a working friendship with Jane Addams and a close relation with a surrogate mother, the pioneering women's sociologist, Helen Campbell.

For the fourteen years between 1895 and 1909 Gilman did not publish any fiction. Instead, she criss-crossed the country as a lecturer, attended European labour and women's conferences, and developed into the leading American feminist intellectual. Through lectures, articles, and such books as *Women and Economics* (1898), *The Home* (1903), and *Human Work* (1904) she was

---

[15] Quoted in Lane, *'Herland'*, 150. [16] Quoted in Lane, *'Herland'*, 166.

at the cutting edge of feminist reform thought during the Progressive period. By 1909 Gilman was none the less finding it difficult to publish what she wanted to write. Her response was to start her own journal, the *Forerunner*. Between 1909 and 1916 Gilman was the owner, publisher, and author of a monthly periodical. She again began writing stories, one for each issue, in addition to the serialized novels *The Crux* (1910), *What Diantha Did* (1910), and *Benigna Machiavelli* (1914), and the serialized utopian novels *Moving the Mountain* (1911), *Herland* (1915), and *With Her in Ourland* (1916). In the *Forerunner* she also wrote *The Man-Made World or Our Androcentric Culture* (1911) and running commentary in reviews and editorials. The readership was small, perhaps 1,000, and Gilman and her second husband, Houghton Gilman, subsidized the undertaking.

Houghton Gilman was also supportive in other ways. He was a younger cousin and the two had known each other before her marriage to Walter Stetson. They resumed relations after she consulted him for legal advice in 1897. She opened herself to him in an unusually revealing correspondence preceding their marriage in 1900. By this time the author of *Women and Economics* had established herself, and Houghton Gilman, a patent attorney, encouraged her independent career. Their marriage flourished until his death in 1934.

As readers will have the satisfaction of discovering for themselves, Gilman's *Forerunner* stories have features in common but they do not reduce to an indiscriminate blur or to some sort of ur-story. Gilman almost always gives an independent emphasis, a distinguishing insight or turn of phrase, an enlivening resolution to a problem. Her stories, moreover, are not simplified or sugar-coated versions of her non-fiction. Gilman is at her best in the concrete situations and plausible, suggestive, sometimes satiric details of her short stories. In them she did not feel obligated to supply the evolutionary paraphernalia that underpins her non-fiction. Our expectations also change. The kind of proof, the canons of evidence, the tests of validity are one thing in works like *Women and Economics* and quite another in the fiction Gilman creates. In the fiction we are inclined to give Gilman the leeway she needs to criticize and to imagine alternatives.

Gilman writes an engaged fiction. In her stories the situations, settings, and language are those of the respectable white American middle class. In these respects, like George Eliot, Henry James, and Mary E. Wilkins, writers she 'imitated', Gilman is a literary realist. But her *Forerunner* stories also move toward parable, fable, fairy-tale, and satire. They share traits with Horatio Alger, like Gilman a creator of fables of American success, but they also carry on Bellamy's interest in imagining workable alternatives to America's divisive individualism, a project ideologically at odds with Alger. Gilman is in one sense a feminist counter to Alger.

She is also writing in the reform tradition of her great aunts ('great' in both senses of the word), Harriet Beecher Stowe, Catherine Beecher, and Isabel Beecher. Like them Gilman uses fiction to convey a re-vision of women in America. Her great aunts were the most influential disseminators of the domestic ideology Gilman challenges. They were also powerful, complex women who in both their writing and personal lives set an example and helped set Gilman's agenda. As Gillian Brown observes, the kitchen, to take an important example, is the ideological centre of both Stowe's *Uncle Tom's Cabin* and Catherine Beecher's house plans in her influential *A Treatise on Domestic Economy*, whereas the kitchenless apartment is one of Gilman's innovative projects.[17] But Gilman is also carrying into the first decades of the twentieth century the Beecher concern with *The Home*, to use one of Gilman's titles, and with *Women and Economics*, to cite another. Particularly after Mary Perkins finally divorced her Beecher husband, the Beecher family withheld the educational and social support Gilman needed growing up in an impoverished and fatherless family. At the same time, however, the Beechers made a difference to her. In multiple ways, including her creation of ideologically-charged reform fiction, Gilman is a worthy member of a great American family.

To turn to specifics, in her *Forerunner* stories Gilman again and again explores territory ignored in most mainstream fiction.

---

[17] Gillian Brown, *Domestic Individualism: Imagining Self in Nineteenth-Century America* (Berkeley: University of California Press, 1990), 13–38.

Whereas during the early 1890s she was fascinated with court-ship rituals, now at 50 she repeatedly examines the generally overlooked situation of 'the woman of fifty'. In story after story, moreover, Gilman shows her ability to engage us from the start in openings sometimes marked by emotional intensity and loud or quiet crises. Sometimes, as in 'Fulfilment' (1914), she engages us with acute social observation and a facility with language and detail. Gilman typically packs a lot into her initial paragraphs.

Gilman rings ingenious changes on the theme of the comfort-able middle-class woman whose children have married, whose husband is occupied with his business, and who finds that after all the linen is counted and stored, all the guest rooms cleaned, she has thirty more years ahead and what is she to do? Gilman knows that not everyone is prosperous. Perhaps one of her hand-some, energetic widows does not want to live with one or another of her children, confined to second-class status in an unattractive room. The drama in these stories often involves the threat of dependency and the gradual or sudden assertion of indepen-dence as the woman discovers or asserts her ability to do mean-ingful work in the face of the emptiness of her life. Throughout her life she has done her duty, a concept that from Gilman's early poem, 'In Duty Bound' (1883), has functioned as one of her major antagonists. The challenge is to redefine 'duty' into the principled way of life the stories show we can achieve.

In dealing with her antagonists, Gilman energizes stories like 'The Widow's Might' (1911) with a notable charge of feeling against repressive gender expectations and practices. In the process she delights in undercutting the husbands who embody the old patriarchal power, as she does with the Bible-quoting Mr Solomon Bankside of 'According to Solomon' (1909), or the Mr Elder of 'Mrs Elder's Idea' (1912). Gilman, however, is well-aware that the conventional relations do as much damage to men as to women. In 'Their House' (1912) she arranges it so that Mr Waterson is freed from the store he has run in order dutifully to support his family. While he goes on a scientific expedition arranged by his son, Mrs Waterson, instead of selling the store, hires an efficiency expert, expands the small dry goods business into related areas, and, in a lovely reversal, welcomes her returning husband to the spacious new home she has designed to replace the dreary, cramped structure they have previously lived in. The symbolism is unobtrusive and as basic to Gilman's vision as her belief that women can run and develop businesses, which is to say that they can work successfully outside the home and become full human beings.

To show that this mode of empowerment is achievable now, not in a utopian future, Gilman repeatedly goes into the dollars and cents detail of what it costs to have a competent woman manage a communal centre, buy and prepare simple food, and provide a meeting and resting place for the women of the entire countryside; or to buy a New York building, hire as seamstresses skilled women who need money, and, in a co-operative fashion, house and feed them and produce useful, well-made clothes for teachers and professionals.

In her stories, Gilman inspires by showing again and again that women can succeed and by showing in detail how and what to do. Sometimes she has her women work individually, on the model of any small entrepreneur, sometimes communally by tapping into a network of like-minded women with complementary skills, on the model of a small-scale, immediately realizable socialism. As a non-Marxist socialist, Gilman does not believe in class conflict. Her co-operative society is often jump-started by a person of wealth or social prestige. In other works Gilman will have her women save themselves as individuals by satisfying the communal needs of women. Throughout, she has a sure eye for the unmet needs their enterprises can satisfy: the New Home Bakery that brings European quality bread to a midwest town in 'A Partnership' (1914) or the marvelously satiric role of the necktie, that emblem of male confinement, as part of the female-run industry in 'A Council of War' (1913). Far from being threatened by or critical of the emerging consumerism of the fashion industry, Gilman has her women turn clothing and shopping to their own uses. One of her characters, who loves department stores, even asserts her independence from her husband by becoming a paid shopping specialist. Gilman was unable to foresee that the co-opting power of consumer culture would unfortunately thwart the human liberation she believed women would achieve through work.

An index of her view of work is Gilman's interest in recreation. In 'Girls and Land' (1915) she combines her interests by having Dacia Boone take charge and turn the unused family land into a prosperous vacation club for working women. With the profits from this co-operative effort, Dacia, with the help of a Scandinavian designer and woodworker, then uses the timber on the land to manufacture strong, simple, solid, inexpensive furniture. They start small, avoid the notice of the railroads, and prosper. At the end, Dacia, who has earlier lost the man she loves because of her looks, marries her partner. As in many of her stories, in 'Girls and Land' Gilman combines a 'how-to-do-it' story with elements of parable, fable, and fairy tale. As in other stories she is also reminiscent of Horatio Alger in her attention to hard work, the 'quite a sum of money' Dacia earns, and in Dacia's rise from rags to riches, all qualified by Gilman's feminism and her commitment to use value and co-operative effort. The partnership at the end encodes a feminism that posits equality between men and women and that emerges from the woman's demonstrated achievements.

In a related concern, in seeking to do justice to the claims of both individualism and community, Gilman is sensitive to the symbolism of the design of the individual house or apartment and the larger community the dwelling fits into. In her imagined landscape these settings are sometimes urban, sometimes rural. For Gilman the ideal site of house, apartment, or country cottage gives the inhabitants a view of water and green trees. The elevation of a hill or the upper stories of a New York apartment overlooking the Hudson provides the prospect Gilman, anticipating recent bio-theory, values as necessary for human life. Internally, the well-lighted house or apartment provides space so that both partners can be independent. In 'In Two Houses' (1911) this takes the form of connected twin houses, echoing Gilman's proposal before her marriage to Walter Stetson that they should live separately and get together when the sexual urge was strong.

Another feature of Gilman's domestic architecture and ideology is the kitchenless apartment. Instead of the conventional arrangement, Gilman shows the economic, social, and personal advantages of kitchens run by experts, the food delivered by dumb-waiters to individual apartments or to common dining areas for those who want more company. After they thrive in separate cottages, each without a kitchen—the artists' community takes care of the cooking from a central kitchen—in 'The Cottagette' the smell and psychic drain of the new, individual kitchen nearly spoil the developing love between two artists after Malda is persuaded to act like a traditional 'true woman' in order to catch her man. But he saves them by declaring for the freedom they both need, appropriately embodied in a life without kitchen drudgery. In her non-fiction Gilman assumes trained personnel will somehow be glad to do this work, an index of her tendency to push off onto the lower class the unpleasant labour she knows interferes with the creativity of professional women. In any case, as Dolores Hayden has shown in *The Grand Domestic Revolution*, Gilman is an exceptionally gifted popularizer in a tradition that includes such nineteenth-century pioneers as Marie Howland, Mary Livermore, Melusina Peirce, and John Pickering Putnam.

In her domestic architecture, a related structural feature is the absence of a nursery. Gilman values children and motherhood but in stories like 'Making a Change' (1911) she brings alive the near-suicidal price mothers pay in the traditional home. Her solution is the roof-garden nursery run by women with a gift for caring for children. Mothers can then spend time with but not be imprisoned by their children and the children receive care from loving experts, often older women who would otherwise be devalued and functionless. In 'Bee Wise' (1913) Gilman imagines the larger society within which her domestic architecture can function. On the California coast and in the hills above it, Gilman sets a small, ecologically and socially vital community. She is alert to the need for water and to the value of solar and wind power to supply electricity. Women and their men friends co-operate in this suggestive American utopia where people's skills are in harmony with the underlying human needs they meet. In 'Bee Wise', countless other *Forerunner* stories, and *Herland*, Gilman belongs to a tradition of women socialists including her contemporaries, Vida Scudder and Susan Glaspell, a tradition Deborah Rosenfelt shows continues 'through such thirties Old Left women as Meridel Le Sueur, Tess Slesinger, Josephine Herbst, Grace Lumpkin, and Ruth McKenney, to contemporary writers with early ties to the civil rights and anti-war movements and the New Left: Marge Piercy, Grace Paley, Alice Walker and others'.[18]

Within this tradition, Gilman's optimism and her persistent, provocative suggestions for workable change are central parts of her legacy to readers in our own period of post-modern suspicion of hopeful grand designs. 'The Yellow Wall-Paper', for its part, has a particular and contrasting appeal because of its depth, openness, and sense of the painful, qualified liberation of its narrator. The strains and ambivalence that characterize 'The Yellow Wall-Paper' are in tune with current sensibilities that value the exposure of conventional patterns of power even as they are understandably wary of affirmations and closure. The main body of Gilman's subsequent short fiction may put off some readers precisely because the works are positive and feature the closure of practical solutions. On the same grounds, however, this significant reform fiction also offers a new generation of readers a reminder of lost possibilities and an incentive to renewed effort.

[18] Deborah Rosenfelt, 'From the Thirties: Tillie Olsen and the Radical Tradition', in *Feminist Criticism and Social Change*, ed. Judith Newton and Deborah Rosenfelt (New York: Methuen, 1985), 218.

NOTE ON THE TEXT

'The Yellow Wall-Paper' was written in 1890 and appeared first in the *New England Magazine*, ns 5 (January 1892), 647–56, the source for this edition. The story was reprinted in booklet form as *The Yellow Wallpaper* (Boston: Small, Maynard & Co., 1899). In the *New England Magazine* the spelling of 'wall-paper' is inconsistent, a device I have retained since it underscores both elements of this central symbol. The other stories are also reprinted from their first (and usually only) magazine appearance. The one exception is 'An Unnatural Mother', which I was unable to locate in the 16 February 1895 *Impress* version. I have used the *Forerunner* 7 (1916) reprint. The stories following 'The Yellow Wall-Paper' are arranged in order of publication and appear as in the original, except for a few silently corrected typographical errors.

SELECT BIBLIOGRAPHY

POLLY WYNN ALLEN, *Building Domestic Liberty: Charlotte Perkins Gilman's Architectural Feminism* (Amherst: University of Massachusetts Press, 1988).

ELLEN L. BASSUK, 'The Rest Cure: Repetition or Resolution of Victorian Women's Conflicts?', in *The Female Body in Western Culture*, ed. Susan Rubin Suleiman (Cambridge: Harvard University Press, 1985), 139–51.

JEFFREY BERMAN, 'The Unrestful Cure: Charlotte Perkins Gilman and "The Yellow Wallpaper"', in *The Talking Cure: Literary Representations of Psychoanalysis* (New York: New York University Press, 1985), 33–59.

GLORIA A. BIAMONTE, '". . . there is a story, if we could only find it": Charlotte Perkins Gilman's "The Giant Wisteria"', *Legacy*, 5 (1988), 33–43.

GILLIAN BROWN, *Domestic Individualism: Imagining Self in Nineteenth-Century America* (Berkeley: University of California Press, 1990).

LARRY CEPLAIR (ed.), *Charlotte Perkins Gilman: A Nonfiction Reader* (New York: Columbia University Press, 1991).

EUGENIA C. DELAMOTTE, 'Male and Female Mysteries in "The Yellow Wallpaper"', *Legacy*, 5 (1988), 3–13.

SANDRA GILBERT and SUSAN GUBAR, *The Madwoman in the Attic: The Woman Writer and the Nineteenth-Century Literary Imagination* (New Haven: Yale University Press, 1979).

CHARLOTTE PERKINS GILMAN, *The Living of Charlotte Perkins Gilman: An Autobiography*, intro. Ann J. Lane (Madison: University of Wisconsin Press, 1935, 1990).

CATHERINE GOLDEN (ed.), *The Captive Imagination: A Casebook on 'The Yellow Wallpaper'* (New York: The Feminist Press at the City University of New York, 1992).

JANICE HANEY-PERITZ, 'Monumental Feminism and Literature's Ancestral House: Another Look at "The Yellow Wallpaper"', *Women's Studies*, 12 (1986), 271–92.

DOLORES HAYDEN, *The Grand Domestic Revolution: A History of Feminist Designs for American Homes, Neighborhoods, and Cities* (Cambridge: MIT Press, 1981).

ELAINE R. HEDGES, afterword, *The Yellow Wallpaper* (Old Westbury, 1973).

MARY A. HILL, *Charlotte Perkins Gilman: The Making of a Radical Feminist 1860–1896* (Philadelphia: Temple University Press, 1980).

MARY JACOBUS, *Reading Women: Essays in Feminist Criticism* (New York: Columbia University Press, 1986).

JEAN KENNARD, 'Convention Coverage or How to Read Your Own Life', *New Literary History*, 13 (1981), 69–88.

JEANNETTE KING and PAM MORRIS, 'On Not Reading Between the Lines: Models of Reading in "The Yellow Wallpaper"', *Studies in Short Fiction*, 26 (1989), 23–32.

DENISE KNIGHT, 'The Reincarnation of Jane: "Through This"— Gilman's Companion to "The Yellow Wallpaper"', *Women's Studies*, 20 (1992), 287–302.

ANNETTE KOLODNY, 'A Map for Rereading: Or, Gender Interpretation of Literary Texts', *New Literary History*, 11 (1980), 451–67.

ANN J. LANE, *To 'Herland' and Beyond: The Life and Work of Charlotte Perkins Gilman* (New York: Pantheon, 1990).

JULIET A. LANGLEY, '"Audacious Fancies": A Collection of Letters from Charlotte Perkins Gilman to Martha Luther', *Trivia*, 6 (1985), 52–69.

SHERYL L. MEYERING (ed.), *Charlotte Perkins Gilman: The Woman and Her Work* (Ann Arbor: UMI Research Press, 1989).

WALTER BENN MICHAELS, *The Gold Standard and the Logic of Naturalism: American Literature at the Turn of the Century* (Berkeley: University of California Press, 1987).

LYNNE PEARCE and SARA MILLS, 'Marxist-Feminism: Margaret Atwood *Surfacing*, Charlotte Perkins Gilman "The Yellow Wallpaper"', in Sara Mills, Lynne Pearce, Sue Spaull, Elaine Millard, *Feminist Readings/Feminist Reading* (New York: Harvester Wheatsheaf, 1989), 186–226.

SUZANNE POIRIER, 'The Weir Mitchell Rest Cure: Doctor and Patients', *Women's Studies*, 10 (1983), 588–99.

GARY SCHARNHORST, *Charlotte Perkins Gilman* (Boston: Twayne, 1985).
—— *Charlotte Perkins Gilman: A Bibliography* (Metuchen: Scarecrow Press, 1985).

CONRAD SHUMAKER, ' "Too Terribly Good to Be Printed": Charlotte Perkins Gilman's "The Yellow Wallpaper"', *American Literature*, 57 (1985), 588–99.
—— 'Realism, Reform, and the Audience: Charlotte Perkins Gilman's Unreadable Wallpaper', *Arizona Quarterly*, 47 (1991), 81–93.

CAROL SMITH-ROSENBERG, *Disorderly Conduct: Visions of Gender in Victorian America* (New York: Oxford University Press, 1985).

CHARLES WALTER STETSON, *Endure: The Diaries of Charles Walter Stetson*, ed. Mary A. Hill (Philadelphia: Temple University Press, 1985).

PATRICIA VERTINSKY, *The Eternally Wounded Woman: Women, Doctors and Exercise in the Late Nineteenth Century* (Manchester: Manchester University Press, 1990).

CHRONOLOGY

1860 Charlotte Anna Perkins, born 3 July, Hartford, Connecticut, second surviving child of Mary Westcott Perkins and Frederick Beecher Perkins. Great aunts Harriet Beecher Stowe, Catherine Beecher, Isabel Beecher, important reform writers, activists, formulators of domestic ideology. Father deserts family, visiting occasionally thereafter.

1860–78 Impoverished, fatherless family moves 19 times in 18 years, with poor relation stays with Beechers and Westcotts and in rented homes. Mother withholds physical affection. Active fantasy life. Conflicts with older brother, Thomas. Irregular schooling, voracious reading. Infrequent meetings with father, San Francisco and later Boston city librarian, who supplies reading lists on evolution and history.

1873 Parents officially divorced. Accepts mother's prohibition against imagining stories.

1873–5 Family part of co-operative housekeeping group in Providence. Attends stimulating private school in 1874, emphasis on physics and gymnastics.

1879 Attends Rhode Island School of Design (father pays tuition) and later takes academic correspondence courses.

1877–81 Intimate friendship with Martha Luther. July 1881 decides career helping mankind precludes marriage. Lively social life on Boston visits to Uncle Edward Hale.

1882–4 12 January 1882 meets attractive, struggling artist, Walter Stetson. Rejects marriage proposal 29 January but continues to see Stetson, experiencing periods of depression for first time. Tutors, paints and sells cards, studies French, visits gym regularly. Reads Mill, Darwin, Rossetti, and Symonds on the Greek poets.

1883 20 May accepts Stetson but asks for year's delay. Often depressed. Writes 'Of Duty Bound'.

1884 Marries Stetson in Providence, Rhode Island, 2 May. Often 'miserable' before and incapacitated after pregnancy.

1885 Daughter Katherine Beecher Stetson born 23 March. Intensifying depression, arguments, crying, 'hysteria' immediately relieved by late Fall departure for Pasadena, California where, at Grace Channing's invitation, spends rejuvenating winter without Walter, leaving Katherine with mother and nurse.

1886   Condition worsens on return to Providence.

1887   To counter depression, returns to gym, again sells painted greeting cards, begins reading books on women, writes column on suffrage activities, becomes 'absorbed in woman's question'. Believing herself 'sick with brain disease', in April goes to leading neurologist, S. Weir Mitchell, for his rest cure. Rejects Mitchell's warning against intellectual activity. After 'dreadful' summer, decides to end marriage but continues for another year, working out details.

1888   Grace Channing gets her through winter. Spends summer with Grace. 8 October leaves for good for Pasadena with Grace and Katherine. At Christmas Walter tries for reconciliation.

1889   Walter spends year in Pasadena, becoming close and then engaged to Grace. Periodic depression. Gives drawing lessons and modern lit class. Gains 'disciples' among young women reformers.

1890   Reads Bellamy's *Looking Backward*. Publishes satiric poem, 'Similar Cases', in Bellamy's April *Nationalist*. In immediate demand as Nationalist lecturer. Writes 'The Yellow Wall-Paper'. Despite periodic 'wretched health', writes thirty-three short articles and twenty-three poems for reform papers. Joint playwriting with Grace. In December letter states love, need, and 'cracked' heart after Grace leaves for East and Walter.

1891   Publishes 'The Giant Wistaria'. Reads Olive Schreiner. Successful Bay Area lectures. Meets and falls deeply in love 'that way' with San Francisco *Call* writer Adeline Knapp (Delle). September, moves to Oakland. Shares two rooms in boarding-house with Delle, Katherine, and ailing Mrs Perkins. Delle helps with finances. At Delle's urging, starts divorce proceedings.

1892–3   Hearst press stigmatizes her for divorce attempt. Active in Nationalist and Populist politics, organizes women, lectures and writes on women, economics, and ethics. At centre of Bay area intellectuals—Joaquin Miller, Edwin Markham, Helen Howe. Runs boarding-house. Cares for mother, who dies 6 March 1893. Friction culminating in final break with Delle, Summer 1893. 24 October 1893 publishes satirical reform poetry, *In This Our World*.

1894   Supports Pullman strikers, fights Southern Pacific monopoly. Active on board and at first convention of Woman's Congress Assoc. of Pacific Coast. Lectures at Stanford. April, divorce final. May, sends Kate to Walter and Grace, who marry in June. Hearst press resumes attacks. Runs *Impress* with friends Helen Campbell, twenty-one years her senior, and Paul Tyner. For *Impress* writes weekly story 'imitations' and story studies, editorials, reviews, verse.

1895   February, *Impress* folds leaving her thousands in debt. At Jane Addams's invitation moves to Hull House in Chicago. Helps Campbell in 'Little Hell' settlement house. Lectures. Enlarged *In This Our World* published.

1896   Success at Washington, D.C. Women's Suffrage Convention. July–November in England after attending London International Socialist and Labour Congress. Meets Shaw, the Webbs, other prominent Socialists. Invited to join Fabian Society. Gives several speeches.

1897   March, reacquainted with younger cousin, Houghton Gilman, a cultivated attorney. March, leaves on extended, successful lecture tour. Begins intensive correspondence with Houghton.

1898   Writes *Women and Economics* in six weeks. International success brings fame, not fortune. Southern lecture tour. June, vacation with daughter, Kate. Accepts that her depression will recur.

1899   Cross-country lecture tour. Five months in England, part with Houghton.

1900   *Concerning Children*. Pays back California financial debts. Lectures. 12 June, marries Houghton Gilman.

1900–22 Upper West Side Manhattan residences, with Kate 1900–2, 1907, and several vacations.

1900–15 Extensive lecture tours.

1903   *The Home: Its Work and Influence*.

1904   *Human Work*. Ovation at Berlin International Congress of Women. Tours Italy with Kate. Returns to U.S. with Kate for summer.

1905   European lecture tour.

1909–16 Owner, editor, publisher of monthly *Forerunner*.

1910   *What Diantha Did*, serialized *Forerunner* novel.

1911   *The Man-Made World; or, Our Androcentric Culture*, first serialized in *Forerunner*. *The Crux*, serialized *Forerunner* novel; *Moving the Mountain*, utopian novel first serialized in *Forerunner*.

1913   Last European conference, Budapest International Suffrage Convention.

1914   Well-reported NY and London lecture series.

1915   *Herland*, serialized *Forerunner* utopian novel.

1916–17 Supports War, criticizes dissidents, surprising Germano-phobia.

1919–20 Daily columnist for New York *Tribune* syndicate.

1922   Moves to Norwich Town, Connecticut.

1923   *His Religion and Hers*, last published work.

1926–7 Writes and circulates draft of autobiography.

1929   Completes unpublished detective novel, *Unpunished*.

1932   Inoperable breast cancer discovered.

1934   May, Houghton dies. August, moves to Pasadena to be with Kate. Returns to autobiography.

1935   17 August takes life in planned mercy death. October, auto-biography, *The Living of Charlotte Perkins Gilman*, posthumously published.

THE YELLOW WALL-PAPER
and Other Stories

THE YELLOW WALL-PAPER

It is very seldom that mere ordinary people like John and myself secure ancestral halls for the summer.

A colonial mansion, a hereditary estate, I would say a haunted house, and reach the height of romantic felicity—but that would be asking too much of fate!

Still I will proudly declare that there is something queer about it.

Else, why should it be let so cheaply? And why have stood so long untenanted?

John laughs at me, of course, but one expects that in marriage.

John is practical in the extreme. He has no patience with faith, an intense horror of superstition, and he scoffs openly at any talk of things not to be felt and seen and put down in figures.

John is a physician, and *perhaps*—(I would not say it to a living soul, of course, but this is dead paper and a great relief to my mind—) *perhaps* that is one reason I do not get well faster.

You see he does not believe I am sick!

And what can one do?

If a physician of high standing, and one's own husband, assures friends and relatives that there is really nothing the matter with one but temporary nervous depression—a slight hysterical tendency—what is one to do?

My brother is also a physician, and also of high standing, and he says the same thing.

So I take phosphates or phosphites—whichever it is, and tonics, and journeys, and air, and exercise, and am absolutely forbidden to 'work' until I am well again.

Personally, I disagree with their ideas.

Personally, I believe that congenial work, with excitement and change, would do me good.

But what is one to do?

I did write for a while in spite of them; but it *does* exhaust me

New England Magazine, NS 5 (January 1890), 647–56.

a good deal—having to be so sly about it, or else meet with heavy opposition.

I sometimes fancy that in my condition if I had less opposition and more society and stimulus—but John says the very worst thing I can do is to think about my condition, and I confess it always makes me feel bad.

So I will let it alone and talk about the house.

The most beautiful place! It is quite alone, standing well back from the road, quite three miles from the village. It makes me think of English places that you read about, for there are hedges and walls and gates that lock, and lots of separate little houses for the gardeners and people.

There is a *delicious* garden! I never saw such a garden—large and shady, full of box-bordered paths, and lined with long grape-covered arbors with seats under them.

There were greenhouses, too, but they are all broken now.

There was some legal trouble, I believe, something about the heirs and co-heirs; anyhow, the place has been empty for years.

That spoils my ghostliness, I am afraid, but I don't care—there is something strange about the house—I can feel it.

I even said so to John one moonlight evening, but he said what I felt was a *draught*, and shut the window.

I get unreasonably angry with John sometimes. I'm sure I never used to be so sensitive. I think it is due to this nervous condition.

But John says if I feel so, I shall neglect proper self-control; so I take pains to control myself—before him, at least, and that makes me very tired.

I don't like our room a bit. I wanted one downstairs that opened on the piazza and had roses all over the window, and such pretty old-fashioned chintz hangings! but John would not hear of it.

He said there was only one window and not room for two beds, and no near room for him if he took another.

He is very careful and loving, and hardly lets me stir without special direction.

I have a schedule prescription for each hour in the day; he takes all care from me, and so I feel basely ungrateful not to value it more.

He said we came here solely on my account, that I was to have perfect rest and all the air I could get. 'Your exercise depends on your strength, my dear,' said he, 'and your food somewhat on your appetite; but air you can absorb all the time.' So we took the nursery at the top of the house.

It is a big, airy room, the whole floor nearly, with windows that look all ways, and air and sunshine galore. It was nursery first and then playroom and gymnasium, I should judge; for the windows are barred for little children, and there are rings and things in the walls.

The paint and paper look as if a boys' school had used it. It is stripped off—the paper—in great patches all around the head of my bed, about as far as I can reach, and in a great place on the other side of the room low down. I never saw a worse paper in my life.

One of those sprawling flamboyant patterns committing every artistic sin.

It is dull enough to confuse the eye in following, pronounced enough to constantly irritate and provoke study, and when you follow the lame uncertain curves for a little distance they suddenly commit suicide—plunge off at outrageous angles, destroy themselves in unheard of contradictions.

The color is repellant, almost revolting; a smouldering unclean yellow, strangely faded by the slow-turning sunlight.

It is a dull yet lurid orange in some places, a sickly sulphur tint in others.

No wonder the children hated it! I should hate it myself if I had to live in this room long.

There comes John, and I must put this away,—he hates to have me write a word.

We have been here two weeks, and I haven't felt like writing before, since that first day.

I am sitting by the window now, up in this atrocious nursery, and there is nothing to hinder my writing as much as I please, save lack of strength.

John is away all day, and even some nights when his cases are serious.

I am glad my case is not serious!

But these nervous troubles are dreadfully depressing.

John does not know how much I really suffer. He knows there is no *reason* to suffer, and that satisfies him.

Of course it is only nervousness. It does weigh on me so not to do my duty in any way!

I meant to be such a help to John, such a real rest and comfort, and here I am a comparative burden already!

Nobody would believe what an effort it is to do what little I am able,—to dress and entertain, and order things.

It is fortunate Mary is so good with the baby. Such a dear baby!

And yet I *cannot* be with him, it makes me so nervous.

I suppose John never was nervous in his life. He laughs at me so about this wall-paper!

At first he meant to repaper the room, but afterwards he said that I was letting it get the better of me, and that nothing was worse for a nervous patient than to give way to such fancies.

He said that after the wall-paper was changed it would be the heavy bedstead, and then the barred windows, and then that gate at the head of the stairs, and so on.

'You know the place is doing you good,' he said, 'and really, dear, I don't care to renovate the house just for a three months' rental.'

'Then do let us go downstairs,' I said, 'there are such pretty rooms there.'

Then he took me in his arms and called me a blessed little goose, and said he would go down cellar, if I wished, and have it whitewashed into the bargain.

But he is right enough about the beds and windows and things.

It is an airy and comfortable room as any one need wish, and, of course, I would not be so silly as to make him uncomfortable just for a whim.

I'm really getting quite fond of the big room, all but that horrid paper.

Out of one window I can see the garden, those mysterious deep-shaded arbors, the riotous old-fashioned flowers, and bushes and gnarly trees.

Out of another I get a lovely view of the bay and a little private wharf belonging to the estate. There is a beautiful shaded lane that runs down there from the house. I always fancy I see people walking in these numerous paths and arbors, but John has cautioned me not to give way to fancy in the least. He says that with my imaginative power and habit of story-making, a nervous weakness like mine is sure to lead to all manner of excited fancies, and that I ought to use my will and good sense to check the tendency. So I try.

I think sometimes that if I were only well enough to write a little it would relieve the press of ideas and rest me.

But I find I get pretty tired when I try.

It is so discouraging not to have any advice and companionship about my work. When I get really well, John says we will ask Cousin Henry and Julia down for a long visit; but he says he would as soon put fireworks in my pillow-case as to let me have those stimulating people about now.

I wish I could get well faster.

But I must not think about that. This paper looks to me as if it *knew* what a vicious influence it had!

There is a recurrent spot where the pattern lolls like a broken neck and two bulbous eyes stare at you upside down.

I get positively angry with the impertinence of it and the everlastingess. Up and down and sideways they crawl, and those absurd, unblinking eyes are everywhere. There is one place where two breaths didn't match, and the eyes go all up and down the line, one a little higher than the other.

I never saw so much expression in an inanimate thing before, and we all know how much expression they have! I used to lie awake as a child and get more entertainment and terror out of blank walls and plain furniture than most children could find in a toy-store.

I remember what a kindly wink the knobs of our big, old bureau used to have, and there was one chair that always seemed like a strong friend.

I used to feel that if any of the other things looked too fierce I could always hop into that chair and be safe.

The furniture in this room is no worse than inharmonious, however, for we had to bring it all from downstairs. I suppose when this was used as a playroom they had to take the nursery things out, and no wonder! I never saw such ravages as the children have made here.

The wall-paper, as I said before, is torn off in spots, and it sticketh closer than a brother—they must have had perseverance as well as hatred.

Then the floor is scratched and gouged and splintered, the plaster itself is dug out here and there, and this great heavy bed which is all we found in the room, looks as if it had been through the wars.

But I don't mind it a bit—only the paper.

There comes John's sister. Such a dear girl as she is, and so careful of me! I must not let her find me writing.

She is a perfect and enthusiastic housekeeper, and hopes for no better profession. I verily believe she thinks it is the writing which made me sick!

But I can write when she is out, and see her a long way off from these windows.

There is one that commands the road, a lovely shaded winding road, and one that just looks off over the country. A lovely country, too, full of great elms and velvet meadows.

This wallpaper has a kind of subpattern in a different shade, a particularly irritating one, for you can only see it in certain lights, and not clearly then.

But in the places where it isn't faded and where the sun is just so—I can see a strange, provoking, formless sort of figure, that seems to skulk about behind that silly and conspicuous front design.

There's sister on the stairs!

Well, the Fourth of July is over! The people are all gone and I am tired out. John thought it might do me good to see a little company, so we just had mother and Nellie and the children down for a week.

Of course I didn't do a thing. Jennie sees to everything now. But it tired me all the same.

John says if I don't pick up faster he shall send me to Weir Mitchell in the fall.

But I don't want to go there at all. I had a friend who was in his hands once, and she says he is just like John and my brother, only more so!

Besides, it is such an undertaking to go so far.

I don't feel as if it was worth while to turn my hand over for anything, and I'm getting dreadfully fretful and querulous.

I cry at nothing, and cry most of the time.

Of course I don't when John is here, or anybody else, but when I am alone.

And I am alone a good deal just now. John is kept in town very often by serious cases, and Jennie is good and lets me alone when I want her to.

So I walk a little in the garden or down that lovely lane, sit on the porch under the roses, and lie down up here a good deal.

I'm getting really fond of the room in spite of the wallpaper. Perhaps *because* of the wallpaper.

It dwells in my mind so!

I lie here on this great immovable bed—it is nailed down, I believe—and follow that pattern about by the hour. It is as good as gymnastics, I assure you. I start, we'll say, at the bottom, down in the corner over there where it has not been touched, and I determine for the thousandth time that I *will* follow that pointless pattern to some sort of a conclusion.

I know a little of the principle of design, and I know this thing was not arranged on any laws of radiation, or alternation, or repetition, or symmetry, or anything else that I ever heard of.

It is repeated, of course, by the breadths, but not otherwise.

Looked at in one way each breadth stands alone, the bloated curves and flourishes—a kind of 'debased Romanesque' with *delirium tremens*—go waddling up and down in isolated columns of fatuity.

But, on the other hand, they connect diagonally, and the sprawling outlines run off in great slanting waves of optic horror, like a lot of wallowing seaweeds in full chase.

The whole thing goes horizontally, too, at least it seems so, and I exhaust myself in trying to distinguish the order of its going in that direction.

They have used a horizontal breadth for a frieze, and that adds wonderfully to the confusion.

There is one end of the room where it is almost intact, and there, when the crosslights fade and the low sun shines directly upon it, I can almost fancy radiation after all,—the interminable grotesque seem to form around a common centre and rush off in headlong plunges of equal distraction.

It makes me tired to follow it. I will take a nap I guess.

I don't know why I should write this.

I don't want to.

I don't feel able.

And I know John would think it absurd. But I *must* say what I feel and think in some way—it is such a relief!

But the effort is getting to be greater than the relief.

Half the time now I am awfully lazy, and lie down ever so much.

John says I mustn't lose my strength, and has me take cod liver oil and lots of tonics and things, to say nothing of ale and wine and rare meat.

Dear John! He loves me very dearly, and hates to have me sick. I tried to have a real earnest reasonable talk with him the other day, and tell him how I wish he would let me go and make a visit to Cousin Henry and Julia.

But he said I wasn't able to go, nor able to stand it after I got there; and I did not make out a very good case for myself, for I was crying before I had finished.

It is getting to be a great effort for me to think straight. Just this nervous weakness I suppose.

And dear John gathered me up in his arms, and just carried me upstairs and laid me on the bed, and sat by me and read to me till it tired my head.

He said I was his darling and his comfort and all he had, and that I must take care of myself for his sake, and keep well.

He says no one but myself can help me out of it, that I must use my will and self-control and not let any silly fancies run away with me.

There's one comfort, the baby is well and happy, and does not have to occupy this nursery with the horrid wallpaper.

If we had not used it, that blessed child would have! What a fortunate escape! Why, I wouldn't have a child of mine, an impressionable little thing, live in such a room for worlds.

I never thought of it before, but it is lucky that John kept me here after all, I can stand it so much easier than a baby, you see.

Of course I never mention it to them any more—I am too wise,—but I keep watch of it all the same.

There are things in that paper that nobody knows but me, or ever will.

Behind that outside pattern the dim shapes get clearer every day.

It is always the same shape, only very numerous.

And it is like a woman stooping down and creeping about behind that pattern. I don't like it a bit. I wonder—I begin to think—I wish John would take me away from here!

It is so hard to talk with John about my case because he is so wise, and because he loves me so.

But I tried it last night.

It was moonlight. The moon shines in all around just as the sun does.

I hate to see it sometimes, it creeps so slowly, and always comes in by one window or another.

John was asleep and I hated to waken him, so I kept still and watched the moonlight on that undulating wallpaper till I felt creepy.

The faint figure behind seemed to shake the pattern, just as if she wanted to get out.

I got up softly and went to feel and see if the paper *did* move, and when I came back John was awake.

'What is it, little girl?' he said. 'Don't go walking about like that—you'll get cold.'

I thought it was a good time to talk, so I told him that I really was not gaining here, and that I wished he would take me away.

'Why, darling!' said he, 'our lease will be up in three weeks, and I can't see how to leave before.

'The repairs are not done at home, and I cannot possibly leave town just now. Of course if you were in any danger, I could and would, but you really are better, dear, whether you can see it or not. I am a doctor, dear, and I know. You are gaining flesh and color, your appetite is better, I feel really much easier about you.'

'I don't weigh a bit more,' said I, 'nor as much; and my appetite may be better in the evening when you are here, but it is worse in the morning when you are away!'

'Bless her little heart!' said he with a big hug, 'she shall be as sick as she pleases! But now let's improve the shining hours by going to sleep, and talk about it in the morning!'

'And you won't go away?' I asked gloomily.

'Why, how can I, dear? It is only three weeks more and then we will take a nice little trip of a few days while Jennie is getting the house ready. Really dear you are better!'

'Better in body perhaps—' I began, and stopped short, for he sat up straight and looked at me with such a stern, reproachful look that I could not say another word.

'My darling,' said he, 'I beg of you, for my sake and for our child's sake, as well as for your own, that you will never for one instant let that idea enter your mind! There is nothing so dangerous, so fascinating, to a temperament like yours. It is a false and foolish fancy. Can you not trust me as a physician when I tell you so?'

So of course I said no more on that score, and we went to sleep before long. He thought I was asleep first, but I wasn't, and lay there for hours trying to decide whether that front pattern and the back pattern really did move together or separately.

On a pattern like this, by daylight, there is a lack of sequence, a defiance of law, that is a constant irritant to a normal mind.

The color is hideous enough, and unreliable enough, and infuriating enough, but the pattern is torturing.

You think you have mastered it, but just as you get well underway in following, it turns a back-somersault and there you are. It slaps you in the face, knocks you down, and tramples upon you. It is like a bad dream.

The outside pattern is a florid arabesque, reminding one of a fungus. If you can imagine a toadstool in joints, an interminable string of toadstools, budding and sprouting in endless convolutions—why, that is something like it.

That is, sometimes!

There is one marked peculiarity about this paper, a thing nobody seems to notice but myself, and that is that it changes as the light changes.

When the sun shoots in through the east window—I always watch for that first long, straight ray—it changes so quickly that I never can quite believe it.

That is why I watch it always.

By moonlight—the moon shines in all night when there is a moon—I wouldn't know it was the same paper.

At night in any kind of light, in twilight, candlelight, lamplight, and worst of all by moonlight, it becomes bars! The outside pattern I mean, and the woman behind it is as plain as can be.

I didn't realize for a long time what the thing was that showed behind, that dim sub-pattern, but now I am quite sure it is a woman.

By daylight she is subdued, quiet. I fancy it is the pattern that keeps her so still. It is so puzzling. It keeps me quiet by the hour.

I lie down ever so much now. John says it is good for me, and to sleep all I can.

Indeed he started the habit by making me lie down for an hour after each meal.

It is a very bad habit I am convinced, for you see I don't sleep.

And that cultivates deceit, for I don't tell them I'm awake—O no!

The fact is I am getting a little afraid of John.

He seems very queer sometimes, and even Jennie has an inexplicable look.

It strikes me occasionally, just as a scientific hypothesis,—that perhaps it is the paper!

I have watched John when he did not know I was looking, and come into the room suddenly on the most innocent excuses, and I've caught him several times *looking at the paper!* And Jennie too. I caught Jennie with her hand on it once.

She didn't know I was in the room, and when I asked her in a quiet, a very quiet voice, with the most restrained manner possible, what she was doing with the paper—she turned around as if she had been caught stealing, and looked quite angry—asked me why I should frighten her so!

Then she said that the paper stained everything it touched, that she had found yellow smooches on all my clothes and John's, and she wished we would be more careful!

Did not that sound innocent? But I know she was studying that pattern, and I am determined that nobody shall find it out but myself!

Life is very much more exciting now than it used to be. You see I have something more to expect, to look forward to, to watch. I really do eat better, and am more quiet than I was.

John is so pleased to see me improve! He laughed a little the other day, and said I seemed to be flourishing in spite of my wall-paper.

I turned it off with a laugh. I had no intention of telling him it was *because* of the wall-paper—he would make fun of me. He might even want to take me away.

I don't want to leave now until I have found it out. There is a week more, and I think that will be enough.

I'm feeling ever so much better! I don't sleep much at night, for it is so interesting to watch developments; but I sleep a good deal in the daytime.

In the daytime it is tiresome and perplexing.

There are always new shoots on the fungus, and new shades of yellow all over it. I cannot keep count of them, though I have tried conscientiously.

It is the strangest yellow, that wall-paper! It makes me think of all the yellow things I ever saw—not beautiful ones like butter-cups, but old foul, bad yellow things.

But there is something else about that paper—the smell! I noticed it the moment we came into the room, but with so much air and sun it was not bad. Now we have had a week of fog and rain, and whether the windows are open or not, the smell is here.

It creeps all over the house.

I find it hovering in the dining-room, skulking in the parlor, hiding in the hall, lying in wait for me on the stairs.

It gets into my hair.

Even when I go to ride, if I turn my head suddenly and surprise it—there is that smell!

Such a peculiar odor, too! I have spent hours in trying to analyze it, to find what it smelled like.

It is not bad—at first, and very gentle, but quite the subtlest, most enduring odor I ever met.

In this damp weather it is awful, I wake up in the night and find it hanging over me.

It used to disturb me at first. I thought seriously of burning the house—to reach the smell.

But now I am used to it. The only thing I can think of that it is like is the *color* of the paper! A yellow smell.

There is a very funny mark on this wall, low down, near the mopboard. A streak that runs round the room. It goes behind every piece of furniture, except the bed, a long, straight, even *smooch*, as if it had been rubbed over and over.

I wonder how it was done and who did it, and what they did it for. Round and round and round—round and round and round—it makes me dizzy!

I really have discovered something at last.

Through watching so much at night, when it changes so, I have finally found out.

The front pattern *does* move—and no wonder! The woman behind shakes it!

Sometimes I think there are a great many women behind, and sometimes only one, and she crawls around fast, and her crawling shakes it all over.

Then in the very bright spots she keeps still, and in the very shady spots she just takes hold of the bars and shakes them hard.

And she is all the time trying to climb through. But nobody could climb through that pattern—it strangles so; I think that is why it has so many heads.

They get through, and then the pattern strangles them off and turns them upside down, and makes their eyes white!

If those heads were covered or taken off it would not be half so bad.

I think that woman gets out in the daytime!

And I'll tell you why—privately—I've seen her!

I can see her out of every one of my windows!

It is the same woman, I know, for she is always creeping, and most women do not creep by daylight.

I see her in that long shaded lane, creeping up and down. I see her in those dark grape arbors, creeping all around the garden.

I see her on that long road under the trees, creeping along, and when a carriage comes she hides under the blackberry vines.

I don't blame her a bit. It must be very humiliating to be caught creeping by daylight!

I always lock the door when I creep by daylight. I can't do it at night, for I know John would suspect something at once.

And John is so queer now, that I don't want to irritate him. I wish he would take another room! Besides, I don't want anybody to get that woman out at night but myself.

I often wonder if I could see her out of all the windows at once.

But, turn as fast as I can, I can only see out of one at one time.

And though I always see her, she *may* be able to creep faster than I can turn!

I have watched her sometimes away off in the open country, creeping as fast as a cloud shadow in a high wind.

If only that top pattern could be gotten off from the under one! I mean to try it, little by little.

I have found out another funny thing, but I shan't tell it this time! It does not do to trust people too much.

There are only two more days to get this paper off, and I believe John is beginning to notice. I don't like the look in his eyes.

And I heard him ask Jennie a lot of professional questions about me. She had a very good report to give.

She said I slept a good deal in the daytime.

John knows I don't sleep very well at night, for all I'm so quiet!

He asked me all sorts of questions, too, and pretended to be very loving and kind.

As if I couldn't see through him!

Still, I don't wonder he acts so, sleeping under this paper for three months.

It only interests me, but I feel sure John and Jennie are secretly affected by it.

Hurrah! This is the last day, but it is enough. John to stay in town over night, and won't be out until this evening.

Jennie wanted to sleep with me—the sly thing! but I told her I should undoubtedly rest better for a night all alone.

That was clever, for really I wasn't alone a bit! As soon as it was moonlight and that poor thing began to crawl and shake the pattern, I got up and ran to help her.

I pulled and she shook, I shook and she pulled, and before morning we had peeled off yards of that paper.

A strip about as high as my head and half around the room.

And then when the sun came and that awful pattern began to laugh at me, I declared I would finish it to-day!

We go away to-morrow, and they are moving all my furniture down again to leave things as they were before.

Jennie looked at the wall in amazement, but I told her merrily that I did it out of pure spite at the vicious thing.

She laughed and said she wouldn't mind doing it herself, but I must not get tired.

How she betrayed herself that time!

But I am here, and no person touches this paper but me,—not *alive!*

She tried to get me out of the room—it was too patent! But I said it was so quiet and empty and clean now that I believed I would lie down again and sleep all I could; and not to wake me even for dinner—I would call when I woke.

So now she is gone, and the servants are gone, and the things are gone, and there is nothing left but that great bedstead nailed down, with the canvas mattress we found on it.

We shall sleep downstairs to-night, and take the boat home to-morrow.

I quite enjoy the room, now it is bare again.

How those children did tear about here!

This bedstead is fairly gnawed!

But I must get to work.

I have locked the door and thrown the key down into the front path.

I don't want to go out, and I don't want to have anybody come in, till John comes.

I want to astonish him.

I've got a rope up here that even Jennie did not find. If that woman does get out, and tries to get away, I can tie her!

But I forgot I could not reach far without anything to stand on!

This bed will *not* move!

I tried to lift and push it until I was lame, and then I got so angry I bit off a little piece at one corner—but it hurt my teeth.

Then I peeled off all the paper I could reach standing on the floor. It sticks horribly and the pattern just enjoys it! All those strangled heads and bulbous eyes and waddling fungus growths just shriek with derision!

I am getting angry enough to do something desperate. To jump out of the window would be admirable exercise, but the bars are too strong even to try.

Besides I wouldn't do it. Of course not. I know well enough that a step like that is improper and might be misconstrued.

I don't like to *look* out of the windows even—there are so many of those creeping women, and they creep so fast.

I wonder if they all come out of that wall-paper as I did?

But I am securely fastened now by my well-hidden rope—you don't get *me* out in the road there!

I suppose I shall have to get back behind the pattern when it comes night, and that is hard!

It is so pleasant to be out in this great room and creep around as I please!

I don't want to go outside. I won't, even if Jennie asks me to.

For outside you have to creep on the ground, and everything is green instead of yellow.

But here I can creep smoothly on the floor, and my shoulder just fits in that long smooch around the wall, so I cannot lose my way.

Why there's John at the door!

It is no use, young man, you can't open it!

How he does call and pound!

Now he's crying for an axe.

It would be a shame to break down that beautiful door!

'John dear!' said I in the gentlest voice, 'the key is down by the front steps, under a plantain leaf!'

That silenced him for a few moments.

Then he said—very quietly indeed, 'Open the door, my darling!'

'I can't,' said I. 'The key is down by the front door under a plantain leaf!'

And then I said it again, several times, very gently and slowly, and said it so often that he had to go and see, and he got it of course, and came in. He stopped short by the door.

'What is the matter?' he cried. 'For God's sake, what are you doing!'

I kept on creeping just the same, but I looked at him over my shoulder.

'I've got out at last,' said I, 'in spite of you and Jane? And I've pulled off most of the paper, so you can't put me back!'

Now why should that man have fainted? But he did, and right across my path by the wall, so that I had to creep over him every time!

THAT RARE JEWEL

'WHAT are you laughing at, Sherman? You seem to find something endlessly amusing in your smoke-wreaths, or the roof of the piazza, or the sky yonder.'

'Nothing so soothing as smoke, Hal, so simple as boards, or so natural as the sky. I'm laughing about modern girls.'

'Oh! Well, I confess they are funny. But what special phase?'

'Their high-minded social conscientiousness. You know Miss Walker—nice, sensible, jolly girl? She was a very good friend of mine, and I was having all manner of good times with her, when all at once I discovered that she was taking care of my heart all the time, for fear it should get broken. She was afraid to go with me so much, for fear I might think, you know,—that she might think, you know—Bah! It's enough to make a man forswear womankind for ever!'

Harold acquiesced cheerfully. 'Yes,' said he, 'I've noticed it. If it were not for sheer pity—and natural attraction, I suppose—one would let the whole thing go. But if you don't pay a girl some attention, she can't do a single thing, dance, or walk, or have any kind of a time. A fellow has to sit up nights, to divide these wonderful attentions so that nobody can build on them.'

Harold looked out over the beach and the bathers, where, perhaps, even an unceremonious clutch out of the grip of a big wave was being received and built upon as an 'attention.'

Sherman Blake blew other soothing smoke wreaths, softly vanishing as they ascended toward the simple roof and natural sky before mentioned. He was a nice fellow, a very nice fellow indeed, much prized among the numerous young ladies of his acquaintance; and his responsibilities weighed heavily upon him, as we observe. Harold Onthewaite, his friend, was a clever young man, of literary tastes and newspaper necessities; much given to analysis and sweeping deduction.

'You see, Sherman,' said he, 'girls nowadays are awfully complex. There is no naturalness to them. Women were always mysterious enough, heaven knows; but "the higher education" seems to have added an intense self-consciousness of their own intricacy. Where they used to be queer and couldn't account for it, now they are queer and can give you a thousand reasons. It is wearing to a humble, plain, consistent creature like man.'

'You're right, there,' said Sherman. 'If that fair friend of mine had had an inkling of where my heart *was* wandering, she might have saved herself some pains. It is quite pathetic, though, really, to think of the study she wasted on her supposed victim!—the energy gone to waste! Now that I do not call so often, I suppose she thinks I languish! See you at lunch, Hal, I have an engagement.' And young Blake settled his hat a little, and started off briskly to the next hotel.

Harold followed him with his eyes.

'What a shame it is,' he thought, 'that a man can't find a natural, honest woman, either for friend or sweetheart. Honest! If they would only be consistent, I'd ask nothing else!'

Julia Farwell sat by the window of her narrow little room in 'The Water View,' gazing off across the misty blue expanse with a rather perplexed expression. To her entered her mother,— pleasant-faced, well-dressed, serene.

'Are you going to walk with Mr Blake or not, Julia? He is waiting around downstairs, and said he believed you had some such plan for this morning.'

'Well, I don't know, mother. I hate to go with him all the time. He might think'——

'It doesn't seem to me, dear, that you ought to think so much of what he might think. I know you are conscientious about it, but sometimes you seem to me to carry it too far. You are pretty and attractive enough, but so are other girls, and it is a little hard on a friendly young man always to suppose him paying attention. You can't alter society, my dear.'

'I know I can't, mother. But you know well enough that a girl gets blamed for encouraging a man if he does mean anything.'

'Yes, I know that. But do be reasonable! As society is constituted, you can't have the amusements due to a girl of your age without some man's escort. You can't even go to walk alone without being conspicuous. Men like to have it so, too. When they are kind and gentlemanly and polite to a girl, I don't think the girl ought to quarrel with it.'

'Yes, but mother, if they are in earnest, if they really want to— to marry you, they have only the same way to show it; and you are supposed to understand.'

'Now, my dear, you are absurd! In the first place, you *do* understand well enough when a man means that. And, in the second place, it seems to me scarcely—well, maidenly, to be assuming that every man who offers you some small attention wants to marry you. I may be old-fashioned, but it seems to me unbecoming to quarter the ground in advance, analyze every look and word, and try to take care of a man's heart that may be miles away. The world is not on your shoulders, dear. Keep within your own proper limits, and let them take care of themselves.'

'Wouldn't you like to come with us, mother? I shall not go far.'

'No, thank you, dear, I do not feel like it this morning. See that you don't wet your feet.'

So Miss Farwell and Mr Blake set forth in the clear sunshine and fresh sea-breeze. They walked along the ever-inviting rocks, and found them too populous with other pairs; they walked through stony meadows, full of golden-rod and sumach, and found them too bare and hot; they walked down cool woodland roads, and were moved to gather flowers there, and to rest under the shimmering green roof of widespread pines. She made a lapful of their fragrant burden, and arranged great clusters to carry back with her. He took off his hat, the better to feel the gentle wind, and laid himself admiringly at her feet. And, finding words for the occasion, he spoke out manfully, called her 'Julia,' told her she knew he loved her, and asked her to be his wife.

'Indeed—indeed, I did not know it, Mr Blake! If I had I should have saved you this. I do not—can not—it must be "no." I had no idea it was so much to you—believe me!'

There was an ominous silence, while the young man pulled up little bunches of thin wood grass and pushed them into the ground again with his stick.

'I hope you are not angry, Mr Blake? I do like you very much, and I am so sorry.'

'Thank you. I appreciate your—kindness.'

And, as further conversation seemed difficult, they walked silently back together.

He made his adieux with careful politeness, hoping he should see her again in the winter, and went straightway to his room and his valise.

His companion sought her mother.

'Why, Julia, what has happened? You look tired out. Did you go too far?'

'Yes, mother, I did go too far, it appears; or Mr Blake did. It is just as I told you—just as I was afraid. And when I—couldn't, he was angry—actually angry and sarcastic. He acted just as if I had led him on and played with him; and you know well enough how careful I have been!'

'Don't be silly, Julia. It is not wicked, child. You can't help it if you have offers. I had five myself, and I'm sure I didn't encourage them. It's nothing to grieve over, dear!'

'It is something to grieve over, mother, to have things so that a girl cannot live naturally and honestly, try as she may. I don't care, I'm going to enjoy the rest of my life as best I can, and not bother.'

'A very sensible conclusion, my dear, and I hope you will keep to it. You will be far happier and more comfortable, and it will not hurt your chances, I promise you. Of all things, don't be odd.'

When Harold looked in to remind his friend of lunch time, he found him packing violently.

'What's up now, Sherm?' he inquired. 'You don't look exactly permanent.'

'I am going to take the afternoon train,' said he, briefly.

'Anything happened? Has—oh, I see! I'm awfully sorry, Sherm!' And Harold's hand-clasp was a small bit of human comfort, after all. Sherman returned the pressure vigorously, walked to the window and looked out through panes that seemed uncommonly dim, and then burst out suddenly: 'Don't waste your sympathy, old fellow! I'm hurt, of course; but I'm almost more angry, to be so fooled and led by the nose like a—freshman!'

Harold looked a world of interest, but was shy of speaking. But, as something seemed necessary, he tried one word—'Jilted?'

'I should think so! Jilted! If ever a man was sure and careful and warranted in speaking, I was. Why, she has gone about with me all summer, danced and walked and ridden, and—why, you must have noticed it; everybody has noticed it!'

'Yes,' said Harold, 'I noticed it. I'm awfully sorry.'

'It's more than the pain, Hal. It's the general disappointment. What is a man to expect, to hope for anywhere, when women are like this? And then we are blamed for not marrying!'

'Yes, that's what amuses me,' said Harold. 'We'd marry, be glad to marry, and marry young, too, if women were what they used to be.'

'And the wretched idiots that talk about it miss the whole point. It's not expense and frivolity and incapableness—those are bad enough—it's this cursed, double-faced dishonesty. Lead a man on with the openest, baldest encouragement, till he's fool enough really to show his heart, and then they're so sorry! Well, I'm twenty-eight, and this is my third lesson. If I need another, I shall deserve it.'

'And then they always offer to be sisters, and want to keep your friendship,' echoed Hal. 'Why can't they be honest even there, and show a little natural triumph, if that was their game?'

The girls at that resort were the poorer by two young men, which was a serious diminution where one had to cover so many.

Sherman finished his packing and his lunch, and left that evening. Harold went with him, disgusted with womankind.

'If they would only be consistent!' said he, 'that's all I'd ask!'

THE UNEXPECTED

I

'It is the unexpected which happens,' says the French proverb. I like the proverb, because it is true—and because it is French.

Edouard Charpentier is my name.

I am an American by birth, but that is all. From infancy, when I had a French nurse; in childhood, when I had a French governess; through youth, passed in a French school; to manhood, devoted to French art, I have been French by sympathy and education.

France—modern France—and French art—modern French art—I adore!

My school is the 'pleine-aire,' and my master, could I but find him, is M. Duchesne. M. Duchesne has had pictures in the Salon for three years, and pictures elsewhere, eagerly bought, and yet Paris knows not M. Duchesne. We know his house, his horse, his carriage, his servants and his garden-wall, but he sees no one, speaks to no one; indeed, he has left Paris for a time, and we worship afar off.

I have a sketch by this master which I treasure jealously—a pencil sketch of a great picture yet to come. I await it.

M. Duchesne paints from the model, and I paint from the model, exclusively. It is the only way to be firm, accurate, true. Without the model we may have German fantasy or English domesticity, but no modern French art.

It is hard, too, to get models continually when one is but a student after five years' work, and one's pictures bring francs indeed, but not dollars.

Still, there is Georgette!

There, also, were Emilie and Pauline. But now it is Georgette, and she is adorable!

'Tis true, she has not much soul; but, then, she has a charming body, and 'tis that I copy.

Georgette and I get on together to admiration. How much better is this than matrimony for an artist! How wise is M. Daudet!

Antoine is my dearest friend. I paint with him, and we are happy. Georgette is my dearest model. I paint from her, and we are happy.

Into this peaceful scene comes a letter from America, bringing much emotion.

It appears I had a great-uncle there, in some northeastern corner of New England. Maine? No; Vermont.

And it appears, strangely enough, that this northeastern great-uncle was seized in his old age with a passion for French art; at least I know not how else to account for his hunting me up through a lawyer and leaving me some quarter of a million when he died.

An admirable great-uncle!

But I must go home and settle the property; that is imperative. I must leave Paris, I must leave Antoine, I must leave Georgette!

Could anything be further from Paris than a town in Vermont? No, not the Andaman Islands.

And could anything be further from Antoine and Georgette than the family of great-cousins I find myself among?

But one of them—ah, Heaven! some forty-seventh cousin who is so beautiful that I forget she is an American, I forget Paris, I forget Antoine—yes, and even Georgette! Poor Georgette! But this is fate.

This cousin is not like the other cousins. I pursue, I inquire, I ascertain.

Her name is Mary D. Greenleaf. I shall call her Marie.

And she comes from Boston.

But, beyond the name, how can I describe her? I have seen beauty, yes, much beauty, in maid, matron and model, but I never saw anything to equal this country girl. What a figure!

No, not a 'figure'—the word shames her. She has a body, the body of a young Diana, and a body and a figure are two very different things. I am an artist, and I have lived in Paris, and I know the difference.

The lawyers in Boston can settle that property, I find.

The air is delightful in northern Vermont in March. There are mountains, clouds, trees. I will paint here a while. Ah, yes; and I will assist this shy young soul!

'Cousin Marie,' say I, 'come, let me teach you to paint!'

'It would be too difficult for you, Mr Carpenter—it would take too long!'

'Call me Edouard!' I cry. 'Are we not cousins? Cousin Edouard, I beg of you! And nothing is difficult when you are with me, Marie—nothing can be too long at your side!'

'Thanks, cousin Edward, but I think I will not impose on your good nature. Besides, I shall not stay here. I go back to Boston, to my aunt.'

I find the air of Boston is good in March, and there are places of interest there, and rising American artists who deserve encouragement. I will stay in Boston a while to assist the lawyers in settling my property; it is necessary.

I visit Marie continually. Am I not a cousin?

I talk to her of life, of art, of Paris, of M. Duchesne. I show her my precious sketch.

'But,' says she, 'I am not wholly a wood nymph, as you seem fondly to imagine. I have been to Paris myself—with my uncle—years since.'

'Fairest cousin,' say I, 'if you had not been even to Boston, I should still love you! Come and see Paris again—with me!' And then she would laugh at me and send me away. Ah, yes! I had come even to marriage, you see!

I soon found she had the usual woman's faith in those conventions. I gave her 'Artists' Wives.' She said she had read it. She laughed at Daudet and me!

I talked to her of ruined geniuses I had known myself, but she said a ruined genius was no worse than a ruined woman! One cannot reason with young girls!

Do not believe I succumbed without a struggle. I even tore myself away and went to New York. It was not far enough, I fear. I soon came back.

She lived with an aunt—my adorable little precisian!—with a horrible strong-minded aunt, and such a life as I led between them for a whole month!

I call continually. I bury her in flowers. I take her to the theatre, aunt and all. And at this the aunt seemed greatly surprised, but I disapprove of American familiarities. No; my wife—and wife she must be—shall be treated with punctilious respect.

Never was I so laughed at and argued with in my life as I was laughed at by that dreadful beauty, and argued with by that dreadful aunt.

The only rest was in pictures. Marie would look at pictures always, and seemed to have a real appreciation of them, almost an understanding, of a sort. So that I began to hope—dimly and faintly to hope—that she might grow to care for mine. To have a wife who would care for one's art, who would come to one's studio—but, then, the models! I paint from the model almost entirely, as I said, and *I* know what women are about models, without Daudet to tell me!

And this prudish New England girl! Well, she might come to the studio on stated days, and perhaps in time I might lead her gently to understand.

That I should ever live to commit matrimony!

But Fate rules all men.

I think that girl refused me nine times. She always put me off with absurd excuses and reasons: said I didn't know her yet; said we should never agree; said I was French and she was American; said I cared more for art than I did for her! At that I earnestly assured her that I would become an organ-grinder or a bank-clerk rather than lose her—and then she seemed downright angry, and sent me away again.

Women are strangely inconsistent!

She always sent me away, but I always came back.

After about a month of this torture, I chanced to find her, one soft May twilight, without the aunt, sitting by a window in the fragrant dusk.

She had flowers in her hand—flowers I had sent her—and sat looking down at them, her strong, pure profile clear against the saffron sky.

I came in quietly, and stood watching, in a rapture of hope and admiration. And while I watched I saw a great pearl tear roll down among my violets.

That was enough.

I sprang forward, I knelt beside her, I caught her hands in mine, I drew her to me, I cried, exultantly: 'You love me! And I—ah, God! how I love you!'

Even then she would have put me from her. She insisted that I did not know her yet, that she ought to tell me—but I held her close and kissed away her words, and said: 'You love me, perfect one, and I love you. The rest will be right.'

Then she laid her white hands on my shoulders, and looked deep into my eyes.

'I believe that is true,' said she; 'and I will marry you, Edward.'

She dropped her face on my shoulder then—that face of fire and roses—and we were still.

II

It is but two months' time from then; I have been married a fortnight. The first week was heaven—and the second was hell! O my God! my wife! That young Diana to be but——! I have borne it a week. I have feared and despised myself. I have suspected and hated myself. I have discovered and cursed myself. Aye, and cursed her, and *him*, whom this day I shall kill!

It is now three o'clock. I cannot kill him until four, for he comes not till then.

I am very comfortable here in this room opposite—very comfortable; and I can wait and think and remember.

Let me think.

First, to kill him. That is simple and easily settled.

Shall I kill her?

If she lived, could I ever see her again? Ever touch that hand—those lips—that, within two weeks of marriage——? No, she shall die!

And, if she lived, what would be before her but more shame, and more, till she felt it herself?

Far better that she die!

And I?

Could I live to forget her? To carry always in my heart a black stone across that door? To rise and rise, and do great work—*alone!*

Never! I cannot forget her!

Better die with her, even now.

Hark! Is that a step on the stair? Not yet.

My money is well bestowed. Antoine is a better artist than I, and a better man, and the money will widen and lighten a noble life in his hands.

And little Georgette is provided for. How long ago, how faint and weak, that seems! But Georgette loved me, I believe, at least for a time—longer than a week.

To wait—until four o'clock!

To think—I have thought; it is all arranged!

These pistols, that she admired but day before yesterday, that we practised with together, both loaded full. What a shot she is! I believe she can do everything!

To wait—to think—to remember.

Let me remember.

I knew her a week, wooed her a month, have been married a fortnight.

She always said I didn't know her. She was always on the point of telling me something, and I would not let her. She seemed half repentant, half in jest—I preferred to trust her. Those clear, brown eyes—clear and bright, like brook water with the sun through it! And she would smile so! 'Tis not that I must remember.

Am I sure? Sure! I laugh at myself.

What would you call it, you—any man? A young woman steals from her house, alone, every day, and comes privately, cloaked and veiled, to this place, this den of Bohemians, this building of New York studios! Painters? I know them—I am a painter myself.

She goes to this room, day after day, and tells me nothing.

I say to her gently: 'What do you do with your days, my love?'

'Oh, many things,' she answers; 'I am studying art—to please you!'

That was ingenious. She knew she might be watched.

I say, 'Cannot I teach you?' and she says, 'I have a teacher I used to study with. I must finish. I want to surprise you!' So she would soothe me—to appearance.

But I watch and follow, I take this little room. I wait, and I see.

Lessons? Oh, perjured one! There is no tenant of that room but yourself, and to it *he* comes each day.

Is that a step? Not yet. I watch and wait. This is America, I say, not France. This is my wife. I will trust her. But the man comes every day. He is young. He is handsome—handsome as a fiend.

I cannot bear it. I go to the door. I knock. There is no response. I try the door. It is locked. I stoop and look through the key-hole. What do I see? Ah, God! The hat and cloak of that man upon a chair, and then only a tall screen. Behind that screen, low voices!

I did not go home last night. I am here to-day—with these!

That is a step. Yes! Softly, now. He has gone in. I heard her speak. She said: 'You are late, Guillaume!'

Let me give them a little time.

Now—softly—I come, friends. *I* am not late!

III

Across the narrow passage I steal, noiselessly. The door is unlocked this time. I burst in.

There stands my young wife, pale, trembling, startled, unable to speak.

There is the handsome Guillaume—behind the screen. My fingers press the triggers. There is a sharp double report. Guillaume tumbles over, howling, and Marie flings herself between us.

'Edward! One moment! Give me a moment for my life! The pistols are harmless, dear—blank cartridges. I fixed them myself. I saw you suspected. But you've spoiled my surprise. I shall have to tell you now. This is my studio, love. Here is the picture you have the sketch of. *I* am "M. Duchesne"—Mary Duchesne Greenleaf Carpenter—and this is my model!'

IV

We are very happy in Paris, with our double studio. We sometimes share our models. We laugh at M. Daudet.

CIRCUMSTANCES ALTER CASES

I

'ARE you going to let a wretched prejudice like this stand against my love?' he asked; 'an empty impersonal sex-prejudice against a man's lifelong devotion? You say you love me, and yet you won't marry me because I don't agree with you in all your ideas! A pretty kind of love!'

'I am not defending my special variety of love,' she answered, slowly. 'I never pretended it was all absorbing, or everlasting, or in any way equal to a man's lifelong devotion. I am, unfortunately, one of those much-berated New England women who have learned to think as well as feel; and to me, at least, marriage means more than a union of hearts and bodies—it must mean minds, too. It would be a never-ending grief to me, starvation and bitter pain, to have you indifferent or contemptuous to my most earnest thoughts and beliefs. You see, I should love you enough to care.'

'Yes, I see! I see a great deal!' he replied, walking over to the hearth and leaning his arm against the mantel. He seemed to borrow fire from the glowing coals, for he came back and began again with restrained intensity:

'It is another instance of this cursed modern education! The women of to-day develop their minds until they are stronger than heart and body together—too strong to yield to a healthy love. And so they live, and so they die, and who is the better for it!'

'My dear George, you feel so keenly that it makes you unjust. You are not fair to women. It is that, more than anything else, which stands between us. If you are not fair now, to your heart's idol, your queen and all that, what *would* you be to your wife?'

She leaned back against the dull bronze green of the great chair, a lovely picture in the soft firelight, and looked at him steadily. Youth; health and beauty were in the up-turned face, and the free fine curves of body and limb showed that modern education had trained something besides intellect.

He turned over several things in his mind before replying. It was really difficult. Masculine habits of thought, dominant for centuries, were strong within him. He was a just man in most things, and he knew it. But his sense of chivalry and love for her moved him to soften what was most natural to say; and, under all, the individual soul could but admit some truth in her accusation.

'I can't talk any more on this theme to-night,' he said at last. 'But once convict me of an instance of clear injustice to your sex, and I will own you are right—and that it is wiser for us to live apart. Come, won't you sing to me a little before I go?'

'With all my heart,' said she. 'You see it is with all my heart, not my head, so we don't quarrel over music!'

He suppressed an impatient rejoinder, and they went to the piano.

II

George Saunders and his friend Howard Clarke—schoolmates, college chums, and partners at law—were strolling the beach next day below the high bluff where stood the imposing 'cottage' of Hilda Warde.

She was, as she had said, one of those New England women who are so disproportionately numerous that they cannot marry at home, while to take them away would go far toward depopulating the country.

They are a singular race. Violating every law of woman's existence according to the canons, they still live, and often present a favorable contrast to their married sisters in both health and happiness. As to usefulness, of course, they have none. No trifles in the way of personal achievement can counterbalance the delinquency of unmarried women. They live, and Hilda bade fair to finally join their ranks, for she was twenty-seven, travelled, cultured, experienced, and 'peculiar.'

Clarke had loved her, vainly, and gotten safely over it, much to his astonishment. Saunders had loved her at the same time, and did still—not wholly in vain, for she at least professed to love him; but still she would not marry.

'Howard,' he said, after they had strolled a gloomy mile, comforted only by their cigars, 'do you think she cares for me or not?'

'Doesn't she say so?' inquired Howard.

'Yes, she says so, but she doesn't act so. If a woman really loves, she doesn't hesitate over a matter of opinion. There isn't one woman in a hundred to-day, here at least, with a heart as big as a button! I am glad I am going abroad.'

'Have you made up your mind when to start?'

'I shall start to-night if I can't get anything more definite from Hilda. I'll take the early boat to Boston, and leave by the Wednesday steamer—the Ithuriel. I had a berth engaged with the privilege of countermanding, and only came down here in hopes——' He broke off, and looked wearily out to sea.

'It's too bad, George!' cried Howard. 'There isn't a woman in christendom that's worth the sacrifice you are making! You would have been one of the first lawyers in the country before this, and nobody knows what politically, if you hadn't wasted these years on that heartless jilt! Look at that Ashford case you lost. I know why you lost it. Nothing on earth but sleeplessness and misery. It's as bad as murder! Talk about justice! If women got the justice they are so anxious for, there wouldn't be many of them left.'

'Stop!' said Saunders. 'She is a woman, and I love her. For my sake, be still.' And they were still for another gloomy mile, till they caught sight of Hilda herself, on the edge of the cliff above them, walking with a swift, free grace, her figure outlined clearly against the sky. She saw them presently, and began to descend a steep little path, motioning back their start to help her.

'I was coming down anyway,' she said, 'and, besides, it is easier for one to come down than for two to come up. But I want to rest a moment, for I've been to Shark Rock, and then a story to tell and an opinion to ask.'

They ensconced themselves in a shaded and windless corner, and Miss Warde was about to begin, when she espied a new-made friend of theirs, somewhat a lion in the little place, standing uncertainly a short way off, his hat in his hand.

He was a young Russian, wealthy, noble, and famous in his own country, but now a lifelong exile, making a tool of what had been a weapon before—his pen.

'Won't you join us, Count Stefan?' asked Hilda. 'I want an audience to-day.'

So the three gentlemen, after a moment's talk, settled themselves at her feet and she began her story.

'It is only a little one,' she said, 'but a true story; and I want your honest opinions on the merits of the case. *Honest*—mind you!

'There was a young man, good and clever and all that, but a little queer and opinionated. He had great notions of the work he was going to do, and really showed some promise, though nobody believed in his reformatory ideas or his ability either—he was so indefinite. Well, he met a young woman.'

'Of course,' remarked Saunders.

'Fate!' said Clarke.

'He was fortunate,' murmured the Count.

'Now, you must not interrupt,' frowned Hilda. 'This is a test case, and I want your calmest judgment. This young woman fell in love with him, and—I won't say made up her mind, for that was not her method—but she wanted to marry him. She was a fine girl, handsome and clever, a genius in her line. She was musical, and they might have been great friends but for that. But he was a rabid reformer, and she cared for nothing but love and music; so he didn't want to marry her, though he could not but love her in a way, she was so good and beautiful and—well, a strongly feminine nature.

'They were intimate friends and talked with all the freedom of the philosopher on one side and the artist on the other. He found out how things were going, and told her freely his plans and hopes; how he was resolved never to marry, that she was to him but a dear friend—everything as clear as daylight.

'But our young woman had her own plans and hopes. To do her justice, she didn't believe in his projects at all, and felt sure she could make him both powerful and happy by marrying him; so she went to work. Her methods were simple. She just took advantage of the freedom of their friendship to play upon his masculine nature. She had no scruples of any kind in such a case.

She loved him, and him alone, and meant to marry him—that was all.

'Of course, it was only a matter of time. He struggled manfully, made engagements and broke them, left her and returned again; she always managed, by appealing to sympathy or friendship, or by a blank, reproachful silence, to get him to come and see her once more. After a while he felt his honor was engaged, and then he stuck to it, and married her. He loved her somewhat, you understand, through it all; only he knew——'

'Knew what?' from the Count, whose quiet eyes never left her face.

'Knew how it would end.'

'How did it end?' asked Saunders, rather bitterly.

'Just as he feared. It upset his work and health and everything. He wasn't earning much anyway, and that bothered him, as it always does. There was a child, of course; and between the extra care and unusual demands, and the miserable state of mind he was in, it quite ruined him. He just went insane and killed himself—one of those excitable, nervous temperaments, you know.

'That's all the story. What I want of you gentlemen is an opinion on the relative guilt of the two parties.'

'Guilt of the one party, you mean,' said Saunders, harshly. 'He was weak, no doubt—most men are in a similar case—but she was the one to blame!'

'She didn't force him to marry her,' objected Hilda, mildly. 'He might have escaped or refused.'

'And where could he have gone, pray, to escape a hunter like that—even if he had the means, which I understand he hadn't? And as to refusing—she led him on till he *couldn't* refuse—in honor! No, indeed. Get a man into the hands of a woman like that, and he can neither escape nor refuse.'

'I agree with George,' said Howard Clarke. 'The girl was altogether to blame.'

'Do I understand,' inquired the Count, with his perfect accent, 'that she made the proposal of marriage?'

'She did,' said Hilda.

'And that he explained to her that he did not love her in that way, and that he was unfit and unwilling to marry?'

'Clearly and repeatedly,' said Hilda.

'And that, after being led into one engagement, he broke it and left her, only to be pulled back again?'

'He did.'

'I am forced to agree with these gentlemen against the lady. She was most cruelly to blame.'

Hilda's eyes dwelt on him a moment admiringly, as he uttered the quiet but impressive syllables. Then she studied the other speakers.

'It makes no difference in a case like that,' Saunders broke out, 'whether it's a man or a woman. To play on a person like that and win him against his will through his worst and weakest nature! She was a criminal!'

'But she loved him,' said Hilda.

'Love! Do you call *that* love? To ruin a man's life!' Mr Saunders's horror overcame him and he became speechless.

Hilda Warde sat quiet for a few minutes. 'And you, Mr Clarke?'

'Of course I say the same. Sorry, to a woman, but she was a selfish wretch!'

Hilda heaved a long sigh.

'Well, my friends,' she said at length, 'I hope you are honest. I have made one error in my story—just a trifle. The facts are all the same, but the sexes are reversed. It is the story of my friend May Henderson and her husband.'

The Count looked mildly surprised, and seemed trying to rebuild the tale on the new basis in his mind.

But Saunders spoke out vehemently.

'Why, Hilda, it's not the same case at all. John Henderson's a capital fellow—a real genius. And his wife was a nervous hypochondriac. It was the kindest thing she ever did—her departure.'

Hilda regarded him softly with her great brown eyes.

'But she used to be a paragon of health, and of most brilliant promise. And she told him she did not wish to marry—was not able or willing.'

Saunders laughed scornfully.

'Plenty of girls would say that,' he answered. 'She was a beautiful creature, and he had a perfect right to marry her if he could. She need not let him if she really did not want to—it's a free country!'

'I am so glad it is a free country,' said Hilda, rising. 'I am quite satisfied with your answer, George. Don't you think it will do for that single instance you mentioned last night?'

'I see,' he replied, in a restrained voice. 'A very pretty little trap!'

'It's a wholly different matter when you change the sex,' cried Mr Clarke, vehemently. 'It alters—er—everything!'

'So I see,' said Hilda.

'But, madame,' the Count quietly interposed, 'you say the tale remains the same—identical?'

'Exactly the same, Count Stefan.'

'Then surely the judgment is the same—the man was so the criminal!'

'Excuse me—I must bid you good-bye,' here broke in Mr Saunders. 'I am going to Boston to-night, and sail Wednesday, as I told you. Howard is going to walk down with me.'

The farewells were soon said, and somewhat coldly.

'Shall we not go back together?' asked Mr Clarke, seeing her also preparing to start.

'Thank you, no,' said she, 'I am going by the upper path.'

'May I accompany you?' asked the Count.

'If you care for climbing—and a high wind,' she answered.

And they went together.

THE GIANT WISTARIA

'MEDDLE not with my new vine, child! See! Thou hast already broken the tender shoot! Never needle or distaff for thee, and yet thou wilt not be quiet!'

The nervous fingers wavered, clutched at a small carnelian cross that hung from her neck, then fell despairingly.

'Give me my child, mother, and then I will be quiet!'

'Hush! hush! thou fool—some one might be near! See—there is thy father coming, even now! Get in quickly!'

She raised her eyes to her mother's face, weary eyes that yet had a flickering, uncertain blaze in their shaded depths.

'Art thou a mother and hast no pity on me, a mother? Give me my child!'

Her voice rose in a strange, low cry, broken by her father's hand upon her mouth.

'Shameless!' said he, with set teeth. 'Get to thy chamber, and be not seen again to-night, or I will have thee bound!'

She went at that, and a hard-faced serving woman followed, and presently returned, bringing a key to her mistress.

'Is all well with her,—and the child also?'

'She is quiet, Mistress Dwining, well for the night, be sure. The child fretteth endlessly, but save for that it thriveth with me.'

The parents were left alone together on the high square porch with its great pillars, and the rising moon began to make faint shadows of the young vine leaves that shot up luxuriantly around them; moving shadows, like little stretching fingers, on the broad and heavy planks of the oaken floor.

'It groweth well, this vine thou broughtest me in the ship, my husband.'

'Aye,' he broke in bitterly, 'and so doth the shame I brought thee! Had I known of it I would sooner have had the ship founder beneath us, and have seen our child cleanly drowned, than live to this end!'

'Thou art very hard, Samuel, art thou not afeard for her life? She grieveth sore for the child, aye, and for the green fields to walk in!'

'Nay,' said he grimly, 'I fear not. She hath lost already what is more than life; and she shall have air enough soon. To-morrow the ship is ready, and we return to England. None knoweth of our stain here, not one, and if the town hath a child unaccounted for to rear in decent ways—why, it is not the first, even here. It will be well enough cared for! And truly we have matter for thankfulness, that her cousin is yet willing to marry her.'

'Hast thou told him?'

'Aye! Thinkest thou I would cast shame into another man's house, unknowing it? He hath always desired her, but she would none of him, the stubborn! She hath small choice now!'

'Will he be kind, Samuel? can he—'

'Kind? What call'st thou it to take such as she to wife? Kind! How many men would take her, an' she had double the fortune? and being of the family already, he is glad to hide the blot forever.'

'An' if she would not? He is but a coarse fellow, and she ever shunned him.'

'Art thou mad, woman? She weddeth him ere we sail to-morrow, or she stayeth ever in that chamber. The girl is not so sheer a fool! He maketh an honest woman of her, and saveth our house from open shame. What other hope for her than a new life to cover the old? Let her have an honest child, an' she so longeth for one!'

He strode heavily across the porch, till the loose planks creaked again, strode back and forth, with his arms folded and his brows fiercely knit above his iron mouth.

Overhead the shadows flickered mockingly across a white face among the leaves, with eyes of wasted fire.

'O, George, what a house! what a lovely house! I am sure it's haunted! Let us get that house to live in this summer! We will have Kate and Jack and Susy and Jim of course, and a splendid time of it!'

Young husbands are indulgent, but still they have to recognize facts.

'My dear, the house may not be to rent; and it may also not be habitable.'

'There is surely somebody in it. I am going to inquire!'

The great central gate was rusted off its hinges, and the long drive had trees in it, but a little footpath showed signs of steady usage, and up that Mrs Jenny went, followed by her obedient George. The front windows of the old mansion were blank, but in a wing at the back they found white curtains and open doors. Outside, in the clear May sunshine, a woman was washing. She was polite and friendly, and evidently glad of visitors in that lonely place. She 'guessed it could be rented— didn't know.' The heirs were in Europe, but 'there was a lawyer in New York had the lettin' of it.' There had been folks there years ago, but not in her time. She and her husband had the rent of their part for taking care of the place. 'Not that they took much care on't either, but keepin' robbers out.' It was furnished throughout, old-fashioned enough, but good; and if they took it she could do the work for 'em herself, she guessed—'if *he* was willin'!'

Never was a crazy scheme more easily arranged. George knew that lawyer in New York; the rent was not alarming; and the nearness to a rising sea-shore resort made it a still pleasanter place to spend the summer.

Kate and Jack and Susy and Jim cheerfully accepted, and the June moon found them all sitting on the high front porch.

They had explored the house from top to bottom, from the great room in the garret, with nothing in it but a rickety cradle, to the well in the cellar without a curb and with a rusty chain going down to unknown blackness below. They had explored the grounds, once beautiful with rare trees and shrubs, but now a gloomy wilderness of tangled shade.

The old lilacs and laburnums, the spirea and syringa, nodded against the second-story windows. What garden plants survived were great ragged bushes or great shapeless beds. A huge wistaria vine covered the whole front of the house. The trunk, it was too large to call a stem, rose at the corner of the porch by the high steps, and had once climbed its pillars; but now the pillars were wrenched from their places and held rigid and helpless by the tightly wound and knotted arms.

It fenced in all the upper story of the porch with a knitted wall of stem and leaf; it ran along the eaves, holding up the gutter that had once supported it; it shaded every window with heavy green; and the drooping, fragrant blossoms made a waving sheet of purple from roof to ground.

'Did you ever see such a wistaria!' cried ecstatic Mrs Jenny. 'It is worth the rent just to sit under such a vine,—a fig tree beside it would be sheer superfluity and wicked extravagance!'

'Jenny makes much of her wistaria,' said George, 'because she's so disappointed about the ghosts. She made up her mind at first sight to have ghosts in the house, and she can't find even a ghost story!'

'No,' Jenny assented mournfully; 'I pumped poor Mrs Pepperill for three days, but could get nothing out of her. But I'm convinced there is a story, if we could only find it. You need not tell me that a house like this, with a garden like this, and a cellar like this, isn't haunted!'

'I agree with you,' said Jack. Jack was a reporter on a New York daily, and engaged to Mrs Jenny's pretty sister. 'And if we don't find a real ghost, you may be very sure I shall make one. It's too good an opportunity to lose!'

The pretty sister, who sat next him, resented. 'You shan't do anything of the sort, Jack! This is a *real* ghostly place, and I won't have you make fun of it! Look at that group of trees out there in the long grass—it looks for all the world like a crouching, hunted figure!'

'It looks to me like a woman picking huckleberries,' said Jim, who was married to George's pretty sister.

'Be still, Jim!' said that fair young woman. 'I believe in Jenny's ghost as much as she does. Such a place! Just look at this great wistaria trunk crawling up by the steps here! It looks for all the world like a writhing body—cringing—beseeching!'

'Yes,' answered the subdued Jim, 'it does, Susy. See its waist,—about two yards of it, and twisted at that! A waste of good material!'

'Don't be so horrid, boys! Go off and smoke somewhere if you can't be congenial!'

'We can! We will! We'll be as ghostly as you please.' And forthwith they began to see bloodstains and crouching figures so plentifully that the most delightful shivers multiplied, and the fair enthusiasts started for bed, declaring they should never sleep a wink.

'We shall all surely dream,' cried Mrs Jenny, 'and we must all tell our dreams in the morning!'

'There's another thing certain,' said George, catching Susy as she tripped over a loose plank; 'and that is that you frisky creatures must use the side door till I get this Eiffel tower of a portico fixed, or we shall have some fresh ghosts on our hands! We found a plank here that yawns like a trap-door—big enough to swallow you,—and I believe the bottom of the thing is in China!'

The next morning found them all alive, and eating a substantial New England breakfast, to the accompaniment of saws and hammers on the porch, where carpenters of quite miraculous promptness were tearing things to pieces generally.

'It's got to come down mostly,' they had said. 'These timbers are clean rotted through, what ain't pulled out o' line by this great creeper. That's about all that holds the thing up.'

There was clear reason in what they said, and with a caution from anxious Mrs Jenny not to hurt the wistaria, they were left to demolish and repair at leisure.

'How about ghosts?' asked Jack after a fourth griddle cake. 'I had one, and it's taken away my appetite!'

Mrs Jenny gave a little shriek and dropped her knife and fork.

'Oh, so had I! I had the most awful—well, not dream exactly, but feeling. I had forgotten all about it!'

'Must have been awful,' said Jack, taking another cake. 'Do tell us about the feeling. My ghost will wait.'

'It makes me creep to think of it even now,' she said. 'I woke up, all at once, with that dreadful feeling as if something were going to happen, you know! I was wide awake, and hearing every little sound for miles around, it seemed to me. There are so many strange little noises in the country for all it is so still. Millions of crickets and things outside, and all kinds of rustles in the trees! There wasn't much wind, and the moonlight came through in my three great windows in three white squares on the black old floor, and those fingery wistaria leaves we were talking of last night just seemed to crawl all over them. And—O, girls, you know that dreadful well in the cellar?'

A most gratifying impression was made by this, and Jenny proceeded cheerfully:

'Well, while it was so horridly still, and I lay there trying not to wake George, I heard as plainly as if it were right in the room, that old chain down there rattle and creak over the stones!'

'Bravo!' cried Jack. 'That's fine! I'll put it in the Sunday edition!'

'Be still!' said Kate. 'What was it, Jenny? Did you really see anything?'

'No, I didn't, I'm sorry to say. But just then I didn't want to. I woke George, and made such a fuss that he gave me bromide, and said he'd go and look, and that's the last I thought of it till Jack reminded me,—the bromide worked so well.'

'Now, Jack, give us yours,' said Jim. 'Maybe, it will dovetail in somehow. Thirsty ghost, I imagine; maybe they had prohibition here even then!'

Jack folded his napkin, and leaned back in his most impressive manner.

'It was striking twelve by the great hall clock—' he began.

'There isn't any hall clock!'

'O hush, Jim, you spoil the current! It was just one o'clock then, by my old-fashioned repeater.'

'Waterbury! Never mind what time it was!'

'Well, honestly, I woke up sharp, like our beloved hostess, and tried to go to sleep again, but couldn't. I experienced all those moonlight and grasshopper sensations, just like Jenny, and was wondering what could have been the matter with the supper, when in came my ghost, and I knew it was all a dream! It was a female ghost, and I imagine she was young and handsome, but all those crouching, hunted figures of last evening ran riot in my brain, and this poor creature looked just like them. She was all wrapped up in a shawl, and had a big bundle under her arm,— dear me, I am spoiling the story! With the air and gait of one in frantic haste and terror, the muffled figure glided to a dark old bureau, and seemed taking things from the drawers. As she turned, the moonlight shone full on a little red cross that hung from her neck by a thin gold chain—I saw it glitter as she crept noiselessly from the room! That's all.'

'O Jack, don't be so horrid! Did you really? Is that all! What do you think it was?'

'I am not horrid by nature, only professionally. I really did. That was all. And I am fully convinced it was the genuine, legitimate ghost of an eloping chambermaid with kleptomania!'

'You are too bad, Jack!' cried Jenny. 'You take all the horror out of it. There isn't a "creep" left among us.'

'It's no time for creeps at nine-thirty a.m., with sunlight and carpenters outside! However, if you can't wait till twilight for your creeps, I think I can furnish one or two,' said George. 'I went down cellar after Jenny's ghost!'

There was a delighted chorus of female voices, and Jenny cast upon her lord a glance of genuine gratitude.

'It's all very well to lie in bed and see ghosts, or hear them,' he went on. 'But the young householder suspecteth burglars, even though as a medical man he knoweth nerves, and after Jenny dropped off I started on a voyage of discovery. I never will again, I promise you!'

'Why, what *was* it?'

'Oh, George!'

'I got a candle—'

'Good mark for the burglars,' murmured Jack.

'And went all over the house, gradually working down to the cellar and the well.'

'Well?' said Jack.

'Now you can laugh; but that cellar is no joke by daylight, and a candle there at night is about as inspiring as a lightning-bug in the Mammoth Cave. I went along with the light, trying not to fall into the well prematurely; got to it all at once; held the light down and *then* I saw, right under my feet—(I nearly fell over her, or walked through her, perhaps),—a woman, hunched up under a shawl! She had hold of the chain, and the candle shone on her hands—white, thin hands,—on a little red cross that hung from her neck—*vide* Jack! I'm no believer in ghosts, and I firmly object to unknown parties in the house at night; so I spoke to her rather fiercely. She didn't seem to notice that, and I reached down to take hold of her,—then I came upstairs!'

'What for?'

'What happened?'

'What was the matter?'

'Well, nothing happened. Only she wasn't there! May have been indigestion, of course, but as a physician I don't advise any one to court indigestion alone at midnight in a cellar!'

'This is the most interesting and peripatetic and evasive ghost I ever heard of!' said Jack. 'It's my belief she has no end of silver tankards, and jewels galore, at the bottom of that well, and I move we go and see!'

'To the bottom of the well, Jack?'

'To the bottom of the mystery. Come on!'

There was unanimous assent, and the fresh cambrics and pretty boots were gallantly escorted below by gentlemen whose jokes were so frequent that many of them were a little forced.

The deep old cellar was so dark that they had to bring lights, and the well so gloomy in its blackness that the ladies recoiled.

'That well is enough to scare even a ghost. It's my opinion you'd better let well enough alone!' quoth Jim.

'Truth lies hid in a well, and we must get her out,' said George. 'Bear a hand with the chain?'

Jim pulled away on the chain, George turned the creaking windlass, and Jack was chorus.

'A wet sheet for this ghost, if not a flowing sea,' said he. 'Seems to be hard work raising spirits! I suppose he kicked the bucket when he went down!'

As the chain lightened and shortened there grew a strained silence among them; and when at length the bucket appeared, rising slowly through the dark water, there was an eager, half reluctant peering, and a natural drawing back. They poked the gloomy contents. 'Only water.'

'Nothing but mud.'

'Something—'

They emptied the bucket up on the dark earth, and then the girls all went out into the air, into the bright warm sunshine in front of the house, where was the sound of saw and hammer, and the smell of new wood. There was nothing said until the men joined them, and then Jenny timidly asked:

'How old should you think it was, George?'

'All of a century,' he answered. 'That water is a preserva-
tive,—lime in it. Oh!—you mean?—Not more than a month; a
very little baby!'

There was another silence at this, broken by a cry from the
workmen. They had removed the floor and the side walls of the
old porch, so that the sunshine poured down to the dark stones
of the cellar bottom. And there, in the strangling grasp of the
roots of the great wistaria, lay the bones of a woman, from whose
neck still hung a tiny scarlet cross on a thin chain of gold.

AN EXTINCT ANGEL

THERE was once a species of angel inhabiting this planet, acting as 'a universal solvent' to all the jarring, irreconcilable elements of human life.

It was quite numerous; almost every family had one; and, although differing in degree of seraphic virtue, all were, by common consent, angels.

The advantages of possessing such a creature were untold. In the first place, the chances of the mere human being in the way of getting to heaven were greatly increased by these semi-heavenly belongings; they gave one a sort of lien on the next world, a practical claim most comforting to the owner.

For the angels of course possessed virtues above mere humanity; and because the angels were so well-behaved, therefore the owners were given credit.

Beside this direct advantage of complimentary tickets up above were innumerable indirect advantages below. The possession of one of these angels smoothed every feature of life, and gave peace and joy to an otherwise hard lot.

It was the business of the angel to assuage, to soothe, to comfort, to delight. No matter how unruly were the passions of the owner, sometimes even to the extent of legally beating his angel with 'a stick no thicker than his thumb,' the angel was to have no passion whatever—unless self-sacrifice may be called a passion, and indeed it often amounted to one with her.

The human creature went out to his daily toil and comforted himself as he saw fit. He was apt to come home tired and cross, and in this exigency it was the business of the angel to wear a smile for his benefit—a soft, perennial, heavenly smile.

By an unfortunate limitation of humanity the angel was required, in addition to such celestial duties as smiling and soothing, to do kitchen service, cleaning, sewing, nursing, and other mundane tasks. But these things must be accomplished without the slightest diminution of the angelic virtues.

Kate Field's Washington (23 September 1891), 199–200.

The angelic virtues, by the way, were of a curiously paradoxical nature.

They were inherent. A human being did not pretend to name them, could not be expected to have them, acknowledged them as far beyond his gross earthly nature; and yet, for all this, he kept constant watch over the virtues of the angel, wrote whole books of advice for angels on how they should behave, and openly held that angels would lose their virtues altogether should they once cease to obey the will and defer to the judgment of human kind.

This looks strange to us to-day as we consider these past conditions, but then it seemed fair enough; and the angels—bless their submissive, patient hearts!—never thought of questioning it.

It was perhaps only to be expected that when an angel fell the human creature should punish the celestial creature with unrelenting fury. It was so much easier to be an angel than to be human, that there was no excuse for an angel's falling, even by means of her own angelic pity and tender affection.

It seems perhaps hard that the very human creature the angel fell on, or fell with, or fell to—however you choose to put it—was as harsh as anyone in condemnation of the fall. He never assisted the angel to rise, but got out from under and resumed his way, leaving her in the mud. She was a great convenience to walk on, and, as was stoutly maintained by the human creature, helped keep the other angels clean.

This is exceedingly mysterious, and had better not be inquired into too closely.

The amount of physical labor of a severe and degrading sort required of one of these bright spirits, was amazing. Certain kinds of work—always and essentially dirty—were relegated wholly to her. Yet one of her first and most rigid duties was the keeping of her angelic robes spotlessly clean.

The human creature took great delight in contemplating the flowing robes of the angels. Their changeful motion suggested to him all manner of sweet and lovely thoughts and memories; also, the angelic virtues above mentioned were supposed largely to inhere in the flowing robes. Therefore flow they must, and the ample garments waved unchecked over the weary limbs of the wearer, the contiguous furniture and the stairs. For the angels unfortunately had no wings, and their work was such as required a good deal of going up and down stairs.

It is quite a peculiar thing, in contemplating this work, to see how largely it consisted in dealing with dirt. Yes, it does seem strange to this enlightened age; but the fact was that the angels waited on the human creatures in every form of menial service, doing things as their natural duty which the human creature loathed and scorned.

It does seem irreconcilable, but they reconciled it. The angel was an angel and the work was the angel's work, and what more do you want?

There is one thing about the subject which looks a little suspicious: The angels—I say it under breath—were not very bright!

The human creatures did not like intelligent angels—intelligence seemed to dim their shine, somehow, and pale their virtues. It was harder to reconcile things where the angels had any sense. Therefore every possible care was taken to prevent the angels from learning anything of our gross human wisdom.

But little by little, owing to the unthought-of consequences of repeated intermarriage between the angel and the human being, the angel longed for, found and ate the fruit of the forbidden tree of knowledge.

And in that day she surely died.

The species is now extinct. It is rumored that here and there in remote regions you can still find a solitary specimen—in places where no access is to be had to the deadly fruit; but the race as a race is extinct.

Poor dodo!

THE ROCKING-CHAIR

A WAVING spot of sunshine, a signal light that caught the eye at once in a waste of commonplace houses, and all the dreary dimness of a narrow city street.

Across some low roof that made a gap in the wall of masonry, shot a level, brilliant beam of the just-setting sun, touching the golden head of a girl in an open window.

She sat in a high-backed rocking-chair with brass mountings that glittered as it swung, rocking slowly back and forth, never lifting her head, but fairly lighting up the street with the glory of her sunlit hair.

We two stopped and stared, and, so staring, caught sight of a small sign in a lower window—'Furnished Lodgings.' With a common impulse we crossed the street and knocked at the dingy front door.

Slow, even footsteps approached from within, and a soft girl-ish laugh ceased suddenly as the door opened, showing us an old woman, with a dull, expressionless face and faded eyes.

Yes, she had rooms to let. Yes, we could see them. No, there was no service. No, there were no meals. So murmuring monot-onously, she led the way up-stairs. It was an ordinary house enough, on a poor sort of street, a house in no way remarkable or unlike its fellows.

She showed us two rooms, connected, neither better nor worse than most of their class, rooms without a striking feature about them, unless it was the great brass-bound chair we found still rocking gently by the window.

But the gold-haired girl was nowhere to be seen.

I fancied I heard the light rustle of girlish robes in the inner chamber—a breath of that low laugh—but the door leading to this apartment was locked, and when I asked the woman if we could see the other rooms she said she had no other rooms to let.

A few words aside with Hal, and we decided to take these two, and move in at once. There was no reason we should not. We

Worthington's Illustrated, 1 (May 1893), 453–9.

were looking for lodgings when that swinging sunbeam caught our eyes, and the accommodations were fully as good as we could pay for. So we closed our bargain on the spot, returned to our deserted boarding-house for a few belongings, and were settled anew that night.

Hal and I were young newspaper men, 'penny-a-liners,' part of that struggling crowd of aspirants who are to literature what squires and pages were to knighthood in olden days. We were winning our spurs. So far it was slow work, unpleasant and ill-paid—so was squireship and pagehood, I am sure; menial service and laborious polishing of armor; long running afoot while the master rode. But the squire could at least honor his lord and leader, while we, alas! had small honor for those above us in our profession, with but too good reason. We, of course, should do far nobler things when these same spurs were won!

Now it may have been mere literary instinct—the grasping at 'material' of the pot-boiling writers of the day, and it may have been another kind of instinct—the unacknowledged attraction of the fair unknown; but, whatever the reason, the place had drawn us both, and here we were.

Unbroken friendship begun in babyhood held us two together, all the more closely because Hal was a merry, prosaic, clear-headed fellow, and I sensitive and romantic.

The fearless frankness of family life we shared, but held the right to unapproachable reserves, and so kept love unstrained.

We examined our new quarters with interest. The front room, Hal's, was rather big and bare. The back room, mine, rather small and bare.

He preferred that room, I am convinced, because of the window and the chair. I preferred the other, because of the locked door. We neither of us mentioned these prejudices.

'Are you sure you would not rather have this room?' asked Hal, conscious, perhaps, of an ulterior motive in his choice.

'No, indeed,' said I, with a similar reservation; 'you only have the street and I have a real "view" from my window. The only thing I begrudge you is the chair!'

'You may come and rock therein at any hour of the day or night,' said he magnanimously. 'It is tremendously comfortable, for all its black looks.'

It was a comfortable chair, a very comfortable chair, and we both used it a great deal. A very high-backed chair, curving a little forward at the top, with heavy square corners. These corners, the ends of the rockers, the great sharp knobs that tipped the arms, and every other point and angle were mounted in brass.

'Might be used for a battering-ram!' said Hal.

He sat smoking in it, rocking slowly and complacently by the window, while I lounged on the foot of the bed, and watched a pale young moon sink slowly over the western housetops.

It went out of sight at last, and the room grew darker and darker till I could only see Hal's handsome head and the curving chair-back move slowly to and fro against the dim sky.

'What brought us here so suddenly, Maurice?' he asked, out of the dark.

'Three reasons,' I answered. 'Our need of lodgings, the suitability of these, and a beautiful head.'

'Correct,' said he. 'Anything else?'

'Nothing you would admit the existence of, my sternly logical friend. But I am conscious of a certain compulsion, or at least attraction, in the case, which does not seem wholly accounted for, even by golden hair.'

'For once I will agree with you,' said Hal. 'I feel the same way myself, and I am not impressionable.'

We were silent for a little. I may have closed my eyes,—it may have been longer than I thought, but it did not seem another moment when something brushed softly against my arm, and Hal in his great chair was rocking beside me.

'Excuse me,' said he, seeing me start. 'This chair evidently "walks," I've seen 'em before.'

So had I, on carpets, but there was no carpet here, and I thought I was awake.

He pulled the heavy thing back to the window again, and we went to bed.

Our door was open, and we could talk back and forth, but presently I dropped off and slept heavily until morning. But I must have dreamed most vividly, for he accused me of rocking in his chair half the night; said he could see my outline clearly against the starlight.

'No,' said I, 'you dreamed it. You've got rocking-chair on the brain.'

'Dream it is, then,' he answered cheerily. 'Better a nightmare than a contradiction; a vampire than a quarrel! Come on, let's go to breakfast!'

We wondered greatly as the days went by that we saw nothing of our golden-haired charmer. But we wondered in silence, and neither mentioned it to the other.

Sometimes I heard her light movements in the room next mine, or the soft laugh somewhere in the house; but the mother's slow, even steps were more frequent, and even she was not often visible.

All either of us saw of the girl, to my knowledge, was from the street, for she still availed herself of our chair by the window. This we disapproved of, on principle, the more so as we left the doors locked, and her presence proved the possession of another key. No; there was the door in my room! But I did not mention the idea. Under the circumstances, however, we made no complaint, and used to rush stealthily and swiftly up-stairs, hoping to surprise her. But we never succeeded. Only the chair was often found still rocking, and sometimes I fancied a faint sweet odor lingering about, an odor strangely saddening and suggestive. But one day when I thought Hal was there I rushed in unceremoniously and caught her. It was but a glimpse—a swift, light, noiseless sweep—she vanished into my own room. Following her with apologies for such a sudden entrance, I was too late. The envious door was locked again.

Our landlady's fair daughter was evidently shy enough when brought to bay, but strangely willing to take liberties in our absence.

Still, I had seen her, and for that sight would have forgiven much. Hers was a strange beauty, infinitely attractive yet infinitely perplexing. I marveled in secret, and longed with painful eagerness for another meeting; but I said nothing to Hal of my surprising her—it did not seem fair to the girl! She might have some good reason for going there; perhaps I could meet her again.

So I took to coming home early, on one excuse or another, and inventing all manner of errands to get to the room when Hal was not in.

But it was not until after numberless surprises on that point, finding him there when I supposed him downtown, and noticing something a little forced in his needless explanations, that I began to wonder if he might not be on the same quest.

Soon I was sure of it. I reached the corner of the street one evening just at sunset, and—yes, there was the rhythmic swing of that bright head in the dark frame of the open window. There also was Hal in the street below. She looked out, she smiled. He let himself in and went up-stairs.

I quickened my pace. I was in time to see the movement stop, the fair head turn, and Hal standing beyond her in the shadow.

I passed the door, passed the street, walked an hour—two hours—got a late supper somewhere, and came back about bedtime with a sharp and bitter feeling in my heart that I strove in vain to reason down. Why he had not as good a right to meet her as I it were hard to say, and yet I was strangely angry with him.

When I returned the lamplight shone behind the white curtain, and the shadow of the great chair stood motionless against it. Another shadow crossed—Hal—smoking. I went up.

He greeted me effusively and asked why I was so late. Where I got supper. Was unnaturally cheerful. There was a sudden dreadful sense of concealment between us. But he told nothing and I asked nothing, and we went silently to bed.

I blamed him for saying no word about our fair mystery, and yet I had said none concerning my own meeting. I racked my brain with questions as to how much he had really seen of her; if she had talked to him; what she had told him; how long she had stayed.

I tossed all night and Hal was sleepless too, for I heard him rocking for hours, by the window, by the bed, close to my door. I never knew a rocking-chair to 'walk' as that one did.

Towards morning the steady creak and swing was too much for my nerves or temper.

'For goodness' sake, Hal, do stop that and go to bed!'

'What?' came a sleepy voice.

'Don't fool!' said I, 'I haven't slept a wink to-night for your everlasting rocking. Now do leave off and go to bed.'

'Go to bed! I've been in bed all night and I wish you had! Can't you use the chair without blaming me for it?'

And all the time I *heard* him rock, rock, rock, over by the hall door!

I rose stealthily and entered the room, meaning to surprise the ill-timed joker and convict him in the act.

Both rooms were full of the dim phosphorescence of reflected moonlight; I knew them even in the dark; and yet I stumbled just inside the door, and fell heavily.

Hal was out of bed in a moment and had struck a light.

'Are you hurt, my dear boy?'

I was hurt, and solely by his fault, for the chair was not where I supposed, but close to my bedroom door, where he must have left it to leap into bed when he heard me coming. So it was in no amiable humor that I refused his offers of assistance and limped back to my own sleepless pillow. I had struck my ankle on one of those brass-tipped rockers, and it pained me severely. I never saw a chair so made to hurt as that one. It was so large and heavy and ill-balanced, and every joint and corner so shod with brass. Hal and I had punished ourselves enough on it before, especially in the dark when we forgot where the thing was standing, but never so severely as this. It was not like Hal to play such tricks, and both heart and ankle ached as I crept into bed again to toss and doze and dream and fitfully start till morning.

Hal was kindness itself, but he would insist that he had been asleep and I rocking all night, till I grew actually angry with him.

'That's carrying a joke too far,' I said at last. 'I don't mind a joke, even when it hurts, but there are limits.'

'Yes, there are!' said he, significantly, and we dropped the subject.

Several days passed. Hal had repeated meetings with the gold-haired damsel; this I saw from the street; but save for these bitter glimpses I waited vainly.

It was hard to bear, harder almost than the growing estrangement between Hal and me, and that cut deeply. I think that at last either one of us would have been glad to go away by himself, but neither was willing to leave the other to the room, the chair, the beautiful unknown.

Coming home one morning unexpectedly, I found the dull-faced landlady arranging the rooms, and quite laid myself out to make an impression upon her, to no purpose.

'That is a fine old chair you have there,' said I, as she stood mechanically polishing the brass corners with her apron.

She looked at the darkly glittering thing with almost a flash of pride.

'Yes,' said she, 'a fine chair!'

'Is it old!' I pursued.

'Very old,' she answered briefly.

'But I thought rocking-chairs were a modern American invention!' said I.

She looked at me apathetically.

'It is Spanish,' she said, 'Spanish oak, Spanish leather, Spanish brass, Spanish——.' I did not catch the last word, and she left the room without another.

It was a strange ill-balanced thing, that chair, though so easy and comfortable to sit in. The rockers were long and sharp behind, always lying in wait for the unwary, but cut short in front; and the back was so high and so heavy on top, that what with its weight and the shortness of the front rockers, it tipped forward with an ease and a violence equally astonishing.

This I knew from experience, as it had plunged over upon me during some of our frequent encounters. Hal also was a sufferer, but in spite of our manifold bruises, neither of us would have had the chair removed, for did not she sit in it, evening after evening, and rock there in the golden light of the setting sun.

So, evening after evening, we two fled from our work as early as possible, and hurried home alone, by separate ways, to the dingy street and the glorified window.

I could not endure forever. When Hal came home first, I, lingering in the street below, could see through our window that lovely head and his in close proximity. When I came first, it was to catch perhaps a quick glance from above—a bewildering smile—no more. She was always gone when I reached the room, and the inner door of my chamber irrevocably locked.

At times I even caught the click of the latch, heard the flutter of loose robes on the other side; and sometimes this daily disappointment, this constant agony of hope deferred, would bring me to my knees by that door, begging her to open to me, crying to her in every term of passionate endearment and persuasion that tortured heart of man could think to use.

Hal had neither word nor look for me now, save those of studied politeness and cold indifference, and how could I behave otherwise to him, so proven to my face a liar?

I saw him from the street one night, in the broad level sunlight, sitting in that chair, with the beautiful head on his shoulder. It was more than I could bear. If he had won, and won so utterly, I would ask but to speak to her once, and say farewell to both for ever. So I heavily climbed the stairs, knocked loudly, and entered at Hal's 'Come in!' only to find him sitting there alone, smoking—yes, smoking in the chair which but a moment since had held her too!

He had but just lit the cigar, a paltry device to blind my eyes.

'Look here, Hal,' said I, 'I can't stand this any longer. May I ask you one thing? Let me see her once, just once, that I may say good-bye, and then neither of you need see me again!'

Hal rose to his feet and looked me straight in the eye. Then he threw that whole cigar out of the window, and walked to within two feet of me.

'Are you crazy,' he said, '*I* ask her! *I!* I have never had speech of her in my life! And *you*—' He stopped and turned away.

'And I what?' I would have it out now whatever came.

'And you have seen her day after day—talked with her—I need not repeat all that my eyes have seen!'

'You need not, indeed,' said I. 'It would tax even your invention. I have never seen her in this room but once, and then but for a fleeting glimpse—no word. From the street I have seen her often—with you!'

He turned very white and walked from me to the window, then turned again.

'I have never seen her in this room for even such a moment as you own to. From the street I have seen her often—*with you!*'

We looked at each other.

'Do you mean to say,' I inquired slowly, 'that I did not see you just now sitting in that chair, by that window, with her in your arms?'

'Stop!' he cried, throwing out his hand with a fierce gesture. It struck sharply on the corner of the chair-back. He wiped the blood mechanically from the three-cornered cut, looking fixedly at me.

'I saw you,' said I.

'You did not!' said he.

I turned slowly on my heel and went into my room. I could not bear to tell that man, my more than brother, that he lied.

I sat down on my bed with my head on my hands, and presently I heard Hal's door open and shut, his step on the stair, the front door slam behind him. He had gone, I knew not where, and if he went to his death and a word of mine would have stopped him, I would not have said it. I do not know how long I sat there, in the company of hopeless love and jealousy and hate.

Suddenly, out of the silence of the empty room, came the steady swing and creak of the great chair. Perhaps—it must be! I sprang to my feet and noiselessly opened the door. There she sat by the window, looking out, and—yes—she threw a kiss to some one below. Ah, how beautiful she was! How beautiful! I made a step toward her. I held out my hands, I uttered I know not what—when all at once came Hal's quick step upon the stairs.

She heard it, too, and, giving me one look, one subtle, mysterious, triumphant look, slipped past me and into my room just as Hal burst in. He saw her go. He came straight to me and I thought he would have struck me down where I stood.

'Out of my way,' he cried. 'I will speak to her. Is it not enough to see?'—he motioned toward the window with his wounded hand—'Let me pass!'

'She is not there,' I answered. 'She has gone through into the other room.'

A light laugh sounded close by us, a faint, soft, silver laugh, almost at my elbow.

He flung me from his path, threw open the door, and entered. The room was empty.

'Where have you hidden her?' he demanded. I coldly pointed to the other door.

'So her room opens into yours, does it?' he muttered with a bitter smile. 'No wonder you preferred the "view"! Perhaps I can open it too?' And he laid his hand upon the latch.

I smiled then, for bitter experience had taught me that it was always locked, locked to all my prayers and entreaties. Let him kneel there as I had! But it opened under his hand! I sprang to his side, and we looked into—a closet, two by four, as bare and shallow as an empty coffin!

He turned to me, as white with rage as I was with terror. I was not thinking of him.

'What have you done with her?' he cried. And then contemptuously—'That I should stop to question a liar!'

I paid no heed to him, but walked back into the other room, where the great chair rocked by the window.

He followed me, furious with disappointment, and laid his hand upon the swaying back, his strong fingers closing on it till the nails were white.

'Will you leave this place?' said he.

'No,' said I.

'I will live no longer with a liar and a traitor,' said he.

'Then you will have to kill yourself,' said I.

With a muttered oath he sprang upon me, but caught his foot in the long rocker, and fell heavily.

So wild a wave of hate rose in my heart that I could have trampled upon him where he lay—killed him like a dog—but with a mighty effort I turned from him and left the room.

When I returned it was broad day. Early and still, not sunrise yet, but full of hard, clear light on roof and wall and roadway. I stopped on the lower floor to find the landlady and announce my immediate departure. Door after door I knocked at, tried and opened; room after room I entered and searched thoroughly; in all that house, from cellar to garret, was no furnished room but ours, no sign of human occupancy. Dust, dust, and cobwebs everywhere. Nothing else.

With a strange sinking of the heart I came back to our own door.

Surely I heard the landlady's slow, even step inside, and that soft, low laugh. I rushed in.

The room was empty of all life; both rooms utterly empty.

Yes, of all life; for, with the love of a lifetime surging in my heart, I sprang to where Hal lay beneath the window, and found him dead.

Dead, and most horribly dead. Three heavy marks—blows—three deep, three-cornered gashes—I started to my feet—even the chair had gone!

Again the whispered laugh. Out of that house of terror I fled desperately.

From the street I cast one shuddering glance at the fateful window.

The risen sun was gilding all the housetops, and its level rays, striking the high panes on the building opposite, shone back in a calm glory on the great chair by the window, the sweet face, down-dropped eyes, and swaying golden head.

DESERTED

Mrs Ellphalet Johnson was a very hardworking woman—even her nextdoor neighbors admitted that. Her chimney blackened the soft morning air as early as any in town; her wash fluttered white under the apple boughs long before breakfast. That is, before Ellphalet's breakfast.

Ellphalet kept store. He preferred keeping store to farming because he could sit down more. In the store it was all in the way of business. His customers sat down on every available object—the counter, the sugar barrel, the cracker box, even the cask of molasses, but not on that last until the counter and other things were full.

There were a few chairs around the store in the rear and vast political measures were discussed there—matters far beyond the reach of Mrs Johnson's busy feminine brain.

The house was over the store. The stairs connecting the two came down in the end where the store was, and when a customer came in who wanted not a seat but service Mr Ellphalet Johnson would tip back his chair a little further, open the stair door and say, 'Maria!'

Then Mrs Johnson would hurry down and attend to the customer. Mrs Johnson had a good head in a servile sort of way and usually kept the accounts. This she did after the store was closed and the children were in bed.

But in spite of all her efforts Ellphalet got into difficulties. He never fully explained to her what these difficulties were, but they were such as induced him to transfer the family bank account and business liabilities to her name.

This, he explained with lofty comprehensiveness, was merely a matter of form, and quite essential for the safety of the children.

'And Maria,' he added, seeking to bring the conversation to a more comprehensible level, 'there's a lady over at Clark's, a Miss Burton, who wants board in a private family, and I told her she could come here. I knew the spare room was suitable, and one more or less wouldn't make any difference to you.'

'But I wanted mother for a while this summer!' urged Maria. 'She'd be such a help preservin' and with the baby.'

Ellphalet grinned.

'Well, I don't want your mother,' said he: 'not by a long chalk. And this lady is to pay a dollar a day right along and you're to bank it in your name—here's the book.'

Maria took the book and looked at it. Eight hundred dollars were set down already to her credit.

'Why, 'Liphalet, where'd you get this?' she exclaimed.

'Sold the river lot,' he answered, and tipped back his chair to its farthest, looking at her with narrowed eyes from under the brim of his hat.

A dull red color rose on Mrs Johnson's faded face.

'That was my lot,' said she slowly. 'My father gave it to me when he died and I never meant to have had it sold in the world.'

'You don't know nothin' about business an' never will,' said Ellphalet. 'But now you pay 'tention to this and see if you can understand it. Here's the deeds of this house, store an' all an' all the furniture and stock. All in your name. Now, the reason of it is that I've got creditors who might clean me out any time, but if I can tide over this year I'll get over it all right. For this year the hull property's in your name and none of my creditors can touch it. See? As to that lot 'twan't no more yours than this house was or the farm—they all come from your father, but when you married me it made 'em mine, and it ought to. A man supports the family. He's got to hold the property. But for this year it's in your name.'

The year passed slowly. Mrs Johnson grew to understand somewhat of the value of her position and to do more and more of the business.

In truth, though she never owned to her most intimate friend that 'Liphalet drinked!' this sad fact was now becoming painfully apparent.

Much had Mrs Johnson suffered in the fifteen years of her laborious marriage. She had worked, on the average, fifteen hours a day, and lost much sleep besides. She had put into the family all its real estate, and really kept the store. She had borne and reared four children and lost two, and out of all this she had learned nothing until what she thought the last straw turned out to be a blessing in disguise. That was the lady boarder. If Mr Johnson had dreamed of that worthy woman's real position he would never have placed his conservative spare chamber at her disposal.

But he did not suspect, and never learned until it was too late.

She was a lawyer, and in spite of the absolute prohibition of all brain work for three months, she had brought with her a few little calf-bound books from force of habit.

So it chanced that Mrs Johnson, in the invigorating freshness of new acquaintance, was led to read somewhat in the penal and civil codes of her native State. Moreover, the boarder, moved by a strong sense of human kindness to this struggling woman and seeing the responsibilities of life with wider reach, urged upon her a new view of her duties to her children and the world.

Wherefore, it came to pass that when Ellphalet waked up one morning very late, indeed, after a little heavier drinking than was usual to him, and called vainly, with quite advanced profanity, for his faithful wife, he found her not in attendance.

Somewhat sobered by surprise he arose and searched the house.

No wife, no child, no boarder!

And a little later, to his incredulous horror and amazement, he discovered that the house and store, stock, furniture and farm had been sold over his head, and the proceeds had disappeared with his wife.

She left him a letter, however, in which it was set forth that if he gave up drinking and became a self-supporting citizen she would gladly receive him again as a husband—on her own terms.

In the meantime she would allow him $30 a month, to be paid to him personally on application to her lawyer, whose address she enclosed.

For herself she had gone into business independently, and should do well by the children.

Ellphalet read the letter repeatedly.

The name of the lawyer confused him.
'Elizabeth!' said he. 'Elizabeth Burton! Great Scott!'
Then the deserted husband took up the burden of life.
It made a new man of him.

AN ELOPEMENT

THE little town of Midgeville was full of excitement. The women made hasty and unwarranted calls on one another to discuss the subject of the hour; and the men were more numerous than usual in the 'store,' considering the time of day.

Even the minister was much exercised in his mind; and he had more reason than most of the others for Belle Jenkins had been his right-hand woman in church and Sunday-schools.

Not that she was over-pious—not nearly as pious as old Sister Greenman, or Widow Peters, but she had been widely and practically useful, and an overworked minister appreciates that.

And that she should suddenly vary the monotony of her quiet, busy life by so strange and unlooked for a step as this was unaccountable.

'Have you heard,' asked eager Miss Pendleton of Mrs Andrews, 'have you heard the news?'

Mrs Andrews, by blessed chance, had not, and Miss Pendleton unburdened herself triumphantly. 'Belle Jenkins has eloped!'

'Well, of all things,' said Mrs Andrews, and then she followed up this exclamation by the question which was on everybody's lips. 'Who with?'

'That's just what we don't know yet,' Miss Pendleton answered, shaking her lean little head till her earrings rattled. 'There's nobody missin' in the village, so she must a joined somebody somewheres else.' She left home in the middle of the night, it appears—before day at any rate, and walked to Barnford and took train for Boston—that is, we think it's for Boston. She took the Boston train at any rate. How we happen to know that much is only chance.

'Old Miss Merrit, that's been sick so long, you know, was lookin' out the winder some time in the night—she thinks 'twas near mornin'—and see her go by the gate, walkin' real fast. She says she'd swear to her step anywhere. There's no other woman in town can walk so fast and such long steps like a man.

'Miss Merrit thought of hollerin' to her, but she'd got clean past before she could open the window, and she just concluded there was somebody sick down in the Holler and they'd sent for her. You know she's a splendid nurse.

'And then Mr Winterbottom come home early this morning from Barnford, and he was waitin' for the up train when the other one come in and just as 'twas startin' off, there come a woman runnin' with a bag and just scrambled onto the last car—much as her life was worth.

'He run forward to help her—or to stop her, more likely—and he says 'twas Belle Jenkins!

'She had a veil on and she just rushed inside the car, but he says he'd know her anywhere. You know she nursed his wife last winter. She's the best nurse, for a young woman, I ever saw.'

Miss Pendleton paused for breath, and Mrs Andrews returned to her original inquiry:

'Who can it be she's gone with? John Martin was payin' attention to her, but it ain't him. She hasn't had a beau from anywhere else, has she?'

'Nobody knows,' said Miss Pendleton. 'She's been away from home a good deal these last years, and her mother has been real anxious about her often. She's had correspondence, her mother says, with a doctor from Boston that Mrs Elder in Barnford had for awhile, and Belle was nursin' her and met him. And her mother thinks it's him.'

But ain't it awful! Belle's mother had the sympathy of the community, yet it is doubtful if she deserved it. She was a close-fisted, narrow-minded woman, and had kept her daughters with a strictness suitable only to an old-fashioned nursery, regardless of her twenty-three years.

She lived with her sister, both able-bodied sturdy New England women, in a little house on the outskirts of the town, ran a farm successfully, rented a larger house in Barnford, and with all this abundance lived as penuriously as if she had depended on the few dollars Belle earned by nursing.

For some people insisted on paying her, she did so much and so well. Belle never complained, and therefore the busy-tongued town knew nothing of how the mother demanded every cent she earned and allowed her so little that the poor girl's shabbiness was taken to indicate the same miserly spirit as actuated her parent. Nothing of the years of repression and exaction, the constant watching and critical supervision, the hard, loveless life that made Belle's home, was known in the town, or the violent quarrel between her and her mother that last evening because she refused to show a letter at her mother's harsh demand. If they had known her life they might not have found it strange that so young a woman immersed herself in church work and the care of the sick.

Now she had eloped, and no one ever knew with whom. No news of the lost girl came to the home of her childhood for some years.

Then information was brought, and by the proud Miss Pendleton. 'I've had a letter from my cousin in Boston,' said she to the eager sewing circle. 'And what do you think! Belle Jenkins never eloped at all—that is, not with a man. She just went to the hospital and studied to be a trained nurse, and now she gets $20 a week and expenses! And she's been to Europe with a crippled girl and her mother! And she says when her mother needs her she'll come and do for her—not before!'

'Well, I never!' said the sewing circle.

THROUGH THIS

THE dawn colors creep up my bedroom wall, softly, slowly.

Darkness, dim gray, dull blue, soft lavender, clear pink, pale yellow, warm gold—sunlight.

A new day.

With the great sunrise great thoughts come.

I rise with the world. I live, I can help. Here close at hand lie the sweet home duties through which my life shall touch the others! Through this man made happier and stronger by my living; through these rosy babies sleeping here in the growing light; through this small, sweet, well-ordered home, whose restful influence shall touch all comers; through me too, perhaps—there's the baker, I must get up, or this bright purpose fades.

How well the fire burns! Its swift kindling and gathering roar speak of accomplishment. The rich odor of coffee steals through the house.

John likes morning-glories on the breakfast table—scented flowers are better with lighter meals. All is ready—healthful, dainty, delicious.

The clean-aproned little ones smile milky-mouthed over their bowls of mush. John kisses me good-bye so happily.

Through this dear work, well done, I shall reach, I shall help—but I must get the dishes done and not dream.

'Good morning! Soap, please, the same kind. Coffee, rice, two boxes of gelatine. That's all, I think. Oh—crackers! Good morning.'

There, I forgot the eggs! I can make these go, I guess. Now to soak the tapioca. Now the beets on, they take so long. I'll bake the potatoes—they don't go in yet. Now babykins must have her bath and nap.

A clean hour and a half before dinner. I can get those little nightgowns cut and basted. How bright the sun is! Amaranth lies on the grass under the rosebush, stretching her paws among the warm, green blades. The kittens tumble over her. She's brought them three mice this week. Baby and Jack are on the warm grass too—happy, safe, well. Careful, dear! Don't go away from little sister!

By and by when they are grown, I can—O there! the bell!

Ah, well!—yes—I'd like to have joined. I believe in it, but I can't now. Home duties forbid. This is my work. Through this, in time—there's the bell again, and it waked the baby!

As if I could buy a sewing machine every week! I'll put out a bulletin, stating my needs for the benefit of agents. I don't believe in buying at the door anyway, yet I suppose they must live. Yes, dear! Mamma's coming!

I wonder if torchon would look better, or Hamburg? It's softer but it looks older. Oh, here's that knit edging grandma sent me. Bless her dear heart!

There! I meant to have swept the bed-room this morning so as to have more time to-morrow. Perhaps I can before dinner. It does look dreadfully. I'll just put the potatoes in. Baked potatoes are so good! I love to see Jack dig into them with his little spoon.

John says I cook steak better than anyone he ever saw.

Yes, dear?

Is that so? Why, I should think they'd *know* better. Can't the people do anything about it?

Why no—not *personally*—but I should think *you* might. What are men for if they can't keep the city in order.

Cream on the pudding, dear?

That was a good dinner. I like to cook. I think housework is noble if you do it in a right spirit.

That pipe must be seen to before long. I'll speak to John about it. Coal's pretty low, too.

Guess I'll put on my best boots, I want to run down town for a few moments—in case mother comes and can stay with baby. I wonder if mother wouldn't like to join that—she has time enough. But she doesn't seem a bit interested in outside things. I ought to take baby out in her carriage, but it's so heavy with Jack, and yet Jack can't walk a great way. Besides, if mother comes I needn't. Maybe we'll all go in the car—but that's such an undertaking! Three o'clock!

Jack! Jack! Don't do that—here—wait a moment.

I ought to answer Jennie's letter. She writes such splendid things, but I don't go with her in half she says. A woman cannot do that way and keep a family going. I'll write to her this evening.

Of course, if one *could*, I'd like as well as anyone to be in those great live currents of thought and action. Jennie and I were full of it in school. How long ago that seems. But I never thought then of being so happy. Jennie isn't happy, I know—she can't be, poor thing, till she's a wife and mother.

O, there comes mother! Jack, deary, open the gate for Grandma! So glad you could come, mother dear! Can you stay awhile and let me go down town on a few errands?

Mother looks real tired. I wish she would go out more and have some outside interests. Mary and the children are too much for her, I think. Harry ought not to have brought them home. Mother needs rest. She's brought up one family.

There, I've forgotten my list, I hurried so. Thread, elastic, buttons; what was that other thing? Maybe I'll think of it.

How awfully cheap! How can they make them at that price! Three, please. I guess with these I can make the others last through the year. They're so pretty, too. How much are these? Jack's got to have a new coat before long—not to-day.

O, dear! I've missed that car, and mother can't stay after five! I'll cut across and hurry.

Why, the milk hasn't come, and John's got to go out early to-night. I wish election was over.

I'm sorry, dear, but the milk was so late I couldn't make it. Yes, I'll speak to him. O, no, I guess not; he's a very reliable man, usually, and the milk's good. Hush, hush, baby! Papa's talking!

Good night, dear, don't be too late.

> Sleep, baby, sleep!
> The large stars are the sheep,
> The little stars are the lambs, I guess,
> And the fair moon is the shepherdess.
> Sleep, baby, sleep!

How pretty they look. Thank God, they keep so well.

It's no use, I can't write a letter to-night—especially to Jennie. I'm too tired. I'll go to bed early. John hates to have me wait up for him late. I'll go now, if it is before dark—then get up early to-morrow and get the sweeping done. How loud the crickets are! The evening shades creep down my bedroom wall—softly—slowly.

Warm gold—pale yellow—clear pink—soft lavender—dull blue—dim gray–darkness.

THE MISLEADING OF
PENDLETON OAKS

There's many a trick to the red, red fox—
    The white snake well can please—
And the tree-toad hides behind the box
    Beside your very knees.
But the smiling guile of a witch-eyed girl
    Is deeper far than these.

                    The Second Daughter

It all came of not understanding a new country.

When Pendleton Oaks came to Santa Barbara from home he
came direct.

That is, he did not stop in Boston or New York, or even
Chicago—in fact, he did not come across country at all, but
through the Gulf and over the Isthmus.

He preferred to travel that way. Therefore to him Santa
Barbara and her customs were the United States of America. He
took no note of certain cities on the Atlantic seaboard otherwise
known to fame.

Preconceived opinions are not useful in traveling. They are
good furniture in home life, however. Which is why you find so
many of them there.

When a man is a stranger and a pilgrim, and the people of a
country are kind to him, he ought to treat their local customs
with respect; but Pendleton Oaks did not do this.

He held that at home they knew how to live, but that in Santa
Barbara all men were *yahoos*—savages. So he came to the
Orchester tennis court in the clothes he wore in the stable, and
lifted, slightly, to the Orchester girls, the hat of a ranchman.
Pendleton enjoyed his ranch, and was proud of it. He wrote large
letters home of the yard-long grape bunches, and the eucalyptus
tree that grows thirty feet in a year.

Impress (6 October 1894), 4–5; imitation of Rudyard Kipling, see
Appendix A.

But he did not mention the Orchester girls. There were two of them, Maisie and Maud. It was a pity that both their names began with M. You will see the reason later.

Santa Barbara was gay that winter. The Delmars were there with their new bowling alley, and the beautiful Miss Easter and her sister Lou and Ella Sandhurst, and the Conway girl that sang.

There were young men, too, but most of them were only Americans. Still, the dancing parties were very pleasant, and the bowling parties in between; for the Orchester girls attended all these festivities, and so did Pendleton Oaks.

It was not his fault that he could not tell which one of them preferred him. He knew which one he preferred, and said so, clearly, to the rest of the fellows. Miss Maud was the one for him. And yet, sometimes, when Miss Maisie was more than commonly gracious, he wished again that he knew which one preferred him. One did, that was certain. Or else it was both. Certain little notes and invitations—all proper enough in their way—seemed to him to speak volumes in the first person, as well as phrases in the third, but all these much-regarded missives were signed only with an M. 'M. Orchester.'

And the writing he could not distinguish.

That is what comes of being twins and having one writing-master.

It was the valentine party that he expected to settle it. A valentine party is a good thing when properly conducted. The Orchester girls had one once, when every guest was treated to a separate surprise. But that isn't the story I'm telling. Pendleton Oaks had never attended a valentine party before. They do not have them at home.

And he was not good at joking. However, when the valentine first came it made him quite happy.

He knew now.

He knew now that she must care for him, or she never would have written such beautiful verses. And if he was not quite sure yet as to whether it was Miss Maisie or Miss Maud—why the occasion would settle that matter forever. For did not it say that he should know her then at last; and did not that suffice to illumine the Past with a new intelligence, and fill the Future with most roseate light?

When a man is as young as Pendleton Oaks and thinks as much of himself, a valentine like that is rather fetching.

Here it is:

> Blessed St. Valentine once a year
> Banisheth shame and scattereth fear
> Biddeth each maiden reveal her heart,
> Sweet St. Valentine! Kind thou art!
> If I a Valentine write for thee
> Wilt thou not wear a flower for me?
> A passion flower of scarlet bright,
> Wear it for me on Wednesday night.
> There thou'lt see thy Valentine,
> And thou wilt know her by this sign:
> That she for thee will surely wear
> An azure love knot in her hair.
> O red is the color for love and for lover.
> And blue is for truth the wide world over!
> See thou forget not the token and sign,
> Thy faithful lover and Valentine.

That settled it.

A girl who could write like that must be a Genius, he was sure of that; and he knew she was a Beauty. Whichever of them it was, the beauty was undeniable; and that is more than could be said of Miss Delmars. Yet her costumes came from Paris.

When Pendleton Oaks first read that valentine he was fairly awed by its grandeur.

You see when a man cannot rhyme two words even with the aid of a T square, he is impressionable on that side.

The worst of it was that it went to his head. He couldn't hold it. Now that is bad.

> You may let out your horse on a falling incline,
> Or your sail on the hurricane's wing,
> But the tongue you should hold
> Till the doom-record's told.
> For the tongue is a different thing.

Now if Pendleton Oaks had known that! But he didn't.

First he told the Galoot. The Galoot threw back his head and snorted. Pendleton would have rebelled with violence, but the Galoot was a bigger man. So he demanded an explanation.

The Galoot looked at him for a few moments, visibly bursting; but withheld his information, and went off, snorting at intervals.

Then, after a while, Pendleton told Exeter. Exeter looked at him very earnestly and opened his mouth as if to speak. He did not speak, however, to any purpose,—merely congratulated him on his prowess with the fair, and seemed anxious to get away.

Afterwards he and the Galoot were seen to roll in the alfalfa, with uproarious outcry.

Pendleton felt hurt. But he could not keep it to himself.

The thing was so deucedly clever—and—it was too good to keep, really.

So he told it to Forsyth. Then it came out.

Forsyth was more merciful, or not so self-restrained. Perhaps he thought it was too good to keep, also. At any rate he showed him his copy.

It is as well to pause here. There *are* emotions which no rude pen should seek to paint for the heartless beholder.

When a young man, and such a young man as Pendleton Oaks, receives a valentine from the object of his affections—even granting that he is not quite sure which she is—he is naturally complimented.

But when he finds that every last one of the regular dancing party set has received the same thing, it is not nice. Pendleton Oaks experienced various sensations, of a kind quite new in his history. After a while they consoled him.

'Come,' said they all, led by the Galoot's cheerful voice, 'let's go in a body, and wear that red thing unanimously, and pay our respects to the fair deceiver as one man.'

This was a fine plan. They were not to show any consciousness of having betrayed the crafty secret, but simply to surround and overwhelm the perpetrator. ' 'Tis sport to see the engineer hoist with his own petard,' hummed little Mortarson as they went, and the Galoot punched him, for the tune was atrocious.

Meanwhile the Orchester house was full of light inside, and the Orchester girls were apparently in the best of spirits, both Miss Maud and Miss Maisie.

Which of them had put the little 'M' to so many dainty missives is not here told, and as the girls gathered in the big bedrooms and laid their 'things' elbow deep on the beds, there was no hint of other mischief toward than it has pleased God to put in the young female heart at all times.

To this scene came Pendleton and his brethren in iniquity, exulting hugely that they had risen to the occasion.

> And she for thee will surely wear
> An azure love knot in her hair,

hummed little Mortarson as the crucial moment approached. The Galoot punched him for his sins.

Into the great parlors they marched in a body, each wearing upon his front a scarlet passion flower, and gloating over the forthcoming discomfiture of the wily fair.

These were but men, however, and the Orchester girls were Women.

Every woman in that room wore a knot of blue ribbon in her hair.

A DAY'S BERRYIN'

THE sun was very hot on the round humpy little hills above 'the smut.' It was hot enough down there, on the black cracked surface of the peat bog; or where the still blacker pools reflected the cloudless sky in filmy lustre.

But up here it was hotter, and the lovely white moss crumbled under foot as you walked on it.

'That moss makes first-rate kindlin' if you keep it dry,' said Dothea Hopkins, crushing through the brittle masses. 'That is, I've always heard say it did—I ain't never tried it.'

'Goodness! how hot 'tis up here!' ejaculated her sister in reply. She was a little thin woman, and apparently nimbler than Dothea, whose square back was now bent low over the huckleberry bushes, while a brisk, hopping sound in the six-quart pail she wore at her waist told of the day's work being already begun. 'Yes, it takes just such sun to sweeten the berries,' Dothea replied. 'They're real good this year. It's rained some, so they ain't little, and now it's hot enough so s't they'll be sweet.' She rolled a few about in the palm of her large hand, blew off the bits of leaf and twig and put them in her mouth.

'I like these better'n the blueb'rys, don't you?' she said.

'Well, I do' know's I do,' responded her sister, still panting a little from her climb up the hill, and looking gingerly about her for the very thickest place to pick in.

Dothea's big pail had ceased to thump and rattle, and only gave forth a dull soft sound, long before Almira had found a spot to her liking. Once settled, however, she picked steadily and with care. You did not have to pick over Almira's berries—they could go on the table at once.

'The swamp blues is the best, *I* think,' pursued Almira. 'Them big bushes you can bend down and sit on—I used to when I was little. But after all I do' know's they're any better'n the low blues—the real little ones that knock against your shoes so heavy.'

Impress (13 October 1894), 4–5; imitation of Mary E. Wilkens, see Appendix A.

'The black ones is the best,' said Dothea firmly. 'Blueb'rys is good for a change, I admit, but for steady wear, 'n above all for cookin', give me good black huckleberries!'

'O, for cookin', of course, I thought you meant jest a matter of taste,' said Almira, and they relapsed into silence, moving farther away from each other and picking steadily.

It was hot. The big stones crusted with lichen, that lay in the midst of the huckleberry patches, were too hot to sit on comfortably, and the stiff little juniper trees filled the dry air with aromatic breath. In the shade, a few large speckled mosquitoes lurked hungrily.

'It's an awful bad year for mosquitoes,' suddenly burst out Almira. 'Down stairs where I live in the city they've got screen doors and screen windows and nettin's over the beds, and then they complain.'

'Is that Hines girl married yet?' inquired Dothea, brightening up at the mention of her sister's tenants.

'No, she ain't,' said Almira.

Almira Hopkins had married a 'city feller' in her youth; and while she never said much of her life with him and mourned him decorously in whole, half and quarter mourning when he died; still it was observed that she did not marry again.

'Marriage,' she would say sagely, 'is a lott'ry. I've got a house and lot, and I'm independent—why should I marry again?' Yet Almira had plenty of chances, for her 'city house' was a solid attraction, and her domestic skill was added to year by year with marvelous new recipes. Still she serenely declined any further experiment, making no explanation, and lived up stairs in her small city home, in two or three slant-roofed rooms, renting the lower part.

'She ain't, and *I* don't think it's likely she will,' continued Almira, 'with that mother of her'n. How much did I tell you about her, anyway?'

'Only that she was strong-minded and queer, and hadn't a beau for all her good looks. But Bijah Sterns sells 'em potatoes; he knew her mother when they lived over in Pendleton, and he says she's got a beau now. Has she?'

'Well, it's hard tellin',' answered Almira slowly, 'but I'll tell you what I know about it. That girl works like a horse anyway.

Her mother frets to have her work so hard; but she will do it, and I suppose there's reason good. Did you bring anythin' to drink, Dothea, or shall I hev to go down to the spring?'

'There's cold tea, lots of it,' replied Dothea. 'We didn't git started till near noon time, anyhow; and we might as well eat now as ever, if you're ready. I've filled this pail, anyhow, and we want the one with the things in it.'

So they sat down together in a shady spot, kept off the mosquitoes as best they might with waving of sweet-fern bushes, and continued to discuss the Hines girl's marriage.

'She's a good girl for all she's so queer,' pursued Almira, 'and her mother has kept her awful strict. Then when she come of age she kind of asserted herself, and done as she pleased. She don't do no manner of harm; only she won't be put upon as if she was a child any more. Her room is on the top floor with me and she pays reg'lar board to her mother. Pays some of the bills beside I guess, and does consid'able of the housework; but she's real independent and her mother can't abide it. She is a domineerin' sort of woman, *I* think, for all her religion.

'Well, when this young feller began to come—he was a photographer and good at his business, they said; but he had no faculty, and his folks were not up to what Mis' Hines wanted for her daughter.

'Anyhow, when he first come Mis' Hines never thought her Car'line would take up with him; and she was awful polite—kind of patronizin', *I* think. Car'line didn't like it, for she wasn't encouragin' him much, but her mother would ask him to tea, and set and talk with him Sunday evenin's while Car'line went to church. She would go to church regular and he wouldn't, not even for her company, it appears. So she'd go just the same to all the services, and her mother'd keep him to tea, as I say, and to spend the evenin'.

'Car'line never altered what she was doin' fer any man, or woman either. I never saw a young person so sot.

'Well, it run along, and bye 'n bye it begun to look as if she would have him after all. Then Mis' Hines turned right around. She'd been doin' all she could to encourage him, it looked to be, before that; more'n Car'line did by a long chalk. But now she thought the girl was goin' to have him, she began to behave—

well, it was most peculiar, *I* think. Why, she told Car'line that he couldn't stay to tea no more, and that she'd got to tell him so! And here he'd been comin' right along every Sunday, and she keepin' him to tea as a reg'lar thing!'

'Well, of all things!' said Dothea. Dothea was unimaginative—unromantic. She had lived with her mother until that good woman, after five years in her chair and two in her bed, had died and left her the little house and a tiny bit in the bank. She was a nurse by profession, not from choice, particularly, but because she had been a nurse for seven years. This story of Almira's seemed to stir some faint memory in her broad breast, for she sat up straighter, shook the flakes of pie crust off her brown gingham apron, and asked, with some eagerness:

'What did she do?'

'Do? Why she had to tell him, of course. It come tea time, and we was thinkin', of course, he was goin' to stay, and there was no plate set, and Car'line's mother just rung the bell and said nothin'. So she had to tell him.'

'What'd he do?' asked Dothea, eagerly.

'Oh, of course he said he wouldn't come any more. But Car'line held her head right up straight. I heard 'em, 'cause they was in the front hall, and I was up stairs lookin' out the window. "I pay my board here," says Car'line, "and if I can't receive my friends here where I board, I will board somewhere else!"

'So he's comin' yet, but her mother don't speak to him, and I think he feels kinder stiff there now.'

Dothea sighed a long, slow sigh.

'When'd Bijah Sterns get back from Idaho,' asked Almira, suddenly.

Dothea colored a little.

'Last June,' said she.

'And is he waitin' on you agin?' eagerly inquired Almira.

'He has called once or twice,' slowly assented Dothea, looking far over the sun-burned meadows to where the white, dusty road lay like a piece of faded tape between its yellow-green border.

An old horse jogged slowly along in the sun, and a man sat dozing over the reins, his elbows on his knees.

'Come, let's go home,' said she suddenly. 'There's berries enough, and it looks as if 't was goin' to shower.'

It was black in the north, and the air was hotter than ever. So they gathered up the pails, and reached the road by the shortest cut, the sweet fern breathing fragrant remonstrance, as they crushed it under foot.

'Why, Dothea! and here's Almira, too!' said Bijah Sterns, from his wagon, overtaking them, as they walked single file in the narrow footpath by the fence, the dust rising in clouds from the laden grass.

'Get right in, and lem'me take you home. It's goin' to shower.'

'How lucky 't you should come along!' said Almira. 'It's a special providence, *I* think.'

Almira was rather nearsighted.

FIVE GIRLS

'THERE won't be many more such good times as these for us,' said Olive Sargent, mournfully hugging her knees as she sat on the floor under the big Victory; 'we've got to go out into the cold world presently and earn our livings.'

'I don't mind earning the living a bit,' pretty Molly Edgerton asserted; 'I like to, and I shall never give it up; but I do hate to be separated the way we shall be. I wish we needn't.' And Molly dusted the crumbs of her luncheon from her spotless gingham apron.

The other girls always had charcoal on their aprons, or water colors, or oil, or dabs of clay; even sometimes all of these; but Molly's was always clean. To be sure, her work was mostly pencil drawing, the making of delicately beautiful designs for jewelry, for fans, for wood carving, for lace even—she was a born designer, and made the other girls green with envy.

Then Serena Woods opened her mouth and spoke. Serena was going to be an architect; indeed she was one already in a modest way, having planned the school-house in her native town, and also the dwelling of her married sister. To be sure, the sister did sometimes complain to intimate friends of certain minor deficiencies in the edifice, but what is that to a rising architect whose brain glows with enthusiasm and lives in a luminous cloud of architraves, pediments, and façades. She spoke slowly, looking down from her perch on a high stool. 'Girls, let's not separate. Let's go and live together in a house of our own. I'll build it.'

'O do!' said Julia Morse, 'I'll decorate it! We shall each have a room in our favorite color, with most appropriate designs, and the rooms down stairs shall be a real sermon and poem in one!' And Julia gushed on with fervid descriptions of her proposed scheme of mural decoration, while the others joined in rapturous applause.

Impress (1 December 1894), 4–5; imitation of Louisa May Alcott, see Appendix A.

Then Maud Annersley joined in. Maud was a tall, pale, slender girl, with dark, thoughtful, blue eyes and a quiet voice. She was a painter, and had had a picture in the last exhibition which had won approval from the best critics. 'Do you know,' she said earnestly, 'that we really might do this thing? We are all good friends and used to rooming together for these two years. We know all we mean to each other and when to stop—when to let each other alone. We've all got to earn our living, as Olive says, and it would be cheaper to earn it together than it would apart.' And Maud rinsed her biggest brush in the turpentine cup with severe decision.

Olive rose to her feet tempestuously.

'I do believe we could!' she said, her blue eyes lighting with sudden fervor. 'What is to hinder our joining forces and working on together, having the sweetest, grandest, most useful life in the world! We could club our funds, go to some nice place where land is cheap, and Serena could really plan for us one of those splendid compound houses that are so beautiful and convenient. We could arrange it with studios, all as they should be, and other artists could rent them of us to help on. You know I shall have some money as soon as I'm twenty-one; and I'd rather invest it so than any way I know.' Olive stopped for breath, flushed and triumphant; and the others looked at each other with new earnestness.

'We're talking of an awfully serious thing,' said Maud. 'It would mean living, you know, really living right along;' and she scraped her palette softly as she talked, making a beautiful mixed tint of the spotty little dabs of burnt sienna, cadmium and terre vert. 'There is no reason we should not do it though. But it ought to mean for life, and we're not all going to be single, I hope.'

Beautiful Maud, with her pale, sweet, oval face and wealth of soft, glistening, chestnut hair, had seen her lover buried, and turned to her chosen art as a life-long companion. But, she could speak all the more earnestly to her heart free friends; though there was a tell-tale blush on pretty Mollie's cheek, and Julia looked a little conscious as she spoke.

'Well anyway,' said the last named damsel, with rather a defiant tone; 'if we do marry we don't mean to give up our work I hope. I mean to marry some time, perhaps—but I don't mean to cook! I mean to decorate always, and make lots of money and hire a housekeeper.'

'I don't see,' said Mollie dimpling softly, 'why that should be an obstacle. Couldn't we have a house so big and beautiful and live so happily and get to be so famous that—that—if any one wanted to marry us they could come there too?'

'What sort of compound fractions do you think we are?' demanded Serena. 'Any one marry us indeed! It would take five to marry us, Mollie!'

'Now stop joking, girls,' said Olive. 'We are all grown and trained. We all want to always work—indeed, some of us have got to. Now, honestly, why shouldn't we build a sort of apartment home you know, a beautiful "model tenement" affair, artistic and hygenic and esthetic and everything else; with central kitchens and all those things; and studios and rooms for ourselves, and a hall to exhibit in and so on. Then we could have suites of apartments for families and let them; and bye and bye, if we are families, we can occupy those ourselves and let the others!'

And Olive hugged the headless Victory in her enthusiasm while the girls applauded rapturously.

Then what a happy year they had before their course at the Institute was finished! Such innumerable plans and elevations; such glowing schemes of color, such torrents of design for carving and painting and modelling, such wild visions of decoration, where races and epochs and styles waltzed madly together in interminable procession.

The class work went on, of course, and Maud's great picture won the first prize at the exhibition, though no one guessed that the lovely walls in the background were from one of Serena's least practicable elevations, and that the group of girls in front were the future owners thereof. There was a troubadour in it also, but he was purely imaginary; though Maud did tell Mollie that he was the fortunate youth that was going to marry them.

It was but a year or two before the lovely plan came true, for after all there was nothing impossible in it. Between them all there was money enough to buy the lot and build the house, and the 'families' consented to hire apartments therein to such an extent as to furnish all the funds for running expenses.

Julia Morse's redoubtable Aunt Susan came down from her New Hampshire home to keep house in the new mansion, and declared that she never had had half a chance to show what was in her before.

Olive's widowed mother made the dearest of chaperones for the girls, and their long parlor rang with music and merriment on the pleasant winter evenings.

The studios were easy to let also, and the velveteen coat and loose blouse became as frequent in the long halls as the paint-daubed gingham apron. Also the troubadour materialized in the shape of a most angelic-voiced singing master, who occupied a room on the top floor; and who, though he did not marry them all, as was aforetime suggested, did marry Olive in due season and stayed in the same pleasant quarters thereafter. Only a 'family' was evicted, so to speak, for their convenience, and Olive's room was let to an aspiring little sister of the troubadour.

Pretty Mollie followed suit in a few months more—it took some time to convince her devoted but conservative lover that they could just as well have a suite in this beautiful great home cluster as in a flat near the park. Every girl of them married, as years passed on; even Maud, who forgot her early sorrow in a newer, deeper joy.

But live together they did, and work together always, with various breaks and lapses, as the sweet home cares sometimes interfered with working hours, and the charming little kindergarten in the south wing grew fuller and fuller.

'There's nothing like planning things for life,' said Olive one still June evening in after years, as the same five girls sat together on the rose shadowed porch; older, but no less earnest in their work and their love for each other.

'That's so,' said Serena heartily—especially when you do the things you plan.'

ONE WAY OUT

SHE sat quite silent for a little after his last remark, with that silence which suggests the retention of many things most pertinent to the matter in hand, but not always of an agreeable nature.

Her cousin—she had quite returned to the old habit of thinking of him as a cousin,—regardless of the few weeks after their betrothal in which he had seemed to become luminous and large, a hero, a lover, such as one reads about. She had read about many, and delighted in the change from the old child love between them to this new feeling, half combined with, half separated from the first, yet so palpably another.

'What's the matter?' he inquired lightly enough, yet with a certain suppressed anxiety in his voice. 'It does seem, May, as if nothing I said suited you in these days. You used not to be so—captious—when we were just cousins.'

It was a trifle—the merest trifle, and of itself surely inadequate to send such a multitude of feelings to the heart of the hearer.

She made no sign of emotion however, beyond a quick look at the earnest yet boyish face beside her, with its rather petulant expression. In what way was it possible, she thought coldly, for this man to have become so—so distasteful,—in so short a time. She had had the warmest affection for him as a boy, and surely but a few short weeks ago she had had a love far warmer and of larger meaning. Now she groped hurriedly about in her heart for either feeling, and to her astonishment found only a pale sense of justice to the human creature by her side, whom she knew loved her, and who had done her no harm whatever, save for a hapless jarring on certain minor chords of her life, which perhaps she was foolish to so resent.

Then as she saw the disconsolate droop of his big shoulders, and noted how he sat over the fire and relieved his mind by carefully picking the perfectly arranged cannel coal into a score of flaming fragments, greatly to their mutual discomfort, two strong sensations rose uppermost. The one a sense of accumu-

Impress (29 December 1894), 4–5; imitation of Henry James, see Appendix A.

lated outrage based on no one act of discourtesy or forgetfulness; on nothing that was unworthy of her cousin or her lover, but that sweepingly admitted its inability to show just cause of offence and at the same time protested before high heaven that any man should be able to so trample on every minor peculiarity, so fail to apprehend, so perversely misapply, so succeed in distilling perpetual unrest into the cup of life he had but now lifted to her lips. The very talk they had been having—what had he said? Nothing in which any listener would find cause even for displeasure, yet which left her wrung and angry as from a bitter dispute. Then following this causeless rage, which raged the more at its own causelessness, came a great wave of ante-betrothal tenderness, the warm affection of her childhood for the big cousin who had always been so good to her. He was good to her now, he had never failed to be kind, tender, patient, self-sacrificing; there was nothing wrong except—except—ah yes, that was it. She had over-estimated his love and her own. They loved each other of course, and always would, but he was perfectly right in the speech that hurt her so just now—they were happier, she was less fretful and hard to please, when they were only cousins.

She rose and went to him, kneeling on the rug by his side, and laid one hand on his knee, the other about his neck.

'Bert, dear,' she said, 'Do you know I think you've just hit it. I was nicer when we were only cousins, and so were you. Now don't let's be miserable or make any more mistakes as to how we feel. I love you dearly, as I always did, and you do me, I know. Nobody knows we were engaged and nobody need know why we aren't; but really, Bert, I think we were both naturally mistaken—don't you? Now, don't be sulky, you dear boy. You'll thank me some day, really. Come—let's be just cousins again—and always.'

He rose to his feet without a word and began to walk up and down with his hands in his pockets and a puzzled frown on his brow. She watched him narrowly, feeling sure she should recognize any signs of pain, and with a queer tugging sort of wish that he would stop striding about, take his hands out of his pockets and come and take possession of her hands, as he did once; assure her that it was he who was wrong—that he had been a wretched failure so far, and that he wasn't half good enough for her, but—

and the tugging wish became an absolute cry for something of that look in his eyes which had so burned itself into hers a month or more ago.

But when he came and stood over her there was no such look visible, only a rueful sort of expression, and, she fancied a glimmer of relief. And what he said,—alas for the ineffable stupidity of the most considerate of men! dull creatures whose efforts to console and spare are often productive of quite the subtlest pangs in life,—what he said was only in tones of the tenderest compunction: 'Are you sure you won't care?'

He mistrusted that he had entered a frying pan the instant the words were uttered and precipitated himself nimbly into the fire by adding: 'care too much, I mean!'

For one wild moment, she longed to hurt his honest heart by assuring him that it would not cost her a moment's uneasiness; and truly what grief she had fled utterly, as she realized anew the utter misapprehension in which her life might have been passed had she failed to save them both from such mis-step.

'Bert, you dear old, uncomplimentary goose!—it's you who ought to be a mass of ruin, if you weren't too visibly thankful at my being wise enough for two! Of course, I shall care some. A woman hates to make a mistake like that. But it's well found out now, and you and I will always love each other dearly, as we always have. It's all right, isn't it? Come shake hands on the new cousinship, dear.'

He took her hand and held it a moment, saying with an unreliable voice: 'May—you are the best friend a fellow ever had—I hope—I hope that you will find some one that is good enough for you!'

She looked at his perturbed countenance and broke into a little laugh.

'Any one would think to hear you, Bert Howard, that I could not possibly sustain the state of single-cousinship without serious distress of mind. You are such a goose that I have a great mind to punish you.'

'What will you do to me?' he asked, standing with his back to the fire and looking down at her. The leaping flames which followed his unseemly use of the poker were brighter than the much draped lamp, whose profuse silken petticoats and copious laces gave somehow the impression of a skirt dance—motionless but suggestive. Her fair face, lit by the rosy flames, was turned up at him mockingly.

'What will I do? I will upbraid you with being a feather-headed inconstant boy, deluding your pet cousin into the notion that she was fonder of you than is really the case. Or I would, if I were not so grateful to you for finding it out in time, and being so palpably miserable that I could not choose but see it?'

'I was not miserable,' he protested, flushing. 'I was as happy as could be, only—you don't imagine I wanted to get out of it, do you?'

'No, indeed, I don't!' she hastily replied, 'It is all right, dear boy; don't feel badly. You didn't do a thing but just what was natural under the circumstances. It is I who have found out that I do not feel as I did—that's all. If you had acted like Uncle Chester, now, I never would have forgiven you!'

'What did he do?' demanded her listener.

'Do? Why he found out there was insanity or something in the family of the girl he was engaged to, and just calmly broke it off. She found out the reason and went mad on the spot—lamentable corroboration of his theory, was it not? If I knew of any such danger as that, I'd never marry anybody—would you? But you and I come from the same people, so it's as broad as it's long. I wonder if you had had any notions about our family spectre, if you would have sought to escape me on good humanitarian grounds, instead of sticking closer than a brother till I found out how little I really cared—or you either.'

There was quite a silence at this, broken by her suddenly asking him if he enjoyed Dr Henderson's lectures on 'Consumption and Heredity.'

He looked up at her with an eager questioning glance quickly restrained.

'That's ours, you know,' said she, 'my poor mother and father and yours,—what do they say about the heredity, Bert?'

He drew himself up to his full height, assumed his most professional manner and informed her in choice scientific terminology that the latest theory was that only tendencies were transmissible and those could be overcome by education. He talked with great freedom and prolixity until she yawned behind her hand and sent him home.

'It's all very interesting,' said she, 'I'm glad you feel that way—I had really begun to feel horrid about it. Good night, Bert.'

'Good night, May,' he said, and kissed her very lightly.

She stood looking in the fire, the medical terms still ringing in her ears.

'Too bad,' she said, 'I ought to have known better. He didn't care except cousin fashion, nor I.'

He went home under the moonlight, over the snow. It was light enough, but very cold.

AN UNPATENTED PROCESS

OF course there was an alarming discrepancy between their characters—everybody could see that fast enough. They were about as well calculated to get along together as an eight-day clock and a California rainy season. She was accuracy itself; mathematics were no better than a weather bureau compared to her methods, and he—well a weather bureau was mathematics compared to his.

The things that fellow forgot, and left open, and untied, and hung in the wrong place, and misdirected, and over-drew and failed to connect, would shingle Tophet—supposing that the roof of that place has any analogy to its flooring. And her friends told her so, most freely, and with that brimming tenderness of regard and intense devotion to one's best interests that prompts one's friends on such occasions.

'For a woman of your temperament,' they told her, 'it is suicide—rank suicide. You'll die in a year of nervous exhaustion. He'll put your bonnet in the butter dish, bring home preserved barberries when you order beans and buy you a piano lamp with the money you gave him to pay the coal bill. You'll die, Nettie! No, don't you do it.'

But Nettie Hines was not going to be deterred from marrying the man of her choice by any such paltry objections as these. Hers was a devotion such as you read about it in those beautiful stories of the troubadours. Had she been betrothed to him and he been converted in one of those revivals of Peter the Hermit, and gone off to lead a sanctified life in the Turk-and-Sepulchre line, she would have remained faithful to him for seventeen years, and never mentioned the little delay when he returned.

Whether she could have reached the summit of complacency of the lady who received not only her long absent and imprisoned lord, but also the beautiful and infatuated sultaness who delivered him, I do not know, but she was never put to that kind of a test. Hank Richardson was not that sort of a man, not by a long

Impress (12 January 1895), 4–5; imitation of Mark Twain, see Appendix A.

chalk. He had just as good stuff in him as she had, in his way; and was as faithful as that fellow with the barrel hoops around him in the fairy story. He wouldn't have brought home a sultaness under any consideration whatever,—not if he was engaged to be married to Nettie Hines.

So she stuck to it that she would marry him, and marry him she did, in spite of a few characteristic vicissitudes on the occasion of the nuptial ceremonies. You see, he was a doctor, and a real good one; he never slipped up on a case when he once got his mind on it. Hank's mind was a regular sleuth-hound for following the idea he was after; but if he lost the scent anywhere he'd just run around and paw the air and howl—it was really pitiful. They tried to get married two or three times, but Hank slipped up on it, and it was awfully mortifying to Nettie. But she made up her mind to have him, and she did. The first time he was more excusable, because of not having had any experience, and perhaps not rightly appreciating the importance a young girl attaches to a little matter of ceremony like that.

Women are so much more sensitive to these social minutiae than men are. It was an outrageous storm that night, there's no denying it; and living as they did, in the country, it was difficult and really somewhat dangerous to get around.

The minister got there all right; it meant something to him of course in the way of direct returns; and the guests arrived in great numbers—country people don't mind a little weather when it's a question of sociability—but Hank never showed up at all. So after awhile Nettie's brothers set out to look for his body, knowing that he was no hand to drive, and more than likely had gone off in some other direction, and might have made a mistake and harnessed the blind plough horse, and perhaps even then be lying stark and cold in some sheeted drift by the roadside. They went clear to his house, to find out when he started, and Hank came down and opened the door, half dressed.

'Man alive, what are you doin' here!' said they.

'Doin'?' said he, 'why goin' to bed of course. It's time.'

'Don't you know it's your wedding night?' said they.

'Why yes,' said he, in that quiet, courteous, reasonable, sweet-tempered way of his, that endeared him to all hearts in spite of his innocent eccentricities; 'why yes, I know that, but it rained so I thought they wouldn't have it.'

The boys had to laugh, but Nettie was mad and wouldn't be married that night at all, when they did bring him.

Next time he was interested in a case of smallpox and sent word that he was sorry, but he really couldn't leave his patient.

But finally the thing was managed, and nobody was better pleased than Hank when it was all safely accomplished.

Nettie had insisted on one thing though, and she'd saved money enough from her school teaching during these vicissitudes to be able to compass it: this was that they should go off somewhere for a year before they settled down. So he arranged to pursue his medical studies abroad, and she got the tickets and the guide-books and rate-cards and time-tables and schedules, and they got started in about two weeks' time from the date set. She didn't chafe any under that, for she had allowed a month to make sure. Nettie was the most reasonable woman I ever saw.

When they really did start; when the gang plank was off and all those dear friends one has on those occasions had stood around to the last moment and made you feel every emotion you had in your bosom several times over, and were now standing all along the edge of the pier to make you feel them over again—or maybe a new one—I thought I saw a peculiar expression of— well, of scientific enthusiasm, in Nettie's eye, as she held him securely by the arm. I was one of those friends; but then they wanted to see me there, and I never make a fool of myself at such times.

You see, after all, they were kindred spirits, though their walks in life were different. Nettie was a born educator, and just as fond of educating as he was of doctoring. She didn't stop at children either; so when I saw that look I got at the reason of her patience and determination; the reason besides her undying affection. It became evident to me that she considered his faults eradicable, and intended to eradicate them.

He came home in a year's time, as intended. He wrote on to have the house open on the fifteenth of April, and that they'd be there on the 10.30 a.m. train, but his folks just gave out that Hank was likely to get back this spring, and were as surprised as anybody to see them come.

They looked well, both of them. She regarded him with a sort of triumphant admiration, as a woman will a man that she's plumb proud of; not a shadow of anxiety or doubt. But she'd a kind of a worn look too, same as Paracelsus might, or Archimedes, or any of those absorbed experimentalists.

As for him, his face was fairly illuminated. There was such a glory of determination about him, such an air of high resolve and definite purpose, that one was led to expect immortal deeds at once.

'Is the house all ready?' he asked his mother when he'd kissed her properly and answered everybody's questions; and we all stood around with our smiles getting a little tired—just a little.

'Why yes,' said she, kind of dazed though, he looked at her so, sharp 'we fixed it all, not being very busy—but we didn't hardly expect you yet a while, dear.'

'I dare say not,' said he smiling, 'but here we are, and I hope Simley has sent up the office book-shelves I ordered to match the other set, and Jenks put out my new sign. Do you want to stop and order at White's, Nettie, or would you rather come down in the morning?'

'I guess the morning will do,' said she, with such a reposeful, restful look as would do your heart good to see, a real luxurious sort of expression—kind of bee-in-clovery—and they all went off without a vestige of shawl or umbrella or railroad novel left behind them. He had even remembered to leave out her sun umbrella when he sent up the baggage, and opened it for her as they started off.

My sister said that when they got home there was a great bowl of violets on Nettie's bureau, and that Nettie turned to him and said, 'How did you know I liked violets?' and he said, 'You told me so in the art gallery of Munich that day when we were talking about flower painting. It was—June 21st, I think,' and Nettie just threw her arms around his neck and cried.

We all thought it was a miracle, or that maybe he had been changed at nurse, or something of that sort; but my sister found out the whole process after a while and told me. You may think it is strange for a brother and sister to be so confidential, but then she was only being a sister to me for a while—she isn't that now. And it wasn't in human nature for Nettie not to tell, for an achievement like that in one year is a thing to make the meekest Moses as boastful as a healthy newspaper. Nettie never really boasted; but you could see she was proud and gradually we learned the details of the process.

'It was only a question of relating brain action,' said she modestly, 'and not nearly so hard as doing it to a child where you have to wait for years of growth. My husband has a splendid brain, and a well trained one too, only he had never been taught to focus and carry at the same time. He could focus all right and forget to carry, or he could carry all right and forget to focus. It's a trick of the mind, like patting your head and rubbing on your chest at the same time. Most of us do this more or less well, but Mr Richardson didn't take to it naturally, and nobody ever trained him.'

My sister—that was—was extremely awed by this opening. She hasn't a scientific mind herself, but I have never cast it up at her. You see I don't need any professional treatment myself. I never forget anything, but letters to mail, and to order the coal, and little things like that,—same as any man does.

'How did you begin?' asked my sister.

Nettie looked back over her path of victory and smiled: 'I took care of everything without his knowing it, and arranged a series of openings for him to forget in. He did, of course.

'The first time he missed connection he lost me, and it made a great impression on him. The second time, it left me in great danger; the third, I should have been dead—but for having planned it myself. That was in the Catacombs. These things made a deep impression on him. I planned so that there were no innocent lapses—only awful ones. Then I began a carefully prepared series of things to remember—good, loud things, to rouse his neglected powers of observation and retention. For instance, whenever we came to our room in the hotel I wrapped the match box in scarlet paper. I made a sign that said 'matches' in big letters. Then I put matches on the floor and on the stove and on the bureau and on the desk—on everything there was in the room.

'What are you doing?' said he.

'Arranging the matches,' said I calmly, and went on. Finally, I put them on the table by the bed near the light and begged his approval. He was unsuspecting and interested, but I talked about those matches and their location on that table till his brain revolted. Then I would ask him, at irregular intervals, but suddenly, where those matches were put; and after a while he could remember at once, even when I changed the position, and the color, and finally the thing itself. You see, the startling irregularity of my actions aroused a new interest, and my carefully adjusted inquiries did not let it die out. In time, he could remember every item of furniture in a room we had left a month before, and things that I had said about them, and it never tired him a bit.

'Then I began on errands and things that you have to remember ahead instead of backwards; beginning with urgent demands for conspicuous things to be brought at once, and gradually shading off till the mere mention of a thing once would ensure its production at the desired time.

'He saw through it all pretty soon and was as eager as I was; and soon got to enjoy the exercises. He's in splendid condition now, and if I keep him in regular practice for another year I think it will be absolutely successful.'

And Nettie beamed and glowed like a young mother. She was a young mother, in course of time; and, if you'll believe me, Hank Richardson could tell you that baby's age as well as he could the increase in the local death rate.

But if I tell you any more, perhaps you'll discredit the whole story.

AN UNNATURAL MOTHER

'DON'T tell me!' said old Mis' Briggs, with a forbidding shake of the head; 'no mother that was a mother would desert her own child for anything on earth!'

'And leaving it a care on the town, too!' put in Susannah Jacobs, 'as if we hadn't enough to do to take care of our own!'

Miss Jacobs was a well-to-do old maid, owning a comfortable farm and homestead, and living alone with an impoverished cousin acting as general servant, companion and protegée. Mis' Briggs, on the contrary, had had thirteen children, five of whom remained to bless her, so that what maternal feeling Miss Jacobs might lack, Mis' Briggs could certainly supply.

'I should think,' piped little Martha Ann Simmons, the village dressmaker, 'that she might a saved her young one first and then tried what she could do for the town.'

Martha had been married, had lost her husband, and had one sickly boy to care for.

The youngest Briggs girl, still unmarried at thirty-six, and in her mother's eyes a most tender infant, now ventured to make a remark.

'You don't any of you seem to think what she did for all of us—if she hadn't left hers we should all have lost ours, sure.'

'You ain't no call to judge, Maria Melia,' her mother hastened to reply; 'you've no children of your own, and you can't judge of a mother's duty. No mother ought to leave her child, whatever happens. The Lord gave it to her to take care of—he never gave her other people's. You nedn't tell me!'

'She was an unnatural mother!' repeated Miss Jacobs harshly, 'as I said to begin with.'

'What is the story?' asked the City Boarder. The City Boarder was interested in stories from a business point of view, but they did not know that. 'What did this woman do?' she asked.

There was no difficulty in eliciting particulars. The difficulty was rather in discriminating amidst their profusion and

Impress (16 February 1895), 4–5, rpt. from *Forerunner* 7 (November 1916).

contradictoriness. But when the City Boarder got it clear in her mind it was somewhat as follows:

The name of the much condemned heroine was Esther Greenwood, and she lived and died here in Toddsville.

Toddsville was a mill village. The Todds lived on a beautiful eminence overlooking the little town, as the castles of robber barons on the Rhine used to overlook their little towns. The mills and the mill hands' houses were built close along the bed of the river. They had to be pretty close, because the valley was a narrow one, and the bordering hills were too steep for travel, but the water power was fine. Above the village was the reservoir, filling the entire valley save for a narrow road beside it, a fair blue smiling lake, edged with lilies and blue flag, rich in pickerel and perch. This lake gave them fish, it gave them ice, it gave the power that ran the mills that gave the town its bread. Blue Lake was both useful and ornamental.

In this pretty and industrious village Esther had grown up, the somewhat neglected child of a heart-broken widower. He had lost a young wife, and three fair babies before her—this one was left him, and he said he meant that she should have all the chance there was.

'That was what ailed her in the first place!' they all eagerly explained to the City Boarder. 'She never knew what 'twas to have a mother, and she grew up a regular tomboy! Why she used to roam the country for miles around, in all weather like an Injun! And her father wouldn't take no advice!'

This topic lent itself to eager discussion. The recreant father, it appeared, was a doctor, not their accepted standby, the resident physician of the neighborhood, but an alien doctor, possessed of 'views.'

'You never heard such things as he advocated,' Miss Jacobs explained. 'He wouldn't give no medicines, hardly; said "nature" did the curing—he couldn't.'

'And he couldn't either—that was clear,' Mrs Briggs agreed. 'Look at his wife and children dying on his hands, as it were! "Physician heal thyself," I say.'

'But, mother,' Maria Amelia put in, 'she was an invalid when he married her, they say; and those children died of polly—polly—what's that thing that nobody can help?'

'That may all be so,' Miss Jacobs admitted, 'but all the same it's a doctor's business to give medicine. If "nature" was all that was wanted, we needn't have any doctor at all!'

'I believe in medicine and plenty of it. I always gave my children a good clearance, spring and fall, whether anything ailed 'em or not, just to be on the safe side. And if there was anything the matter with 'em they had plenty more. I never had anything to reproach myself with on that score,' stated Mrs Briggs, firmly. Then as a sore of concession to the family graveyard, she added piously, 'The Lord giveth and the Lord taketh away.'

'You should have seen the way he dressed that child!' pursued Miss Jacobs. 'It was a reproach to the town. Why, you couldn't tell at a distance whether it was a boy or a girl. And barefoot! He let that child go barefoot till she was so big we was actually mortified to see her.'

It appeared that a wild, healthy childhood had made Esther very different in her early womanhood from the meek, well-behaved damsels of the little place. She was well enough liked by those who knew her at all, and the children of the place adored her, but the worthy matrons shook their heads and prophesied no good of a girl who was 'queer.'

She was described with rich detail in reminiscence, how she wore her hair short till she was fifteen—'just shingled like a boy's—it did seem a shame that girl had no mother to look after her—and her clo'se was almost a scandal, even when she did put on shoes and stockings.' 'Just gingham—brown gingham—and *short*!'

'I think she was a real nice girl,' said Maria Amelia. 'I can remember her just as well! She was *so* nice to us children. She was five or six years older than I was, and most girls that age won't have anything to do with little ones. But she was as kind and pleasant. She'd take us berrying and on all sorts of walks, and teach us new games and tell us things. I don't remember any one that ever did us the good she did!'

Maria Amelia's thin chest heaved with emotion; and there were tears in her eyes; but her mother took her up somewhat sharply.

'That sounds well I must say—right before your own mother that's toiled and slaved for you! It's all very well for a young thing that's got nothing on earth to do to make herself agreeable to young ones. That poor blinded father of hers never taught her to do the work a girl should—naturally he couldn't.'

'At least he might have married again and given her another mother,' said Susannah Jacobs, with decision, with so much decision in fact that the City Boarder studied her expression for a moment and concluded that if this recreant father had not married again it was not for lack of opportunity.

Mrs Simmons cast an understanding glance upon Miss Jacobs, and nodded wisely.

'Yes, he ought to have done that, of course. A man's not fit to bring up children, anyhow—How can they? Mothers have the instinct—that is, all natural mothers have. But, dear me! There's some as don't seem to *be* mothers—even when they have a child!'

'You're quite right, Mis' Simmons,' agreed the mother of thirteen. 'It's a divine instinct, I say. I'm sorry for the child that lacks it. Now this Esther. We always knew she wan't like other girls—she never seemed to care for dress and company and things girls naturally do, but was always philandering over the hills with a parcel of young ones. There wan't a child in town but would run after her. She made more trouble 'n a little in families, the young ones quotin' what Aunt Esther said, and tellin' what Aunt Esther did to their own mothers, and she only a young girl. Why she actually seemed to care more for them children than she did for beaux or anything—it wasn't natural!'

'But she did marry?' pursued the City Boarder.

'Marry! Yes, she married finally. We all thought she never would, but she did. After the things her father taught her it did seem as if he'd ruined *all* her chances. It's simply terrible the way that girl was trained.'

'Him being a doctor,' put in Mrs Simmons, 'made it different, I suppose.'

'Doctor or no doctor,' Miss Jacobs rigidly interposed, 'it was a crying shame to have a young girl so instructed.'

'Maria Melia,' said her mother, 'I want you should get me my smelling salts. They're up in the spare chamber, I believe—

When your Aunt Marcia was here she had one of her spells—don't you remember?—and she asked for salts. Look in the top bureau drawer—they must be there.'

Maria Amelia, thirty-six, but unmarried, withdrew dutifully, and the other ladies drew closer to the City Boarder.

'It's the most shocking thing I ever heard of,' murmured Mrs Briggs. 'Do you know he—a father—actually taught his daughter how babies come!'

There was a breathless hush.

'He did,' eagerly chimed in the little dressmaker, 'all the particulars. It was perfectly awful!'

'He said,' continued Mrs Briggs, 'that he expected her to be a mother and that she ought to understand what was before her!'

'He was waited on by a committee of ladies from the church, married ladies, all older than he was,' explained Miss Jacobs severely. 'They told him it was creating a scandal in the town—and what do you think he said?'

There was another breathless silence.

Above, the steps of Maria Amelia were heard, approaching the stairs.

'It ain't there, Ma!'

'Well, you look in the high boy and in the top drawer; they're somewhere up there,' her mother replied.

Then, in a sepulchral whisper:

'He told us—yes, ma'am, I was on that committee—he told us that until young women knew what was before them as mothers they would not do their duty in choosing a father for their children! That was his expression—"choosing a father!" A nice thing for a young girl to be thinking of—a father for her children!'

'Yes, and more than that,' inserted Miss Jacobs, who, though not on the committee, seemed familiar with its workings. 'He told them——' But Mrs Briggs waved her aside and continued swiftly——

'He taught that innocent girl about—the Bad Disease! Actually!'

'He did!' said the dressmaker. 'It got out, too, all over town. There wasn't a man here would have married her after that.'

Miss Jacobs insisted on taking up the tale. 'I understand that he said it was "to protect her!" Protect her, indeed! Against matrimony! As if any man alive would want to marry a young girl who knew all the evil of life! I was brought up differently, I assure you!'

'Young girls should be kept innocent!' Mrs Briggs solemnly proclaimed. 'Why, when I was married I knew no more what was before me than a babe unborn and my girls were all brought up so, too!'

Then, as Maria Amelia returned with the salts, she continued more loudly, 'but she did marry after all. And a mighty queer husband she got, too. He was an artist or something, made pictures for the magazines and such as that, and they do say she met him first out in the hills. That's the first 'twas known of it here, anyhow—them two trapesing about all over; him with his painting things! They married and just settled down to live with her father, for she vowed she wouldn't leave him, and he said it didn't make no difference where he lived, he took his business with him.'

'They seemed very happy together,' said Maria Amelia.

'Happy! Well, they might have been, I suppose. It was a pretty queer family, I think.' And her mother shook her head in retrospection. 'They got on all right for a while; but the old man died, and those two—well, I don't call it housekeeping—the way they lived!'

'No,' said Miss Jacobs. 'They spent more time out of doors than they did in the house. She followed him around everywhere. And for open love making——'

They all showed deep disapproval at this memory. All but the City Boarder and Maria Amelia.

'She had one child, a girl,' continued Mrs Briggs, 'and it was just shocking to see how she neglected that child from the beginnin'. She never seemed to have no maternal feelin' at all!'

'But I thought you said she was very fond of children,' remonstrated the City Boarder.

'Oh, *children*, yes. She'd take up with any dirty faced brat in town, even to them Kanucks. I've seen her again and again with a whole swarm of the mill hands' young ones round her, goin' on some picnic or other—"open air school," she used to call it—

Such notions as she had. But when it come to her own child! Why——' Here the speaker's voice sank to a horrified hush. 'She never had no baby clo'se for it! Not a single sock!'

The City Boarder was interested. 'Why, what did she do with the little thing?'

'The Lord knows!' answered old Mis' Briggs. 'She neved would let us hardly see it when 'twas little, 'Shamed too, I don't doubt. But that's strange feelin's for a mother. Why, I was so proud of my babies! And I kept 'em lookin' so pretty! I'd a-sat up all night and sewed and washed, but I'd a had my children look well!' And the poor old eyes filled with tears as she thought of the eight little graves in the churchyard, which she never failed to keep looking pretty, even now. 'She just let that young one roll round in the grass like a puppy with hardly nothin' on! Why, a squaw does better. She does keep 'em done up for a spell! That child was treated worse'n an Injun! We all done what we could, of course. We felt it no more'n right. But she was real hateful about it, and we had to let her be.'

'The child died?' asked the City Boarder.

'Died! Dear no! That's it you saw going by; a great strappin' girl she is, too, and promisin' to grow up well, thanks to Mrs Stone's taking her. Mrs Stone always thought a heap of Esther. It's a mercy to the child that she lost her mother, I do believe! How she ever survived that kind of treatment beats all! Why that woman never seemed to have the first spark of maternal feeling to the end! She seemed just as fond of the other young ones after she had her own as she was before, and that's against nature. The way it happened was this. You see they lived up the valley nearer to the lake than the village. He was away, and was coming home that night, it seems, driving from Drayton along the lake road. And she set out to meet him. She must a walked up to the dam to look for him; and we think maybe she saw the team clear across the lake. Maybe she thought he could get to the house and save little Esther in time—that's the only explanation we ever could put on it. But this is what she did; and you can judge for yourselves if any mother in her senses *could* ha' done such a thing! You see 'twas the time of that awful disaster, you've read of it, likely, that destroyed three villages. Well, she got to the dam and see that 'twas givin' way—she was always great for knowin' all such things. And she just turned and ran. Jake Elder was up on the hill after a stray cow, and he seen her go. He was too far off to imagine what ailed her, but he said he never saw a woman run so in his life.

'And, if you'll believe it, she run right by her own house— never stopped—never looked at it. Just run for the village. Of course, she may have lost her head with the fright, but that wasn't like her. No, I think she had made up her mind to leave that innocent baby to die! She just ran down here and give warnin', and, of course, we sent word down valley on horseback, and there was no lives lost in all three villages. She started to run back as soon as we was 'roused, but 'twas too late then.

'Jake saw it all, though he was too far off to do a thing. He said he couldn't stir a foot, it was so awful. He seen the wagon drivin' along as nice as you please till it got close to the dam, and then Greenwood seemed to see the danger and whipped up like mad. He was the father, you know. But he wasn't quite in time—the dam give way and the water went over him like a tidal wave. She was almost to the gate when it struck the house and her,—and we never found her body nor his for days and days. They was washed clear down river.

'Their house was strong and it stood a little high, and had some big trees between it and the lake too. It was moved off the place and brought up against the side of the stone church down yonder, but 'twant wholly in pieces. And that child was found swimmin' round in its bed, most drowned, but not quite. The wonder is, it didn't die of a cold, but it's here yet—must have a strong constitution. Their folks never did nothing for it—so we had to keep it here.'

'Well, now, mother,' said Maria Amelia Briggs. 'It does seem to me that she did her duty. You know yourself that if she hadn't give warnin' all three of the villages would a' been cleaned out— a matter of fifteen hundred people. And if she'd stopped to lug that child, she couldn't have got here in time. Don't you believe she was thinkin' of those mill-hands' children?'

'Maria 'Melia, I'm ashamed of you!' said old Mis' Briggs. 'But you ain't married and ain't a mother. A mother's duty is to her

own child! She neglected her own to look after other folks—the
Lord never gave her them other children to care for!'

'Yes,' said Miss Jacobs, 'and here's her child, a burden on the
town! She was an unnatural mother!'

THREE THANKSGIVINGS

ANDREW'S letter and Jean's letter were in Mrs Morrison's lap.
She had read them both, and sat looking at them with a varying
sort of smile, now motherly and now unmotherly.

'You belong with me,' Andrew wrote. 'It is not right that
Jean's husband should support my mother. I can do it easily
now. You shall have a good room and every comfort. The old
house will let for enough to give you quite a little income of your
own, or it can be sold and I will invest the money where you'll get
a deal more out of it. It is not right that you should live alone
there. Sally is old and liable to accident. I am anxious about you.
Come on for Thanksgiving—and come to stay. Here is the
money to come with. You know I want you. Annie joins me in
sending love. ANDREW.'

Mrs Morrison read it all through again, and laid it down with
her quiet, twinkling smile. Then she read Jean's.

'Now, mother, you've got to come to us for Thanksgiving this
year. Just think! You haven't seen baby since he was three
months old! And have never seen the twins. You won't know
him—he's such a splendid big boy now. Joe says for you to come,
of course. And, mother, why won't you come and live with us?
Joe wants you, too. There's the little room upstairs; it's not very
big, but we can put in a Franklin stove for you and make you
pretty comfortable. Joe says he should think you ought to sell
that white elephant of a place. He says he could put the money
into his store and pay you good interest. I wish you would,
mother. We'd just love to have you here. You'd be such a comfort to me, and such a help with the babies. And Joe just loves
you. Do come now, and stay with us. Here is the money for the
trip.—Your affectionate daughter,

JEANNIE.'

Mrs Morrison laid this beside the other, folded both, and
placed them in their respective envelopes, then in their several
well-filled pigeon-holes in her big, old-fashioned desk. She

turned and paced slowly up and down the long parlor, a tall woman, commanding of aspect, yet of a winningly attractive manner, erect and light-footed, still imposingly handsome.

It was now November, the last lingering boarder was long since gone, and a quiet winter lay before her. She was alone, but for Sally; and she smiled at Andrew's cautious expression, 'liable to accident.' He could not say 'feeble' or 'ailing,' Sally being a colored lady of changeless aspect and incessant activity.

Mrs Morrison was alone, and while living in the Welcome House she was never unhappy. Her father had built it, she was born there, she grew up playing on the broad green lawns in front, and in the acre of garden behind. It was the finest house in the village, and she then thought it the finest in the world.

Even after living with her father at Washington and abroad, after visiting hall, castle and palace, she still found the Welcome House beautiful and impressive.

If she kept on taking boarders she could live the year through, and pay interest, but not principal, on her little mortgage. This had been the one possible and necessary thing while the children were there, though it was a business she hated.

But her youthful experience in diplomatic circles, and the years of practical management in church affairs, enabled her to bear it with patience and success. The boarders often confided to one another, as they chatted and tatted on the long piazza, that Mrs Morrison was 'certainly very refined.'

Now Sally whisked in cheerfully, announcing supper, and Mrs Morrison went out to her great silver tea-tray at the lit end of the long, dark mahogany table, with as much dignity as if twenty titled guests were before her.

Afterward Mr Butts called. He came early in the evening, with his usual air of determination and a somewhat unusual spruceness. Mr Peter Butts was a florid, blonde person, a little stout, a little pompous, sturdy and immovable in the attitude of a self-made man. He had been a poor boy when she was a rich girl; and it gratified him much to realize—and to call upon her to realize—that their positions had changed. He meant no unkindness, his pride was honest and unveiled. Tact he had none.

She had refused Mr Butts, almost with laughter, when he proposed to her in her gay girlhood. She had refused him, more gently, when he proposed to her in her early widowhood. He had always been her friend, and her husband's friend, a solid member of the church, and had taken the small mortgage on the house. She refused to allow him at first, but he was convincingly frank about it.

'This has nothing to do with my wanting you, Delia Morrison,' he said. 'I've always wanted you—and I've always wanted this house, too. You won't sell, but you've got to mortgage. By and by you can't pay up, and I'll get it—see? Then maybe you'll take me—to keep the house. Don't be a fool, Delia. It's a perfectly good investment.'

She had taken the loan. She had paid the interest. She would pay the interest if she had to take boarders all her life. And she would not, at any price, marry Peter Butts.

He broached the subject again that evening, cheerful and undismayed. 'You might as well come to it, Delia,' he said. 'Then, we could live right here just the same. You aren't so young as you were, to be sure; I'm not, either. But you are as good a housekeeper as ever—better—you've had more experience.'

'You are extremely kind, Mr Butts,' said the lady, 'but I do not wish to marry you.'

'I know you don't,' he said. 'You've made that clear. You don't, but I do. You've had your way and married the minister. He was a good man, but he's dead. Now you might as well marry me.'

'I do not wish to marry again, Mr Butts; neither you nor anyone.'

'Very proper, very proper, Delia,' he replied. 'It wouldn't look well if you did—at any rate, if you showed it. But why shouldn't you? The children are gone now—you can't hold them up against me any more.'

'Yes, the children are both settled now, and doing nicely,' she admitted.

'You don't want to go and live with them—either one of them—do you?' he asked.

'I should prefer to stay here,' she answered.

'Exactly! And you can't! You'd rather live here and be a grandee—but you can't do it. Keepin' house for boarders isn't any better than keepin' house for me, as I see. You'd much better marry me.'

'I should prefer to keep the house without you, Mr Butts.'

'I know you would. But you can't, I tell you. I'd like to know what a woman of your age can do with a house like this—and no money? You can't live eternally on hens' eggs and garden truck. That won't pay the mortgage.'

Mrs Morrison looked at him with her cordial smile, calm and non-committal. 'Perhaps I can manage it,' she said.

'That mortgage falls due two years from Thanksgiving, you know.'

'Yes—I have not forgotten.'

'Well, then, you might just as well marry me now, and save two years of interest. It'll be my house, either way—but you'll be keepin' it just the same.'

'It is very kind of you, Mr Butts. I must decline the offer none the less. I can pay the interest, I am sure. And perhaps—in two years' time—I can pay the principal. It's not a large sum.'

'That depends on how you look at it,' said he. 'Two thousand dollars is considerable money for a single woman to raise in two years—*and* interest.'

He went away, as cheerful and determined as ever; and Mrs Morrison saw him go with a keen light in her fine eyes, a more definite line to that steady, pleasant smile.

Then she went to spend Thanksgiving with Andrew. He was glad to see her. Annie was glad to see her. They proudly installed her in 'her room,' and said she must call it 'home' now.

This affectionately offered home was twelve by fifteen, and eight feet high. It had two windows, one looking at some pale gray clapboards within reach of a broom, the other giving a view of several small fenced yards occupied by cats, clothes and children. There was an ailanthus tree under the window, a lady ailanthus tree. Annie told her how profusely it bloomed. Mrs Morrison particularly disliked the smell of ailanthus flowers. 'It doesn't bloom in November,' said she to herself. 'I can be thankful for that!'

Andrew's church was very like the church of his father, and Mrs Andrew was doing her best to fill the position of minister's wife—doing it well, too—there was no vacancy for a minister's mother.

Besides, the work she had done so cheerfully to help her husband was not what she most cared for, after all. She liked the people, she liked to manage, but she was not strong on doctrine. Even her husband had never known how far her views differed from his. Mrs Morrison had never mentioned what they were.

Andrew's people were very polite to her. She was invited out with them, waited upon and watched over and set down among the old ladies and gentlemen—she had never realized so keenly that she was no longer young. Here nothing recalled her youth, every careful provision anticipated age. Annie brought her a hot-water bag at night, tucking it in at the foot of the bed with affectionate care. Mrs Morrison thanked her, and subsequently took it out—airing the bed a little before she got into it. The house seemed very hot to her, after the big, windy halls at home.

The little dining-room, the little round table with the little round fern-dish in the middle, the little turkey and the little carving-set—game-set she would have called it—all made her feel as if she was looking through the wrong end of an opera-glass.

In Annie's precise efficiency she saw no room for her assistance; no room in the church, no room in the small, busy town, prosperous and progressive, and no room in the house. 'Not enough to turn round in!' she said to herself. Annie, who had grown up in a city flat, thought their little parsonage palatial. Mrs Morrison grew up in the Welcome House.

She stayed a week, pleasant and polite, conversational, interested in all that went on.

'I think your mother is just lovely,' said Annie to Andrew.

'Charming woman, your mother,' said the leading church member.

'What a delightful old lady your mother is!' said the pretty soprano.

And Andrew was deeply hurt and disappointed when she announced her determination to stay on for the present in her old home. 'Dear boy,' she said, 'you mustn't take it to heart. I love to be with you, of course, but I love my home, and want to keep it as long as I can. It is a great pleasure to see you and Annie so well settled, and so happy together. I am most truly thankful for you.'

'My home is open to you whenever you wish to come, mother,' said Andrew. But he was a little angry.

Mrs Morrison came home as eager as a girl, and opened her own door with her own key, in spite of Sally's haste.

Two years were before her in which she must find some way to keep herself and Sally, and to pay two thousand dollars and the interest to Peter Butts. She considered her assets. Here was the house—the white elephant. It *was* big—very big. It was profusely furnished. Her father had entertained lavishly like the Southern-born, hospitable gentleman he was; and the bedrooms ran in suites—somewhat deteriorated by the use of boarders, but still numerous and habitable. Boarders—she abhorred them. They were people from afar, strangers and interlopers. She went over the place from garret to cellar, from front gate to backyard fence.

The garden had great possibilities. She was fond of gardening, and understood it well. She measured and estimated.

'This garden,' she finally decided, 'with the hens, will feed us two women and sell enough to pay Sally. If we make plenty of jelly, it may cover the coal bill, too. As to clothes—I don't need any. They last admirably. I can manage. I can *live*—but two thousand dollars—*and* interest!'

In the great attic was more furniture, discarded sets put there when her extravagant young mother had ordered new ones. And chairs—uncounted chairs. Senator Welcome used to invite numbers to meet his political friends—and they had delivered glowing orations in the wide, double parlors, the impassioned speakers standing on a temporary dais, now in the cellar; and the enthusiastic listeners disposed more or less comfortably on these serried rows of 'folding chairs,' which folded sometimes, and let down the visitor in scarlet confusion to the floor.

She sighed as she remembered those vivid days and glittering nights. She used to steal downstairs in her little pink wrapper and listen to the eloquence. It delighted her young soul to see her father rising on his toes, coming down sharply on his heels, hammering one hand upon the other; and then to hear the fusilade of applause.

Here were the chairs, often borrowed for weddings, funerals, and church affairs, somewhat worn and depleted, but still numerous. She mused upon them. Chairs—hundreds of chairs. They would sell for very little.

She went through her linen room. A splendid stock in the old days; always carefully washed by Sally; surviving even the boarders. Plenty of bedding, plenty of towels, plenty of napkins and tablecloths. 'It would make a good hotel—but I *can't* have it so—I *can't*! Besides, there's no need of another hotel here. The poor little Haskins House is never full.'

The stock in the china closet was more damaged than some other things, naturally; but she inventoried it with care. The countless cups of crowded church receptions were especially prominent. Later additions these, not very costly cups, but numerous, appallingly.

When she had her long list of assets all in order, she sat and studied it with a clear and daring mind. Hotel—boarding-house—she could think of nothing else. School! A girls' school! A boarding school! There was money to be made at that, and fine work done. It was a brilliant thought at first, and she gave several hours, and much paper and ink, to its full consideration. But she would need some capital for advertising; she must engage teachers—adding to her definite obligation; and to establish it, well, it would require time.

Mr Butts, obstinate, pertinacious, oppressively affectionate, would give her no time. He meant to force her to marry him for her own good—and his. She shrugged her fine shoulders with a little shiver. Marry Peter Butts! Never! Mrs Morrison still loved her husband. Some day she meant to see him again—God willing—and she did not wish to have to tell him that at fifty she had been driven into marrying Peter Butts.

Better live with Andrew. Yet when she thought of living with Andrew, she shivered again. Pushing back her sheets of figures and lists of personal property, she rose to her full graceful height and began to walk the floor. There was plenty of floor to walk. She considered, with a set deep thoughtfulness, the town and the townspeople, the surrounding country, the hundreds upon hundreds of women whom she knew—and liked, and who liked her.

It used to be said of Senator Welcome that he had no enemies; and some people, strangers, maliciously disposed, thought it no credit to his character. His daughter had no enemies, but no one had ever blamed her for her unlimited friendliness. In her father's wholesale entertainments the whole town knew and admired his daughter; in her husband's popular church she had come to know the women of the countryside about them. Her mind strayed off to these women, farmers' wives, comfortably off in a plain way, but starving for companionship, for occasional stimulus and pleasure. It was one of her joys in her husband's time to bring together these women—to teach and entertain them.

Suddenly she stopped short in the middle of the great high-ceiled room, and drew her head up proudly like a victorious queen. One wide, triumphant, sweeping glance she cast at the well-loved walls—and went back to her desk, working swiftly, excitedly, well into the hours of the night.

Presently the little town began to buzz, and the murmur ran far out into the surrounding country. Sunbonnets wagged over fences; butcher carts and pedlar's wagon carried the news farther; and ladies visiting found one topic in a thousand houses.

Mrs Morrison was going to entertain. Mrs Morrison had invited the whole feminine population, it would appear, to meet Mrs Isabelle Carter Blake, of Chicago. Even Haddleton had heard of Mrs Isabelle Carter Blake. And even Haddleton had nothing but admiration for her.

She was known the world over for her splendid work for children—for the school children and the working children of the country. Yet she was known also to have lovingly and wisely reared six children of her own—and made her husband happy in his home. On top of that she had lately written a novel, a popular novel, of which everyone was talking; and on top of that she was an intimate friend of a certain conspicuous Countess—an Italian.

It was even rumored, by some who knew Mrs Morrison better than others—or thought they did—that the Countess was coming, too! No one had known before that Delia Welcome was a school-mate of Isabel Carter, and a life-long friend; and that was ground for talk in itself.

The day arrived, and the guests arrived. They came in hundreds upon hundreds, and found ample room in the great white house.

The highest dream of the guests was realized—the Countess had come, too. With excited joy they met her, receiving impressions that would last them for all their lives, for those large widening waves of reminiscence which delight us the more as years pass. It was an incredible glory—Mrs Isabelle Carter Blake, *and* a Countess!

Some were moved to note that Mrs Morrison looked the easy peer of these eminent ladies, and treated the foreign nobility precisely as she did her other friends.

She spoke, her clear quiet voice reaching across the murmuring din, and silencing it.

'Shall we go into the east room? If you will all take chairs in the east room, Mrs Blake is going to be so kind as to address us. Also perhaps her friend—'

They crowded in, sitting somewhat timorously on the unfolded chairs.

Then the great Mrs Blake made them an address of memorable power and beauty, which received vivid sanction from that imposing presence in Parisian garments on the platform by her side. Mrs Blake spoke to them of the work she was interested in, and how it was aided everywhere by the women's clubs. She gave them the number of these clubs, and described with contagious enthusiasm the inspiration of their great meetings. She spoke of the women's club houses, going up in city after city, where many associations meet and help one another. She was winning and convincing and most entertaining—an extremely attractive speaker.

Had they a women's club there? They had not.

Not *yet*, she suggested, adding that it took no time at all to make one.

They were delighted and impressed with Mrs Blake's speech, but its effect was greatly intensified by the address of the Countess.

'I, too, am American,' she told them; 'born here, reared in England, married in Italy.' And she stirred their hearts with a vivid account of the women's clubs and associations all over Europe, and what they were accomplishing. She was going back soon, she said, the wiser and happier for this visit to her native land, and she should remember particularly this beautiful, quiet town, trusting that if she came to it again it would have joined the great sisterhood of women, 'whose hands were touching around the world for the common good.'

It was a great occasion.

The Countess left next day, but Mrs Blake remained, and spoke in some of the church meetings, to an ever widening circle of admirers. Her suggestions were practical.

'What you need here is a "Rest and Improvement Club," ' she said. 'Here are all you women coming in from the country to do your shopping—and no place to go to. No place to lie down if you're tired, to meet a friend, to eat your lunch in peace, to do your hair. All you have to do is organize, pay some small regular due, and provide yourselves with what you want.'

There was a volume of questions and suggestions, a little opposition, much random activity.

Who was to do it? Where was there a suitable place? They would have to hire someone to take charge of it. It would only be used once a week. It would cost too much.

Mrs Blake, still practical, made another suggestion. 'Why not combine business with pleasure, and make use of the best place in town, if you can get it? I *think* Mrs Morrison could be persuaded to let you use part of her house; it's quite too big for one woman.'

Then Mrs Morrison, simple and cordial as ever, greeted with warm enthusiasm by her wide circle of friends.

'I have been thinking this over,' she said. 'Mrs Blake has been discussing it with me. My house is certainly big enough for all of you, and there am I, with nothing to do but entertain you. Suppose you formed such a club as you speak of—for Rest and Improvement. My parlors are big enough for all manner of meetings; there are bedrooms in plenty for resting. If you form such a club I shall be glad to help with my great, cumbersome house, shall be delighted to see so many friends there so often; and I think I could furnish accommodations more cheaply than you could manage in any other way.'

Then Mrs Blake gave them facts and figures, showing how much clubhouses cost—and how little this arrangement would cost. 'Most women have very little money, I know,' she said, 'and they hate to spend it on themselves when they have; but even a little money from each goes a long way when it is put together. I fancy there are none of us so poor we could not squeeze out, say ten cents a week. For a hundred women that would be ten dollars. Could you feed a hundred tired women for ten dollars, Mrs Morrison?'

Mrs Morrison smiled cordially. 'Not on chicken pie,' she said. 'But I could give them tea and coffee, crackers and cheese for that, I think. And a quiet place to rest, and a reading room, and a place to hold meetings.'

Then Mrs Blake quite swept them off their feet by her wit and eloquence. She gave them to understand that if a share in the palatial accommodation of the Welcome House, and as good tea and coffee as old Sally made, with a place to meet, a place to rest, a place to talk, a place to lie down, could be had for ten cents a week each, she advised them to clinch the arrangement at once before Mrs Morrison's natural good sense had overcome her enthusiasm.

Before Mrs Isabelle Carter Blake had left, Haddleton had a large and eager women's club, whose entire expenses, outside of stationery and postage, consisted of ten cents a week *per capita*, paid to Mrs Morrison. Everybody belonged. It was open at once for charter members, and all pressed forward to claim that privileged place.

They joined by hundreds, and from each member came this tiny sum to Mrs Morrison each week. It was very little money, taken separately. But it added up with silent speed. Tea and coffee, purchased in bulk, crackers by the barrel, and whole cheeses—these are not expensive luxuries. The town was full of Mrs Morrison's ex-Sunday-school boys, who furnished her with the best they had—at cost. There was a good deal of work, a good deal of care, and room for the whole supply of Mrs Morrison's diplomatic talent and experience. Saturdays found the Welcome House as full as it could hold, and Sundays found Mrs Morrison in bed. But she liked it.

A busy, hopeful year flew by, and then she went to Jean's for Thanksgiving.

The room Jean gave her was about the same size as her haven in Andrew's home, but one flight higher up, and with a sloping ceiling. Mrs Morrison whitened her dark hair upon it, and rubbed her head confusedly. Then she shook it with renewed determination.

The house was full of babies. There was little Joe, able to get about, and into everything. There were the twins, and there was the new baby. There was one servant, over-worked and cross. There was a small, cheap, totally inadequate nursemaid. There was Jean, happy but tired, full of joy, anxiety and affection, proud of her children, proud of her husband, and delighted to unfold her heart to her mother.

By the hour she babbled of their cares and hopes, while Mrs Morrison, tall and elegant, in her well-kept old black silk, sat holding the baby or trying to hold the twins. The old silk was pretty well finished by the week's end. Joseph talked to her also, telling her how well he was getting on, and how much he needed capital, urging her to come and stay with them; it was such a help to Jeannie; asking questions about the house.

There was no going visiting here. Jeannie could not leave the babies. And few visitors; all the little suburb being full of similarly overburdened mothers. Such as called found Mrs Morrison charming. What she found them, she did not say. She bade her daughter an affectionate good-bye when the week was up, smiling at their mutual contentment.

'Good-bye, my dear children,' she said. 'I am so glad for all your happiness. I am thankful for both of you.'

But she was more thankful to get home.

Mr Butts did not have to call for his interest this time, but he called none the less.

'How on earth'd you get it, Delia?' he demanded. 'Screwed it out o' these club-women?'

'Your interest is so moderate, Mr Butts, that it is easier to meet than you imagine,' was her answer. 'Do you know the average interest they charge in Colorado? The women vote there, you know.'

He went away with no more personal information than that; and no nearer approach to the twin goals of his desire than the passing of the year.

'One more year, Delia,' he said; 'then you'll have to give in.'

'One more year!' she said to herself, and took up her chosen task with renewed energy.

The financial basis of the undertaking was very simple, but it would never have worked so well under less skilful management. Five dollars a year these country women could not have faced, but ten cents a week was possible to the poorest. There was no difficulty in collecting, for they brought it themselves; no unpleasantness in receiving, for old Sally stood at the receipt of custom and presented the covered cash box when they came for their tea.

On the crowded Saturdays the great urns were set going, the mighty array of cups arranged in easy reach, the ladies filed by, each taking her refection and leaving her dime. Where the effort came was in enlarging the membership and keeping up the attendance; and this effort was precisely in the line of Mrs Morrison's splendid talents.

Serene, cheerful, inconspicuously active, planning like the born statesman she was, executing like a practical politician, Mrs Morrison gave her mind to the work, and thrived upon it. Circle within circle, and group within group, she set small classes and departments at work, having a boys' club by and by in the big room over the woodshed, girls' clubs, reading clubs, study clubs, little meetings of every sort that were not held in churches, and some that were—previously.

For each and all there was, if wanted, tea and coffee, crackers and cheese; simple fare, of unvarying excellence, and from each and all, into the little cashbox, ten cents for these refreshments. From the club members this came weekly; and the club members, kept up by a constant variety of interests, came every week. As to numbers, before the first six months was over The Haddleton Rest and Improvement Club numbered five hundred women.

Now, five hundred times ten cents a week is twenty-six

hundred dollars a year. Twenty-six hundred dollars a year would not be very much to build or rent a large house, to furnish five hundred people with chairs, lounges, books and magazines, dishes and service; and with food and drink even of the simplest. But if you are miraculously supplied with a club-house, furnished, with a manager and servant on the spot, then that amount of money goes a long way.

On Saturdays Mrs Morrison hired two helpers for half a day, for half a dollar each. She stocked the library with many magazines for fifty dollars a year. She covered fuel, light, and small miscellanies with another hundred. And she fed her multitude with the plain viands agreed upon, at about four cents apiece.

For her collateral entertainments, her many visits, the various new expenses entailed, she paid as well; and yet at the end of the first year she had not only her interest, but a solid thousand dollars of clear profit. With a calm smile she surveyed it, heaped in neat stacks of bills in the small safe in the wall behind her bed. Even Sally did not know it was there.

The second season was better than the first. There were difficulties, excitements, even some opposition, but she rounded out the year triumphantly. 'After that,' she said to herself, 'they may have the deluge if they like.'

She made all expenses, made her interest, made a little extra cash, clearly her own, all over and above the second thousand dollars.

Then did she write to son and daughter, inviting them and their families to come home to Thanksgiving, and closing each letter with joyous pride: 'Here is the money to come with.'

They all came, with all the children and two nurses. There was plenty of room in the Welcome House, and plenty of food on the long mahogany table. Sally was as brisk as a bee, brilliant in scarlet and purple; Mrs Morrison carved her big turkey with queenly grace.

'I don't see that you're over-run with club women, mother,' said Jeannie.

'It's Thanksgiving, you know; they're all at home. I hope they are all as happy, as thankful for their homes as I am for mine,' said Mrs Morrison.

Afterward Mr Butts called. With dignity and calm unruffled, Mrs Morrison handed him his interest—and principal.

Mr Butts was almost loath to receive it, though his hand automatically grasped the crisp blue check.

'I didn't know you had a bank account,' he protested, somewhat dubiously.

'Oh, yes; you'll find the check will be honored, Mr Butts.'

'I'd like to know how you got this money. You *can't* 'a' skinned it out o' that club of yours.'

'I appreciate your friendly interest, Mr Butts; you have been most kind.'

'I believe some of these great friends of yours have lent it to you. You won't be any better off, I can tell you.'

'Come, come, Mr Butts! Don't quarrel with good money. Let us part friends.'

And they parted.

ACCORDING TO SOLOMON

' "HE THAT rebuketh a man afterwards shall find more favor than he that flattereth with his tongue," ' said Mr Solomon Bankside to his wife Mary.

'It's the other way with a woman, I think;' she answered him, 'you might put that in.'

'Tut, tut, Molly,' said he; ' "Add not unto his words,"—do not speak lightly of the wisdom of the great king.'

'I don't mean to, dear, but—when you hear it all the time'—

' "He that turneth away his ear from the law, even his prayer shall be an abomination," ' answered Mr Bankside.

'I believe you know every one of those old Proverbs by heart,' said his wife with some heat. 'Now that's *not* disrespectful!— they *are* old!—and I do wish you'd forget some of them!'

He smiled at her quizzically, tossing back his heavy silver-gray hair with the gesture she had always loved. His eyes were deep blue and bright under their bushy brows; and the mouth was kind—in its iron way. 'I can think of at least three to squelch you with, Molly,' said he, 'but I won't.'

'O I know the one you want! "A continual dropping in a very rainy day and a contentious woman are alike!" I'm *not* contentious, Solomon!'

'No, you are not,' he frankly admitted. 'What I really had in mind was this—"A prudent wife is from the Lord," and "He that findeth a wife findeth a good thing; and obtaineth favor of the Lord." '

She ran around the table in the impulsive way years did not alter, and kissed him warmly.

'I'm not scolding you, my dear,' he continued; 'but if you had all the money you'd like to give away—there wouldn't be much left!'

'But look at what you spend on me!' she urged.

'That's a wise investment—as well as a deserved reward,' her husband answered calmly. ' "There is that scattereth and yet increaseth," you know, my dear; "And there is that withholdeth more than is meet—and it tendeth to poverty!" Take all you get my dear—it's none too good for you.'

He gave her his goodbye kiss with special fondness, put on his heavy satin-lined overcoat and went to the office.

Mr Solomon Bankside was not a Jew; though his last name suggested and his first seemed to prove it; also his proficiency in the Old Testament gave color to the idea. No; he came from Vermont; of generations of unbroken New England and old English Puritan ancestry, where the Solomons and Isaacs and Zedekiahs were only mitigated by the Standfasts and Praise-the-Lords. Pious, persistent pig-headed folk were they, down all the line.

His wife had no such simple pedigree. A streak of Huguenot blood she had (some of the best in France, though neither of them knew that), a grandmother from Albany with a Van to her name; a great grandmother with a Mac; and another with an O'; even a German cross came in somewhere. Mr Bankside was devoted to genealogy, and had been at some pains to dig up these facts—the more he found the worse he felt, and the lower ran his opinion of Mrs Bankside's ancestry.

She had been a fascinating girl; pretty, with the dash and piquancy of an oriole in a May apple-tree; clever and efficient in everything her swift hands touched; quite a spectacular house-keeper; and the sober, long-faced young downeasterner had married her with a sudden decision that he often wondered about in later years. So did she.

What he had not sufficiently weighed at the time, was her spirit of incorrigible independence, and a light-mindedness which, on maturer judgment, he could almost term irreligious. His conduct was based on principle, all of it; built firmly into habit and buttressed by scriptural quotations. Hers seemed to him as inconsequent as the flight of a moth. Studying it, in his solemn conscientious way, in the light of his genealogical re-searches, he felt that all her uncertainties were accounted for, and that the error was his—in having married too many kinds of people at once.

They had been, and were, very happy together none the less: though sometimes their happiness was a little tottery. This was one of the times. It was the day after Christmas, and Mrs Bankside entered the big drawing room, redolent of popcorn and evergreen, and walked slowly to the corner where the fruits of yesterday were lovingly arranged; so few that she had been able to give—so many that she had received.

There were the numerous pretty interchangeable things given her by her many friends; 'presents,' suitable to any lady. There were the few perfectly selected ones given by the few who knew her best. There was the rather perplexing gift of Mrs MacAvelly. There was her brother's stiff white envelope enclosing a check. There were the loving gifts of children and grand-children.

Finally there was Solomon's.

It was his custom to bestow upon her one solemn and expensive object, a boon as it were, carefully selected, after much thought and balancing of merits; but the consideration was spent on the nature of the gift—not on the desires of the recipient. There was the piano she could not play, the statue she did not admire, the set of Dante she never read, the heavy gold bracelet, the stiff diamond brooch—and all the others. This time it was a set of sables, costing even more than she imagined.

Christmas after Christmas had these things come to her; and she stood there now, thinking of that procession of unvalued valuables, with an expression so mixed and changeful it resembled a kaleidoscope. Love for Solomon, pride in Solomon, respect for Solomon's judgment and power to pay, gratitude for his unfailing kindness and generosity, impatience with his always giving her this one big valuable permanent thing, when he knew so well that she much preferred small renewable cheap ones; her personal dislike of furs, the painful conviction that brown was not becoming to her—all these and more filled the little woman with what used to be called 'conflicting emotions.'

She smoothed out her brother's check, wishing as she always did that it had come before Christmas, so that she might buy more presents for her beloved people. Solomon liked to spend money on her—in his own way; but he did not like to have her spend money on him—or on anyone for that matter. She had asked her brother once, if he would mind sending her his Christmas present beforehand.

'Not on your life, Polly!' he said. 'You'd never see a cent of it!

You can't buy 'em many things right on top of Christmas, and it'll be gone long before the next one.'

She put the check away and turned to examine her queerest gift. Upon which scrutiny presently entered the donor.

'I'm ever so much obliged, Benigna,' said Mrs Bankside. 'You know how I love to do things. It's a loom, isn't it? Can you show me how it works?'

'Of course I can, my dear; that's just what I ran in for—I was afraid you wouldn't know. But you are so clever with your hands that I'm sure you'll enjoy it. I do.'

Whereat Mrs MacAvelly taught Mrs Bankside the time-honored art of weaving. And Mrs Bankside enjoyed it more than any previous handicraft she had essayed.

She did it well, beginning with rather coarse and simple weaves; and gradually learning the finer grades of work. Despising as she did the more modern woolens, she bought real wool yarn of a lovely red—and made some light warm flannelly stuff in which she proceeded to rapturously enclose her little grandchildren.

Mr Bankside warmly approved, murmuring affectionately, ' "She seeketh wool and flax—she worketh willingly with her hands." '

He watched little Bob and Polly strenuously 'helping' the furnace man to clear the sidewalk, hopping about like red-birds in their new caps and coats; and his face beamed with the appositeness of his quotation, as he remarked, ' "She is not afraid of the snow for her household, for all her household are clothed with scarlet!" ' and he proffered an extra, wholly spontaneous kiss, which pleased her mightily.

'You dear man!' she said with a hug; 'I believe you'd rather find a proverb to fit than a gold mine!'

To which he triumphantly responded: ' "Wisdom is better than rubies; and all the things that may be desired are not to be compared to it." '

She laughed sweetly at him. 'And do you think wisdom stopped with that string of proverbs?'

'You can't get much beyond it,' he answered calmly. 'If we lived up to all there is in that list we shouldn't be far out, my dear!'

Whereat she laughed again, smoothed his gray mane, and kissed him in the back of his neck. 'You *dear* thing!' said Mrs Bankside.

She kept herself busy with the new plaything as he called it. Hands that had been rather empty were now smoothly full. Her health was better, and any hint of occasional querulousness disappeared entirely; so that her husband was moved to fresh admiration of her sunny temper, and quoted for the hundredth time, ' "She openeth her mouth with wisdom, and in her tongue is the law of kindness." '

Mrs MacAvelly taught her to make towels. But Mrs Bankside's skill outstripped hers; she showed inventive genius and designed patterns of her own. The fineness and quality of the work increased; and she joyfully replenished her linen chest with her own handiwork.

'I tell you, my dear,' said Mrs MacAvelly, 'if you'd be willing to sell them you could get almost *any* price for those towels. With the initials woven in. I know I could get you orders— through the Woman's Exchange, you know!'

Mrs Bankside was delighted. 'What fun!' she said. 'And I needn't appear at all?'

'No, you needn't appear at all—do let me try.'

So Mrs Bankside made towels of price, soft, fine, and splendid, till she was weary of them; and in the opulence of constructive genius fell to devising woven belts of elaborate design.

These were admired excessively. All her women friends wanted one, or more; the Exchange got hold of it, there was a distinct demand; and finally Mrs MacAvelly came in one day with a very important air and a special order.

'I don't know what you'll think, my dear,' she said, 'but I happen to know the Percys very well—the big store people, you know; and Mr Percy was talking about those belts of yours to me;—of course he didn't know they are yours; but he said (the Exchange people told him I knew, you see), "If you can place an order with that woman, I can take all she'll make and pay her full price for them. Is she poor?" he asked. "Is she dependent on her work?" And I told him, "Not altogether." And I think he thinks it an interesting case! Anyhow, there's the order. Will you do it?'

Mrs Bankside was much excited. She wanted to very much, but dreaded offending her husband. So far she had not told him of her quiet trade in towels; but hid and saved this precious money—the first she had ever earned.

The two friends discussed the pros and cons at considerable length; and finally with some perturbation, she decided to accept the order.

'You'll never tell, Benigna!' she urged. 'Solomon would never forgive me, I'm afraid.'

'Why of course I won't—you needn't have a moment's fear of it. You give them to me—I'll stop with the carriage you see; and I take them to the Exchange—and he gets them from there.'

'It seems like smuggling!' said Mrs Bankside delightedly. 'I always did love to smuggle!'

'They say women have no conscience about laws, don't they?' Mrs MacAvelly suggested.

'Why should we?' answered her friend. 'We don't make 'em— nor God—nor nature. Why on earth should we respect a set of silly rules made by some men one day and changed by some more the next?'

'Bless us, Polly! Do you talk to Mr Bankside like that?'

'Indeed I don't!' answered her hostess, holding out a particularly beautiful star-patterned belt to show to advantage. 'There are lots of things I don't say to Mr Bankside—"A man of understanding holdeth his peace" you know—or a woman.'

She was a pretty creature, her hair like that of a powdered marchioness, her rosy cheeks and firm slight figure suggesting a charmer in Dresden china.

Mrs MacAvelly regarded her admiringly. ' "Where there is no wood the fire goeth out; so where there is no tale bearer the strife ceaseth," ' she proudly offered, 'I can quote that much myself.'

But Mrs Bankside had many misgivings as she pursued her audacious way; the busy hours flying away from her, and the always astonishing checks flying toward her in gratifying accumulation. She came down to her well-planned dinners gracious and sweet; always effectively dressed; spent the cosy quiet evenings with her husband, or went out with him, with a manner of such increased tenderness and charm that his heart warmed anew to the wife of his youth; and he even relented a little toward her miscellaneous ancestors.

As the days shortened and darkened she sparkled more and more; with little snatches of song now and then; gay ineffectual strumming on the big piano; sudden affectionate darts at him, with quaintly distributed caresses.

'Molly!' said he, 'I don't believe you're a day over twenty! What makes you act so?'

'Don't you like it, So?' she asked him. That was the nearest she ever would approximate to his name.

He did like it, naturally, and even gave her an extra ten dollars to buy Christmas presents with; while he meditated giving her an electric runabout;—to her!—who was afraid of a wheelbarrow!

When the day arrived and the family were gathered together, Mrs Bankside, wearing the diamond brooch, the gold bracelet, the point lace handkerchief—everything she could carry of his accumulated generosity—and such an air of triumphant mystery that the tree itself was dim beside her; handed out to her astonished relatives such an assortment of desirable articles that they found no words to express their gratitude.

'Why, *Mother!*' said Jessie, whose husband was a minister and salaried as such, 'Why, *Mother*—how did you know we wanted just that kind of a rug!—and a sewing-machine *too!* And this lovely suit—and—and—why *Mother!*'

But her son-in-law took her aside and kissed her solemnly. He had wanted that particular set of sociological books for years— and never hoped to get them; or that bunch of magazines either.

Nellie had 'married rich;' she was less ostentatiously favored; but she had shown her thankfulness a week ago—when her mother had handed her a check.

'Sh, sh! my dear!' her mother had said, 'Not one word. I know! What pleasant weather we're having.'

This son-in-law was agreeably surprised, too; and the other relatives, married and single; while the children rioted among their tools and toys, taking this Christmas like any other, as a season of unmitigated joy.

Mr Solomon Bankside looked on with growing amazement, making computations in his practiced mind; saying nothing whatever. Should he criticize his wife before others?

But when his turn came—when gifts upon gifts were offered to him—sets of silken handkerchiefs (he couldn't bear the touch of a silk handkerchief!), a cabinet of cards and chips and counters of all sorts (he never played cards), an inlaid chess-table and ivory men (the game was unknown to him), a gorgeous scarf-pin (he abominated jewelery), a five pound box of candy (he never ate it), his feelings so mounted within him, that since he would not express and could not repress them, he summarily went up stairs to his room.

She found him there later, coming in blushing, smiling, crying a little too—like a naughty but charming child.

He swallowed hard as he looked at her; and his voice was a little strained.

'I can take a joke as well as any man, Molly. I guess we're square on that. But—my dear!—where did you get it?'

'Earned it,' said she, looking down, and fingering her lace handkerchief.

'Earned it! My wife, earning money! How—if I may ask?'

'By my weaving, dear—the towels and the belts—I sold 'em. Don't be angry—nobody knows—my name didn't appear at all! Please don't be angry!—It isn't wicked, and it was such fun!'

'No—it's not wicked, I suppose,' said he rather grimly. 'But it is certainly a most mortifying and painful thing to me—most unprecedented.'

'Not so unprecedented, Dear,' she urged, 'Even the woman you think most of did it! Don't you remember "She maketh fine linen and selleth it—and delivereth girdles unto the merchants!"'

Mr Bankside came down handsomely.

He got used to it after a while, and then he became proud of it. If a friend ventured to suggest a criticism, or to sympathize, he would calmly respond, ' "The heart of her husband doth safely trust in her, so that he shall have no need of spoil. Give her of the fruit of her hands, and let her own works praise her in the gates." '

THE COTTAGETTE

'Why not?' said Mr Mathews. 'It is far too small for a house, too pretty for a hut, too—unusual—for a cottage.'

'Cottagette, by all means,' said Lois, seating herself on a porch chair. 'But it is larger than it looks, Mr Mathews. How do you like it, Malda?'

I was delighted with it. More than delighted. Here this tiny shell of fresh unpainted wood peeped out from under the trees, the only house in sight except the distant white specks on far off farms, and the little wandering village in the river-threaded valley. It sat right on the turf,—no road, no path even, and the dark woods shadowed the back windows.

'How about meals?' asked Lois.

'Not two minutes' walk,' he assured her, and showed us a little furtive path between the trees to the place where meals were furnished.

We discussed and examined and exclaimed, Lois holding her pongee skirts close about her—she needn't have been so careful, there wasn't a speck of dust,—and presently decided to take it.

Never did I know the real joy and peace of living, before that blessed summer at 'High Court.' It was a mountain place, easy enough to get to, but strangely big and still and far away when you were there.

The working basis of the establishment was an eccentric woman named Caswell, a sort of musical enthusiast, who had a summer school of music and the 'higher thought.' Malicious persons, not able to obtain accommodations there, called the place 'High C.'

I liked the music very well, and kept my thoughts to myself, both high and low, but 'The Cottagette' I loved unreservedly. It was so little and new and clean, smelling only of its fresh-planed boards—they hadn't even stained it.

There was one big room and two little ones in the tiny thing, though from the outside you wouldn't have believed it, it looked so small; but small as it was it harbored a miracle—a real bath-room with water piped from mountain springs. Our windows opened into the green shadiness, the soft brownness, the bird-inhabited quiet flower-starred woods. But in front we looked across whole counties—over a far-off river—into another state. Off and down and away—it was like sitting on the roof of some-thing—something very big.

The grass swept up to the door-step, to the walls—only it wasn't just grass of course, but such a procession of flowers as I had never imagined could grow in one place.

You had to go quite a way through the meadow, wearing your own narrow faintly marked streak in the grass, to reach the town-connecting road below. But in the woods was a little path, clear and wide, by which we went to meals.

For we ate with the highly thoughtful musicians, and highly musical thinkers, in their central boarding-house nearby. They didn't call it a boarding-house, which is neither high nor musi-cal; they called it 'The Calceolaria.' There was plenty of that growing about, and I didn't mind what they called it so long as the food was good—which it was, and the prices reasonable—which they were.

The people were extremely interesting—some of them at least; and all of them were better than the average of summer boarders.

But if there hadn't been any interesting ones it didn't matter while Ford Mathews was there. He was a newspaper man, or rather an ex-newspaper man, then becoming a writer for maga-zines, with books ahead.

He had friends at High Court—he liked music—he liked the place—and he liked us. Lois liked him too, as was quite natural. I'm sure I did.

He used to come up evenings and sit on the porch and talk.

He came daytimes and went on long walks with us. He estab-lished his workshop in a most attractive little cave not far beyond us,—the country there is full of rocky ledges and hollows,—and sometimes asked us over to an afternoon tea, made on a gipsy fire.

Lois was a good deal older than I, but not really old at all, and she didn't look her thirty-five by ten years. I never blamed her for not mentioning it, and I wouldn't have done so, myself, on any account. But I felt that together we made a safe and reasonable household. She played beautifully, and there was a piano in our big room. There were pianos in several other little cottages about—but too far off for any jar of sound. When the wind was right we caught little wafts of music now and then; but mostly it was still—blessedly still about us. And yet that Calceolaria was only two minutes off—and with raincoats and rubbers we never minded going to it.

We saw a good deal of Ford and I got interested in him, I couldn't help it. He was big. Not extra big in pounds and inches, but a man with big view and a grip—with purpose and real power. He was going to do things. I thought he was doing them now, but he didn't—this was all like cutting steps in the ice-wall, he said. It had to be done, but the road was long ahead. And he took an interest in my work too, which is unusual for a literary man.

Mine wasn't much. I did embroidery and made designs.

It is such pretty work! I like to draw from flowers and leaves and things about me; conventionalize them sometimes, and sometimes paint them just as they are,—in soft silk stitches.

All about up here were the lovely small things I needed; and not only these, but the lovely big things that make one feel so strong and able to do beautiful work.

Here was the friend I lived so happily with, and all this fairy land of sun and shadow, the free immensity of our view, and the dainty comfort of the Cottagette. We never had to think of ordinary things till the soft musical thrill of the Japanese gong stole through the trees, and we trotted off to the Calceolaria.

I think Lois knew before I did.

We were old friends and trusted each other, and she had had experience too.

'Malda,' she said, 'let us face this thing and be rational.' It was a strange thing that Lois should be so rational and yet so musical—but she was, and that was one reason I liked her so much.

'You are beginning to love Ford Mathews—do you know it?'

I said yes, I thought I was.

'Does he love you?'

That I couldn't say. 'It is early yet,' I told her. 'He is a man, he is about thirty I believe, he has seen more of life and probably loved before—it may be nothing more than friendliness with him.'

'Do you think it would be a good marriage?' she asked. We had often talked of love and marriage, and Lois had helped me to form my views—hers were very clear and strong.

'Why yes—if he loves me,' I said. 'He has told me quite a bit about his family, good western farming people, real Americans. He is strong and well—you can read clean living in his eyes and mouth.' Ford's eyes were as clear as a girl's, the whites of them were clear. Most men's eyes, when you look at them critically, are not like that. They may look at you very expressively, but when you look at them, just as features, they are not very nice.

I liked his looks, but I liked him better.

So I told her that as far as I knew it would be a good marriage—if it was one.

'How much do you love him?' she asked.

That I couldn't quite tell,—it was a good deal,—but I didn't think it would kill me to lose him.

'Do you love him enough to do something to win him—to really put yourself out somewhat for that purpose?'

'Why—yes—I think I do. If it was something I approved of. What do you mean?'

Then Lois unfolded her plan. She had been married,—unhappily married, in her youth; that was all over and done with years ago; she had told me about it long since; and she said she did not regret the pain and loss because it had given her experience. She had her maiden name again—and freedom. She was so fond of me she wanted to give me the benefit of her experience—without the pain.

'Men like music,' said Lois; 'they like sensible talk; they like beauty of course, and all that,—'

'Then they ought to like you!' I interrupted, and, as a matter of fact they did. I knew several who wanted to marry her, but she said 'once was enough.' I don't think they were 'good marriages' though.

'Don't be foolish, child,' said Lois, 'this is serious. What they care for most after all is domesticity. Of course they'll fall in love with anything; but what they want to marry is a homemaker.

Now we are living here in an idyllic sort of way, quite conducive to falling in love, but no temptation to marriage. If I were you— if I really loved this man and wished to marry him, I would make a home of this place.'

'Make a home?—why it *is* a home. I never was so happy anywhere in my life. What on earth do you mean, Lois?'

'A person might be happy in a balloon, I suppose,' she replied, 'but it wouldn't be a home. He comes here and sits talking with us, and it's quiet and feminine and attractive—and then we hear that big gong at the Calceolaria, and off we go slopping through the wet woods—and the spell is broken. Now you can cook.' I could cook. I could cook excellently. My esteemed Nara had rigorously taught me every branch of what is now called 'domestic science;' and I had no objection to the work, except that it prevented my doing anything else. And one's hands are not so nice when one cooks and washes dishes,—I need nice hands for my needlework. But if it was a question of pleasing Ford Mathews—

Lois went on calmly. 'Miss Caswell would put on a kitchen for us in a minute, she said she would, you know, when we took the cottage. Plenty of people keep house up here,—we can if we want to.'

'But we don't want to,' I said, 'we never have wanted to. The very beauty of the place is that it never had any house-keeping about it. Still, as you say, it would be cosy on a wet night, we could have delicious little suppers, and have him stay—'

'He told me he had never known a home since he was eighteen,' said Lois.

That was how we came to install a kitchen in the Cottagette. The men put it up in a few days, just a lean-to with a window, a sink and two doors. I did the cooking. We had nice things, there is no denying that; good fresh milk and vegetables particularly, fruit is hard to get in the country, and meat too, still we managed nicely; the less you have the more you have to manage—it takes time and brains, that's all.

Lois likes to do housework, but it spoils her hands for practicing, so she can't; and I was perfectly willing to do it—it was all in the interest of my own heart. Ford certainly enjoyed it. He dropped in often, and ate things with undeniable relish. So I was pleased, though it did interfere with my work a good deal. I always work best in the morning; but of course housework has to be done in the morning too; and it is astonishing how much work there is in the littlest kitchen. You go in for a minute, and you see this thing and that thing and the other thing to be done, and your minute is an hour before you know it.

When I was ready to sit down the freshness of the morning was gone somehow. Before, when I woke up, there was only the clean wood smell of the house, and then the blessed out-of-doors: now I always felt the call of the kitchen as soon as I woke. An oil stove will smell a little, either in or out of the house; and soap, and—well you know if you cook in a bedroom how it makes the room feel differently? Our house had been only bedroom and parlor before.

We baked too—the baker's bread was really pretty poor, and Ford did enjoy my whole wheat, and brown, and especially hot rolls and gems. It was a pleasure to feed him, but it did heat up the house, and me. I never could work much—at my work—baking days. Then, when I did get to work, the people would come with things,—milk or meat or vegetables, or children with berries; and what distressed me most was the wheelmarks on our meadow. They soon made quite a road—they had to of course, but I hated it—I lost that lovely sense of being on the last edge and looking over—we were just a bead on a string like other houses. But it was quite true that I loved this man, and would do more than this to please him. We couldn't go off so freely on excursions as we used, either; when meals are to be prepared someone has to be there, and to take in things when they come. Sometimes Lois stayed in, she always asked to, but mostly I did. I couldn't let her spoil her summer on my account. And Ford certainly liked it.

He came so often that Lois said she thought it would look better if we had an older person with us; and that her mother could come if I wanted her, and she could help with the work of course. That seemed reasonable, and she came. I wasn't very fond of Lois's mother, Mrs Fowler, but it did seem a little conspicuous, Mr Mathews eating with us more than he did at the Calceolaria. There were others of course, plenty of them dropping in, but I didn't encourage it much, it made so much more work. They would come in to supper, and then we would have musical evenings. They offered to help me wash dishes, some of them, but a new hand in the kitchen is not much help, I preferred to do it myself; then I knew where the dishes were.

Ford never seemed to want to wipe dishes; though I often wished he would.

So Mrs Fowler came. She and Lois had one room, they had to,—and she really did a lot of the work, she was a very practical old lady.

Then the house began to be noisy. You hear another person in a kitchen more than you hear yourself, I think,—and the walls were only boards. She swept more than we did too. I don't think much sweeping is needed in a clean place like that; and she dusted all the time; which I know is unnecessary. I still did most of the cooking, but I could get off more to draw, out-of-doors; and to walk. Ford was in and out continually, and, it seemed to me, was really coming nearer. What was one summer of interrupted work, of noise and dirt and smell and constant meditation on what to eat next, compared to a lifetime of love? Besides—if he married me—I should have to do it always, and might as well get used to it.

Lois kept me contented, too, telling me nice things that Ford said about my cooking. 'He does appreciate it so,' she said.

One day he came around early and asked me to go up Hugh's Peak with him. It was a lovely climb and took all day. I demurred a little, it was Monday, Mrs Fowler thought it was cheaper to have a woman come and wash, and we did, but it certainly made more work.

'Never mind,' he said, 'what's washing day or ironing day or any of that old foolishness to us? This is walking day—that's what it is.' It was really, cool and sweet and fresh,—it had rained in the night,—and brilliantly clear.

'Come along!' he said. 'We can see as far as Patch Mountain I'm sure. There'll never be a better day.'

'Is anyone else going?' I asked.

'Not a soul. It's just us. Come.'

I came gladly, only suggesting—'Wait, let me put up a lunch.'

'I'll wait just long enough for you to put on knickers and a short skirt,' said he. 'The lunch is all in the basket on my back.

I know how long it takes for you women to "put up" sandwiches and things.'

We were off in ten minutes, light-footed and happy: and the day was all that could be asked. He brought a perfect lunch, too, and had made it all himself. I confess it tasted better to me than my own cooking; but perhaps that was the climb.

When we were nearly down we stopped by a spring on a broad ledge, and supped, making tea as he liked to do out-of-doors. We saw the round sun setting at one end of a world view, and the round moon rising at the other; calmly shining each on each.

And then he asked me to be his wife.—

We were very happy.

'But there's a condition!' said he all at once, sitting up straight and looking very fierce. 'You mustn't cook!'

'What!' said I. 'Mustn't cook?'

'No,' said he, 'you must give it up—for my sake.'

I stared at him dumbly.

'Yes, I know all about it,' he went on, 'Lois told me. I've seen a good deal of Lois—since you've taken to cooking. And since I would talk about you, naturally I learned a lot. She told me how you were brought up, and how strong your domestic instincts were—but bless your artist soul dear girl, you have some others!' Then he smiled rather queerly and murmured, 'surely in vain the net is spread in the sight of any bird.'

'I've watched you, dear, all summer;' he went on, 'it doesn't agree with you.

'Of course the things taste good—but so do my things! I'm a good cook myself. My father was a cook, for years—at good wages. I'm used to it you see.

'One summer when I was hard up I cooked for a living—and saved money instead of starving.'

'O ho!' said I, 'that accounts for the tea—and the lunch!'

'And lots of other things,' said he. 'But you haven't done half as much of your lovely work since you started this kitchen business, and—you'll forgive me, dear—it hasn't been as good. Your work is quite too good to lose; it is a beautiful and distinctive art, and I don't want you to let it go. What would you think of me if I gave up my hard long years of writing for the easy competence of a well-paid cook!'

I was still too happy to think very clearly. I just sat and looked at him. 'But you want to marry me?' I said.

'I want to marry you, Malda,—because I love you—because you are young and strong and beautiful—because you are wild and sweet and—fragrant, and—elusive, like the wild flowers you love. Because you are so truly an artist in your special way, seeing beauty and giving it to others. I love you because of all this, because you are rational and highminded and capable of friendship,—and in spite of your cooking!'

'But—how do you want to live?'

'As we did here—at first,' he said. 'There was peace, exquisite silence. There was beauty—nothing but beauty. There were the clean wood odors and flowers and fragrances and sweet wild wind. And there was you—your fair self, always delicately dressed, with white firm fingers sure of touch in delicate true work. I loved you then. When you took to cooking it jarred on me. I have been a cook, I tell you, and I know what it is. I hated it—to see my wood-flower in a kitchen. But Lois told me about how you were brought up to it and loved it, and I said to myself, "I love this woman; I will wait and see if I love her even as a cook." And I do, Darling: I withdraw the condition. I will love you always, even if you insist on being my cook for life!'

'O I don't insist!' I cried. 'I don't want to cook—I want to draw! But I thought—Lois said—How she has misunderstood you!'

'It is not true, always, my dear,' said he, 'that the way to a man's heart is through his stomach; at least it's not the only way. Lois doesn't know everything, she is young yet! And perhaps for my sake you can give it up. Can you sweet?'

Could I? Could I? Was there ever a man like this?

THE WIDOW'S MIGHT

JAMES had come on to the funeral, but his wife had not; she could not leave the children—that is what he said. She said, privately, to him, that she would not go. She never was willing to leave New York except for Europe or for Summer vacations; and a trip to Denver in November—to attend a funeral—was not a possibility to her mind.

Ellen and Adelaide were both there: they felt it a duty—but neither of their husbands had come. Mr Jennings could not leave his classes in Cambridge, and Mr Oswald could not leave his business in Pittsburg—that is what they said.

The last services were over. They had had a cold, melancholy lunch and were all to take the night train home again. Meanwhile the lawyer was coming at four to read the will.

'It is only a formality. There can't be much left,' said James.

'No,' agreed Adelaide, 'I suppose not.'

'A long illness eats up everything,' said Ellen, and sighed. Her husband had come to Colorado for his lungs years before and was still delicate.

'Well,' said James rather abruptly, 'What are we going to do with Mother?'

'Why, of course—' Ellen began, 'We *could* take her. It would depend a good deal on how much property there is—I mean, on where she'd want to go. Edward's salary is more than needed now,' Ellen's mental processes seemed a little mixed.

'She can come to me if she prefers, of course,' said Adelaide. 'But I don't think it would be very pleasant for her. Mother never did like Pittsburg.'

James looked from one to the other.

'Let me see—how old is Mother?'

'Oh she's all of fifty,' answered Ellen, 'and much broken, I think. It's been a long strain, you know.' She turned plaintively to her brother. 'I should think you could make her more comfortable than either of us, James—with your big house.'

Forerunner, 2:1 (January 1911), 1–5.

'I think a woman is always happier living with a son than with a daughter's husband,' said Adelaide. 'I've always thought so.'

'That is often true,' her brother admitted. 'But it depends.' He stopped, and the sisters exchanged glances. They knew upon what it depended.

'Perhaps if she stayed with me, you could——help some,' suggested Ellen.

'Of course, of course, I could do that,' he agreed with evident relief. 'She might visit between you——take turns——and I could pay her board. About how much ought it to amount to? We might as well arrange everything now.'

'Things cost awfully in these days,' Ellen said with a criss-cross of fine wrinkles on her pale forehead. 'But of course it would be only just *what* it costs. I shouldn't want to *make* anything.'

'It's work and care, Ellen, and you may as well admit it. You need all your strength——with those sickly children and Edward on your hands. When she comes to me, there need be no expense, James, except for clothes. I have room enough and Mr Oswald will never notice the difference in the house bills——but he does hate to pay out money for clothes.'

'Mother must be provided for properly,' her son declared. 'How much ought it to cost——a year——for clothes.'

'You know what your wife's cost,' suggested Adelaide, with a flicker of a smile about her lips.

'Oh, *no*,' said Ellen. 'That's no criterion! Maude is in society, you see. Mother wouldn't *dream* of having so much.'

James looked at her gratefully. 'Board——and clothes——all told; what should you say, Ellen?'

Ellen scrabbled in her small black hand bag for a piece of paper, and found none. James handed her an envelope and a fountain pen.

'Food——just plain food materials——costs all of four dollars a week now——for one person,' said she. 'And heat——and light—— and extra service. I should think six a week would be the *least*, James. And for clothes and carfare and small expenses——I should say——well, three hundred dollars!'

'That would make over six hundred a year,' said James slowly. 'How about Oswald sharing that, Adelaide?'

Adelaide flushed. 'I do not think he would be willing, James. Of course if it were absolutely necessary——'

'He has money enough,' said her brother.

'Yes, but he never seems to have any outside of his business—and he has his own parents to carry now. No—I can give her a home, but that's all.'

'You see, you'd have none of the care and trouble, James,' said Ellen. 'We—the girls—are each willing to have her with us, while perhaps Maude wouldn't care to, but if you could just pay the money——'

'Maybe there's some left after all,' suggested Adelaide. 'And this place ought to sell for something.'

'This place' was a piece of rolling land within ten miles of Denver. It had a bit of river bottom, and ran up towards the foothills. From the house the view ran north and south along the precipitous ranks of the 'Big Rockies' to westward. To the east lay the vast stretches of sloping plain.

'There ought to be at least six or eight thousand dollars from it, I should say,' he concluded.

'Speaking of clothes,' Adelaide rather irrelevantly suggested, 'I see Mother didn't get any new black. She's always worn it as long as I can remember.'

'Mother's a long time,' said Ellen. 'I wonder if she wants anything, I'll go up and see.'

'No,' said Adelaide, 'She said she wanted to be let alone—and rest. She said she'd be down by the time Mr Frankland got here.'

'She's bearing it pretty well,' Ellen suggested, after a little silence.

'It's not like a broken heart,' Adelaide explained. 'Of course Father meant well——'

'He was a man who always did his duty,' admitted Ellen. 'But we none of us—loved him—very much.'

'He is dead and buried,' said James. 'We can at least respect his memory.'

'We've hardly seen Mother—under that black veil.' Ellen went on. 'It must have aged her. This long nursing.'

'She had help toward the last—a man nurse,' said Adelaide.

'Yes, but a long illness is an awful strain—and Mother never was good at nursing. She has surely done her duty,' pursued Ellen.

'And now she's entitled to a rest,' said James, rising and walking about the room. 'I wonder how soon we can close up affairs here—and get rid of this place. There might be enough in it to give her almost a living—properly invested.'

Ellen looked out across the dusty stretches of land.

'How I did hate to live here!' she said.

'So did I,' said Adelaide.

'So did I,' said James.

And they all smiled rather grimly.

'We don't any of us seem to be very—affectionate, about Mother,' Adelaide presently admitted, 'I don't know why it is— we never were an affectionate family, I guess.'

'Nobody could be affectionate with Father,' Ellen suggested timidly.

'And Mother—poor Mother! She's had an awful life.'

'Mother has always done her duty,' said James in a determined voice, 'and so did Father, as he saw it. Now we'll do ours.'

'Ah,' exclaimed Ellen, jumping to her feet. 'Here comes the lawyer, I'll call Mother.'

She ran quickly upstairs and tapped at her mother's door.

'Mother, oh Mother,' she cried. 'Mr Frankland's come.'

'I know it,' came back a voice from within. 'Tell him to go ahead and read the will. I know what's in it. I'll be down in a few minutes.'

Ellen went slowly back downstairs with the fine criss-cross of wrinkles showing on her pale forehead again, and delivered her mother's message.

The other two glanced at each other hesitatingly, but Mr Frankland spoke up briskly.

'Quite natural, of course, under the circumstances. Sorry I couldn't get to the funeral. A case on this morning.'

The will was short. The estate was left to be divided among the children in four equal parts, two to the son and one each to the daughters after the mother's legal share had been deducted, if she were still living. In such case they were furthermore directed to provide for their mother while she lived. The estate, as described, consisted of the ranch, the large, rambling house on it, with all the furniture, stock and implements, and some $5,000 in mining stocks.

'That is less than I had supposed,' said James.

'This will was made ten years ago,' Mr Frankland explained. 'I have done business for your father since that time. He kept his faculties to the end, and I think that you will find that the property has appreciated. Mrs McPherson has taken excellent care of the ranch, I understand—and has had some boarders.'

Both the sisters exchanged pained glances.

'There's an end to all that now,' said James.

At this moment, the door opened and a tall black figure, cloaked and veiled, came into the room.

'I'm glad to hear you say that Mr McPherson kept his faculties to the last, Mr Frankland,' said the widow. 'It's true. I didn't come down to hear that old will. It's no good now.'

They all turned in their chairs.

'Is there a later will, madam?' inquired the lawyer.

'Not that I know of. Mr McPherson had no property when he died.'

'No property! My dear lady—four years ago he certainly had some.'

'Yes, but three years and a-half ago he gave it all to me. Here are the deeds.'

There they were, in very truth—formal and correct, and quite simple and clear—for deeds, James R. McPherson, Sr, had assuredly given to his wife the whole estate.

'You remember that was the panic year,' she continued. 'There was pressure from some of Mr McPherson's creditors; he thought it would be safer so.'

'Why—yes,' remarked Mr Frankland, 'I do remember now his advising with me about it. But I thought the step unnecessary.'

James cleared his throat.

'Well, Mother, this does complicate matters a little. We were hoping that we could settle up all the business this afternoon— with Mr Frankland's help—and take you back with us.'

'We can't be spared any longer, you see, Mother,' said Ellen.

'Can't you deed it back again, Mother,' Adelaide suggested, 'to James, or to—all of us, so we can get away?'

'Why should I?'

'Now, Mother,' Ellen put in persuasively, 'we know how badly you feel, and you are nervous and tired, but I told you this morning when we came, that we expected to take you back with us. You know you've been packing——'

'Yes, I've been packing,' replied the voice behind the veil.

'I dare say it was safer—to have the property in your name—technically,' James admitted, 'but now I think it would be the simplest way for you to make it over to me in a lump, and I will see that Father's wishes are carried out to the letter.'

'Your father is dead,' remarked the voice.

'Yes, Mother, we know—we know how you feel,' Ellen ventured.

'I am alive,' said Mrs McPherson.

'Dear Mother, it's very trying to talk business to you at such a time. We all realize it,' Adelaide explained with a touch of asperity, 'But we told you we couldn't stay as soon as we got here.'

'And the business has to be settled,' James added conclusively.

'It is settled.'

'Perhaps Mr Frankland can make it clear to you,' went on James with forced patience.

'I do not doubt that your mother understands perfectly,' murmured the lawyer. 'I have always found her a woman of remarkable intelligence.'

'Thank you, Mr Frankland. Possibly you may be able to make my children understand that this property—such as it is—is mine now.'

'Why assuredly, assuredly, Mrs McPherson. We all see that. But we assume, as a matter of course, that you will consider Mr McPherson's wishes in regard to the disposition of the estate.'

'I have considered Mr McPherson's wishes for thirty years,' she replied. 'Now, I'll consider mine. I have done my duty since the day I married him. It it eleven hundred days—to-day.' The last with sudden intensity.

'But madam, your children——'

'I have no children, Mr Frankland. I have two daughters and a son. These two grown persons here, grown up, married, having children of their own—or ought to have—were my children. I did my duty by them, and they did their duty by me—and would yet, no doubt.' The tone changed suddenly. 'But they don't have to. I'm tired of duty.'

The little group of listeners looked up, startled.

'You don't know how things have been going on here,' the voice went on. 'I didn't trouble you with my affairs. But I'll tell you now. When your father saw fit to make over the property to me—to save it—and when he knew that he hadn't many years to live, I took hold of things. I had to have a nurse for your father—and a doctor coming: the house was a sort of hospital, so I made it a little more so. I had a half a dozen patients and nurses here—and made money by it. I ran the garden—kept cows—raised my own chickens—worked out doors—slept out of doors. I'm a stronger woman to-day than I ever was in my life!'

She stood up, tall, strong and straight, and drew a deep breath.

'Your father's property amounted to about $8,000 when he died,' she continued. 'That would be $4,000 to James and $2,000 to each of the girls. That I'm willing to give you now—each of you—in your own name. But if my daughters will take my advice, they'd better let me send them the yearly income—in cash—to spend as they like. It is good for a woman to have some money of her own.'

'I think you are right, Mother,' said Adelaide.

'Yes indeed,' murmured Ellen.

'Don't you need it yourself, Mother?' asked James, with a sudden feeling of tenderness for the stiff figure in black.

'No, James, I shall keep the ranch, you see. I have good reliable help. I've made $2,000 a year—clear—off it so far, and now I've rented it for that to a doctor friend of mine—woman doctor.'

'I think you have done remarkably well, Mrs McPherson—wonderfully well,' said Mr Frankland.

'And you'll have an income of $2,000 a year,' said Adelaide incredulously.

'You'll come and live with me, won't you,' ventured Ellen.

'Thank you, my dear, I will not.'

'You're more than welcome in my big house,' said Adelaide.

'No thank you, my dear.'

'I don't doubt Maude will be glad to have you,' James rather hesitatingly offered.

'I do. I doubt it very much. No thank you, my dear.'

'But what *are* you going to do?'

Ellen seemed genuinely concerned.

'I'm going to do what I never did before. I'm going to *live!*'

With a firm swift step, the tall figure moved to the windows and pulled up the lowered shades. The brilliant Colorado sunshine poured into the room. She threw off the long black veil.

'That's borrowed,' she said. 'I didn't want to hurt your feelings at the funeral.'

She unbuttoned the long black cloak and dropped it at her feet, standing there in the full sunlight, a little flushed and smiling, dressed in a well-made traveling suit of dull mixed colors.

'If you want to know my plans, I'll tell you. I've got $6,000 of my own. I earned it in three years—off my little rancho-sanitarium. One thousand I have put in the savings bank—to bring me back from anywhere on earth, and to put me in an old lady's home if it is necessary. Here is an agreement with a cremation company. They'll import me, if necessary, and have me duly—expurgated—or they don't get the money. But I've got $5,000 to play with, and I'm going to play.'

Her daughters looked shocked.

'Why Mother——'

'At your age——'

James drew down his upper lip and looked like his father.

'I knew you wouldn't any of you understand,' she continued more quietly. 'But it doesn't matter any more. Thirty years I've given you—and your father. Now I'll have thirty years of my own.'

'Are you—are you sure you're—well, Mother,' Ellen urged with real anxiety.

Her mother laughed outright.

'Well, really well, never was better, have been doing business up to to-day—good medical testimony that. No question of my sánity, my dears! I want you to grasp the fact that your mother is a Real Person with some interests of her own and half a lifetime yet. The first twenty didn't count for much—I was growing up and couldn't help myself. The last thirty have been—hard. James perhaps realizes that more than you girls, but you all know it. Now, I'm free.'

'Where *do* you mean to go, Mother?' James asked.

She looked around the little circle with a serene air of decision and replied.

'To New Zealand. I've always wanted to go there,' she pursued. 'Now I'm going. And to Australia—and Tasmania—and Madagascar—and Terra del Fuego. I shall be gone some time.'

They separated that night—three going East, one West.

THE JUMPING-OFF PLACE

Two new guests were expected at The Jumping-off Place that night. The establishment was really too full already of Professors, Professorins and—shall we take a lingual liberty and say Professorinii?

The extra ones however had special claims in the mind of Miss Shortridge; claims well weighed by her when she answered their letters.

The Reverend Joseph Whitcomb had been one of her oldest and most honored friends; her minister for some thirty years. She could remember as if of yesterday the hot still Sunday in late May when he was installed in the white wooden church; the warm approval of the entire congregation, with the possible exception of the two oldest deacons and Miss Makepeace—whose name belied her; the instant and continuous adoration of the women, young and old; their artless efforts to attract his attention, win his favor—she herself among the eagerest, worshipping devoutly and afar;—and the chill that fell upon them all when after a few years of this idolatry he brought home a wife after his vacation absence.

A higher call, with a higher salary attached, had taken him to the big city afterward, and in later days she had sat under him there, still worshipping, though with a chastened adoration. It was nine years since she had left that city:——

He had heard of the excellence of her accommodation, his letter read; the quiet intellectual atmosphere of the place—could she be his old parishioner, Miss Shortridge, of Brooktown? And could she put him up for a week or so?

Then she had asked one of the young unmarried Professors if he would mind having his bill reduced three dollars, and sleeping in the woodshed chamber, for a week; and by a comfortable coincidence of desires he was very glad to.

The other letter she was slower in answering.

'Can it be possible that you are the Jean Shortridge I used to know in Brooktown?' this ran. 'Perhaps you won't remember me—Bessie Moore that was—then Mrs Paul Olcott—now Mrs Weatherby. I'm not at all strong, and I've heard of your place as being so refined and quiet, with really excellent food and beds, and very reasonable prices. Could you give me a nice room for two weeks or a month—a large comfortable room, near a bathroom corner room if possible, and not too many stairs—and what would you charge an old friend?'

There was just one such room unrented, and that was Miss Shortridge's own. With a fortitude rare among those who give board and lodging, she always retained for herself a restful, convenient, quiet room; and enjoyed it.

She read Mrs Weatherby's letter over more than once, her amused smile growing as she studied it.

'I believe I will,' she said to herself at length, 'just for the fun of it. I can manage to dress in the garret for a little while. It won't affect my sleeping, anyhow.'

So she wrote to both that for a week's time she would gladly accommodate them, and found continuing entertainment in the days before their coming in memories and speculations.

'You're not really going to give up your room at last,' protestingly inquired Mrs Professor Joran, who had tried vainly to secure it for a friend.

'Only for a week,' Miss Shortridge explained, 'and under rather exceptional circumstances: The lady coming was a—I have known her since early girlhood.'

The advent of Dr Whitcomb excited more discussion, and was hailed with a better grace, as no one begrudged the young unmarried Professor's room, while many had desired Miss Shortridge's. They were all extremely polite to their entertainer, however, she not being, so to speak, a professional; taking only a few during the summer months to accommodate; and accommodating beyond the dreams of local competitors.

No professional comments reached her ears regarding the expected arrivals, but she in her own mind, dwelt upon them with growing interest. She remembered Bessie Moore with sharp, almost painful clearness, from the day she was 'teacher's pet' in school, up through her pink and ringleted girlhood, to the white delicacy of her beauty as a bride.

Miss Shortridge had seen her twice as a bride—and as long as she lived would remember those occasions. She could see her still, at nineteen, standing there in soft veiled whiteness, her small face, pink as a rose beneath the tulle, beside Paul Olcott with his slim young dignity and serious, intellectual face; while she, plain Jean Shortridge, sat, watching, with a pain in her heart that she had honestly believed would kill her.

Not dying, she had gone away to work; and twelve years later found her comfortably established in the office of Horace Weatherby; his trusted, valued and fairly well-paid secretary.

Slowly, and not unnaturally, through long association she had grown to think more and more of this rather burly and florid gentleman, a successful man, cold and peremptory with subordinates, yet always distinctly courteous to a woman of any class.

As a married man her thoughts of him had been but distantly admiring; when she knew him a widower she had allowed herself to sympathize, afar; when he grew more gracious and approachable with the passing of time, why then—'What an uncommon old fool I must have been!' said Miss Shortridge to herself, as she summoned those days before her.

Yet she was not old then, only thirty-five, and if a fool, by no means an uncommon one. She had lived in a fool's paradise for a while, it is true, building castles in Spain out of the veriest sticks and straws of friendliness. And then one day, in a burst of exceptional cordiality, he had invited her to his wedding. And she had gone, veiled, shrinking behind a pillar, scarce able to force herself there, yet wholly unable to stay away.

There was the big, impressive church, her church too, though she hardly knew it with these accessories of carpets, canopies, carriages, crowds; its heaped flowers and triumphant bursts of music. And then, up the aisle, pinker and plumper than ever, in tightly gleaming pearl gray satin, with pearls and lace and a profusion of orange blossoms—Bessie Moore again!

And that was more than twenty years ago!

As the slow train struggled on from little town to little town, its crushed commuters scattering like popped corn at every station, Mrs Horace Weatherby speculated more and more as to the impressive clerical figure a few seats in front of her. The broad square shoulders, the thick gray hair with a wave that was almost a curl—surely she had seen them somewhere.

Sudden need for a glass of water took her down the aisle beyond him, and a returning view brought recognition.

'Dr Whitcomb!—Oh this *is* a pleasure! Do you remember an old parishioner?'

The reverend gentleman rose to the occasion with that marked deference and suave address which had always distinguished his manner to ladies. Remember her! He did indeed. Had he not twice had the privilege of marrying her—with its invaluable perquisite!

Mrs Weatherby could still blush at fifty-three, and did so, prettily.

'It's a great pleasure to meet you, I'm sure,' she said; and then in a burst of intuition—'perhaps you're going to Jean Shortridge's too!'

He complimented her on her marvelous perception—'I am indeed! And you also?—What a pleasure!'

'I've heard such nice things of her place,' said the lady. 'Some friends of mine knew a Professor's family from Lincoln, Nebraska, that went there—they said it was ideal!'

'We are very fortunate, I am sure,' agreed Dr Whitcomb, 'though our stay is but a short one.'

'If I like it I shall stay,' the lady asserted, smiling. 'She'd never turn out an old friend.'

'You have known her a long time?' he inquired.

'O mercy, yes! Since we were babies. She was such a plain little thing—poor dear!—with her hair combed straight back, and a skimpy little pigtail. Grew up plain, too—as you may remember! She had a Sunday school class, you know, in your church. She was a good girl, and clever in a way; clever at books; but not at all brilliant. I think—I don't know as it's any harm to say it after all these years—but I *think* she was very much in love with my first husband—before he married me, of course.'

Dr Whitcomb looked gravely interested, and made appropriate murmurs as occasion allowed.

'She went to the city to work after that,' continued the lady in continuous flow, 'and the next I heard of her—years later—she was secretary to Mr Weatherby—or had been. That was before

I married him. And then—when did I hear of her next? O, yes. My sister met her somewhere about ten years ago. She must have been all of fifty then!—How time does fly!'

'The lady must be much older than you, I am sure,' said Dr Whitcomb.

'Yes, she is; quite a little; but I'm old enough!' She smiled archly.

'Exactly old enough—and not a bit more,' he promptly agreed.

'Luly said she was a perfect wreck!' Mrs Weatherby continued. 'Looked sixty instead of fifty, and *so* shabby! I don't know what she's done with herself since, I'm sure, but she's somehow got the place at Crosswater (where they have that scientific summer school—fish and things—) and takes boarders in summer—that's all I know.'

'It will be very interesting for you to see her again,' he suggested. 'So many old memories.'

'Some very sad ones, Dr Whitcomb,' murmured the lady, and was easily led or rather was not to be withheld from confiding to his practiced ear the sorrows of her life.

As a recipient of women's griefs Dr Whitcomb was past master; and this assortment was not a novel one. The first husband had proved a consumptive. There were four little children, three little graves, one grown son, always delicate, now haunting the southwest in search of health; with even more of a shadow on his mother's face in speaking of him than his invalidism alone seemed to justify.

Then the husband's early death—her utter loss—her loneliness—did he blame her for marrying again?

Indeed he did not. Marriage was an honorable estate; women especially needed a protecting arm. He trusted that her later happiness had overcome the memory of pain.

But here the appeal to his sympathies was stronger than before.

'O, Dr Whitcomb! You don't know! I can never tell anyone all I've been through! I lived with Mr Weatherby for twenty years—it was a martyrdom, Dr Whitcomb!'

The worthy doctor had a fairly accurate knowledge of his former wealthy parishioner's life and character, and he nodded his head in grave sympathy, the long clean-shaven upper lip pursed solemnly.

'It was not only drink, Dr Whitcomb—that I could have forgiven!—It is such a relief to speak to you!—Of course I never say a word against him—but you know!'

'I do indeed, Mrs Weatherby. You have my sincerest sympathy. You have suffered much—but suffering often leads us Heavenward!'

Meanwhile the lady did not forget a truth long known to her—that men like sympathy as well as women—and presently drew from him the admission that his health was far from good, asthma admitted, other troubles merely hinted at; and that widower-hood was also lonely.

He did not, however, confide to her the uncertain condition of his financial outlook; his lifelong inability to save; his increasing difficulty in finding a pulpit to satisfy his pride—or even his necessity.

Nor did she, for all her fluent recital, hint at the sad deficiencies revealed when the estate of the late Horace Weatherby came to settlement; which was indeed unnecessary, for he had heard these facts.

The Crosswater stage took them, swaying and joggling in its lean-cushioned seats, through the shadowy afternoon woods and along a sluggish brook that curved through encroaching bushes and spread lazily out in successive ponds, starred with white lilies.

When the road seemed to stop short off and end nowhere, with only blue water and blue sky as alternatives, a short turn round a bunch of cedars brought them to Miss Shortridge's door.

'Why, Jean Shortridge! I'd never have known you in the world!' cried Mrs Weatherby, trying to kiss her affectionately, and somehow missing it as her hostess turned to greet Dr Whitcomb.

'I am delighted to meet you again, Miss Shortridge,' he said, holding her hand impulsively in both his. 'How well you look! How young—if you will pardon me—how young you look!'

Even Mrs Weatherby, jealously scrutinizing her old friend, could not deny that there was something in what he said. Her own bright color and plump outlines had long since given way to the dragging softness of a face well nursed, but little used; expressing only the soft negation of an old child; and her figure now took shape more from the stays without than from the frame within.

Jean Shortridge stood erect and lightly upon her feet. She moved with swift alertness, and carried herself with agility. Her face was healthily weatherbeaten; high colored from sun and wind; her eyes bright and steady.

She was cordial, but not diffuse; installed them presently in their respective rooms, and sat smiling and well-gowned at the head of her table when they came to supper.

In the days that followed the new guests learned from the old ones much of their hostess's present and recent achievements. This was her third season here, it appeared, and she was regarded as a wonder; she had bought this old place—mortgaged—and was understood to be paying the mortgage, or to have paid it; she was liked and respected in the little community and considered a solid citizen in spite of her wild eccentricity—she slept out of doors!

All this was commonly known, but what Mrs Weatherby wanted to know, and, if the truth must be told, Dr Whitcomb also, was the tale of those years unaccounted for since Jean Shortridge had last been 'sighted'—and set down as an absolute wreck.

It was extremely difficult to get Miss Shortridge's ear. Her bedchamber on the roof of a porch was inaccessible to others, and she sought that skyey chamber immediately after supper. She was a-foot at dawn and at work, really at work, in her garden. Not a rose garden this, but several acres of highly cultivated land, which the active lady 'worked with her hands,' enough to satisfy the most ardent Tolstoyan.

Small time had she for casual conversation save at meals, and then competition was heavy.

So Mrs Weatherby must needs content herself, during a too short week of good air, good sleep, good food, and good company, with a very pretty campaign of 'friendliness' directed against that smoothly defended fortress of Dr Whitcomb's elderly affections.

Well used was the plump widow to these lines of attack; but even better used was he to all the arts of courteous evasion. Not for nothing had he been a popular minister for nearly fifty years.

It was Friday evening (they had arrived on a Saturday) before, at Dr Whitcomb's direct solicitation, Miss Shortridge agreed to give him an hour, Mrs Weatherby promptly chipping in to urge 'her room' as an excellent place for a talk.

It was; and Miss Shortridge in her own favorite chair looked more than ever the hostess; cordial, friendly, quite at ease.

'Now, Jean Shortridge!' Mrs Weatherby began, 'we are old friends, and you needn't make any mystery with us. We want to know what you *did*—what on earth you did—to—well—to *arrive* like this!'

'Is this what you call "arriving"?' asked Miss Shortridge. 'I'm simply a hard-working woman with her living to earn—and earning it!'

'And a benefactor to society in that process!' blandly interposed the clergyman.

'So is every honest worker, surely!' she suggested, 'but I know what you mean, Mrs Weatherby—I met your sister some seven or eight years ago—and I fancy she gave a pretty bad account of me.'

'A sad account, Jean—not bad. She said you were not looking at all well.'

'No, I was not looking well—nor feeling well—nor doing well,' Miss Shortridge admitted.

'And now you are all three,' said Dr Whitcomb, with an inclination of the head and his admiring smile.

She laughed happily. 'Thank you—I am,' she frankly agreed. 'Well, this is what happened. I was fifty, practically—forty-eight, that is—no money—no health—no happiness.' Here her eyes rested a moment on Mrs Weatherby's soft sagging face. 'You see I never married and all I had earned was spent as it came; for mother for a long time—and doctors. I had no talent in particular, and it was increasingly hard to get work as a stenographer. They want them young and quick and pretty. So—it seemed to me then that I had come to the jumping-off place.'

Her hearers exchanged glances.

'Yes, that's why I named the place—but it's a good name anyhow—and then I got hold of a book—found it by chance in the public library——' Miss Shortridge paused and heaved a large sigh. 'That *was* a book!' she said.

'What was it?' eagerly inquired Mrs Weatherby.

'It was called "The Woman of Fifty"; author, one "A. J. Smith." But that book was written for *me*! It told me what to do and I did it—and it was all true.'

'What was it? Oh, do tell us! What did you do?' Mrs Weatherby urged.

'I began to live,' said Miss Shortridge. 'You see I thought my life was ended—such as it was—and pitied myself abominably. I got a new notion out of the book—that there was just as much life as ever there was, and it was mine; health—power—success—happiness.'

'And so you "demonstrated"—is that the phrase?' Dr Whitcomb asked benignly.

'And so I went to work,' she replied.

'Work isn't always easy to get, is it?' inquired Mrs Weatherby.

'Oh, yes—the kind I did. I selected a healthy suburban town—with a good library—and took a kitchen job for five months. Made my own terms—a good reading lamp and a place to sleep out of doors. I worked hard, slept well, ate good food, and saved money. Every evening I read an hour.'

'May we ask what you read?' asked Dr Whitcomb.

'About nature; about health; about market gardening; and the lives of people who dared to be different. That was a good winter! By June I had over a hundred dollars. All that summer I lived on it. I tramped, rode on trolley cars, lived out of doors—rested. How I rested! Never before in my life had I learned what this world was really like.'

'In wet spells I'd board at some farm house. And I gradually settled on the place where I wanted to live the next year—the man was a market gardener—I wanted to learn the business. I worked out doors and in that year; no time to read, slept like a log, grew strong—saved money.

'I got acquainted, too, and learned a lot about horses and pigs and hens, as well as garden stuff. By the end of the second year I had 450 dollars and some experience. Then I went in with a woman who took summer boarders. She rented me her garden, I furnished enough for the house to pay for it; and I could sell what I had left. I made a lot that year.

'Then I heard of this place, got it on good terms (it was heavily mortgaged you see), and—well, I've paid the mortgage. I own it clear.'

'A magnificent record!' said Dr Whitcomb.

'But how hard you have worked—how hard you work now!' Mrs Weatherby exclaimed. 'I don't see how you stand it.'

'I like it, you see,' said their hostess. 'I like it while I'm doing it, I make a good living by it, and I've got something to look forward to. When I've saved enough I'm going to take a year off, and travel.'

'But—it's not like having a family,' Mrs Weatherby ventured.

'No, it's not. I wish I had a family. . . . But since I haven't— why, I might as well have a life of my own. By the time I'm sixty I mean to take that year abroad I speak of. After that I'll keep on earning. Buy me an annuity, perhaps. There is a home for old people in Los Angeles, I've heard, that's pretty near perfect. I might go there to finish up.'

She looked so cheerful, so alert, so capable and assured, and full of hope, so perplexingly young in spite of her gray hair, that Mrs Weatherby was puzzled in her estimate of age.

'Aren't you older than I am, Jean,' she said. 'You used to be.'

Jean laughed. 'Certainly I am. I'm fifty-seven; you're fifty-three. We've both got many years to look forward to.'

'I don't see how you work such financial miracles, Miss Shortridge,' the clergyman protested. 'Surely it is not open to every woman of middle age to achieve independence as easily.'

'Perhaps they wouldn't all find it easy,' she answered. 'It did take some courage, and a definite, sustaining purpose. But the way is wide open. You see I have three lines of work: I raise vegetables and fruits and sell them during the summer. I preserve and can all I do not sell or use, and the boarders during the summer are a great help. By the way, Mrs Weatherby, are you to take the morning stage, or the afternoon?

'Why, I was hoping you'd let me stay longer,' said that lady lamely; 'I'm very comfortable here; it has done me ever so much good.'

'I am sorry, but I cannot spare the room,' Miss Shortridge replied.

Dr Whitcomb did not wait for her to ask his hour of leaving— 'The morning stage, if you please; and I am extremely grateful for this pleasant visit. It has been a great pleasure, too, to renew our old acquaintance.'

He was up betimes next morning, early enough to find Miss Shortridge in her well kept garden hard at work. He begged a few moments' talk with her, and used his best powers to attract and hold her attention. He spoke of the changes of life; of her long, patient struggle to support herself and care for her mother; of her phenomenal enterprise and success.

She listened gravely, picking her beans with a deft, practiced hand, and stepping slowly along between the dew-wet rows, while he followed.

Then in deeper, softer tones he referred to his own life; to the pain of loss and loneliness; the injury to his work. He longed for true companionship to the end of the journey. Would she, for the time of rich autumnal peace, be his companion?

It is said that all women have at least one offer of marriage; but Jean Shortridge never expected to receive her first at fifty-seven. She thanked him sincerely for the compliment he paid her, but was not inclined to accept it.

He urged her to take time; to think it over. This was no boyish appeal, but a calm proposal for the joining of their declining years; no mad young passion, but real friendship; understanding; a warm, appreciative affection; she must think it over.

He went away on the morning stage, Mrs Weatherby accompanying him, at some inconvenience in the matter of packing.

Miss Shortridge considered her first offer of marriage for a full week, and then declined it.

'Why should I?' she said to herself. 'I always hated nursing. Let Bessie have him, too!'

But Bessie failed this time.

IN TWO HOUSES

THE blank, boarded windows, with which the two old Marshall houses faced, or rather sided, each other, told no tales of midnight danger; but shrill infant screams were more successful.

'Fire! Fire! O Lawdy, Lawdy, de house is afire!' yelled little black Polly, her red-tied pigtails seeming to bristle and prance with horror.

'Be still, child!' said Miss Diana sternly. 'Hold your tongue— we can put this out. Be still, I tell you!'

With a clear head and a strong hand she proceeded to assail the leaping flames in the back kitchen, but could not at the same time capture and quiet the vociferous Polly, who ran out into the moonlit silence of the back yard, shrieking to heaven that they would all be burned alive. The dark house next door stirred inwardly, it would seem reluctantly.

Distant knocks and cries were heard: 'Mas'r Marshall! Mas'r Marshall! De house afire nex' door! Dat lady'll be bun in her baid! O Mas'r Marshall!'

Steps were heard; a moving light glimmered through the cracks of the close-shuttered windows and presently a tall man, somewhat incomplete in costume, leaped over the high brick wall and rushed in, followed by an old negro in a state of uncontrolled excitement.

Miss Diana Marshall paused in her task, smoky and dishevelled, but a commanding figure none the less.

'I thank you for your kind intentions, Dr Blair,' she said. 'There is not the least necessity for assistance.' Neither of the men paid any attention to her; Dr Marshall Blair taking hold with swift intelligence, while the old negro rushed about so madly that he seemed rather to spread the flames than to quench them, adding his cries to Polly's.

'Get out, Polyphemus!' said his master at length. 'Go out there and choke that child! I can put this out if you'll let it alone.'

Forerunner, 2:7 (July 1911), 1–7.

Polyphemus took himself off at the word, and a sudden silence fell upon him and Polly as they withdrew behind the smoke house.

'Just pass me the water—let me throw it,' the visitor commanded, and Miss Marshall, grim and silent, did as she was told. In a few moments the flames were entirely extinguished.

'There is no great damage done,' he remarked on examination.

'I did not think there would be,' replied Miss Marshall. 'I could have put the fire out easily without any man's assistance; but I couldn't stop that foolish child.'

'No,' he politely agreed, 'it is impossible to stop a woman's tongue—even when very young.'

She regarded him coldly. Her thick, coppery hair was in a condition only to be described as tousled; a towel-girt wrapper and shapeless bedroom slippers formed her costume; but the free grace of her athletic body, and the rich color of health and sudden exertion made her a lovely picture for all that. Perhaps the glint of anger in her clear eyes heightened it; at any rate, he looked at her with admiration, though it seemed strangely reluctant.

'I apologise for my intrusion,' he said. 'Kindly excuse me. I supposed the house was in danger.'

'I thank you for your interest in the house, Dr Blair. As you see, it is still standing.'

He bowed with as much dignity as a black-smooched shirt and suspender-belted trousers allowed, and withdrew; taking the high wall with energy, if not grace. His servant must have rejoined him by some easier means, for the sound of severe reproof was presently heard. 'The next time you get me out of bed on any such fool's errand will be your last day in this house!' stormed his master, with that disregard for likelihood which is often to be observed in those who scold. Pacificatory 'Yassirs' trailed off into silence as doors slammed shut, and darkness reigned again.

Diana Marshall felt an equal rage against her domestic imp of mischief, to whose carelessness the fire was evidently due; but the small, cowed figure that slunk back into the dismantled kitchen at her call was so pathetic in its remorseful terror, that she sent the child to bed with few words.

'If I was fool enough to take in that ridiculous infant, I must at least be wise enough to put up with her,' she said to herself, trying with much cold water to remove the soot from her hands, and the angry flush from her cheeks.

'The *idea* of his coming in like that! The *idea!*'

It was a long time before she could sleep again; and all that her sad-eyed mother had told her of these old houses and the old quarrels within them, rose and revolved in her mind as she lay staring into the dark. She seemed to see them appear before her, the proud old Englishman, Blair Marshall, with his grant of land, his big stone house, and his twin sons, the pride of his heart and apple of his eye. For one of them he built the second house, identical with the first—close to it, connected with a bridge— that bridge which now gaped broken between them.

Marshall's Folly it was called even then—as folk are apt to consider foolish anything unusual. 'You can't make any two families live together, not even by a bridge!' the neighbors said.

Identical houses, equally beautiful in furniture and decor- ation, standing in the great estate with wooded hills and rolling fields; monuments of parental love and pride, they were left to young Vance and Gregory on their father's death.

Within a year they had quarreled, quarreled over a cousin— Diana Blair. Vance married her. Vance lived on the estate and Diana Marshall was his granddaughter and sole heir. Gregory became a traveler, bringing home in course of years a brilliant wife from France. Gregory's one child, a daughter, married a Blair; and Gregory's grandson was Dr Marshall Blair, Diana's second cousin and next neighbor. Between them rose a higher wall than six feet of brick, a wider gulf than that between the sawed-off planks of the once connecting bridge; a wall of hatred, a chasm of total strangeness.

Diana's mother was a Massachusetts girl, won by the hand- some Virginian in what she afterwards called a moment of delirium. She bore a bitter widowhood during her husband's frequent absences; suffered a more bitter wifehood when he was at home; and reared her daughter to hate men in general and Marshalls in particular.

'You can't escape the name unless you marry, and I hope you never will!' her mother said to her, 'and you can't wholly escape the nature—though you have enough Wentworth to match it, I believe. But I pray Heaven you may steer clear of all Marshalls and their Follies!'

The girl grew up, a wild, free thing, on the old place; wild enough even to scale the wall and secretly study the shut-up house next door. It made her shiver—it was so like their own—and yet so different.

'It's like a Siamese twin,' she used to say to herself. 'A dead one! Ugh!'

After her husband's unregretted death Mrs Marshall took Diana back to Massachusetts and gave her the college education she herself had relinquished for love, and always regretted. Then they had gone to England, traveled, studied, living always in the company of women; efficient, contented, successful women; where the girl heard more and more of the delinquencies and offenses of menkind.

When she was twenty-eight her mother died; and Diana, now well established professionally as a writer, felt a strong desire to return to her childhood's home; but first made careful inquiries by letter as to the house next door, learning that it was still blank and vacant. She lived there quite alone, a handsome hermit, hunting, fishing, swimming in the deep cold lake that formed part of the boundary between the places, living on the garden products, on canned goods and biscuit, with what she added with line and gun; and working happily on her Book—a book she had been planning for ten years.

She grew to love the once gloomy house, standing now wide-windowed to the sun and air; most of its handsome furniture still covered and packed away as her mother had left it. She loved the wide, far view—trees, trees, trees; blue curve on blue curve of distant mountain; not another building in sight save the dark house next door. The space, the quiet delighted her; the freedom from all interruption.

'But why no servants?' wrote her friend and classmate, Miss Jane Cass, of Boston. 'Surely you cannot keep that great place clean!—and what sort of food to live on! My dear, you'll break down! It must be unsanitary, and aren't you afraid?'

'My dear old Jane,' Diana answered, 'I don't suppose you ever were alone—really alone—in your life. It is glorious, simply glorious! My morning bath is a dive into the cleanest lake you ever saw, my meals are largely from the garden. I do employ an old darky to take care of that, his name is Polyphemus, he used to belong to us, or his parents did. My bread is pure wheat biscuit—better than any other kind; meat I get by shooting or fishing—better living you never saw. Also I have plenty of excellent canned goods for emergencies.

'And the comfort—the utter luxury—of having a house of one's *own*! You have never known it, my poor old Jane—I fear you never will. You see, I don't care at all for what my ancestors thought or what my present relatives or other persons think; this house is now arranged exactly to suit *me*; and I mean to live here, mostly, for the rest of my days. Unless my cousin, Marshall Blair, should come back and prove a disagreeable neighbor.

'Of course I wish I had children. You know how I love them; but not at the price most women pay. I can always adopt, you know. For pure pleasure, I have my music, an excellent resource. Sometimes I wish I had chosen singing instead of writing. But now I have both!

'As to fear—I never knew it. And as to health—you should see me! It was always good, and grows daily better. Come when you can, and we'll be bachelor maids together.'

So feeling, proud and happy in her green solitude, with hasty sandals on bare feet and a blue bathrobe about her, she had raced down to the lake one glittering morning, only to see, poised on her favorite diving place, the straight, white body of a man. He leaped, rose, curved, and swept into the water, swimming with easy pride. She returned to the house, furious, and called Polyphemus.

'There is a man in the lake,' she said; 'you go and tell him this is private property.'

Polyphemus seemed at a loss.

'Ya'as, Miss Dina,' he said, shifting from one foot to the other. 'Ya'asm! But, Miss Dina—dat man am Mars' Marshall Blair!'

Slow rage rose and gathered in her heart. Her lovely lake was no longer hers alone, her solitude was spoiled, and by a man; above all by a Marshall.

Polyphemus eyed her apologetically. 'And if you please, Miss Dina,' he went on, backing a little away from her, 'I goin' to bring another nigger to run this yer garden. I'm 'bleeged to work for Mars' Marshall now.'

She paid him on the spot and returned to her room, the day's work spoiled. That very afternoon, ranging with her gun, well on her side of the estate, she had found a small scared colored child, howling dismally.

Being interrogated, she told a dismal tale of having no parents and no home; of being beaten and sent off by those who had cared for her. 'They done tun me loose, Miss Dina, an' I got no whar to go! an' I dun bring your milk, Miss Dina!' Diana had taken her in, finding the diminutive imp quite as useful in most ways as old Polyphemus.

She avoided the lake thereafter, choosing a small pool in another quarter for her beloved sun-rise bath, and plunged into her work with fresh determination.

Should she, Diana Marshall, be disturbed by the mere adjacent presence of a man? Indeed, no!

Polyphemus, who wholly disapproved of his young mistress swimming in that cold and lonely lake, never told his master of the discovery, and Dr Blair continued to monopolize the quiet water.

He had been educated in England and France, had made his reputation there, and then gradually turned from the practise of medicine to research work. He, too, had remembered the old place in Virginia, with the big comfortable home belonging to him, and the dark empty shell next door, visited once in his youth, when the estate was settled.

'Just the thing,' he said to himself. 'I can experiment all I please; no one will be about to bother me. And when I've got this thing worked out!——'

But first he made careful inquiry about the house across the wall. 'If that female cousin of mine is at home, I won't live there!' he determined. But he heard that no one had lived there for ten years, and came home rejoicing. Old Polyphemus presented himself humbly as the natural retainer of the place, and was promptly employed.

'Can you cook?—and clean—really clean, you understand? I'll have no woman slopping about in my house!'

'O, ya'as, sir—Lawdy, ya'as, sir! I kin cook bettern any woman you eber saw, sir!' the old nigger assured him. And because of the proven excellence of his cooking many deficiencies were overlooked in other lines.

Dr Blair settled down enthusiastically in the old house, conscious of pleasant little thrills of race memory and a comfortable feeling of home. Many rooms he kept shut up; those he used, he furnished in a manner suggesting a laboratory or hospital more than a home, and the great garrets he consecrated to his research work—to slow, careful, continuous experiment and observation, requiring the arbitrary matchmaking of many mice, much time and no interruption.

He lived well, under the ministrations of the old negro. For exercise he rode far and wide, and found his relaxation and deepest pleasure in his violin. He had scarcely been settled three days, and had not unpacked that beloved instrument, when he heard one evening, rising through the magnolia-scented air, the soft, rich tones of a deep contralto voice. He called Polyphemus. 'Look here—there's someone in the other house!'

'Ya'as, sir; jes' so, sir. It are Miss Dina, sir.'

'Name of a pig!' said Marshall Blair, which was certainly unfair, as pigs are seldom called Diana.

He meditated upon it. 'Confound all women,' said he to himself. 'Feeble, sickly, sentimental, selfish, shallow, idle, luxurious, empty-headed, useless trash! And confound This One in particular—spoiling my quiet!' Then he laughed grimly. 'If she comes over here we'll let out the mice, Polyphemus,' he said. 'Don't ever let me hear a word about her.'

But Polyphemus was sorely exercised in his mind.

'Dere dey bof are—juxtacomposed to-gedder—and dere dey stick! An' bein' cousins, and bof Blairs *an'* Marshalls, and dis yer property needin' to be looked after and wukked de wust way! Lawdy! Lawdy!'

But just as young Polly's guileless praises of 'Mars Marshall nex' door' were met with prompt reproof and tabooed utterly, so were old Polyphemus' more artful suggestions sharply rebuffed.

'I tell you, I want to hear nothing about that woman!' said Dr Blair. 'Not a word. I hope never to set eyes upon her!'

Polyphemus, taking needed rest at hours when his master was engrossed with mice, revolved matters solemnly in the dark recesses of his mind.

'He ain't even willin' to *see* her,' he said to himself; 'an' she as hansome as a picter. De Lawd must provide some way to bring dem young people togedder!'

Dr Blair succeeded in not seeing his cousin until the night of the conflagration, an event which he strove utterly to dismiss from his mind.

'Two fool women together,' he summarized them. 'Might have burned down both houses by their confounded carelessness. I hope I shall never see her again!'

None the less, he was glad when he did see her again—one hot, still, summer night, when the broad moonlight and the oppressive heat had tempted him to the lake. He lay too long, perhaps, with arms outstretched, enjoying the spring-fed coldness of the water, for a fierce pain shot through suddenly crippled limbs as he struck out for the bank.

He sank, rose, shouted for help with a hopeless thought of Polyphemus' deafness; sank again, rose struggling weakly, and saw through half-blinded eyes a great white figure shoot down through the moonlight and dive after him.

She reached him, rose with him, struck out strongly and brought him safe to land, worked over him there, till at last his eyes opened again to a humiliating spectacle. She was holding his tongue out: Polyphemus, summoned by Polly's frantic cries, was there, pumping his master's arms up and down. He experienced great distress of body—and more of mind. She disappeared on the instant, her tall white figure shining in the moonlight, sternly Greek in outline under the wet swathing of her nightdress, vanishing through the trees like a veritable nymph.

'I certinly am ashamed of you, Mars' Marshall,' said the old negro, when once his charge was safe. 'Here you might 'a died without ever wakin' me up, if it hadn't been for that lady! And she havin' to jump out'n her baid and run down yer, bar-footed, to pull you outen de water. Mighty lucky she's such a good swimmer!'

In place of that lively gratitude toward one's preserver which is supposed to move the heart of the rescued, Dr Blair felt only an intense mortification and anger. To be caught like a drowning rat—he, who could swim for miles—and to be dragged to land, pulled out, and laboriously resuscitated—by a woman! He thought of how he must have looked, helpless, sodden, with his tongue forcibly pulled out. It was hideously humiliating.

Go to her he would not, but he wrote a courteous note, expressing his obligation in decent terms, though not in warm ones, begging her 'to accept the thanks due for saving a worthless life.'

She replied with equal courtesy and coldness, also with equal ambiguity. 'Pray do not speak of it. It will equal, I trust, your attempt to rescue my house. My efforts are wholly unworthy of mention.'

'Women must have the last word,' he said grimly, and let it go at that, putting the note in the fire. But he remembered every word of it.

After that the work went on steadily in the two houses. The click of the typewriter resounded faintly on one side of the wall, and the smell of many mice rose like an undesirable incense on the other.

Polyphemus shook his white head, meditating in the old garden. 'It did seem like the han' o' Providence—dat yer fire, and den dis yer drownin' upset it all. Hit certainly am a shame! In course, a man don' like to be beholden to a woman dat a-way; it ain't natural. Lawdy! Lawdy! What we guine to do? I must go see dat Voodoo woman after all!'

The hand of Providence soon became strangely active, however, for before many days he approached his master with much timidity, announcing, 'If you please, sir, dat good-fer-nuffin Polly chile next door say 'at Miss Dina sick.'

'I dare say,' replied Dr Blair, coldly, going on with his supper; 'women are always sick.'

'Yass, sir; but Miss Dina ain't never been sick in her life before, and she's takin' on turrble; she's clean outn' her haid— just hear to dat, sir!'

The deep contralto voice he had heard so often with irresistible pleasure rose now in sudden, reckless melody; stopped short; broke into laughter; began to sing again, a queer, low chant.

Dr Blair dropped knife and napkin and rushed into his laboratory, bringing out a long-untouched medicine case; then scaled the wall once more.

He found her standing at the head of the great stairway, brilliantly arrayed in some rich ball dress of a previous generation, with cheeks flaming pink and glittering eyes. She took him for a dangerous assailant, and he was obliged to use all his strength to subdue without hurting her.

He had her quiet at last, and she lay staring at him with fierce eyes, till the sedative he forcibly administered made the white lids close.

Polly, under close questioning, showed as much terror as if she were being blamed for her mistress's condition, and it was only by the exercise of unusual gentleness and the gift of a shining half-dollar that he was able to get any facts in the case.

It appeared that her mistress had been well as usual up to dinner time; had grown more and more flushed and excited ever since, and had been in considerable pain. 'She been powerful sick, sir; she sut'nly have!'

'What did she eat for dinner?'

'Some can' soup, and some fish—fraish dis mornin', sir; and some green peas—I picked 'em myself.'

'Show me the can.'

'Lawdy, sah, I frowed it away.'

'Go and get it.'

'I can't, sir. I frowed it down de dry well whar I always frow 'em.'

His opinion was clear.

'That deadly canned stuff, I don't doubt. Serves anybody right who uses it. I think she's in no danger now.' But he had sat by her all night, noting the pulse, the temperature, the action of the lungs; trying to make his knowledge of poisons agree with his theories of the malign composition of canned soup.

She slept heavily most of the following day, and when she opened her eyes he was sitting calmly by her window, reading. She made no sound, no movement, but watched him for a few moments, uncertain whether he was not part of the wild dream which had been drifting through her mind. Then she realized, with a sense of unmeasured amazement, that Marshall Blair was making himself perfectly at home in her house—in her room.

Lying quite still, she spoke calmly. 'To what do I owe the honor of this visit, Dr Blair?'

He rose, looked at his watch, and came to her bedside. 'To the fact that you have been suddenly and dangerously ill, and I was the only physician within reach. I make no apologies. If you will allow me, I will take your pulse and temperature once more.'

He popped the little thermometer into her mouth before she could say anything further, and held her wrist with an abstracted air, counting.

'I guess you'll do,' he said. 'It was a case of poison; from eating canned goods I think. You really had a rather close call. I advise your lying still another day, and taking nothing but milk for the rest of the week. Good morning.'

He was gone.

She lay still for some time, trying to think, but finding both head and body strangely weak, and presently slept again.

Small Polly waited upon her with spaniel-like devotion. 'Don't look so like a scared mouse, Polly,' Miss Diana told her. 'Anybody's think you were to blame for my being sick.'

'O, Lawdy, no, ma'am—I ain't! I didn't! Please 'scuse me, ma'am,' said Polly, still wearing an air of dark remorse.

Diana Marshall remained quiet the next day, as advised, and also lived on milk for a week, her principal entertainment during this time being the melodious sound of her cousin's violin and his pleasant baritone voice, which rose to her window in the still evenings.

At the end of that week Dr Blair's solo was interrupted by the appearance of his recent patient before his door.

'Good evening,' said she calmly; 'I've come over to thank you for taking care of me when I needed it, and to say that I think we are making melodramatic fools of ourselves.'

He rose and bowed.

'Thank you for your good opinion. Won't you be seated?'

'Not till I know if you share the opinion,' she said. 'You and I are not children, and we are, I believe, second cousins. I abominate men; but you seem to be a decent sort, and not intrusive.'

'And I abominate women,' he replied, 'but I will say you are the least objectionable of the kind I ever knew.'

'You don't disturb my writing, and I don't disturb your mice—I hope.'

'Not in the least.'

'But it does seem a pity to miss the music we might have. I want so much to try accompanying your violin.'

'I have been secretly wishing you would, for a month,' said Dr Blair.

Evenings of mutual music are a pleasant close to days of diverse toil. They played together, they sang together, they talked together, and each learned a real respect for the other's character, together with a deep sympathy for their kindred prejudices.

'If you weren't a woman, Cousin Diana, I really believe I'd ask you to marry me,' he said one night.

'If you weren't a man, I might consider it,' she replied.

'I have taken seven oaths that no woman should ever live in my house,' said he.

'And I, that no man should ever live in mine,' she answered.

'I am a scientist, and no family cares must ever interfere with my work,' he continued.

'I am a writer, and will never be any man's housekeeper,' said she.

'Yet these are happy evenings when the day's work is over,' he urged.

'They certainly are,' she agreed.

'It can't go on this way,' he said.

'Why can't it?' she demanded.

For answer, he suddenly leaned over and kissed her.

There was a silence.

'I see that you are not above Shakesperian argument, Dr Blair.'

'I am glad you admit we are lovers, Cousin Diana.'

'But I will not marry you, Cousin Marshall.'

'It is only a formality, Cousin Diana. What you really don't want to do is to keep house for me, and I assure you I don't want you to. But suppose—just for the sake of argument—that we went through that little formality and then continued to live as we do now?'

'In two houses?'

'Why not? There is the bridge—we can mend it.'

'Well,' said Diana, 'on those conditions—and merely as a formality——'

So they mended the bridge.

After the wedding old Polyphemus withdrew young Polly to the depths of the woods, a dim place, utterly removed, and addressed her with solemnity:

'Now dis yere thing am accomplished, I'se obliged to chastize you for all you' foolishness.'

'I never done nothin' but what you told me to,' she pleaded.

'You are a mizzerble, good for nuffin' female child,' he declared. 'Couldn't you do nuffin' without over-doin' it? Did I tell you to let de house get all a burnin' before you hollered fire? Did I tell you to pison Miss Dina till she near went out of her haid forever, with your double doses? Heah am I, a-wearin' myself to a shadder and a-riskin' my immortal soul to bring dese yere houses togedder, what natchally belong togedder, and you pretty neah to ruin everything with yo' foolishness! You come heah to me!'

And Polly wailed loud and long beneath the severity of an ungrateful grandfather.

TURNED

IN HER soft-carpeted, thick-curtained, richly furnished chamber, Mrs Marroner lay sobbing on the wide, soft bed.

She sobbed bitterly, chokingly, despairingly; her shoulders heaved and shook convulsively; her hands were tight-clenched; she had forgotten her elaborate dress, the more elaborate bed-cover; forgotten her dignity, her self-control, her pride. In her mind was an overwhelming, unbelievable horror, an immeasurable loss, a turbulent, struggling mass of emotion.

In her reserved, superior, Boston-bred life she had never dreamed that it would be possible for her to feel so many things at once, and with such trampling intensity.

She tried to cool her feelings into thoughts; to stiffen them into words; to control herself—and could not. It brought vaguely to her mind an awful moment in the breakers at York Beach, one summer in girlhood, when she had been swimming under water and could not find the top.

In her uncarpeted, thin-curtained, poorly furnished chamber on the top floor, Gerta Petersen lay sobbing on the narrow, hard bed.

She was of larger frame than her mistress, grandly built and strong; but all her proud, young womanhood was prostrate now, convulsed with agony, dissolved in tears. She did not try to control herself. She wept for two.

If Mrs Marroner suffered more from the wreck and ruin of a longer love—perhaps a deeper one; if her tastes were finer, her ideals loftier; if she bore the pangs of bitter jealousy and outraged pride, Gerta had personal shame to meet, a hopeless future, and a looming present which filled her with unreasoning terror.

She had come like a meek young goddess into that perfectly ordered house, strong, beautiful, full of good will and eager obedience, but ignorant and childish—a girl of eighteen.

Forerunner, 2:9 (September 1911), 1–6.

Mr Marroner had frankly admired her, and so had his wife. They discussed her visible perfections and as visible limitations with that perfect confidence which they had so long enjoyed. Mrs Marroner was not a jealous woman. She had never been jealous in her life—till now.

Gerta had stayed and learned their ways. They had both been fond of her. Even the cook was fond of her. She was what is called 'willing,' was unusually teachable and plastic; and Mrs Marroner, with her early habits of giving instruction, tried to educate her somewhat.

'I never saw anyone so docile,' Mrs Marroner had often commented. 'It is perfection in a servant, but almost a defect in character. She is so helpless and confiding.'

She was precisely that; a tall, rosy-cheeked baby; rich womanhood without, helpless infancy within. Her braided wealth of dead-gold hair, her grave blue eyes, her mighty shoulders, and long, firmly moulded limbs seemed those of a primal earth spirit; but she was only an ignorant child, with a child's weakness.

When Mr Marroner had to go abroad for his firm, unwillingly, hating to leave his wife, he had told her he felt quite safe to leave her in Gerta's hands—she would take care of her.

'Be good to your mistress, Gerta,' he told the girl that last morning at breakfast. 'I leave her to you to take care of. I shall be back in a month at latest.'

Then he turned, smiling, to his wife. 'And you must take care of Gerta, too,' he said. 'I expect you'll have her ready for college when I get back.'

This was seven months ago. Business had delayed him from week to week, from month to month. He wrote to his wife, long, loving, frequent letters; deeply regretting the delay, explaining how necessary, how profitable it was; congratulating her on the wide resources she had; her well-filled, well-balanced mind; her many interests.

'If I should be eliminated from your scheme of things, by any of those "acts of God" mentioned on the tickets, I do not feel that you would be an utter wreck,' he said. 'That is very comforting to me. Your life is so rich and wide that no one loss, even a great one, would wholly cripple you. But nothing of the sort is likely to happen, and I shall be home again in three weeks—if this thing gets settled. And you will be looking so lovely, with that eager light in your eyes and the changing flush I know so well—and love so well! My dear wife! We shall have to have a new honeymoon—other moons come every month, why shouldn't the mellifluous kind?'

He often asked after 'little Gerta,' sometimes enclosed a picture postcard to her, joked his wife about her laborious efforts to educate 'the child'; was so loving and merry and wise——

All this was racing through Mrs Marroner's mind as she lay there with the broad, hemstitched border of fine linen sheeting crushed and twisted in one hand, and the other holding a sodden handkerchief.

She had tried to teach Gerta, and had grown to love the patient, sweet-natured child, in spite of her dullness. At work with her hands, she was clever, if not quick, and could keep small accounts from week to week. But to the woman who held a Ph.D., who had been on the faculty of a college, it was like baby-tending.

Perhaps having no babies of her own made her love the big child the more, though the years between them were but fifteen.

To the girl she seemed quite old, of course; and her young heart was full of grateful affection for the patient care which made her feel so much at home in this new land.

And then she had noticed a shadow on the girl's bright face. She looked nervous, anxious, worried. When the bell rang she seemed startled, and would rush hurriedly to the door. Her peals of frank laughter no longer rose from the area gate as she stood talking with the always admiring tradesmen.

Mrs Marroner had labored long to teach her more reserve with men, and flattered herself that her words were at last effective. She suspected the girl of homesickness; which was denied. She suspected her of illness, which was denied also. At last she suspected her of something which could not be denied.

For a long time she refused to believe it, waiting. Then she had to believe it, but schooled herself to patience and understanding. 'The poor child,' she said. 'She is here without a mother—she is so foolish and yielding—I must not be too stern with her.' And she tried to win the girl's confidence with wise, kind words.

But Gerta had literally thrown herself at her feet and begged her with streaming tears not to turn her away. She would admit nothing, explain nothing; but frantically promised to work for Mrs Marroner as long as she lived—if only she would keep her.

Revolving the problem carefully in her mind, Mrs Marroner thought she would keep her, at least for the present. She tried to repress her sense of ingratitude in one she had so sincerely tried to help, and the cold, contemptuous anger she had always felt for such weakness.

'The thing to do now,' she said to herself, 'is to see her through this safely. The child's life should not be hurt any more than is unavoidable. I will ask Dr Bleet about it—what a comfort a woman doctor is! I'll stand by the poor, foolish thing till it's over, and then get her back to Sweden somehow with her baby. How they do come where they are not wanted—and don't come where they are wanted!' And Mrs Marroner, sitting along in the quiet, spacious beauty of the house, almost envied Gerta.

Then came the deluge.

She had sent the girl out for needed air toward dark. The late mail came; she took it in herself. One letter for her—her husband's letter. She knew the postmark, the stamp, the kind of typewriting. She impulsively kissed it in the dim hall. No one would suspect Mrs Marroner of kissing her husband's letters—but she did, often.

She looked over the others. One was for Gerta, and not from Sweden. It looked precisely like her own. This struck her as a little odd, but Mr Marroner had several times sent messages and cards to the girl. She laid the letter on the hall table and took hers to her room.

'My poor child,' it began. What letter of hers had been sad enough to warrant that?

'I am deeply concerned at the news you send.' What news to so concern him had she written? 'You must bear it bravely, little girl. I shall be home soon, and will take care of you, of course. I hope there is no immediate anxiety—you do not say. Here is money, in case you need it. I expect to get home in a month at latest. If you have to go, be sure to leave your address at my office. Cheer up—be brave—I will take care of you.'

The letter was typewritten, which was not unusual. It was unsigned, which was unusual. It enclosed an American bill— fifty dollars. It did not seem in the least like any letter she had ever had from her husband, or any letter she could imagine him writing. But a strange, cold feeling was creeping over her, like a flood rising around a house.

She utterly refused to admit the ideas which began to bob and push about outside her mind, and to force themselves in. Yet under the pressure of these repudiated thoughts she went down-stairs and brought up the other letter—the letter to Gerta. She laid them side by side on a smooth dark space on the table; marched to the piano and played, with stern precision, refusing to think, till the girl came back. When she came in, Mrs Marroner rose quietly and came to the table. 'Here is a letter for you,' she said.

The girl stepped forward eagerly, saw the two lying together there, hesitated, and looked at her mistress.

'Take yours, Gerta. Open it, please.'

The girl turned frightened eyes upon her.

'I want you to read it, here,' said Mrs Marroner.

'Oh, ma'am—— No! Please don't make me!'

'Why not?'

There seemed to be no reason at hand, and Gerta flushed more deeply and opened her letter. It was long; it was evidently puzzling to her; it began 'My dear wife.' She read it slowly.

'Are you sure it is your letter?' asked Mrs Marroner. 'Is not this one yours? Is not that one—mine?'

She held out the other letter to her.

'It is a mistake,' Mrs Marroner went on, with a hard quietness. She had lost her social bearings somehow; lost her usual keen sense of the proper thing to do. This was not life, this was a nightmare.

'Do you not see? Your letter was put in my envelope and my letter was put in your envelope. Now we understand it.'

But poor Gerta had no antechamber to her mind; no trained forces to preserve order while agony entered. The thing swept over her, resistless, overwhelming. She cowered before the out-raged wrath she expected; and from some hidden cavern that wrath arose and swept over her in pale flame.

'Go and pack your trunk,' said Mrs Marroner. 'You will leave my house to-night. Here is your money.'

She laid down the fifty-dollar bill. She put with it a month's wages. She had no shadow of pity for those anguished eyes, those tears which she heard drop on the floor.

'Go to your room and pack,' said Mrs Marroner. And Gerta, always obedient, went.

Then Mrs Marroner went to hers, and spent a time she never counted, lying on her face on the bed.

But the training of the twenty-eight years which had elapsed before her marriage; the life at college, both as student and teacher; the independent growth which she had made, formed a very different background for grief from that in Gerta's mind.

After a while Mrs Marroner arose. She administered to herself a hot bath, a cold shower, a vigorous rubbing. 'Now I can think,' she said.

First she regretted the sentence of instant banishment. She went upstairs to see if it had been carried out. Poor Gerta! The tempest of her agony had worked itself out at last as in a child, and left her sleeping, the pillow wet, the lips still grieving, a big sob shuddering itself off now and then.

Mrs Marroner stood and watched her, and as she watched she considered the helpless sweetness of the face; the defenseless, unformed character; the docility and habit of obedience which made her so attractive—and so easily a victim. Also she thought of the mighty force which had swept over her; of the great process now working itself out through her; of how pitiful and futile seemed any resistance she might have made.

She softly returned to her own room, made up a little fire, and sat by it, ignoring her feelings now, as she had before ignored her thoughts.

Here were two women and a man. One woman was a wife; loving, trusting, affectionate. One was a servant; loving, trusting, affectionate: a young girl, an exile, a dependent; grateful for any kindness; untrained, uneducated, childish. She ought, of course, to have resisted temptation; but Mrs Marroner was wise enough to know how difficult temptation is to recognize when it comes in the guise of friendship and from a source one does not suspect.

Gerta might have done better in resisting the grocer's clerk; had, indeed, with Mrs Marroner's advice, resisted several. But where respect was due, how could she criticize? Where obedience was due, how could she refuse—with ignorance to hold her blinded—until too late?

As the older, wiser woman forced herself to understand and extenuate the girl's misdeed and foresee her ruined future, a new feeling rose in her heart, strong, clear, and overmastering; a sense of measureless condemnation for the man who had done this thing. He knew. He understood. He could fully foresee and measure the consequences of his act. He appreciated to the full the innocence, the ignorance, the grateful affection, the habitual docility, of which he deliberately took advantage.

Mrs Marroner rose to icy peaks of intellectual apprehension, from which her hours of frantic pain seemed far indeed removed. He had done this thing under the same roof with her—his wife. He had not frankly loved the younger woman, broken with his wife, made a new marriage. That would have been heart-break pure and simple. This was something else.

That letter, that wretched, cold, carefully guarded, unsigned letter: that bill—far safer than a check—these did not speak of affection. Some men can love two women at one time. This was not love.

Mrs Marroner's sense of pity and outrage for herself, the wife, now spread suddenly into a perception of pity and outrage for the girl. All that splendid, clean young beauty, the hope of a happy life, with marriage and motherhood; honorable independence, even—these were nothing to that man. For his own pleasure he had chosen to rob her of her life's best joys.

He would 'take care of her' said the letter? How? In what capacity?

And then, sweeping over both her feelings for herself, the wife, and Gerta, his victim, came a new flood, which literally lifted her to her feet. She rose and walked, her head held high. 'This is the sin of man against woman,' she said. 'The offense is against womanhood. Against motherhood. Against—the child.'

She stopped.

The child. His child. That, too, he sacrificed and injured—doomed to degradation.

Mrs Marroner came of stern New England stock. She was not a Calvinist, hardly even a Unitarian, but the iron of Calvinism was in her soul: of that grim faith which held that most people had to be damned 'for the glory of God.'

Generations of ancestors who both preached and practiced stood behind her; people whose lives had been sternly moulded to their highest moments of religious conviction. In sweeping bursts of feeling they achieved 'conviction,' and afterward they lived and died according to that conviction.

When Mr Marroner reached home, a few weeks later, following his letters too soon to expect an answer to either, he saw no wife upon the pier, though he had cabled; and found the house closed darkly. He let himself in with his latch-key, and stole softly upstairs, to surprise his wife.

No wife was there.

He rang the bell. No servant answered it.

He turned up light after light; searched the house from top to bottom; it was utterly empty. The kitchen wore a clean, bald, unsympathetic aspect. He left it and slowly mounted the stair, completely dazed. The whole house was clean, in perfect order, wholly vacant.

One thing he felt perfectly sure of—she knew.

Yet was he sure? He must not assume too much. She might have been ill. She might have died. He started to his feet. No, they would have cabled him. He sat down again.

For any such change, if she had wanted him to know, she would have written. Perhaps she had, and he, returning so suddenly, had missed the letter. The thought was some comfort. It must be so. He turned to the telephone, and again hesitated. If she had found out—if she had gone—utterly gone, without a word—should he announce it himself to friends and family?

He walked the floor; he searched everywhere for some letter, some word of explanation. Again and again he went to the telephone—and always stopped. He could not bear to ask: 'Do you know where my wife is?'

The harmonious, beautiful rooms reminded him in a dumb, helpless way of her; like the remote smile on the face of the dead. He put out the lights; could not bear the darkness; turned them all on again.

It was a long night—

In the morning he went early to the office. In the accumulated mail was no letter from her. No one seemed to know of anything unusual. A friend asked after his wife—'Pretty glad to see you, I guess?' He answered evasively.

About eleven a man came to see him; John Hill, her lawyer. Her cousin, too. Mr Marroner had never liked him. He liked him less now, for Mr Hill merely handed him a letter, remarked, 'I was requested to deliver this to you personally,' and departed, looking like a person who is called on to kill something offensive.'

'I have gone. I will care for Gerta. Good-bye. Marion.'

That was all. There was no date, no address, no postmark; nothing but that.

In his anxiety and distress he had fairly forgotten Gerta and all that. Her name aroused in him a sense of rage. She had come between him and his wife. She had taken his wife from him. That was the way he felt.

At first he said nothing, did nothing; lived on alone in his house, taking meals where he chose. When people asked him about his wife he said she was traveling—for her health. He would not have it in the newspapers. Then, as time passed, as no enlightenment came to him, he resolved not to bear it any longer, and employed detectives. They blamed him for not having put them on the track earlier, but set to work, urged to the utmost secrecy.

What to him had been so blank a wall of mystery seemed not to embarrass them in the least. They made careful inquiries as to her 'past,' found where she had studied, where taught, and on what lines; that she had some little money of her own, that her doctor was Josephine L. Bleet, M.D., and many other bits of information.

As a result of careful and prolonged work, they finally told him that she had resumed teaching under one of her old professors; lived quietly, and apparently kept boarders; giving him town, street, and number, as if it were a matter of no difficulty whatever.

He had returned in early spring. It was autumn before he found her.

A quiet college town in the hills, a broad, shady street, a pleasant house standing in its own lawn, with trees and flowers about it. He had the address in his hand, and the number showed clear on the white gate. He walked up the straight gravel path and rang the bell. An elderly servant opened the door.

'Does Mrs Marroner live here?'

'No, sir.'

'This is number twenty-eight?'

'Yes, sir.'

'Who does live here?'

'Miss Wheeling, sir.'

Ah! Her maiden name. They had told him, but he had forgotten.

He stepped inside. 'I would like to see her,' he said.

He was ushered into a still parlor, cool and sweet with the scent of flowers, the flowers she had always loved best. It almost brought tears to his eyes. All their years of happiness rose in his mind again; the exquisite beginnings; the days of eager longing before she was really his; the deep, still beauty of her love.

Surely she would forgive him—she must forgive him. He would humble himself; he would tell her of his honest remorse—his absolute determination to be a different man.

Through the wide doorway there came in to him two women. One like a tall Madonna, bearing a baby in her arms.

Marion, calm, steady, definitely impersonal; nothing but a clear pallor to hint of inner stress.

Gerta, holding the child as a bulwark, with a new intelligence in her face, and her blue, adoring eyes fixed on her friend—not upon him.

He looked from one to the other dumbly.

And the woman who had been his wife asked quietly:

'What have you to say to us?'

MAKING A CHANGE

'WA-A-A-A! Waa-a-a-aaa!'

Frank Gordins set down his coffee cup so hard that it spilled over into the saucer.

'Is there no way to stop that child crying?' he demanded.

'I do not know of any,' said his wife, so definitely and politely that the words seemed cut off by machinery.

'*I do*,' said his mother with even more definiteness, but less politeness.

Young Mrs Gordins looked at her mother-in-law from under her delicate level brows, and said nothing. But the weary lines about her eyes deepened; she had been kept awake nearly all night, and for many nights.

So had he. So, as a matter of fact, had his mother. She had not the care of the baby—but lay awake wishing she had.

'There's no need at all for that child's crying so, Frank. If Julia would only let me——'

'It's no use talking about it,' said Julia. 'If Frank is not satisfied with the child's mother he must say so—perhaps we can make a change.'

This was ominously gentle. Julia's nerves were at the breaking point. Upon her tired ears, her sensitive mother's heart, the grating wail from the next room fell like a lash—burnt in like fire. Her ears were hypersensitive, always. She had been an ardent musician before her marriage, and had taught quite successfully on both piano and violin. To any mother a child's cry is painful; to a musical mother it is torment.

But if her ears were sensitive, so was her conscience. If her nerves were weak her pride was strong. The child was her child, it was her duty to take care of it, and take care of it she would. She spent her days in unremitting devotion to its needs, and to the care of her neat flat; and her nights had long since ceased to refresh her.

Again the weary cry rose to a wail.

'It does seem to be time for a change of treatment,' suggested the older woman acidly.

'Or a change of residence,' offered the younger, in a deadly quiet voice.

'Well, by Jupiter! There'll be a change of some kind, and p. d. q.!' said the son and husband, rising to his feet.

His mother rose also, and left the room, holding her head high and refusing to show any effects of that last thrust.

Frank Gordins glared at his wife. His nerves were raw, too. It does not benefit any one in health or character to be continuously deprived of sleep. Some enlightened persons use that deprivation as a form of torture.

She stirred her coffee with mechanical calm, her eyes sullenly bent on her plate.

'I will not stand having Mother spoken to like that,' he stated with decision.

'I will not stand having her interfere with my methods of bringing up children.'

'Your methods! Why, Julia, my mother knows more about taking care of babies than you'll ever learn! She has the real love of it—and the practical experience. Why can't you *let* her take care of the kid—and we'll all have some peace!'

She lifted her eyes and looked at him; deep inscrutable wells of angry light. He had not the faintest appreciation of her state of mind. When people say they are 'nearly crazy' from weariness, they state a practical fact. The old phrase which describes reason as 'tottering on her throne,' is also a clear one.

Julia was more near the verge of complete disaster than the family dreamed. The conditions were so simple, so usual, so inevitable.

Here was Frank Gordins, well brought up, the only son of a very capable and idolatrously affectionate mother. He had fallen deeply and desperately in love with the exalted beauty and fine mind of the young music teacher, and his mother had approved. She too loved music and admired beauty.

Her tiny store in the savings bank did not allow of a separate home, and Julia had cordially welcomed her to share in their household.

Here was affection, propriety and peace. Here was a noble

devotion on the part of the young wife, who so worshipped her husband that she used to wish she had been the greatest musician on earth—that she might give it up for him! She had given up her music, perforce, for many months, and missed it more than she knew.

She bent her mind to the decoration and artistic management of their little apartment, finding her standards difficult to maintain by the ever-changing inefficiency of her help. The musical temperament does not always include patience; nor, necessarily, the power of management.

When the baby came her heart overflowed with utter devotion and thankfulness; she was his wife—the mother of his child. Her happiness lifted and pushed within till she longed more than ever for her music for the free pouring current of expression, to give forth her love and pride and happiness. She had not the gift of words.

So now she looked at her husband, dumbly, while wild visions of separation, of secret flight—even of self-destruction—swung dizzily across her mental vision. All she said was 'All right, Frank. We'll make a change. And you shall have—some peace.'

'Thank goodness for that, Jule! You do look tired, Girlie—let Mother see to His Nibs, and try to get a nap, can't you?'

'Yes,' she said. 'Yes . . . I think I will.' Her voice had a peculiar note in it. If Frank had been an alienist, or even a general physician, he would have noticed it. But his work lay in electric coils, in dynamos and copper wiring—not in woman's nerves—and he did not notice it.

He kissed her and went out, throwing back his shoulders and drawing a long breath of relief as he left the house behind him and entered his own world.

'This being married—and bringing up children—is not what it's cracked up to be.' That was the feeling in the back of his mind. But it did not find full admission, much less expression.

When a friend asked him, 'All well at home?' he said, 'Yes, thank you—pretty fair. Kid cries a good deal—but that's natural, I suppose.'

He dismissed the whole matter from his mind and bent his faculties to a man's task—how he can earn enough to support a wife, a mother, and a son.

At home his mother sat in her small room, looking out of the window at the ground glass one just across the 'well,' and thinking hard.

By the disorderly little breakfast table his wife remained motionless, her chin in her hands, her big eyes staring at nothing, trying to formulate in her weary mind some reliable reason why she should not do what she was thinking of doing. But her mind was too exhausted to serve her properly.

Sleep—Sleep—Sleep—that was the one thing she wanted. Then his mother could take care of the baby all she wanted to, and Frank could have some peace. . . . Oh, dear! It was time for the child's bath.

She gave it to him mechanically. On the stroke of the hour she prepared the sterilized milk, and arranged the little one comfortably with his bottle. He snuggled down, enjoying it, while she stood watching him.

She emptied the tub, put the bath apron to dry, picked up all the towels and sponges and varied appurtenances of the elaborate performance of bathing the first-born, and then sat staring straight before her, more weary than ever, but growing inwardly determined.

Greta had cleared the table, with heavy heels and hands, and was now rattling dishes in the kitchen. At every slam the young mother winced, and when the girl's high voice began a sort of doleful chant over her work, young Mrs Gordins rose to her feet with a shiver, and made her decision.

She carefully picked up the child and his bottle, and carried him to his grandmother's room.

'Would you mind looking after Albert?' she asked in a flat, quiet voice; 'I think I'll try to get some sleep.'

'Oh, I shall be delighted,' replied her mother-in-law. She said it in a tone of cold politeness, but Julia did not notice. She laid the child on the bed and stood looking at him in the same dull way for a little while, then went out without another word.

Mrs Gordins, senior, sat watching the baby for some long moments. 'He's a perfectly lovely child!' she said softly, gloating over his rosy beauty. 'There's not a *thing* the matter with him! It's just her absurd ideas. She's so irregular with him! To think of letting that child cry for an hour! He is nervous because she is. And of course she couldn't feed him till after his bath—of course not!'

She continued in these sarcastic meditations for some time, taking the empty bottle away from the small wet mouth, that sucked on for a few moments aimlessly, and then was quiet in sleep.

'I could take care of him so that he'd *never* cry!' she continued to herself, rocking slowly back and forth. 'And I could take care of twenty like him—and enjoy it! I believe I'll go off somewhere and do it. Give Julia a rest. Change of residence, indeed!'

She rocked and planned, pleased to have her grandson with her, even while asleep.

Greta had gone out on some errand of her own. The rooms were very quiet. Suddenly the old lady held up her head and sniffed. She rose swiftly to her feet and sprang to the gas jet—no, it was shut off tightly. She went back to the dining-room—all right there.

'That foolish girl has left the range going and it's blown out!' she thought, and went to the kitchen. No, the little room was fresh and clean; every burner turned off.

'Funny! It must come in from the hall.' She opened the door. No, the hall gave only its usual odor of diffused basement. Then the parlor—nothing there. The little alcove called by the renting agent 'the music room,' where Julia's closed piano and violin case stood dumb and dusty—nothing there.

'It's in her room—and she's asleep!' said Mrs Gordins, senior; and she tried to open the door. It was locked. She knocked— there was no answer; knocked louder—shook it—rattled the knob. No answer.

Then Mrs Gordins thought quickly. 'It may be an accident, and nobody must know. Frank mustn't know. I'm glad Greta's out. I *must* get in somehow!' She looked at the transom, and the stout rod Frank had himself put up for the portieres Julia loved.

'I believe I can do it, at a pinch.'

She was a remarkably active woman of her years, but no memory of earlier gymnastic feats could quite cover the exercise. She hastily brought the step-ladder. From its top she could see in, and what she saw made her determine recklessly.

Grabbing the pole with small strong hands, she thrust her

light frame bravely through the opening, turning clumsily but successfully, and dropping breathlessly and somewhat bruised to the floor, she flew to open the windows and doors.

When Julia opened her eyes she found loving arms around her, and wise, tender words to soothe and reassure.

'Don't say a thing, dearie—I understand. I *understand* I tell you! Oh, my dear girl—my precious daughter! We haven't been half good enough to you, Frank and I! But cheer up now—I've got the *loveliest* plan to tell you about! We *are* going to make a change! Listen now!'

And while the pale young mother lay quiet, petted and waited on to her heart's content, great plans were discussed and decided on.

Frank Gordins was pleased when the baby 'outgrew his crying spells.' He spoke of it to his wife.

'Yes,' she said sweetly. 'He has better care.'

'I knew you'd learn,' said he, proudly.

'I have!' she agreed. 'I've learned—ever so much!'

He was pleased too, vastly pleased, to have her health improve rapidly and steadily, the delicate pink come back to her cheeks, the soft light to her eyes; and when she made music for him in the evening, soft music, with shut doors—not to waken Albert— he felt as if his days of courtship had come again.

Greta the hammer-footed had gone, and an amazing French matron who came in by the day had taken her place. He asked no questions as to this person's peculiarities, and did not know that she did the purchasing and planned the meals, meals of such new delicacy and careful variance as gave him much delight. Neither did he know that her wages were greater than her pre-decessors. He turned over the same sum weekly, and did not pursue details.

He was pleased also that his mother seemed to have taken a new lease of life. She was so cheerful and brisk, so full of little jokes and stories—as he had known her in his boyhood; and above all she was so free and affectionate with Julia, that he was more than pleased.

'I tell you what it is!' he said to a bachelor friend. 'You fellows don't know what you're missing!' And he brought one of them home to dinner—just to show him.

'Do you do all that on thirty-five a week?' his friend demanded.

'That's about it,' he answered proudly.

'Well, your wife's a wonderful manager—that's all I can say. And you've got the best cook I ever saw, or heard of, or ate of— I suppose I might say—for five dollars.'

Mr Gordins was pleased and proud. But he was neither pleased nor proud when someone said to him, with displeasing frankness, 'I shouldn't think you'd want your wife to be giving music lessons, Frank!'

He did not show surprise nor anger to his friend, but saved it for his wife. So surprised and so angry was he that he did a most unusual thing—he left his business and went home early in the afternoon. He opened the door of his flat. There was no one in it. He went through every room. No wife; no child; no mother; no servant.

The elevator boy heard him banging about, opening and shutting doors, and grinned happily. When Mr Gordins came out Charles volunteered some information.

'Young Mrs Gordins is out, Sir; but old Mrs Gordins and the baby—they're upstairs. On the roof, I think.'

Mr Gordins went to the roof. There he found his mother, a smiling, cheerful nursemaid, and fifteen happy babies.

Mrs Gordins, senior, rose to the occasion promptly.

'Welcome to my baby garden, Frank,' she said cheerfully. 'I'm so glad you could get off in time to see it.'

She took his arm and led him about, proudly exhibiting her sunny roof-garden, her sand-pile, and big, shallow, zinc-lined pool; her flowers and vines, her see-saws, swings, and floor mattresses.

'You see how happy they are,' she said. 'Celia can manage very well for a few moments.' And then she exhibited to him the whole upper flat, turned into a convenient place for many little ones to take their naps or to play in if the weather was bad.

'Where's Julia?' he demanded first.

'Julia will be in presently,' she told him, 'by five o'clock anyway. And the mothers come for the babies by then, too. I have them from nine or ten to five.'

He was silent, both angry and hurt.

'We didn't tell you at first, my dear boy, because we knew you wouldn't like it, and we wanted to make sure it would go well. I rent the upper flat, you see—it is forty dollars a month, same as ours—and pay Celia five dollars a week, and pay Dr Holbrook downstairs the same for looking over my little ones every day. She helped me to get them, too. The mothers pay me three dollars a week each, and don't have to keep a nursemaid. And I pay ten dollars a week board to Julia, and still have about ten of my own.'

'And she gives music lessons?'

'Yes, she gives music lessons, just as she used to. She loves it, you know. You must have noticed how happy and well she is now—haven't you? And so am I. And so is Albert. You can't feel very badly about a thing that makes us all happy, can you?'

Just then Julia came in. radiant from a brisk walk, fresh and cheery, a big bunch of violets at her breast.

'Oh, Mother,' she cried, 'I've got tickets and we'll all go to hear Melba—if we can get Celia to come in for the evening.'

She saw her husband, and a guilty flush rose to her brow as she met his reproachful eyes.

'Oh, Frank!' she begged, her arms around his neck. 'Please don't mind! Please get used to it! Please be proud of us! Just think, we're all so happy, and we earn about a hundred dollars a week—all of us together. You see I have Mother's ten to add to the house money, and twenty or more of my own!'

They had a long talk together that evening, just the two of them. She told him, at last, what a danger had hung over them— how near it came.

'And Mother showed me the way out, Frank. The way to have my mind again—and not lose you! She is a different woman herself now that she has her heart and hands full of babies. Albert does enjoy it so! And *you've* enjoyed it—till you found it out!

'And dear—my own love—I don't mind it now at all! I love my home, I love my work, I love my mother, I love you. And as to children—I wish I had six!'

He looked at her flushed, eager, lovely face, and drew her close to him.

'If it makes all of you as happy as that,' he said, 'I guess I can stand it.'

And in after years he was heard to remark, 'This being married and bringing up children is as easy as can be—when you learn how!'

MRS ELDER'S IDEA

DID you ever repeat a word or phrase so often that it lost all meaning to you?

Did you ever eat at the same table, of the same diet, till the food had no taste to you?

Did you ever feel a sudden over-mastering wave of revolt against the ceaseless monotony of your surroundings till you longed to escape anywhere at any cost?

That was the way Mrs Elder felt on this gray, muggy morning, toward the familiar objects about her dining room, the familiar dishes on the table, even, for the moment, at the familiar figure at the other end of it.

It was Mr Elder's idea of a pleasant breakfast to set up his preferred newspaper against the water pitcher, and read it as long as he could continue eating and drinking. Other people were welcome to do the same, he argued; *he* had no objection. It is true that there was but one newspaper.

Mrs Elder was a woman naturally chatty, but skilled in silence. One cannot long converse with an absorbed opposing countenance which meets one's choicest anecdote, some minutes after the event, with a testy 'What's that?'

She sat still, stirring her cool coffee, waiting to ring for it, hot, when he wanted more, and studying his familiar outlines with a dull fascination. She knew every line and tint, every curve and angle, every wrinkle in the loosefitting coat, every moderate change in expression. They were only moderate, nowadays. Never any more did she see the looks she remembered so well, over twenty years ago; looks of admiration, of approval, of interest, of desire to please; looks with a deep kindling fire in them—

'I would thou wert either cold or hot,' she was half consciously repeating to herself.

O yes, he was kind to her in most things; he was fond of her, even, she could admit that. He missed her, when she was not there, or would miss her—she seldom had a chance to test it.

They had no quarrel, no complaint against each other; only a long, slow cooling, as of lava beds; the gradual evaporation of a fine fervor; that process of torpid, tepid, mutual accommodation which is complacently referred to by the wordly wise as 'settling down.'

'Had she no children?' will demand those whose psychological medicine closets hold but a few labels.

'For a Woman: A Husband, Home and Children. Good for whatever ails her.'

'For a Man: Success, Money, A Good Wife.'

'For a Child: Proper Care, Education, A Good Bringing Up.'

There are no other persons to be doctored, and no other remedies.

Now Mrs Elder had had children, four, fulfilling the formula announced by Mr Grant Allen, some years since, that each couple must have four children, merely to preserve the balance of the population; two to replace their parents, and two to die. Two of hers had accordingly; died; and two, living, were now ready to replace their parents; that is they were grown up.

Theodore was of age, and had gone into business already, at a distance. Alice was of age, too; the lesser age allowed the weaker vessel, and also away from home. She was staying with an aunt in Boston, a wealthy aunt who insisted in maintaining her in luxury; but the girl insisted equally upon studying at the Institute of Technology, and threatened an early departure into the proud freedom of self support.

Mrs Elder was fond of children, but these young persons were not children any more. She would have been glad to continue her ministrations; but however motherhood may seek to prolong its period of usefulness, childhood is evanescent; and youth, modern youth, serenely rebellious. The cycle which is supposed to so perfectly round out a woman's life, was closed for the present.

Mr Elder projected a cup, without looking at it, or her; and Mrs Elder rang, poured his coffee, modified it to his liking, and handed it back to him. She even took a fresh cup for herself, but found she did not want it.

There was a heavier shadow than usual between them this morning. As a general thing there was not a real cloud, only the bluish mist of distance in thick air; but now they had had a 'difference,' a decided difference.

Mr Elder's concerns in life had never been similar to his wife's. She had tried, as is held to be the duty of wives, to interest herself in his, but with only a measurable success. Her own preferences had never amounted to more than topics of conversation, to him, and distasteful topics, at that. What was the use of continually talking about things, if you could not have them and ought not to want to?

She loved the city, thick and bustling, the glitter and surge of the big shops with their kaleidoscope exhibition of color and style, that changed even as you looked.

Her fondness for shopping was almost a passion; to her an unending delight; to him, a silly vice.

This attitude was reversed in the matter of tobacco; to him, an unending delight; to her, a silly vice.

They had had arguments upon these lines, but that was years ago.

One of the reasons for Mrs Elder's hard-bitted silence was Mr Elder's extreme dislike of argument. Why argue, when you could not help yourself? that was his position; and not to be able to help herself was hers. How could she shop, to any advantage, when they lived an hour from town, and she had to ask for money to go with, or at least for money to shop with.

Just once in her life had Mrs Elder had an orgy of shopping. A widowed aunt of Mr Elder, who had just paid them a not too agreeable visit, surprised her beyond words with a Christmas present of a hundred dollars. 'It is conditional,' she said grimly, holding the amazing yellow-backed treasure in her bony and somewhat purple hand. 'You're not to tell Herbert a word about it till it's spent. You're to go in town, early in January, some day when the sales are on, and spend it all. And half of it you're to spend on yourself. Promise, now.'

Mrs Elder had promised, but the last condition was a little stretched. She swore she had wanted the movable electric drop light and the little music machine, but Herbert and the children seemed to use them more than she did. Anyhow she had a day's shopping, which was the solace of barren years.

She liked the theatre, too, but that had been so wholly out of the question for so long that it did not trouble her, much.

As for Mr Elder, he had to work in the city to maintain his family, but what he liked above everything else was the country; the real, wild, open country, where you could count your visible neighbors on your fingers, and leave them, visible, but not audible. They had compromised for twenty-two years, by living in Highvale, which was enough like a city to annoy him, and enough like the country to annoy her. She hated the country, it 'got on her nerves.'

Which brings us to the present difference between them.

Theodore being grown up and earning his living; Alice being well on the way to it, and a small expense at present; Mr Elder had concluded that his financial resources would allow of the realization of his fondest hope—retirement. A real retirement, not only officially, from business, and its hated environment; but physically, into the remote and lonely situation which his soul loved. So he had sold his business and bought a farm.

They had talked about it all last evening; at least she had. Mr Elder, as has been stated, was not much of a talker. He had seemed rather more preoccupied than usual during dinner; possibly he did realize in a dim way that the change would be extremely unwelcome to his wife. Then as they settled down to their usual quiet evening, wherein he was supremely comfortable in house-coat; slippers, cigars of the right sort, the books he loved, and a good light at the left back corner of his leather-cushioned chair; and wherein she read as long as she could stand it, sewed as long as she could stand it, and talked as long as he could stand it.

This time, he had, after strengthening himself with a preliminary cigar, heaved a sigh, and faced the inevitable.

'Oh, Grace,' he said, laying down his book, as if this was a minor incident which had just occurred to him, 'I've sold out the business.'

She dropped her work, and looked at him, startled. He went on, wishing to make all clear at once—he did hate discussion.

'Given up for good. It don't cost us much to live, now the children are practically off our hands. You know I've always hated office work; it's a great relief to be done with it, I assure you. . . . And I've bought that farm on Warren Hill. . . . We'll move out by October. I'd have left it till Spring—but I had a splendid chance to sell—and then I didn't dare wait lest I lose the farm. . . . No use keeping up two places. . . . Our lease is out in October, you know.'

He had left little gaps of silence between these blows, not longer than those required to heave up the axe for its full swing; and when he finished Mrs Elder felt as if her head verily rolled in the basket. She moistened her lips, and looked at him rather piteously, saying nothing at first. She could not say anything.

He arose from the easy depth of the chair, and came round the table, giving her a cursory kiss, and a reassuring pat on the shoulder.

'I know you won't like it at first, Grace, but it will do you good—good for your nerves—open air—rest—and a garden. You can have a lovely garden—and' (this was a carefully thought out boon, really involving some intent of sacrifice) 'and company, in summer. Have your friends come out!'

He sat down again feeling that the subject had been fully, fairly and finally discussed. She thought differently. There arose in her a slow, boiling flood of long-suppressed rebellion. He could speak like this—he could do a thing like that—and she was expected to say 'Yes, Herbert' to what amounted to penal servitude for life—to her.

But the habit of a score of years is strong, to say nothing of the habit of several scores of centuries, and out of that surging sea of resistance came only fatuous protests, and inefficacious pleas.

Mr Elder had been making up his mind to take this step for many years, and it was now a fact accomplished. He had decided that it would be good for his wife even it she did not like it; and that conviction gave him added strength.

Against this formidable front of fact and theory she had nothing to advance save a pathetic array of likes and dislikes; feeble neglected things, weak from disuse. But he had generously determined to 'let her talk it out' for that one evening; so she had talked from hour to hour—till she had at last realized that all this talk reached nowhere—the thing was done.

A dull cloud oppressed her dreams; she woke with a sense of impending calamity, and as the remembrance grew, into awakening pain. There was constraint between them at the breakfast table; a cold response from her when he went, with a fine effect of being cheerful and affectionate; and then Mrs Elder was left alone to consider her future.

She was a woman of forty-two, in excellent health, and would have been extremely good-looking if she could have 'dressed the part.' Some women look best in evening dress, some in house gowns, some in street suits; the last was her kind.

She gave her orders for the day listlessly, noting with weary patience the inefficiency of the suburban maid, and then suddenly thinking of how much worse the servant question would become on Warren Hill.

'Perhaps he expects me to do the housework,' she grimly remarked to herself. 'And have company. Company!'

As a matter of fact, Mrs Elder did not enjoy household visitors. They were to her a care, an added strain upon her housekeeping skill. Her idea of company was 'seeing people'; the chance meeting in the street, the friendly face in a theatre crowd, the brisk easily-ended chatter of a 'call,' and now and then a real party—where one could dance. Should she ever dance again?

Mrs Elder always considered it a special providence that brought Mrs Gaylord, a neighbor, in to see her that day; and with her a visiting friend, Mrs MacAvelly, rather a silent person, but sympathetic and suggestive. Mrs Gaylord was profusely interested and even angry at Mr Elder's heartlessness, as she called it; but Mrs MacAvelly had merely assisted in the conversation, by gentle references to this and that story, book and play. Had she seen this? Had she read that? Did she think so and so was right to do what she did?

After they left, Mrs Elder went down town, and bought a magazine or two which had been mentioned, and got a book from the little library.

She read, she was amazed, shocked, fascinated; she read more, and after a week of this inoculation, a strange light dawned upon her mind, quite suddenly and clearly.

'Why not?' she said to herself. And again, 'Why not?' Even in the night she woke and lay smiling, while heavy breathing told of sleep beside her; saying inwardly, 'Why not?'

It was only the end of August; there was a month yet.

She made plans, rapidly but quietly; consulting at length with several of her friends in Highvale, women with large establishments, large purses, and profoundly domestic tastes.

Mrs Gaylord was rapturously interested, introducing her to other friends, and Mrs MacAvelly wrote a little note from the city, mentioning several more; from more than one of these came large encouragement.

She wrote to her daughter also, and her son, whose business brought him to Boston that season. They had a talk in the soft-colored little parlor; Mrs Elder smiling, flushed, eager and excited as a girl, as she announced her plans, under pledge of strictest secrecy.

'I don't care whether you agree or not!' she stoutly proclaimed. 'But I'm going to do it. And you mustn't say one word. He never said a word till it was all done.'

None the less she looked a little anxiously at Theodore. He soon reassured her. 'Bully for you, Mama,' he said. 'You look about sixteen! Go ahead—I'll back you up.'

Alice was profoundly pleased.

'How perfectly splendid, Mama! I'm so proud of you! What glorious times we'll have, won't we just?' And they discussed her plans with enthusiasm and glee.

Toward the middle of September Mr Elder, immersed though he was in frequent visits to that idol of his heart, the farm, began to notice the excitement in his wife's manner. 'I hope you're not tiring yourself too much, packing,' he said, and added, quite affectionately, 'You won't hate it so much after a while, my dear.'

'No, I won't,' she admitted, with an ambiguous smile. 'I think I might even like it, a little while, in Summer.'

About the twentieth of the month she made up her mind to tell him, finding it harder than she had anticipated in the first proud moments of determination.

It was evening again, and he had settled luxuriously into his big chair, surrounded by The Country Gentleman, The Fruit-Grower, and The Breeder and Sportsman. She let him have one cigar, and then—'Herbert.'

He was a moment or two in answering—coming up from the depths of his studies in 'The Profits of Making Honey' with appropriate slowness. 'Yes, Grace, what is it?'

'I am not going with you to the farm.'

He smiled a little wearily. 'Oh, yes you are, my dear; don't make a fuss about the inevitable.'

She flushed at that and gathered courage. 'I have made other arrangements,' she said calmly. 'I am going to board in Boston. I've rented a furnished floor. Theodore is going to hire one room, and Alice one. And we take our meals out. She is to have a position this year. They both approve——' She hesitated a moment, and added breathlessly, 'I'm to be a professional shopper! I've got a lot of orders ahead. I can see my way half through the season already!'

She paused. So did he. He was not good at talking. 'You seem to have it all arranged,' he said drily.

'I have,' she eagerly agreed. 'It's all planned out.'

'Where do I come in?' he asked, after a little.

She took him seriously. 'There is plenty of room for you, dear, and you'll always be welcome. You might like it awhile—in Winter.'

This time it was Mr Elder who spent some hours in stating his likes and dislikes, but she explained how easily he could hire some one to pack and move for him—and how much happier he would be, when once well settled on the farm.

'You can get a nice housekeeper you see—for I shan't be costing you *anything* now!'

'I'm going to town next week,' she added, 'and we hope to see you by Christmas, at latest.'

They did.

They had an unusually happy Christmas, and an unusually happy Summer following. From sullen rage, Mr Elder, in serene rural solitude, simmered down to a grieved state of mind. When he did come to town, he found an eagerly delighted family; and a wife so roguishly young, so attractively dressed, so vivacious and happy and amusing, that the warmth of a sudden Indian Summer fell upon his heart.

Alice and Theodore chuckled in corners. 'Just see Papa making love to Mama! Isn't it impressive?'

Mrs Elder was certainly much impressed by it; and Mr Elder found that two half homes and half a happy wife, were really more satisfying than one whole home, and a whole unhappy wife, withering in discontent.

In her new youth and gaiety of spirit, and her half-remorseful tenderness for him, she grew ever more desirable, and presently the Elder family maintained a city flat and a country home; and spent their happy years between them.

THEIR HOUSE

MR WATERSON'S house was small, owing to the smallness of his income, but it was clean, most violently and meticulously clean, owing to the proficiency of Mrs Waterson as a housekeeper.

Mrs Waterson, in Mr Waterson's house, presented at times the appearance of an Admiral commanding a catboat; at other times she resembled that strictly localized meteorological disturbance, a tempest in a teapot. While her children were young they had furnished something of an outlet for her energies. They were nice children, quiet like their father, conscientious like their mother, of good constitutions, and not difficult to 'raise.' But she had 'raised' them by main force none the less, and during their nonage Mr Waterson had some peace in his house. He had no room of course, nor thought of claiming any, but in such small space as was temporarily allowed him he could read—sometimes.

Now the youngest boy had gone into business, and the youngest girl had suddenly married, using discretion in choice, and developing unexpected obstinacy in carrying out her decision. It is difficult to enforce authority upon a captive whose disobedience means escape.

'You were married at sixteen yourself, mother,' said Jennie junior, and took herself off.

So Mrs Waterson at the age of thirty-nine was left to concentrate her abundant efficiency upon her home and her husband. The house submitted perforce, wearing a cowed and submissive look, with its window-shades drawn to the line, its parlor darkened, its floors scrubbed, swept, or drastically washed, according to their nature. Mr Waterson also submitted—one cannot blame one's wife for being a good housekeeper, even a too good housekeeper.

He was a just man, and a kind one, and so thoroughly imbued with the conviction that woman's place is the home that he never dreamed of criticizing the way in which his wife filled it. Yet if

Forerunner, 3:12 (December 1912), 1–6.

ever a man was unhappy without knowing it, it was John Waterson. His was a studious soul, with the scholar's love of quiet and indifference to dust. He was fitted for high-ceilinged, long-windowed, book-walled libraries, looking out on peaceful lawns, deep-shaded. He liked plenty of room about him, not only for books and papers, but for his personal collections and instruments, and for certain small experiments. Secretly he fostered ambitions for scientific research. Yet all the room he had at his command was one bookcase in the parlor, an oak desk in the attic, and the somewhat begrudged use of the dining-room table after the red cloth was on and the lamp lit, with the condition that he must clean up before going to bed. As for bedroom space, he had his half the bed, less than half the closet, and two drawers in the bureau, the under ones. As Mrs Waterson liked the window shut and he liked it open, as she wanted more bedclothing than he by a pair of blankets, as she liked to go to bed early and he late, they compromised by half-opening the window, dividing the blankets logitudinally, one lying awake or the other being waked up—and were both patiently uncomfortable.

Now that the children were gone, there was really room for him if either of them had thought of having separate apartments, but they never did. The long-cramped Mrs Waterson eagerly arranged her daughter's chamber as a 'spare room,' decked it with all their best, and shut it up. The boys' room was only an attic anyhow and now became a much needed place of storage for Mr Waterson's 'clutter,' as she called it. He called it, in his secret heart, his 'study,' but it was only an attic, hot in summer and cold in winter.

'We ought to have a bigger house, Jennie,' he observed one night, as he had done many times before.

'Well,' said Mrs Waterson, faithfully inserting the *we* to take the edge off her remark, 'when we can afford a bigger house we'll have it.'

She was standing by the bureau combing her thick brown hair, while he lay there, wide awake and a little rebellious, watching her. Of course he could have sat up later, but there were so many directions to remember about the lamp and the stove and the window and to put up all his papers, and not to stumble on the stairs and waken her—which he knew he should infallibly do—that he preferred to come to bed and be done with it.

Hair is beautiful upon the head, smooth-coiled or softly flowing, and Mrs Waterson had 'a fine suit of hair,' but he never quite enjoyed the prosaic motions, swift and monotonous, with which she combed out the tangles, brushed it smooth, and braided it neatly for the night. When she cleaned the comb and wound the thin wisp of loose hairs around her fingers he always felt a sense of distaste—though he had never admitted it to himself. If she felt somewhat the same when he set his lean jaw askew to meet the razor, and masked his features in lather, or when the human form divine was in the ignominious attitude of pulling on a shirt, she never admitted it either. They had no complaint to make of one another, these good people. She was an irreproachable wife, albeit somewhat wearing, as good women often are; he was a model husband, though not pre-eminently successful as a 'provider,' which also is apt to occur. And they had loved each other for twenty-three years.

That they still loved each other neither doubted, but the friction of personal dissimilarity in a too close intimacy had worn and bitten away that golden cord to the merest thread, all unobserved.

Mr Waterson lay still and revolved his secret. Yes, he had better tell her now. The oldest boy, his father's special pride, who had been graduated at twenty and stepped into congenial employment at once with a scientific institution, had sent home a letter with a startling proposition. Couldn't father sell out his business, or let it temporarily, and go with an exploring expedition now forming? He, the son, could get him a small place, he thought, and he would so love to have Dad along. He knew it would be hard on mother, but couldn't mother go to Jennie's, now Jennie had a home?

Mr Waterson had carried the letter in his pocket for some days, pondering hopelessly on this golden opportunity. All his life he had longed for such a chance. It meant a period of freedom, and his patient soul expanded at the thought—time to think, men to talk with who were interested in the same things, growth, study, perhaps some real discovery. But duty held him in his place. He must support his wife, maintain his home, carry on his business.

Before answering, however, he meant to broach the subject to his wife. Perhaps he had a faint, unspoken hope that she might see a way for him to go. Perhaps he felt rather the need of her strong good sense to strengthen him in the way of duty and help him to refuse.

So now, while she stood there, holding her hair in a firm clutch and dragging the comb through it with smart, tearing strokes—he always wondered that she had any hair left—he told her of Jack's letter.

She listened quietly, saying nothing till he had quite finished. Then, when her braid was plaited down to the thin diminishing end, she wrapped her blue kimono close about her and sat down on the edge of the bed, looking at him more lovingly than usual.

'Why don't you do it?' she said, with her brisk smile. 'It would do you good!'

He was much surprised. 'But, my dear—how can I? Here are you—and the house—and the business. If I could sell it—' he added, with a flicker of hope.

Mr Waterson kept a dry goods store, a quiet, reliable old-fashioned dry goods store, which brought in just enough from year to year, and never any more.

'I can sell the business for you,' said his wife cheerfully. 'I'll run it awhile, and sell it—to advantage. Just you try me!'

He believed she could if she set her mind to it.

'But the house—the expenses.'

'I can manage the house, too. Just you try me, John. You put everything in my name and *go!* It's the chance you've always wanted, isn't it?'

It was, without doubt, and he wanted it so much that her cheerful energy and determined optimism wrought him to the pitch of enthusiasm necessary for so great a step.

He put all his property in his wife's name, gave her power of attorney to attend to his affairs, drew half of their savings and started off on the expedition.

He felt like a lad of twenty instead of a man of forty-five. The years rolled off from him with his responsibilities. Eager, clear-minded, full of hope and courage, more like a brother than a father with his son, he set forth with his face to the future.

He had thought himself an elderly man. He felt now like a young one. He had thought himself in duty bound to work always for his wife and family. To his sudden amazement he found that the family cares he had carried for so long rolled off him like a forgotten burden. House, store, business obligations—they had disappeared.

He did think a good deal about his wife at first. So ingrained was his conviction that women should stay at home that it did not seem right to think of her as running a store, and yet he knew she could do it, and do it well. That summer that he had broken his leg she had carried on the business for him most successfully. He wrote some letters of advice, growing shorter and farther apart as the weeks passed. Letters were always difficult and unsatisfying to him. They were even more so to her. She was a woman of deeds rather than words, even spoken ones, and written language was not at all her medium of expression. So she wrote presently to this effect:

'Now, my dear husband, you really can't advise from that distance. I've undertaken the business and it's going nicely. You're off on your expedition and that's going nicely, I judge. Just dismiss this end from your mind, dear. Let's make an agreement right now that if either one of us is sick or injured or needs the other in any way, we'll write or wire at once, but so long as things go all right we won't bother to write unless we feel like it. I know you love me, and I love you, and we'll be glad to see each other again, but for now—just go and play!'

So with a sense of deep though hardly recognized relief, John Waterson let all his personal ties fall loose, and only at rare intervals did he send brief, cheerful letters home, to tell of some wonderful new find they had made, some book he had read, some fruitful talk with other scholars, some work he contemplated. Scant as his opportunities had been, so earnest had been his study along the lines which interested him that he was able to hold his own among these scientists and even to contribute something to their discussions. Now and then he sent her newspaper reports in which the achievements of the expedition were recorded, and in which his own name occasionally appeared.

As he receded from her daily sight, as his always rather perfunctory letters grew few and far between, and as she read of his doings and what others thought of him, he began to loom larger and more attractive in her mind. He would have been surprised indeed to know how she treasured those scant letters now, though far too proud to ask for more after she herself had proposed the lightening of their correspondence. From the first years of their marriage she had not loved her husband as she loved him now.

Then when he wrote to her that there was a chance for him to go still farther, on a long voyage with explorations in another country, which might keep him away another year or two, it took all her strength to send just the right kind of a letter to ensure his going.

'That's *fine*, John,' she said; 'simply *fine*. I am so glad for you. I wouldn't have you miss it for anything. Of course I hate to lose you for so long, but we've had twenty-three years together, and will have all the rest of our lives together; this is perhaps the only time you'll ever have to go where you want to. It's fine for Jack, too, and for you to be together. Don't miss it on my account. Things are going on well here: the business is looking up; my health is fine. I may be able to sell the house—if I don't hear from you to the contrary.'

He really felt a little ashamed to leave her so long, but she seemed so happy, and so—well, he was almost nettled by her serene assurance that she could run the business as well as he could.

Jack was eager to have him go.

'Oh, come on, Dad! Mother's all right. She's having the time of her life. Jennie's there, you know, in case anything should happen, but mother's never sick. And Walter's doing well in the city; he'd help out if she got in trouble with the business. Come along!'

So Mr Waterson, already strengthened and stimulated by congenial occupation, went over seas with the party. He wrote few letters, but he did find time to write a monograph on the single branch of the single subject of which he now really knew as much as any one man, and when this monograph was read at a great international convention, and printed, and praised far and wide by those who knew enough to appreciate it, he sent the accounts of it, with the paper itself, to his wife, and felt that he had not lived in vain.

It was four years before he returned to his home city. Two feelings strove within him, making him alternately happy and miserable. One was a homesick longing for his wife, his house even—almost his store. The other was a shuddering disinclination to go back to what, in this light, looked like a prison. He, who had been a man among men for so long, to go back and be told to shut windows and lock doors and wind clocks—things he always forgot to do, unless so told; he, who had strayed for thousands of miles, with his own luggage and accumulating papers and specimens—he wondered ruefully where he should put them—now dreaded with a real horror to reconfine himself to the bookcase in the parlor, the desk in the attic, the two bureau drawers.

Mrs Waterson meanwhile had had four years to work in, at work which, to her sincere surprise, she had found more congenial than that of forever recooking similar food and reclearing the same rooms, clothes and dishes.

She ran the store a few months on its old lines, then sent for an efficiency expert and spent several days in close consultation with him. She was not content with his report on the store, but asked him his opinion on other businesses in the town, and paid for it.

'Rather an expensive young man, wasn't he?' a conservative friend inquired.

'The most profitable visitor I ever had,' she replied with decision.

She drew more profit from his visit than his direct advice. Hers was a mind that saw the principle of things. She grasped the simple secret of 'efficiency' and proceeded to apply it.

If Mr Waterson had left his business behind him as one dropping a burden, Mrs Waterson left her housekeeping as one escaping from a treadmill. Her natural energies had now for the first time room for full action. Her store blossomed with sudden changes, wisely planned. She enlarged here, altered there, added new features. It became, in a modest way, a department store. To the 'gents' furnishing' department she added a hand laundry—a laundry so safe and sanitary, so quick and clean, that it doubled her trade in that line. If the laundry itself was no great profit—and it was not at first—it added greatly to the profits of the business. With the laundry went naturally a mending bureau; that grew swiftly into a plain-sewing, and that into a dressmaking establishment, all in connection with the background of dry goods.

Exulting in her new freedom, proving her power and finding it increase with use, Mrs Waterson used her first year's profits to add to her building and to acquire an interest in a grocery store next door. The second year she bought out a small hotel which had utterly failed to pay. She made it pay. She knew the kind of manager to hire, and how to manage him, she had her own house-furnishing department to draw on, her grocery business, and her laundry, now solidly flourishing.

The third year saw her department store and her hotel paying handsomely, with a bank account rolling up steadily. She had sold their house, in the second year of her husband's absence, to good advantage, and bought a larger lot, rather on the outskirts of the town, with a long slope down to a quiet river and numbers of old trees. The house on it was of no value, and as soon as she saw her way clear she had it torn down and began to build.

Never in her life had she been so happy, not even when love's fulfillment had for a while stilled that insistent urge within her which always had demanded more to do. Doubtless if she had not had her pleasant family life to look back on, her satisfactory children to be proud of, and her husband—for whom she longed increasingly—to look forward to, all this joyful exertion and new pride would have had its empty side, and left her often lonely. But her domestic conscience was clean; her woman's heart had given and taken to the full, and she found time to enjoy Jennie's baby almost as much as any other grandmother.

Jennie's husband she learned fully to approve of. He was now a general manager in her big store, doing excellent work, and drawing a much higher salary than he had before. The business ran on well, with only such risks and difficulties as roused her to fresh courage and resource.

The house rose with speed. She had been slow and careful in its planning, and now urged the work to completion. He was coming—she wanted it ready for him.

Mr Waterson had not written since announcing the probable date of their return. Why should he? He was coming as fast as letters could, and, if he was delayed here and there, why so would the letters have been. He was coming as fast as he could, and as the slow miles passed, the thoughts of home, the thoughts of her, grew steadily sweeter.

When at last he was on the steamer, with only the ocean between them, the thoughts grew into keen longings. He wanted to see home again, the pleasant town where he had so many friends, where he felt now he could hold his head higher after his scientific honors. He wanted to see his daughter, and his new granddaughter, described as a wonder of the world. Most of all he wanted to see his wife.

Two things he did not long for, though they seemed more endurable as he neared them—his store and the cramped quarters of his home. He wondered if she had sold it, and where they should live.

She met him at the station with a neat electric brougham. 'Ours!' she said. In its seclusion they sat close and held one another so tightly that it hurt.

'Oh, my dear, my dear!' she breathed occasionally. And then he would kiss her again.

How young she looked! How pretty she looked! How cheery and how—smooth! She seemed some way sweeter, less peremptory.

'I've got a surprise for you, John—a big one!'

'I'm not surprised at anything you do, my darling,' he protested. But he was.

The wide grounds, the curving driveway, the tall trees, the glowing banks of flowers, they all surprised him. Then the wide-winged, handsome house, its hospitable hall with the open fire, the big parlors, the dining-room all rich with panelled wood, the pantry and kitchen and laundry—all on one side.

She took him across the hall again, and through a little passage, double-doored. 'The library,' she said. Back of its shelf-lined calm a smaller room. 'Your study, dear!' A little iron stair ran upward. She led him to the floor above. 'Your bedroom, darling.' A roomy bathroom and big closets, with another little passage. 'And this is mine.'

He looked about and caught his breath a little.

'You've done all this,' he said, 'while I was just playing!'

'While you were beginning your real work, dear heart—the work you're going to carry on. While you were making the whole town proud of you—yes, the whole country, if they knew enough. *And* your wife! Why, John!' she held him off and looked at him with wet, shining eyes, 'John, darling, I never appreciated you before. To think of the man you are burying yourself in that old store—just for our sakes! You built the business, John, honest and strong; I've followed your steps. Now you shall really work at what you love—and so will I!

'Surely it's a woman's business to make the home! We ought to have thirty years yet to love each other in!

'This is Our House, John!'

HER BEAUTY

AMARYLLIS was her name.

She used bitterly to reflect, chin on hands, eyes staring gloomily into the ill-natured little mirror—a dull, green-tinted, worse than truthful mirror—that her name was the only beautiful thing about her.

Amaryllis Delong! Some remote Huguenot refugee ancestor put that 'de' into this American family; and an immediate one, her mother, in fact, had insisted on calling her Amaryllis, in the face of the whole town.

A dull face that town had, green-tinted like the old looking-glass, brown and gray of fence and house, though prosperous enough, and contented enough, for the most part.

Not so Amaryllis. She was 'congenitally discontented' her school teacher said—the one that came from Wellesley. She was 'rebellious against Providence' her minister said. She was 'a hard child to bring up' her mother said. She was the most miserable girl alive, she said to herself, lowering into her little glass, which lowered back at her.

It was no use. She had tried every arrangement of that mirror, every angle, every sort of light, from the pink dawn to the pale moon radiance, with two candles and a kerosene lamp as special experiment. She had arranged her hair in every way she knew how; she had tried every costume and combination of costumes she possessed, and as much lack of costume as her conscience permitted—and it was no use. Never once could she bring into that mirror the thing she longed for—beauty.

'Amaryllis is dreadful fond of pretty things,' her mother said discerningly. 'It's a pity she's so plain!'

It was a pity. It grieved her childhood, darkened her girlhood, and now it had crushed and ruined her womanhood.

Because her name was Amaryllis, probably, she had attracted the attention of Weldon Thomas for a little while—the only time of soul-stirring happiness she had ever known. He had asked to

Forerunner, 4:2 (February 1913), 1–5.

be introduced to Miss Amaryllis Delong on the wide foot-worn steps of the First Church after prayer meeting; had talked with her there a moment; had walked home with her; had asked if he might call.

That was all in an evening, a summer evening, when lights were soft and flickering among leaf shadows, and the young face flushing and smiling under the wide hat, had at least the charm of mystery. She must have pleased him then, for he had come to see her once or twice, and the close-blinded parlor, the shaded lamp, the girl's bright, wistful pleasure and happy talk still seemed to hold. Then he asked her to a picnic, and there, alas, she met not only the full daylight, but competition. Among other girls, girls who were round and rosy, soft, alluring and dressed with prompt submission to the prevailing style, Amaryllis was never seen to advantage.

After that he went away on some visit or vacation. After that he only bowed or spoke briefly as they met. After that again he went with Bessy Sharpless and Myra Hall—and now it was all over. He had married Myra.

Myra was undeniably handsome. No one denied it, least of all beauty-worshipping Amaryllis. Myra was smooth and plump; Myra had bright hair that fluffed and curled and blew about her face bewitchingly; Myra had white, regular, shiny teeth, and a round little chin, dimpled hands, small feet in smaller shoes whose high heels captivated the eye—most eyes, that is. And Weldon, who loved beauty almost as well as Amaryllis, who even wrote verses about it, which were printed in The Plainville Watchman, was carried off his feet with a rush. Besides, Myra had practically all the unattached men of the little town at those dapper little feet of hers, and rivalry has charms.

The hope of love died in the heart of Amaryllis, died and was buried under a heavy weight of reticence, a quiet but effective monument of dumb pride.

But the love of beauty did not die. She decided, away out there in middle-western Plainville, to search for beauty and to find it. The only avenues then open to her were books, the books in the little public library, in the minister's library, in the traveling libraries of the Woman's Club. But 'love will find out a way,' more than one kind of love; a girl of eighteen, with a strong character and a heavy disappointment, can do a great deal.

With all the resignation of a nun, she abandoned the thought of happiness, and determined on a life of devotion to her heart's idol, beauty. For right appreciation of this education was required. She determined to go to college. She went to college forthwith, her father rather approving.

'She'll have to teach, I expect,' he said. 'Her face is not her fortune, sure.' And he worked hard to help her.

The girl was proud, and intended to help herself. She took a summer course in dressmaking and worked her way through the last years by helping the girls with their wardrobes.

Teaching was no part of her ambition. When college was over she took a position in a good dressmaking establishment and gained experience if not money. Then she got up a co-operative affair with three other girls, gained more experience, and more money.

In ten years' time Amaryllis was recognized by all Plainville, when they saw her, as an old maid. Even her parents admitted it.

'She's doin' real well, Amaryllis is,' her mother boasted. 'She's sent back to her father all it cost him to start her in college, and pretty nearly clothes me, let alone supportin' herself.'

The clothes of Mrs Delong had indeed waxed in elegance and beauty till her best friends, in the confidence of private friendship, whispered that she was 'a little too dressy.'

In Plainville only young girls, on special occasions, were admired for being 'dressy.' For other persons and seasons any noticeable beauty of apparel was condemned as inappropriate, also as 'conspicuous.' Yet these same people would gladly surround their homes with Canna Indicus and Golden Glow; yes, and with Poinsettias if they would have grown there.

On an ocean steamer a keen young face looked out from hood and rugs and watched the flying, interminable waves with eager eyes. Amaryllis had 'done' better than her parents knew. The dressmaking business, rightly handled, is a gold mine. With garments well made and effective, with a ten per cent. discount for cash and prepayment for all materials required, she had lost no sleep nor cash income from unpaid bills, and her bank account had grown with her reputation. Now she could leave her forewoman, as a sort of partner, in charge of the business, and go to represent the Parisian end.

She knew the language; she had been there often on buying and observing trips, but this time she was to live there, and, at last, to study art. There was no misguided ambition to be a painter. She was no painter, no daughtsman, no artist really, except in the negative sense of appreciation and delight; one may study music without being a musician, surely.

Her trained eye, her business experience, enabled her to send to the home shop its share of Parisian novelties and triumphs, and this required small part of Amaryllis' time. Her real purpose was like that of some rapt 'Bather,' the laying aside of unneeded cumbering things, the stepping into a wide, warm, shimmering sea.

From year to year her business steadied and grew, not a great business, but a small, solid, well-established one, with its full time, its regular patrons, and its waiting list of transient customers. She was able to travel, to study to her heart's content, to meet people, to hear lectures, to read books, to see pictures, to attend plays, to feed her soul with knowledge, and to enjoy as far as it exists in the modern world, the beauty she desired.

On one of her ocean voyages she saw at the captain's table a face that seemed familiar. A woman's face it was, large, over-blown, like a La France rose a day too old; a woman's form, strenuously conventionalized by the last violence of corsets. It was Myra Hall—that was; Myra Thomas now, of course, and Amaryllis watched her with a strange sinking of the heart. Where was Weldon? Was he—could he be—no, Myra was not in black.

She spoke to her, and the stout matron was unfeignedly glad to see her.

'Why, Amaryllis! How stylish you do look! I've heard you were doing wonders, and now I believe it. Did you make that? Will you make me one? How much would it cost—between friends, you know!'

She smiled archly. The round little chin was rounder, larger, manifold; it was, in fact, two chins, and might have been more but for the uncompromising pressure of an ear-lifting lace stock, with 'stiffeners' full four inches long. The small white teeth were much the worse for wear. Her hands were dimpled still, conspicuously so, as the soft tissues expanded; her small feet not so small, however.

'Can't wear my old sizes now, I tell you,' she cheerfully agreed. 'Had a bad case of dropped arch—have to wear these awful things now—doctor's orders!' And she exhibited a pair of those fearsome shoes with which modern science seeks to improve on nature and force reluctant toes to curve and straddle as they never intended.

The bright flying hair was mostly gone, but in its place had come seven other devils worse than the first; a swelling mattress effect, puffs suggestive of upholstery—abundance certainly, but never again the golden shine.

Again Amaryllis' heart sank for Weldon, but not for his life. Myra assured her that he was well, and working hard. 'He's a newspaper man, you see. They can't leave, ever. Yes, Weldon works hard. But he likes it. What? Poetry?' she laughed. 'I guess not. Weldon outgrew that long ago. Guess I laughed him out of it a good deal.'

Amaryllis bade farewell to Myra, who was taking a vacation, she said, and returned to her work in Paris. The cable about her mother's illness brought her home in time only to say good-bye. Her father seemed helpless and lonely after that. In a year's time Amaryllis was alone again, with the old place on her hands. Quite a sum of money awaited her, too; they had had no interest in life but saving, for these last few years.

To her own surprise she felt a deep resurgence of love for the home of her childhood. With eyes trained now in larger views, she saw that the weary ugliness of the town was superficial and transient, while the beauty of the countryside was strong and pure beneath it all. Their own house stood near the road; dust defaced it, noise affronted it, only a few whitened trees and stiff, narrow flowerbeds between their windows and the fence. At the back of the long yard were trees, large trees and old, elms, a walnut, water maples, and beyond the maples flowed a wide, quiet river.

A flame kindled in her eyes. She walked the big place over from corner to corner, from end to end, studying, thinking, looking, with her eyes half shut, her head thrown back as she tried this view and the other.

The island was theirs, too, and the river pasture across. Far over the swale meadow, the low-rolling hills, the sun set even more gloriously than she remembered.

Amaryllis consulted the old lawyer who had been her father's friend; she reckoned up her inheritance, consulted her bank account, and sent for two friends from Boston to come and visit her. One was an architect of growing fame.

Weldon Thomas at forty was frankly considered a failure by his brothers of the press. Newspaper men, however, are not invariably right. He had lost his job on one big daily after another. 'He hasn't snap enough.' 'Lacks ginger.' 'Does good work, but too slow.' 'Trouble with Thomas is he's too old.'

He was, in fact, forty-two. An expensive wife and a residence in New York are not conducive of thrift. The severest economy of one member of the family cannot counterbalance many pleasant indulgences by the party of the second part. Weldon's twenty years in New York left him barely enough to buy a controlling interest in The Plainville Watchman. His city friends thought it a miserable comedown. 'Too bad about old Thomas. He's had to give up work and go down to the country. Bought a rube sheet, I believe. It's a shame.'

He did not feel wholly of that mind as he took up his new duties in the old place. The quiet streets rested him. The arching trees rested him. The cool silence of the nights unutterably rested him. He renewed his acquaintance gradually, more with the place than with the people.

Walking one golden afternoon along the outskirts of the little town he came to a new wall, new to the place he was sure, but softly old to the eye. Above it blossoming boughs curved richly; the gateway gave full view of a deep lawn, far back on which a low, wide house, serene in outline, beautifully white, waited invitingly.

He remembered. 'That Delong girl,' they had told him, had 'fixed up the old place so't you wouldn't know it; tore down the old house and built the queerest thing you ever saw. She must have earned a lot of money, dressmakin'.'

He remembered Amaryllis and what he had heard of her work—he would drop in and see her.

The path curved a little, enough to rest the eye, not enough to annoy the feet. It was only a hundred yards or so, but he stopped more than once to admire the softly changing picture about him, and at the doorstep turned back for a good look. How a mere 'front yard,' however large, could have changed to such a pleasance he could not understand, but the effect had an uplifting sweetness to which his city-starved soul responded with grateful joy.

The house itself was so quiet in its gentle beauty, so restrained and calm, that he made no attempts at analysis, just smiled at the white façade of it, and rang the bell. A soft-voiced colored maid opened the door to him, motioned him to a seat in the broad, hospitable hall, and took his card. Presently she returned to say that he was to come in, and opened a door.

He stopped in the entrance, a quick sigh of pleasure escaping him. A long room, a wide room, a room of just proportions, gracious spaces, blending colors, that were like warmth and flowers and wine, and opposite him a window that was a mighty picture, deep-framed by the broad cushioned seat, the dark casings, the rich hangings. In that picture the river lived before him, veiled here and there by trees; beyond the river beautiful farmland, curving hills, dark woods, the softening splendor of the sun.

A little laugh of pleasure greeted him:

'You like my window.'

He turned to her with a start of pleased surprise. Her kind, clear-cut face glowed with hospitable warmth, perhaps with something more. She reached white hands to him, delicate but strong. Her soft robe swept down from the straight shoulders full of a gentle womanly grace and a discerning color sense; it suited not only her, but the room. She spoke harmony in every tint and line, in the grace of her movements, the stately repose of her quiet beauty, the well-modulated tones of her voice.

The tired man stood and gazed at her, as one drinking thirstily. His soul was stirred and comforted first by that broad stretch of garden ground, then by the gracious house, then by this satisfying restful room, with its windows into heaven, and now he felt in her something like all of them, and something better still.

'Why Amaryllis! How beautiful you are!'

She laughed merrily.

'You always were a poet, Weldon—and good at pretty speeches. Sit down, won't you!'

He would not let go her hand.

'I feel as if I'd been on a horrible long journey,' he told her, 'and this—' he hesitated, and glanced about him with the same satisfaction, concluding:

'I'd just like to sit and look at you for hours!'

'And what would Myra say to that!' she asked him, smiling.

'Didn't you know?' he said. 'I lost her a year ago. May I look at you now?'

MRS HINES'S MONEY

MRS HINES lay quietly on her back, looking sideways out of the window. She was quite conscious of the dull ache in the splinted arms, the bandaged head, but with a strange, unusual sense of peace. Physically she was far from comfortable, but in her mind, in spite of some confusion and regret, was that queer increasing feeling that somehow things were going to be different now— and better.

They had broken it to her, gently and after due delay, that her husband had not survived the accident. She shut her eyes then, turned her head stiffly on the pillow, and they could see the slow salt tears forcing themselves from beneath closed lids, and the close-held lips quivering. Mrs Hines had never complained of her husband. It was quite natural that she should cry. She 'bore up' splendidly, they said. But they did not know why she cried nor what it was she bore up against.

As the lean, small woman with the patient face and iron-gray hair in its two thin little sick-bed braids lay there so still, none of her relatives and attendants knew the crossing currents of emotion that lifted her thin chest with an occasional shuddering sigh.

'Now, Eva, you must be brave!' said her sister, Mrs Arroway. 'It is hard, I know, but you have always done your duty. You have nothing to blame yourself for.'

Her brother, a heavy man with a determined mouth supplemented by an even more determined moustache, added his words of cheer.

'You're left in comfortable circumstances, Eva,' he said. 'Very comfortable circumstances for a woman alone. Jason was better fixed than we knew. I won't worry you with details, but you'll be well taken care of. There's no executor or anything named—I suppose you'll want me to attend to things for you?'

To this she said nothing, but the tears welled afresh, and Mrs

Arroway said: 'Now Frank Peterson, you wait. She's not strong enough to be troubled about anything yet. You go away.'

So Frank went away, and presently, as Mrs Hines seemed to be asleep, her sister went also. Then after awhile Mrs Hines opened her eyes and looked at the drooping fir boughs by the window. Not far beyond them was a slate-colored wooden wall, the windowless side of the next house. She had looked out through those dark fir boughs at that wooden wall ever since she came to this house, a bride, thirty long years ago. Then she was eighteen. Now she was forty-eight.

When the doctor dropped in on his way home, just to see how she was getting along, she whispered that she wanted to see him alone. So he persuaded Mrs Arroway, who sat, large and warm, in a creaky rocking-chair, fanning herself steadily, that a nap would do her good there and then, and sent her to take it.

'Your patient's doing beautifully now,' he said, 'and she'll sleep a bit, too, I think, if she's by herself.'

The nurse was easily disposed of, and Dr Osgood drew his chair closer and looked down, smiling in his wise friendly way on the pale little woman.

'You've known me near thirty years, haven't you, Doctor?'

'I certainly have,' he agreed. 'Sick and well—mostly well, I'm glad to say.'

'And you've known—my family too.'

'Knew your father and mother, and brother and sister, and several cousins—no doubt of it.'

'Well—I'm not crazy—am I, Doctor?'

'Crazy! Certainly not. You've nothing but a few scalp wounds there, and a broken bone or two. You've no fever—you'll be up in no time.'

'Your boy Charles is a real lawyer now, isn't he?' she pursued.

'What *are* you driving at? Yes, Charles is a lawyer all right, and going to be a good one—unless he's too honest.'

'Well, I want to see him, Doctor. Frank tells me that I'm left—fairly well off—and he wants to manage the property—and I prefer to have it in my own hands—absolutely. Can't Charles take care of me?'

'He certainly can, and he'll be glad to. You gave my kids many a good time when they were little—and they're all fond of you. You can count on Charlie. I'll bring him around in the morning.'

With the benefit of her attorney's inquiries and advice Mrs Hines ascertained that she was absolute mistress of the place where she had lived so long, of two other houses and a centrally situated lot, and of some fifty thousand dollars in a reliable bank. He gave her all the details, and some wise advice.

'Is it my very own?' she said. 'I can do just as I please with it all?'

'You can do exactly as you please with every cent of it,' he told her. 'You can sell all you have and give to the poor—but I don't advise it. You can give it all to me—but I won't charge that much.'

Mr Frank Peterson was offended and made that fact conspicuous. Mrs Arroway was offended too, on general principles, that Eva should consult a lawyer when her own brother was one—it looked so bad—it was so inconsiderate.

To their criticisms and protests Mrs Hines opposed no word, only the pale patient face, the set lines of the moutn. She was weak, she was silent under reproach, but she kept on quietly.

As soon as Mrs Hines was up and about she consulted, further, her minister as well as her lawyer, and more than one real estate man. Her own place she sold at once, sold even at what seemed some sacrifice, showing what her sister called 'real hard-heartedness' about it. The other two houses were left in Mr Charles Osgood's hands to rent as before, and Mrs Hines, taking the proceeds of her relinquished home in letters of credit and travelers' checks, summarily departed.

'I never saw anything so unnatural!' her sister protested. 'She won't even say where she's going. She says her lawyer'll forward her letters. Her lawyer, indeed! And her own brother a lawyer all the time! I don't believe she knows what she's doing. I believe her mind's affected.'

But here Dr Osgood satisfied all inquiries. 'Fiddlesticks,' he said. 'She's going off for change, travel, and a complete rest. I advised it. If she doesn't want to tell where she's going, why should she?'

Mrs Hines, in truth, did not know where she was going. She had one settled determination; to make the price of that home which had held her prisoner so long, now carry her as far as it would hold out. Beyond that she had a longing deep and earnest for health—vigorous health—if it could be had at any price. And beyond that, still deeper and more earnest, was the desire to invest her money so that it should do the most good.

'This much I'll spend—just spend!' she told herself, 'I can live easy enough on the rents of the other two, and then I'll put that fifty thousand to work for righteousness. But I've got to get well—*well*—strong, and clearheaded.'

The very first thing she did was to take a 'room and bath' in a New York hotel. She dined rather timidly in the big room with the music, flowers and lights, spent a riotous evening with three new magazines at once, then, with triumphant memories of the compromises and makeshifts of the large, inconvenient, old-fashioned house she had escaped from, she luxuriated in the shining, white-tiled bathroom, the gleaming porcelain tub, the swift, copious rush of the hot water.

'He *wouldn't* have the hot water connected,' she thought. 'He *wouldn't* have a porcelain tub—or even an enameled one. And he could have, just as well!'

Then Mrs Hines crept into a wide smooth luxurious bed, and slept. She slept so deep and sound that on waking there was that sense of coming up from deep waters, of complete detachment.

'Where am I?' was the first thought, with the worried background of a fear that she would be late with Jason's breakfast.

Then she remembered.

She lay perfectly still for awhile, then stretched deliciously, as far as she could reach, to the uttermost corners of the wide bed. How fresh and empty the room smelled! How gently the curtain waved in a soft current of air! Mrs Hines preferred the window open. Jason had preferred it shut.

She looked at her watch, smiled happily, and went to sleep again. Wakening at last an idea struck her—a daring, delightful idea. She would have her breakfast sent up!

For some weeks the little woman rested and freshened herself in unwonted idleness and freedom, and then, feeling strong enough to choose, spent a long Summer, half in the cool uplifting mountains, half by the cool refreshing sea.

How hot it used to be in that house—!

This Summer was divided into three equally pleasant

processes: Rest, exercise and study. She had found out, in the big city, what she wanted to know, and all Summer she was filling her mind with new knowledge.

It came to her as a revelation, the things the world was doing to improve itself. With all her soft little heart she had grieved over the sorrows, the unnecessary sorrows, of humanity; with all her hard little head she had tried to think of ways of helping. But she had had little time or opportunity, and no money, and her ideas had been laughed at as womanish foolishness.

Now she found that men, hard-headed business men and statesmen, doctors and writers and scientific students, were thinking and working along these lines.

She had time now—all there was left. She had freedom. And she had fifty thousand dollars.

A year of travel followed. She was not going to be hasty. She could not afford to make mistakes. So she went methodically about from land to land, supplementing her recent study with more careful observation. *The Survey* and her collateral reading had filled her mind with stirring insight into conditions. The Bureau of Social Service in New York had given her definite lines of inquiry. Now she was learning fast.

'It mustn't be charity,' she said to herself. 'It must be business, good business. It must prove that it will pay.'

When she came back to her home town she felt as if she had changed from a mouse to an elephant, so much stronger she felt, so much wider was her outlook upon life. So detached and upbuilt was she as to feel even a sort of affection for her brother who had always so rudely domineered over her as to check that natural feeling. Her sister, too, no longer seemed a dampener, a clog upon her spirit. That spirit was strong enough now to smile at their limitations and not mind them. Even the town looked pleasant to her—and to her pleased surprise the house by the big fir trees had become a grocery store.

She took two rooms at the best hotel.

Mrs Arroway remonstrated continuously. 'Look here, Julia,' said Mrs Hines at last. 'I'm a woman of fifty, and ought to know my own mind. I prefer to live in this hotel for the present. Now suppose you just make up your mind to it.' She was good-natured but firm, and peace ensued.

There was Charles Osgood and his father; there was the one live minister in town; there was out of many one woman's club with some real ambition to be useful, and the philanthropic associations of the place, such as they were; these were the assets. Ignorance, inertia, prejudice, conservatism and selfishness; these were the liabilities.

It was a large town, or rather, a small city, and small though it was, had many of the disadvantages of large ones, without their ameliorations.

Mrs Hines blew no trumpet. She spent her first season in re-establishing herself in the place on a new basis, in affiliating with church, club and charity, making judicious contributions of money and service. People got to know her. Those who had known her liked her better than they had before.

The only thing she really did that season was to engineer the establishment of a lecture lyceum; the progressive church furnished the auditorium, and Mrs Hines the funds. A number of carefully selected human dynamos were brought to the town, and the local mind was greatly stirred. Before the next Autumn there had risen on that conveniently situated lot of Mrs Hines a building which she quietly announced was a memorial to her husband. It was called simply The Hines Building. Like other memorial buildings she had seen this contained many social conveniences.

The great airy basement was fitted with a swimming-pool and gymnasium; the roof had room for various games, and could be used as a tea-garden. There was an auditorium which could be used for sermon, lecture, mass meeting or theater, and the whole top floor was arranged for dancing or fairs and exhibitions, with a space reserved for the preparation and serving of refreshments.

There was the Hines Circulating Library, an excellent adjunct to the rather meager public one. A committee comprised of Mrs Hines, Charles Osgood, the progressive minister and the extremely progressive librarian they employed, selected the books. If the selection comprised a wide range of sociological works, both in science and fiction, at least no one need read them who did not wish to.

Club rooms, large and small, filled the remaining space.

'There!' said Mrs Hines, when it was done.

The place was opened by an invitation audience that filled the theater, addressed by a group of well-known ministers and philanthropists, followed by a reception in the big ball-room, with refreshments. Everybody went over the building from roof to basement, interested and admiring, and all those interested in social betterment held forth to congenial groups about the things they thought of preeminent importance to the world.

Then Mrs Hines opened accommodations, free, to the two leading philanthropic societies of the town, which offer was accepted promptly. She made the rent of her club rooms so reasonable that one after another the women's clubs grew to use them. 'It was so central,' they delightedly agreed. 'And they could have tea and things when they wanted them—very reasonable, too.'

The wealthy found that that big ballroom was a delightful place to give dances, high, cool, with the whole broad roof for strolling couples between dances. Men's clubs, as well as women's, began to engage rooms; girls' clubs and boys' clubs; classes of various descriptions; lectures, debates and private theatricals were held there.

The library was open evenings, all the evening, and many found it a pleasant place to rest and read, to meet friends, to change for the gymnasium, the dancing-room, the airy restaurant or the more airy roof, at will.

When that ball-room was not engaged by special patrons it was put to good use. Excellent dancing teachers were engaged, a man and wife, and good music furnished by a pianist more definite and regular than a pianola, and a muscular boy with a violin, who supported a widowed mother by that tireless right arm and those quick, strong fingers. Then they had classes, friendly groups of different ages, one which admitted no one under forty, and had more fun than the youngest class of children.

The rents were low, but the patronage was continuous. It was astonishing how popular the place became. There was a club or class-ticket which enabled any regular patron of the building to use the women's parlor upstairs, or the men's lounging room in the basement, and the number of those who took advantage of them was surprising.

The superintendent and his wife, who had a little apartment on the premises, proved both useful and popular, especially in keeping up the interest of the boys' and girls' clubs. Some initiative, some direction, is always valuable.

Boy Scouts and Camp-Fire Girls met there; a 'roque' court on the roof drew increasing memberships; classes in swimming and gymnastics followed one another swiftly. There are never enough places for water sports, and this pool was so big, so clean and fresh, and so enlivened with spring-boards, glistening chutes and all the machinery for clean, natural fun.

From the busy class-rooms, the earnest club-rooms, the gay ball-rooms, the quiet reading rooms, to the shrieks of laughter from the jolly crowds in the basement, the whole space teemed with happy, social life, natural and developing.

Before the year was out Mrs Hines had the pleasure of seeing that her memorial building was going to pay her ten per cent above all expenses, and besides a sinking fund which bade fair to replace her capital in ten years' time.

'Good!' said Mrs Hines. 'Jason wouldn't object to that anyway!'

BEE WISE

'IT's a queer name,' said the man reporter.

'No queerer than the other,' said the woman reporter. 'There are two of them, you know—Beewise and Herways.'

'It reminds me of something,' he said, 'some quotation—do you get it?'

'I think I do,' she said. 'But I won't tell. You have to consider for yourself.' And she laughed quietly. But his education did not supply the phrase.

They were sent down, both of them, from different papers, to write up a pair of growing towns in California which had been built up so swiftly and yet so quietly that it was only now after they were well established and prosperous that the world had discovered something strange about them.

This seems improbable enough in the land of most unbridled and well-spurred reporters, but so it was.

One town was a little seaport, a tiny sheltered nook, rather cut off by the coast hills from previous adoption. The other lay up beyond those hills, in a delightful valley all its own with two most precious streams in it that used to tumble in roaring white during the rainy season down their steep little canyons to the sea, and trickled there, unseen, the rest of the year.

The man reporter wrote up the story in his best descriptive vein, adding embellishments where they seemed desirable, with-holding such facts as appeared to contradict his treatment, and doing his best to cast over the whole a strong sex-interest and the glamor of vague suspicions.

The remarkable thing about the two towns was that their population consisted very largely of women and more largely of children, but there were men also, who seemed happy enough, and answered the questions of the reporters with good-will. They disclaimed, these men residents, anything peculiar or ultra-feminine in the settlements, and one hearty young English-man assured them that the disproportion was no greater than in

England. 'Or in some of our New England towns,' said another citizen, 'where the men have all gone west or to the big cities, and there's a whole township of withering women-folks with a few ministers and hired men.'

The woman reporter questioned more deeply perhaps, perhaps less offensively; at any rate she learned more than the other of the true nature of the sudden civic growth. After both of them had turned in their reports, after all the other papers had sent down representatives, and later magazine articles had been written with impressive pictures, after the accounts of permitted visitors and tourists had been given, there came to be a fuller knowledge than was possible at first, naturally, but no one got a clearer vision of it all than was given to the woman reporter that first day, when she discovered that the Mayor of Herways was an old college mate of hers.

The story was far better than the one she sent in, but she was a lady as well as a reporter, and respected confidence.

It appeared that the whole thing started in that college class, the year after the reporter had left it, being suddenly forced to drop education and take to earning a living. In the senior class was a group of girls of markedly different types, and yet so similar in their basic beliefs and ultimate purposes that they had grown through the four years of college life into a little 'sorority' of their own. They called it 'The Morning Club,' which sounded innocent enough, and kept it secret among themselves. They were girls of strong character, all of them, each with a definite purpose as to her life work.

There was the one they all called 'Mother,' because her whole heart and brain were dominated by the love of children, the thought of children, the wish to care for children; and very close to her was the 'Teacher,' with a third, the 'Nurse,' forming a group within a group. These three had endless discussions among themselves, with big vague plans for future usefulness.

Then there was the 'Minister,' the 'Doctor,' and the far-seeing one they called the 'Statesman.' One sturdy, square-browed little girl was dubbed 'Manager' for reasons frankly prominent, as with the 'Artist' and the 'Engineer.' There were some dozen or twenty of them, all choosing various professions, but all alike in their determination to practice those professions, married or single, and in their vivid hope for better methods of living. 'Advanced' in their ideas they were, even in an age of advancement, and held together in especial by the earnest words of the Minister, who was always urging upon them the power of solidarity.

Just before their graduation something happened. It happened to the Manager, and she called a special meeting to lay it before the club.

The Manager was a plain girl, strong and quiet. She was the one who always overflowed with plans and possessed the unusual faculty of carrying out the plans she made, a girl who had always looked forward to working hard for her own living of choice as well as necessity, and enjoyed the prospect.

'Girls!' said she, when they were all grouped and quiet. 'I've news for you—splendid news! I wouldn't spring it on you like this, but we shall be all broken and scattered in a little while—it's just in time!' She looked around at their eager faces, enjoying the sensation created.

'Say—look here!' she suddenly interjected. 'You aren't any of you engaged, are you?'

One hand was lifted, modestly.

'What does he *do?*' pursued the speaker. 'I don't care who he is, and I know he's all right or you wouldn't look at him—but what does he *do?*'

'He isn't sure yet,' meekly answered the Minister, 'but he's to be a manufacturer, I think.'

'No objection to your preaching, of course.' This was hardly a question.

'He says he'll hear me every Sunday—if I'll let him off at home on weekdays,' the Minister replied with a little giggle.

They all smiled approval.

'He's all right,' the Manager emphatically agreed. 'Now then girls—to put you out of your misery at once—what has happened to me is ten million dollars.'

There was a pause, and then a joyous clapping of hands.

'Bully for you!'

'Hurrah for Margery!'

'You deserve it!'

'Say, you'll treat, won't you?'

They were as pleased as if the huge and sudden fortune were common property.

'Long lost uncle—or what, Marge?'

'Great uncle—my grandmother's brother. Went to California with the 'forty-niners—got lost, for reasons of his own, I suspect. Found some prodigious gold mine—solid veins and nuggets, and spent quiet years in piling it up and investing it.'

'When did he die?' asked the Nurse softly.

He's not dead—but I'm afraid he soon will be,' answered the Manager slowly. 'It appears he's hired people to look up the family and see what they were like—said he didn't propose to ruin any feeble-minded people with all that money. He was pleased to like my record. Said—' she chuckled, 'said I was a man after his own heart! And he's come on here to get acquainted and to make this over before he's gone. He says no dead man's bequest would be as safe as a live man's gift.'

'And he's *given* you all that!'

'Solid and safe as can be. Says he's quite enough left to end his days in peace. He's pretty old . . . Now then, girls——' She was all animation. 'Here's my plan. Part of this property is land, land and water, in California. An upland valley, a little port on the coast—an economic base, you see—and capital to develop it. I propose that we form a combination, go out there, settle, build, manage—make a sample town—set a new example to the world—a place of woman's work and world-work too. . . . What do you say?'

They said nothing for the moment. This was a large proposition.

The Manager went on eagerly: 'I'm not binding you to anything; this is a plain business offer. What I propose to do is to develop that little port, open a few industries and so on, build a reservoir up above and regulate the water supply—use it for power—have great gardens and vineyards. Oh, girls—it's California! We can make a little Eden! And as to Motherhood—' she looked around with a slow, tender smile, 'there's no place better for babies!'

The Mother, the Nurse, and the Teacher all agreed to this.

'I've only got it roughly sketched out in my mind,' pursued the speaker eagerly. 'It will take time and care to work it all out right. But there's capital enough to tide us over first difficulties, and then it shall be just as solid and simple as any other place, a practical paying proposition, a perfectly natural little town, planned, built, and managed—' her voice grew solemn, 'by women—for women—and *children!* A place that will be of real help to humanity.—Oh girls, it's such a chance!'

That was the beginning.

The woman reporter was profoundly interested. 'I wish I could have stayed that year,' she said soberly.

'I wish you had, Jean! But never mind—you can stay now. We need the right kind of work on our little local paper—not just reporting—you can do more than that, can't you?'

'I should hope so!' Jean answered heartily. 'I spent six months on a little country paper—ran the whole thing nearly, except editorials and setting up. If there's room here for me I can tell you I'm coming—day before yesterday!' So the Woman Reporter came to Herways to work, and went up, o'nights, to Beewise to live, whereby she gradually learned in completeness what this bunch of women had done, and was able to prepare vivid little pamphlets of detailed explanations which paved the way for so many other regenerated towns.

And this is what they did:

The economic base was a large tract of land from the sea-coast hills back to the high rich valley beyond. Two spring-fed brooks ran from the opposite ends of the valley and fell steeply to the beach below through narrow cañyons.

The first cash outlay of the Manager, after starting the cable line from beach to hill which made the whole growth possible, was to build a reservoir at either end, one of which furnished drinking water and irrigation in the long summer, the other a swimming pool and a steady stream of power. The powerhouse in the cañon was supplemented by wind-mills on the heights and tide-mill on the beach, and among them they furnished light, heat, and power—clean, economical electric energy. Later they set up a solar engine which furnished additional force, to minimize labor and add to their producing capacity.

For supporting industries, to link them with the world, they had these: First a modest export of preserved fruits, exquisitely prepared, packed in the new fibre cartons which are more sanitary than tin and lighter than glass. In the hills they raised Angora goats, and from their wool supplied a little mill with high-grade down-soft yarn, and sent out fluffy blankets, flannels and knitted garments. Cotton too they raised, magnificent cotton, and silk of the best, and their own mill supplied their principal needs. Small mills, pretty and healthful, with bright-clad women singing at their looms for the short working hours. From these materials the designers and craftswomen, helped by the Artist, made garments, beautiful, comfortable, easy and lasting, and from year to year the demand for 'Beewise' gowns and coats increased.

In a windy corner, far from their homes, they set up a tannery, and from the well-prepared hides of their goats they made various leather goods, gloves and shoes,—'Beewise' shoes, that came to be known at last through the length and breadth of the land— a shoe that fitted the human foot, allowed for free action, and was pleasant to the eye. Many of the townspeople wore sandals and they were also made for merchandise.

Their wooded heights they treasured carefully. A forestry service was started, the whole area studied, and the best rate of planting and cutting established. Their gardens were rich and beautiful; they sold honey, and distilled perfumes.

'This place is to grow in value, not deteriorate,' said the Manager, and she planted for the future.

At first they made a tent city, the tents dyed with rich colors, dry-floored and warm. Later, the Artist and the Architect and the Engineer to the fore, they built houses of stone and wood and heavy sheathing paper, making their concrete of the dead palm leaves and the loose bark of swift-growing eucalyptus, which was planted everywhere and rose over night almost, like the Beanstalk—houses beautiful comfortable, sea-shell clean.

Steadily the Manager held forth to her associates on what she called 'the business end' of their enterprise. 'The whole thing must pay,' she said, 'else it cannot stand—it will not be imitated. We want to show what a bunch of women can do successfully. Men can help, but this time we will manage.'

Among their first enterprises was a guest house, planned and arranged mainly for women and children. In connection with this was a pleasure garden for all manner of games, gymnastics and dancing, with wide courts and fields and roofed places for use in the rainy season.

There was a sanitarium, where the Doctor and the Nurse gathered helpers about them, attended to casual illness, to the needs of child-birth, and to such visitors who came to them as needed care.

Further there was a baby-garden that grew to a kindergarten, and that to a school, and in time the fame of their educational work spread far and wide, and there was a constantly increasing list of applicants. For 'Beewise' was a Residence Club; no one could live there without being admitted by the others.

The beach town, Herways, teemed with industry. At the little pier their small coast steamer landed, bringing such supplies as they did not make, leaving and taking passengers. Where the beach was level and safe they bathed and swam, having a water-pavilion for shelter and refreshment. From beach to hill-top ran a shuttle service of light cars; 'Jacob's Ladder,' they called it.

The broad plan of the Manager was this: with her initial capital to develop a working plant that would then run itself at a profit, and she was surprised to find how soon that profit appeared, and how considerable it was.

Then came in sufficient numbers, friends, relatives, curious strangers. These women had no objection to marrying on their own terms. And when a man is sufficiently in love he sees no serious objection to living in an earthly paradise and doing his share in building up a new community. But the men were carefully selected. They must prove clean health—for a high grade of motherhood was the continuing ideal of the group.

Visitors came, increasing in numbers as accommodations increased. But as the accommodations, even to land for tenting must be applied for beforehand, there was no horde of gaping tourists to vulgarize the place.

As for the working people—there were no others. Everyone in Herways and Beewise worked, especially the women—that was the prime condition of admission; every citizen must be clean physically and morally as far as could be ascertained, but no amount of negative virtues availed them if they were not valuable in social service. So they had eager applications from professional women as fast as the place was known, and some they made room for—in proportion. Of doctors they could maintain but a few; a dentist or two, a handful of nurses, more teachers, several artists of the more practical sort who made beauty for the use of their neighbors, and a few far-reaching world servants, who might live here, at least part of the time, and send their work broadcast, such as poets, writers and composers.

But most of the people were the more immediately necessary workers, the men who built and dug and ran the engines, the women who spun and wove and worked among the flowers, or vice versa if they chose, and those who attended to the daily wants of the community.

There were no servants in the old sense. The dainty houses had no kitchens, only the small electric outfit where those who would might prepare coffee and the like. Food was prepared in clean wide laboratories, attended by a few skilled experts, highly paid, who knew their business, and great progress was made in the study of nutrition, and in the keeping of all the people well. Nevertheless the food cost less than if prepared by many unskilled, ill-paid cooks in imperfect kitchens.

The great art of child-culture grew apace among them with the best methods now known. Froebelian and Montessorian ideas and systems were honored and well used, and with the growing knowledge accumulated by years of observation and experience the right development of childhood at last became not merely an ideal, but a commonplace. Well-born children grew there like the roses they played among, raced and swam and swung, and knew only health, happiness and the joy of unconscious learning.

The two towns filled to their normal limits.

'Here we must stop,' said the Manager in twenty years' time. 'If we have more people here we shall develop the diseases of cities. But look at our financial standing—every cent laid out is now returned, the place is absolutely self-supporting and will grow richer as years pass. Now we'll swarm like the bees and start another—what do you say?'

And they did, beginning another rational paradise in another beautiful valley, safer and surer for the experience behind them.

But far wider than their own immediate increase was the spread of their ideas, of the proven truth of their idea, that a group of human beings could live together in such wise as to decrease the hours of labor, increase the value of the product, ensure health, peace and prosperity, and multiply human happiness beyond measure.

In every part of the world the thing was possible; wherever people could live at all they could live to better advantage. The economic base might vary widely, but wherever there were a few hundred women banded together their combined labor could produce wealth, and their combined motherhood ensure order, comfort, happiness, and the improvement of humanity.

'Go to the ant, thou sluggard, consider her ways and be wise.'

A COUNCIL OF WAR

THERE was an informal meeting of women in a London drawing room, a meeting not over large, between twenty and thirty, perhaps, but of a deadly earnestness. Picked women were these, true and tried, many wearing the broad arrow pin, that badge of shame now turned to honor by sheer heroism. Some would qualify this as 'blind' heroism or 'senseless' heroism. But then, heroes have never been distinguished by a cautious farsightedness or a canny common sense.

No one, not even a one-ideaed physician, could call these women hysterical or morbid. On the contrary they wore a look of calm, uncompromising determination, and were vigorous and healthy enough, save indeed those who had been in prison, and one rather weazened working woman from the north. Still, no one had ever criticized the appearance of the working women, or called them hysterical, as long as they merely worked.

They had been recounting the measures taken in the last seven years, with their results, and though there was no sign of weakening in any face, neither was there any lively hope.

'It is the only way,' said one, a slender pretty woman of over forty, who looked like a girl. 'We've just got to keep it up, that's all.'

'I'm willing enough,' said one who wore the arrow badge, speaking with slow determination. Her courage was proved, and her endurance. 'I'm *willing*—but we've got to be dead certain that it's really the best way.'

'It's the only way!'—protested Lady Horditch, a tall gentle earnest woman, with a pink face and quiet voice.

'They'll ruin us all—they're after the money now.' This from a woman who had none of her own.

'They'll simply kill our leaders—one after another.' One of the working women said that with a break in her voice. She could not lead, but she could follow—to the very end.

'One thing we have done, anyhow—we've forced their hand,'

suggested Mrs Shortham, a pleasant matronly woman who had been most happily married, the mother of a large and fine family, now all grown and established—'we've made the men say what they really think of us—what they've really thought all the time—only they hid it—owing to chivalry.'

'Another thing is that we've brought out the real men—the best ones—we know our friends from our enemies now,' said a clear eyed girl.

'It begins to look like war—in this country, at least,' Lady Horwich remarked.

Little Mrs Wedge suggested:

'It's a sort of strike, *I* think—begging your Ladyship's pardon. They're willing to have us—and use us—on their own terms. But we're on strike now—that's what we are! We're striking for shorter hours,'—she laughed a grim little laugh, intelligent smiles agreed with her, 'and for higher wages, and for' there was a catch in her breath as she looked around at them—'for the Union!'

'Ah!'—and a deep breath all around, a warm handclasp from Lady Horditch who sat next to her, 'Hear, Hear!' from several.

Miss Waltress, a sturdy attractive blonde woman of about thirty, well-known for her highly popular love stories, had been sitting quite silent so far, listening to every word. Now she lifted her head.

'When men began to strike they were in small groups—fiercely earnest, but small and therefore weak. They were frequently violent. They were usually beaten on legal grounds, because of their violence; they were supplemented by others who took their places, or they were starved out—because of their poverty. Why do they so frequently succeed now?'

She looked at Mrs Wedge from Lancashire, and Mrs Wedge looked back at her with a kindling eye.

'Because there's so many of 'em now—and they hang together so well, and they keep on the safe side of the law, *and* they've got the brass.'

Miss Walters nodded. 'Exactly,' said she. 'Now friends, I've got something to suggest to you, something very earnest. Mrs Shortham and I have been talking about it for days,—she has something to say first.'

'I think it comes with as good grace from me as from anybody,' that lady began quietly. 'All of you know how absolutely happy I was with one of the best men God ever made. That shows I'm not prejudiced. And it can't hurt his feelings, now. As to his "memory"—he put me up to most of this, and urged me to publish it—but I—I just *couldn't* while he was alive.'

Most of them had known Hugh Shortham, a tall deep-chested jovial man, always one of the most ardent advocates of the enlargement of women. His big manliness, his efficiency and success, had always made him a tower of strength against those who still talk of 'shorthaired women and long-haired men' as the sole supporters of this cause.

What Mrs Shortham now read was a brief but terrible indictment of what the title called 'The Human Error.' It recounted the evil results of male rule, as affecting the health, beauty, intelligence, prosperity, progress and happiness of humanity, in such clear and terrible terms, with such an accumulating pile of injuries, that faces grew white and lips set in hard steely lines as they listened.

'All this does not in the least militate against the beauty and use of true manhood in right relation to women, nor does it contradict the present superior development of men in all lines of social progress. It does, however, in some sort make out the case against man. There follows the natural corollary that we, the women of to-day, seeing these things, must with all speed possible set ourselves to remove this devastating error in relation, and to establish a free and conscious womanhood for the right service of the world.'

There was a hot silence, with little murmurs of horror at some of the charges she had made, and a stir of new determination. Not all of them, keen as they were for the ballot, deeply as they felt the unnecessary sorrows of women, had ever had the historic panorama of injustice and its deadly consequences so vividly set before them.

'I knew it was bad enough,' broke forth little Mrs Wedge, 'but I never knew it was as bad as *that*. Look at the consequences.'

'That's exactly it, Mrs Wedge! It's the consequences we are looking at. We are tired of these consequences. We want some

new ones!' and Miss Waltress looked around the room, from face
to face.

'I'm ready!' said a pale thin woman with an arrow pin.

They were, every one of them. Then Miss Waltress began.

'What I have to suggest, is a wider, deeper, longer, stronger
strike.'

Mrs Wedge, her eyes fixed on the calm earnest face, drew in
her breath with a big intake.

'Even if we get the ballot in a year—the work is only begun.
Men have had that weapon for a good while now, and they have
not accomplished everything—even for themselves. And if we
do not get it in a year—or five—or ten—are we to do nothing in
all that time save repeat what we have done before? I know the
ballot is the best weapon, but—there are others. There are
enough of us to keep up our previous tactics as long as we hold
it necessary. I say nothing whatever against it. But there are also
enough of us to be doing other things too.

'Here is my suggestion. We need a government within a government; an organization of women, growing and strengthening
against the time when it may come forward in full equality with
that of men; a training school for world politics. This may
become a world-group, holding international meetings and
influencing the largest issues. I speak here only of a definite,
practical beginning in this country.

'Let us form a committee, called, perhaps, "Advisory Committee on Special Measures," or simpler still, we might call
it "Extension Committee"—that tells nothing, and has no
limitations.

'The measures I propose are these:—

'That we begin a series of business undertakings, plain
ordinary, every day businesses—farms, market gardens, greenhouses, small fruits, preserves, confections, bakeries, eating-
houses, boarding and lodging houses, hotels, milliners and
dressmakers' shops, laundries, schools, kindergartens, nurser-
ies—any and every business which women can enter.

'Yes, I know that women are in these things now,—but they
are not united, not organized. This is a great spreading league
of interconnected businesses, with the economic advantages of
such large union.'

'Like a trust,' said Mrs Shortham. 'A woman's trust.'

'Or a Co-operative Society—or a Friendly,' breathed little Mrs Wedge, her cheeks flushing.

'Yes, all this and more. This is no haphazard solitary struggle of isolated women, competing with men, this is a body of women that can grow to an unlimited extent, and be stronger and richer as it grows. But it can begin as small as you please, and without any noise whatever.

'Now see here—you all know how women are sweated and exploited; how they overwork us and underpay us, and how they try to keep us out of trades and professions just as the Americans try to keep out Chinese labor—because they are afraid of being driven out of the market by a lower standard of living.

'Very well. Suppose we take them on their own terms. *Because* we can live on nothing a week and find ourselves—therefore we can cut the ground out from under their feet!'

The bitter intensity of her tones made a little shiver run around the circle, but they all shared her feeling.

'Don't imagine I mean to take over the business of the world—by no means. But I mean to initiate a movement which means on the surface, in immediate results, only some women going into business—that's no novelty! Underneath it means a great growing association with steady increase of power.'

'To what end—as a war measure, I mean?' Lady Horwich inquired.

'To several ends. The most patent, perhaps, is to accumulate the sinews of war. The next is to become owners of halls to speak in, of printing and publishing offices, of paper mills perhaps, of more and more of the necessary machinery needed for our campaign. The third is to train more and more women in economic organization, in the simple daily practice of modern business methods, and to guarantee to more and more of them that foundation stone of all other progress, economic independence. The fourth is to establish in all these businesses as we take them up, *right conditions*—proper hours, proper wages, everything as it should be.'

'Employing women, only?'

'As far as possible, Mrs Wedge. And when men are needed, employing the right kind.'

There was a thoughtful silence.

'It's an ENORMOUS undertaking,' murmured the Honorable Miss Erwood, a rather grim faced spinster of middle age. 'How can you get 'em to do it?'

Miss Waltress met her cheerfully.

'It is enormous, but natural. It does not require a million women to start at once you see; or any unusual undertaking. The advisory central committee will keep books and make plans. Each business, little or big, starts wherever it happens to be needed. The connection is not visible. That connection involves in the first place definite help and patronage in starting, or in increasing the custom of one already started; second, an advantage in buying—which will increase as the allied businesses increase; and then the paying to the central committee of a small annual fee. As the membership increases, all these advantages increase—in arithmetical progression.'

'Is the patronage in your plan confined to our society? or to sympathizers?' pursued Miss Erwood.

'By no means. The very essence of the scheme is to meet general demands to prove the advantage of clean, honest efficiency.

'Now, for instance—' Miss Waltress turned over a few notes she held in a neat package—'here is—let us say—the necktie trade. Now neckties are not laborious to make—as a matter of fact women do make them to-day. Neckties are not difficult to sell. As a matter of fact women frequently sell them. Silk itself was first made use of by a woman, and the whole silk industry might be largely in their hands. Designing, spinning, weaving, dyeing, we might do it all. But in the mere matters of making and selling the present day necktie of mankind, there is absolutely nothing to prevent our stretching out a slow soft hand, and gathering in the business. We might begin in the usual spectacular "feminine" way. A dainty shop in a good street, some fine girls, level-headed ones, who are working for the cause, to sell neckties, or—here is an advertising suggestion—we might call it "The Widows' Shop" and employ only widows. There are always enough of the poor things needing employment.

'Anyhow we establish a trade in neckties, fine neckties, good taste, excellent materials, reliable workmanship. When it is sufficiently prosperous, it branches—both in town and in the provinces—little by little we could build up such a reputation that "Widow Shop Neckties" would have a definite market value the world over. Meanwhile we could have our own workrooms, regular show places—patrons could see the neckties made, short hours, good wages, low prices.'

She was a little breathless, but very eager. 'Now I know you are asking how we are going to make all these things *pay*, for they must, if we are to succeed. You see, in ordinary business each one preys on the others. We propose to have an interconnected group that will help one another—that is where the profit comes. This was only a single instance, just one industry, but now I'll outline a group. Suppose we have a bit of land in some part of the country that is good for small fruit raising, and we study and develop that industry to its best. For the product we open a special shop in town, or at first, perhaps getting patronage by circularizing among our present membership, but winning our market by the goodness of the product and the reasonable price. Then we have a clean, pretty, scientific preserving room, and every bit of the unsold fruit is promptly turned into jam or jelly or syrup, right in sight of the patrons. They can see it done—and take it home, "hot" if they wish to, or mark the jars and have them sent. That would be a legitimate beginning of a business that has practically no limits—and if it isn't a woman's business, I don't know what is!

'Now this could get a big backing of steady orders from boarding houses and hotels managed by women, and gradually more and more of these would be run by our own members. Then we could begin to effect a combination with Summer lodgings—think what missionary work it would be to establish a perfect chain of Summer boarding houses which should be as near perfect as is humanly possible, and all play into one another's hands and into our small market garden local ventures.

'On such a chain of hotels we could found a growing laundry business. In connection with the service required, we could open an Employment Agency; in connection with that a Training School for Modern Employees—not "slaveys," to be "exploited" by the average household, but swift, accurate, efficient, self-respecting young women, unionized and working for our

own patrons. That would lead to club-houses for these girls—
and for other working girls; and step by step, as the circles
widened, we should command a market for our own produce
that would be a tremendous business asset.'

She paused, looking about her, eager and flushed. Mrs
Shortham took up the tale in her calm, sweet voice.

'You see how it opens,' she said. 'Beginning with simple
practical local affairs—a little laundry here, a little bakeshop
there; a fruit garden—honey, vegetables—what you like; with
dressmakers and milliners and the rest. It carries certain definite
advantages from the start; good conditions, wages, hours; and its
range of possible growth is quite beyond our calculations. And it
requires practically no capital. We have simply to plan, to create,
to arrange, and the pledged patronage of say a thousand women
of those now interested would mean backing enough to start any
modest business.'

'There are women among us who have money enough to make
several beginnings,' Lady Horwich suggested.

'There'll be no trouble about that—we have to be sure of the
working plan, that's all,' Miss Erwood agreed.

'There's a-plenty of us workers that could put it through—
with good will!' Mrs Wedge confidently asserted. 'We're doing
most of this work you speak of now, with cruel hours and a dog's
wages. This offers a job to a woman with everything better than
she had before—you'll have no trouble with the workers.'

'But how about the funds?—there might be a great deal of
money in time,' suggested Mrs Doughton-Highbridge. 'Who
would handle it?'

'There would have to be a financial committee of our very
best—names we all know and trust; and then the whole thing
should be kept open and above board, as far as possible.

'There should be certain small return benefits—that would
attract many; a steady increase in the business, and a "war
chest"—the reserve power to meet emergencies.'

'I don't quite see how it would help us to get the ballot,' one
earnest young listener now remarked, and quiet Mrs Shortham
answered out of a full heart.

'Oh, my dear! Don't you see? In the mere matter of funds and
membership it will help. In the very practical question of public

opinion it will help; success in a work of this sort carries conviction with it. It will help as an immense machine for propaganda—all the growing numbers of our employees and fellow-members, all these shops and their spreading patronage. It will help directly as soon as we can own some sort of hall to speak in, in all large towns, and our own publishing house and printing shop. And while we are waiting and working and fighting for the ballot, this would be improving life for more and more women all the time.'

'And it would carry the proof that the good things we want done are practical and *can* be done—it would promote all good legislation,' Miss Waltress added.

'I see; it's all a practical good thing from the start,' said Miss Erwood, rather argumentatively. 'To begin with, it's just plain good work. Furnishes employment and improves conditions. And from that up, there is no top to it—it's education and organization, widening good fellowship and increasing power—I'm for it definitely.'

'It would be a world within a world—ready to come out full-grown a woman's world, clean and kind and safe and service-able,' Lady Horwich murmured, as if to herself. 'Ladies, I move that a committee be appointed forthwith, consisting of Mrs Shortham, Mrs Wedge and Miss Waltress, with power to con-sult as widely as they see fit, and to report further as to this proposition at our next meeting.'

The motion was promptly seconded, as promptly carried, and the women looked at one another with the light of a new hope in their eyes.

FULFILMENT

Two women rocked slowly in the large splint chairs on a breezy corner of the hotel piazza. One sat as if she grew there, as if a rocking-chair were her natural habitat, as if she passed her life occupying rocking-chairs, merely eating and sleeping in the necessary intervals between one sitting and the next; as if, without a rocking-chair, she lacked explanation, missing it as a sailor his ship, or a cowboy his horse.

The other looked comfortable enough, and rocked appreciatively, but her air and her garments suggested other seats: desk-chairs, parlor-car chairs, and no chairs at all—long erect standing, brisk continued walking. There was about her even a subtle suggestion of one running easily, and this in spite of pleasant relaxation, such as one sees in the lines of a sleeping hound.

Mrs Edgar Maxwell, she of the soul affinity to rocking-chairs, was daintily engaged with some bright fancy work, a graceful wildrose wreath on a large linen centerpiece. Her white fingers were dexterously busy, but her eyes were placid pools of contentment.

Her sister, Irma Russell, did nothing. Her vigorous supple hands were quiet, though carrying their clear suggestion of active power, but her eyes were vividly alive.

They talked freely, with increasing intimacy, with a clear view of two long empty stretches of verandah, and neither of them thought that the closed slats of the long green-blinded window beside them concealed a conscienceless novelist. They did not know he was in the hotel, as indeed he intended no one should. He was only waiting over a day to meet a friend, and carefully avoiding the crowds of female admirers, toward whom decent courtesy and business principles compelled some politeness when unescapable.

The term 'conscienceless' is perhaps too severe to describe him; he had an artistic conscience, deep, broad, accurate, relentless, but refused to be bound by the standards of most people.

Mrs Maxwell held her work off from her approving eyes, and drew a happy little sigh of admiration. Her glance dwelt briefly on the green slopes and blue heights about them, then long and tenderly on her boy and girl, playing tennis with the other young folks in the near distance.

'Oh, Irma!' she said. 'If only you were as happy as I am!'

'How do you know I'm not. You haven't seen me for twenty years, you know. Do I look unhappy?'

'Oh, no! I think you look wonderfully well, and you have certainly done well out there.'

'Out there' was California. It seemed the end of the earth to Mrs Maxwell.

Irma smiled. 'You are a dear girl—you always were, Elsie. It's a treat to see you. We haven't had a chance at a good talk for all this while—about half our lives. Pitch in now—tell me about your happiness.'

Elsie laid down her work for a moment and looked lovingly at her sister.

'You always were—different,' she said. 'I remember just as well how we used to talk—just girls! And now we're both forty and over—and here we are together again! But I've nothing to tell—that you don't know.'

'I know the facts, of course,' her sister agreed. 'You wrote me of your engagement, sent wedding cards and baby-cards, and all—and photographs of everybody. But you never were much of a letter-writer—you always did talk better than you wrote, Elsie. What I want you to talk about is first your happiness—and, second, your superiority.'

'My superiority! Why, Irma! What do you mean?'

'Just a little air of "Poor Irma" I detect about you—that's all. I'm perfectly well; I'm doing nicely with my prunes and apricots; I want to know why you think you're happier than I am.'

Elsie met the affectionate quizzical gray eyes with the peaceful conviction of her own soft blue ones. 'You certainly know that, Irma. You've seen Hugh—and the children.'

'Yes, I've seen Hugh and the children—they are dears—I cheerfully agree to that. But what I want is the story of your life.

Come—I've been a day at your house and here a week, getting acquainted all over again—and this is the first clear safe quiet time we've had together. You're just as sweet as ever, and I love to see you so contented—you haven't changed a bit, for all your "Hugh and the children."'

'There isn't anything to tell, Irma, but what you know. Hugh came the year you left. It helped me not to miss you so cruelly. We couldn't marry for some time—he had to save, and I waited. But I was glad to—I'd have waited till now for Hugh. . . . Then we had to struggle along for a good while—you knew that, too, and often helped, bless you! The children came pretty soon—and then we lost little Bobby . . . and the dear baby that never even lived to be named.' The blue eyes filled, but she looked at the gay young tennis players again and turned bravely back to her sister. 'There was waiting, and work, and going without—there always has been a lot of planning and some sacrifices, of course. But there has been love, always, and the blessed children . . . even the grief—we had *together*. . . . It is life, Irma, it is living—and if I seem to say, "Poor Irma!"—which I deny, it is only on that account. A woman who hasn't married, who isn't a mother—I don't care how successful she is—she hasn't *lived*.'

'I see,' said Irma, somewhat drily. 'I thought as much. I wanted you to say it, that's all. And now will you answer me a few questions. How do you spend your time?'

'My time?' Elsie looked at her perplexedly. 'Spend my time? Why, as any woman does.'

'Yes, but specify, please—what do you *do*? Hour by hour—what does your day mean to you?'

The conscienceless novelist behind the green slats had been half dozing on the little hard sofa in the corner, and carrying on a half-hearted skirmish with the rudiments of ordinary people's principles. Now he trampled on those principles, kicked them out entirely, drew forth a worn little note-book, and devoted himself with whole-hearted enthusiasm to the business of listening. 'Invaluable material!' he murmured inaudibly.

'I don't know as I ever thought of it that way,' Elsie said slowly.

'Well—think of it that way now,' her sister urged. 'You get up at—shall we say seven? What do you do—with brain and hand and heart, all day?'

'I—why, I keep house. You know!' protested Elsie.

'Do you make the fire? Get breakfast? Wash and iron?'

'No indeed—of course not. That was one reason Hugh waited. He said his wife was not to be his servant,' quoted Mrs Maxwell proudly.

'I see. Well—what *do* you do?'

'Why—when the children were little there was more to do than there is now—of course, night and day too.'

'You had no nurse?'

'No—we couldn't afford that. Besides, I preferred to care for my children myself—it is a mother's sacred duty, I think. And a pleasure,' she added carefully.

Irma looked at her sister with tender sympathy. She loved her far too much to suggest that for this sacred duty she had never prepared herself by either study or practice, and that in performance of it she had lost fifty per cent. of her children. That would have been cruel—and useless.

'We'll skip the babies, Elsie. Your youngest is fifteen. You haven't had to spend many hours a day on them for ten years or so, now have you? Come—what do you *do* with your time? Twenty-four hours a day; eight out for sleep, one for toilet activities, two for three meals—that leaves thirteen. What do you do for a day's work in thirteen hours?'

'Oh, I'm sure it's not that!' protested Elsie. 'It can't be!'

'Irma produced pencil and paper. 'What time do you get up—seven?'

'Ye—es——' agreed her sister, rather faintly.

'Seven-thirty,' wrote Irma. 'Breakfast at eight?'

'Yes.'

'An hour to eat it?'

'Oh, no—half an hour—the children have to get off—and Hugh. We're always through by eight-thirty.'

'What time is lunch?'

'One o'clock—that doesn't take long either—the children have to hurry—say half an hour.'

'And dinner?'

'Dinner's at seven—Hugh is so often late. I'd like it at six-thirty—on account of the cook—but it's seven.'

'Well, now, my dear sister. I'll give you your evening to play in; but you have from eight-thirty to one, and one-thirty to seven to account for—ten hours. A good working day—what do you do with it?'

'Ten hours!' Elsie would not admit it.

'Ten hours—your own figures. I'll give you another half-hour after breakfast, and after lunch—just to dawdle, read the paper, and so on, but that leaves nine. Now then, Elsie—speak up!'

Elsie spoke up, a little warmly.

'You can't measure housekeeping that way—by hours. Sometimes it's one thing and sometimes another. There is always something to do—always! And then there's one thing you forget—people coming in—and my going out.'

'Exercise—we'll allow an hour for exercise—you don't walk more than an hour a day, do you, sister?'

'I don't mean just walking—one hasn't time to walk much. I mean calling—and shopping.'

'And you haven't any idea how many hours a day—or a week—you call—or shop?'

'No, I haven't. I tell you it's impossible to figure it out that way. And then when the children come home I have to *be there*.' She grasped a thought, and lifted her head rather defiantly. 'That's what housekeeping *is*,' she said proudly. 'It's being there!'

'I see,' said Irma, and wrote it down. (So did the novelist.) 'I'll stop quizzing you as to hours, child—it's evident you never made a time-schedule in your life—much less kept one. Did you ever make a budget? Do you know, as a matter of fact, if your housekeeping is more or less efficient, more or less expensive, than your neighbors?'

Elsie drew herself up, a little hurt. 'I am sure nobody could be more economical than I am. Hugh always says I am such a good manager. I often make my house-dresses myself, and Betty's; and I watch the sales——'

'But you don't know—nor Hugh—anything definite about it? Comparing with other families of the same size—on a similar amount?'

'I'd like to know what you're driving at, Irma. No—we neither of us has made any such calculation. No two families are alike. Each one is a law to itself—has to be. If I am satisfied—and Hugh is—whose business is it besides?'

'Not mine,' agreed Irma cheerfully. 'Excuse me, dear, if I've offended you. I wanted to get at the real working of your life if I could, to compare with mine. Let's take a new tack. Tell me— have you kept up your physical culture?'

'I have not,' said Elsie, a little sharply. 'Motherhood interferes with gymnastics.'

'Are you as strong and active as you used to be?'

'I am not,' still a little sharply. 'You don't seem to understand, Irma—I suppose you can't, not being a mother—that if you have children you can't have everything else.'

'Have you kept up your music? Or your languages?'

'No—for the same reason.'

'Have you learned anything new? Now, Elsie, don't be angry—what I'm getting at is this: You have spent twenty years in one way, I in another. You have certain visible possessions and joys which I have not. You have also had experiences—griefs— cares—which I have not. I'm just trying to see if besides these you have other gains, or if these are the only gains to offset what I may show.'

'I'm not angry with you, Irma—how could I be? You are my only sister, and you've always been good to me. I'll make you all the concessions you wish. Marriage is a mutual compromise, dear. A man gives up his freedom and a woman gives up hers. They have their love—their home—their children. But nobody can have everything.'

'That's a fact—I'll grant you that, Elsie. But tell me one more thing—what do you look forward to?'

'I don't look forward,' protested Elsie stoutly. 'I don't believe in it. "Sufficient unto the day——"'

'"Is the evil thereof"?' asked Irma. 'Please do look forward. You are forty-two. You'll live, I hope, to be twice that. What do you expect to accomplish in the next forty years?' There was a deeper note in her voice.

Elsie dropped her work and looked at her, a little shaken.

'As long as you have lived before—and no preliminary child-hood to wade through! From now on, full grown, experienced, with your home, your happiness, your motherhood achieved; with your housekeeping surely no great burden by this time. With no more children coming and these two fairly grown—

they'll be off your hands entirely soon—college—business—marriage. Then you won't have to "be there" so much, will you? What are you going to do—with forty years of life?'

'I may not live——' suggested Elsie, rather as if it were an agreeable alternative.

'And you may. We're a long-lived lot, all of us. And you know motherhood really adds to the chances of longevity—if you don't die at it. I'll excuse you from the last ten though; after seventy you can rock all the time. Call it thirty years, ten hours a day—or nine—or eight—why Elsie—don't you even *want* to do anything?'

Elsie gave a little nervous laugh. 'I feel like quoting from *Potash and Perlmutter*,' she said, ' "Whadda y' mean do anything?" Come, you leave off questioning me and let's hear all the fine things you've been doing—you never would write about yourself.'

Irma rose and walked softly, smoothly, up and down the piazza, watched with slanting eagerness by the eyes behind the slats. She came back and stood near her sister, leaning against the railing.

'All right—I'll make up for it now. And in the first place, Elsie, I don't want you to think I minimize your happiness—it is a great big splendid slice of life that you've had and I haven't. I'm sorry I've missed it—I'd like to have had that too. Well—here's my record:

'I went to California as you know at twenty-one. Sort of governess-companion. All of our people protested—but I *was* twenty-one—they couldn't stop me. I went because I wanted to grow—and I have grown. I studied the place, the people, the opportunities. I kept at work, saved my salary, added to my capacities. Took that chance to go to Europe with the Cheeseboro kids—saw a lot—learned a lot—got three languages, a world of experience—and a good bit of money. That was at twenty-four.

'Came back to the coast and invested my money in a small private school business.'

'You gave me some of it, you dear thing,' Elsie interrupted, affectionately.

'Oh, well—that was natural. I had enough left to start. I did well with the school, and set up a sort of boarding-school—a health-and-educational stunt, up in the foot-hills. Bought land up there—a fine breezy mesa it is, with an artesian well of its own.

'I worked—but it's work I love. Built on, enlarged my staff, cautiously. Added a sort of winter camp for adults—not invalids. By the time I was thirty I had quite a place up there, a lovely home of my own all by itself on a sort of promontory—with such a garden! O Elsie—you're coming out to see me some day—all of you!

'Then I went very cautiously, used my accumulating experience, invested wisely and slowly. Things move rather quickly out there, but common sense keeps on being useful. As to money I'm very comfortable indeed, and may be rich—rich enough. All sweet, safe, honestly-earned money—my own.

'But that's the least of it. What I'm gladdest of is the *living*. The kind of work I've done has helped people—lots of people— especially children. I've been a sort of foster-mother to hundreds of them, you see, some fifteen years, averaging twenty new ones a year—that's three hundred, besides those in the first five beginning years.

'Also—I adopted some.'

Elsie started. 'And never said a word about it!'

'No—I wanted to see how it would turn out. But I've got four I call my own—took 'em as babies, you know. They're a splendid lot. Two about the age of Tom and Betty—two younger—I'll show you their pictures presently.

'Personally, physically, I mean, I'm a hundred per cent. stronger and more efficient than I used to be. I've trained—years and years of it—in sunlight and mountain air. It's not just strength, but skill. I can climb mountains, ride, shoot, fence, row, swim, play golf, tennis, billiards, dance like a youngster—or a professional. I'm more *alive*, literally, than I was at twenty. I have a good car and can run it as well as the man.

'Then I know more—I've had plenty of time to study. The town is only a half-hour run—the city about an hour.

'I belong to clubs, classes, societies. I'm a citizen, too—I can vote now. I begin to have ambitions of *bigger* service by and by—widening and deepening as I get older. I have plans for when I'm fifty—sixty—seventy.

'As to prunes and apricots—they are growing well—pay well, too. I have a little cannery of my own—and a little settlement of working people near it, and a *crêche* there for the women to tuck the babies in while they work—a jewel of a *crêche*, mind you. And I'm promoting all manner of industries among the women. I've got plans—oh, I couldn't begin to tell you of my plans——!'

'You never did,' said Elsie slowly. 'I—I never dreamed you had spread out so. How splendid of you, Irma!'

'It isn't what I've done that keeps me so happy,' mused her sister. 'It's the things I'm going to do! The widening horizon! Every year I feel stronger, braver, see things more clearly. Life is so—glorious!

'You see, Elsie dear, I have had the babies to love and care for, even if not mine born—they were babies—and I do love them. I have a home, too, a lovely one, with comfort and beauty and peace—and space, too. The one thing I haven't got is the husband—there you are ahead. But I'm not wearing the willow, sister. Life is big enough to bring endless happiness, even without that. Don't you ever show me that "Poor Irma!" look again—now, will you?'

'No——' said Elsie, sitting very quiet, 'I never will.'

There was a hop at the Hotel that night.

Elsie sat among the matrons, watching her son and daughter frisk with the young people.

Irma, dressed to quiet perfection, danced; danced so well that girls, half her age, were envious of her partners.

'What a woman!' said the unprincipled novelist to himself before he danced with her.

'Which is the quickest route to Southern California?' he inquired, after he had danced with her.

A PARTNERSHIP

AFTER the Baby was married—not a real baby, of course, but a girl of twenty-two who could never persuade her parents to call her anything but 'Baby'—Mrs Haven fell to cleaning house.

She set her teeth, put clamps on her heart, and cleaned house from garret to cellar, inclusive. It was so much bigger than it had ever been before, that house. When they moved in, after quite outgrowing their first one, there had been six of them, and a cook and a second girl and a nurse-maid besides. Sometimes there was a trained nurse also, in serious illness. Sometimes there were guests. As the children grew bigger and enjoyed the big house and big yard as children should, they seemed to multiply by some infantile magic into forty children at once—they and their young friends.

Mrs Haven had so completely given her life to her children after the fashion of conscientious American mothers (who can afford it) that she had never once thought of them as an essentially transient possession.

They had liberally appropriated the life she gave them, had grown up as children will, and were now most undeniably gone—all of them. Both boys in business in other cities; both girls married, in other cities, and Othello's occupation gone—clean gone. Also, as she began to find with a pressing sense of loss—her topics of conversation were gone.

She had always held the pleasant theory that marriage was a partnership. Of course it is, in parentage; and she had done her part, her royal share of love and care and service, as faithfully as Mr Haven had paid the bills. But now, as parents, the partnership was closed out. They were has-beens. They could, it is true, read the letters of their absent young people, and discuss their hopes and chances as far as these were confided to them. But talking over occasional letters is not a sufficiently engrossing occupation for really active parents.

After the big house was antiseptically perfect, and four new 'spare rooms' left coldly inviting besides the old one, and the nurse's room, and the nursery itself, Mrs Haven felt a little vacant. She turned to the subject of sewing then, being a busy practical woman. Everything in the line of clothing was put in order, old things cleared out and sent to the proper charities, Mr Haven's wardrobe wisely scrutinized, her own made perfect— that took some time and was fairly interesting while it lasted.

But a vigorous able energetic woman of forty-nine cannot fill all her time with the clothing of her household, especially when her household is reduced to two.

She had been trying not to face it—the *vacancy*. But it kept gaining on her, rising like a tide, and finally it swept her quite off her feet, and she felt as one swimming in a calm gray horizonless sea.

'Gerald!' she burst out one evening, 'how do you *stand* it?'

'Stand what?' he naturally inquired, lowering his newspaper.

'Having them all gone!' she burst out. 'All of them— everything!'

'You are not gone, Margie,' he said affectionately, coming around to kiss her.

She clung to him. 'I don't mean it that way, darling,' she urged remorsefully. 'But things to *do*—you are just my*self*, Gerry, you are not an occupation.'

'Why, there's just as much to do as there ever was, isn't there? I haven't noticed that working hours are any shorter.'

She looked at him, lovingly, but realizing as she never had before the difference in their position. Their partnership in parentage was at an end, but his business went right on. His real partner, Mr Edgers, was a bachelor, yet he had done his half of their common work all these years. They went right on—that partnership—where was hers?

She was sitting by him now, holding his hand as if she was afraid he would go too. He laid the paper down and turned to her definitely, tenderly.

'What is it, Pussy?' he asked. 'Is there something you want? You shall have it.'

'No.' She shook her head slowly. 'There's nothing I want— that I know of. Of course I wouldn't have them back—of all things I wouldn't have had the girls not marry—they all have to go, of course. And I've got you—I can't be unhappy, really—while I have you, dearest. But—what am I to *do?*'

'I don't understand, Margie. Here's the house—as big as it always was. Isn't that—an interest?'

'Why, yes, it's something. But that never was the main interest—I can't begin to mother a house at my age. Besides Agnes and Ellen manage it all right now—it runs on wheels. It's not an occupation for me.'

'Haven't you your friends, and clothes and things? Don't they fill up?'

'Why, yes—and so have you, Gerry. But that's not your *business*. You have your business—mine's gone!'

Mr Haven frowned a little. He was very fond of his wife, and of his home. He had been an excellent father, not only holding up the entire household by his efficient labors outside, but really helping her in her more intimate parental problems.

He missed his children, too, but had merely plunged more actively into the affairs of his office, affairs which opened endlessly before him. And he was extremely conservative.

So far he had never thought of his wife as differing from him in his views. He thought 'woman's place was the home,' and so, apparently, had she. She had always stayed in it, had been continuously busy in it, and apparently happy in it. She still had that home. She still had him. This was only a temporary fit of depression. He must cheer her up.

'I don't see that we can help it, Margie. As you say, you wouldn't have them back. It's the order of nature. I guess all women feel so at first—but they have to get used to it.'

He petted her, drew her close to him.

She was silent for a little, but his words called up a dreary vision. She remembered her own mother, what her life had been, of how little she had ever thought about it, being so immersed in her own. She recalled other elderly women, growing grayer and grayer, slowly fading out, as they 'got used to it.' She thought of the row on the hotel piazzas—middle-aged, elderly, old; rocking, doing fancy work, gossiping,—they were used to it. That gray endless ocean had other women in it, millions of them; some bobbing idly like loose corks, some surrounded by little trays of playthings like the patrons of some German *bad*; some slowly drowning———. She gave a little shiver.

'You must have interests, of course, my dear, and you'll find them—you'll find them.'

He thought of it after he went to bed, thought of it at intervals during the next day, and determined to 'give her a change.' His business was arranged to go on in the hands of Mr Edgers, and they went off for a long foreign tour, together.

That was a very pleasant experience. It did them both good, and it helped Mrs Haven to a more settled frame of mind, a sounder health.

When they returned he plunged with renewed vigor and keen zest into his affairs, and she plunged into that gray ocean. . . .

Then she was asked to address the Women's Central Club, to tell them about her travels, and with some enthusiasm she took up 'club work.' He was pleased to see her returning cheerfulness, to have her chatting gaily across their small bright table of more vital subjects than of old; and, as far as he thought of her problems at all, considered them settled.

They were not settled. The more Mrs Haven used her mind the more mind she had to use. That trip abroad had given her new angles of vision. The people she had met on the steamer, in hotels and trains; the books she was now reading in connection with club papers; the lectures and discussions she heard; all these furnished a stimulus which resulted in growth, surprising growth.

It surprised her, because, in her thought of the lives of women she had always stopped short as most people do, with the mother period. Never until she came to it had she actively realized that life went right on, after motherhood was accomplished.

There was a paper read at one of the State Federation meetings she attended, on 'Ex-Mothers,' which she found arresting indeed. The speaker, a woman some considered dangerously 'advanced,' showed how in the maternal scheme of nature mothers frequently died in the act, as it were—just laid eggs and departed. That in our own early savage period the risks and labors of maternity, with the added toil required of women so shortened their lives that they hardly survived the maternal period. Of them it might be said: 'I lived and bore; and though I died, so that I lived to bear, my daughter lived and bore.' She showed in later civilization women survived the mother period, but sunk their remaining years in the endless work and care of large families without 'modern improvements,' and that it was only to-day, when wealth was larger, families smaller, and education more general, that a new functionary was appearing on the scene—the Ex-Mother.

The paper went on to suggest, what certainly Mrs Haven had never thought of before, that this opened to women a new vista of life, clear human life, in which they were quite free to take up any human function, having fulfilled the feminine.

In two years' time Margaret Haven came to a vital decision. She valued her husband's love, she would on no account neglect his comfort, but she began to feel sure that he had no right to limit her activities during the hours he was away from her by what she now saw to be mere prejudices.

Discussion was rather difficult. She tried her patient best to persuade him to give his consent to her undertaking some business of her own, but he was immovable.

'It's perfect nonsense, Margie,' he insisted. 'Business! What do you want of a business? Don't I earn money enough? Don't I give you money enough? It's absurd—utterly absurd!'

She tried to convince him that it was not for the money, but for the sake of the work—a point of view he was utterly unable to grasp. He could not see why she should not be content to 'improve her mind' eternally.

'Would you want to go to school all your life?' she asked him. 'What is the use of improving my mind if I never *use* it. I tell you, Gerald, I am an able-bodied woman of fifty-one—and I'm going to work.'

Finally he dismissed the subject rather snappily.

'You may do what you please, of course. I can't prevent you— it is a little late to begin to interfere with you now, my dear. Do what you like—but don't expect me to enjoy it. Fortunately I'm doing well enough and people know it—they won't think you are helping me, at any rate.'

She sighed. It would have been ever so much pleasanter if Gerald had been with her in her new hopes—but she could not give them up; she could not settle down to spend twenty or thirty years in 'getting used to it,' even to please him.

They lived in a Middle Western city in a famous wheat district; busy, prosperous, progressive, but undeveloped in many lines. Mr Haven was a dealer in flour, one of many; and so far as his wife knew anything of business, she knew this. Her main interest in the flour had always been lodged in bread—in the last step between the producer and consumer, and when they were 'changing girls' in her young, less experienced days, she had often heard Gerald complain that such first-class flour should go to make such fourth-class food.

The flour of their city was its pride, but the only city that was proud of its bread—as far as she knew, was Vienna.

Spurred by her husband's criticisms, she had long ago perfected herself in the not too abstruse art of bread-making, and took great pride in her 'homemade' rolls, her white and graham and whole-wheat loaves.

In Europe she had been struck with the excellence of the 'baker's bread'—a commodity her mother had taught her to despise; and in discussion with foreign critics had learned to her incredulous mortification that her own country had a very low national standard in breadmaking.

Slowly there had grown in her mind a determination to do something to lift that standard.

'The lady is the loaf-giver, they are always telling us. We ought to give better loaves then. If the man can't we must.'

That is why Mrs Gerald Haven went into the baking business.

She called it 'New Home' bread, and began very simply, paying her excellent cook an extra price for extra work, and selling through the woman's exchange. The orders increased, and she hired an earnest young Norwegian woman to learn in her own kitchen, training her herself as she had the cook.

This was quiet and made no trouble. Mr Haven felt no difference in the domestic regime except heavier fuel bills, which he refused to let her pay—so she put the money in the bank. Her clientele grew and grew, and the boy who came to the back gate with the handcart protested that he needed a horse.

Good bread, like good wine, needs no push and the second year she started a little shop, adding her own especial gingerbread, the 'hot water' gingerbread, smooth, sweet, dark, and as porous as a sponge. Also her own sponge cake, real sponge cake that, soaring aloft on unaided eggs.

This grew, too, to the busy manager's delight and pride; grew quite naturally and safely, on the advertisement that follows the pleased customer.

Almost any woman is glad to avoid the baking if she is sure of getting as good and as reliable products outside; and the New Home Bakery furnished better goods than most of its patrons were able to make.

To Mrs Haven it was a growing joy. Her wide circle of friends approved of the product if they did not approve of the principle and after all, their patronage was worth more than their approval.

She gave a paper at the club, on 'Bread-making, Domestic and Foreign,' which was warmly received. As one of the committee on schools, she addressed the cooking classes of eager young people.

Her supply of 'yesterday's bread' to the Working Girls' Club House was a substantial help to that struggling institution, and the girls said the New Home 'yesterday's' was better than anyone else's to-morrow's.

Meanwhile there was a widening range of study to be kept up. It was perhaps the happiest part of Mrs Haven's work to feel the wonderful sense of *youth* that came with it. Youth is a beginning; it is full of 'first times,' and enjoys them. To her great surprise she found that this new enterprise roused a vivid, eager joy she had not thought ever to feel again, the joy of beginning.

A Social Service lecturer spoke in the town on labor conditions, and disclosed the revolting circumstances in which so much of the baker's bread is made. She was stirred to the depths by this revelation and her ambition took new shape.

With the profits of three years' work and the base of a steadily widening patronage she opened a Model Bakery. She remembered a sign she had seen over a little London dairy: 'The Inspection of the Public is Invited,' and invited it here.

As she must have a delivery wagon in any case she found it cheaper to supply her little shop from a distance than to pay heavy downtown rent for the working place; and placed her bakery farther out, a trim comfortable little building, coolly situated in its own garden, adding to the fresh odors of flower and tree its own tempting bouquet of fragrance. Clean comfortable women worked for reasonable hours, and rested under the trees in their leisure moments.

One girl was detailed to take visitors through the place, and the exquisite shining cleanliness, the glass and marble and nickel fittings, the big gas ovens, only heated for the actual hours of baking, the white-capped, white-uniformed workers, all had their effect on the purchasers.

One of the pleasantest results was an emulous improvement in other bakeries. That kind of competition is indeed 'the life of trade.' Everywhere in the town the standard of bread and of bread-making was raised by this woman's honest work, and her happy pride rose with it.

She did not fade and wither and 'get used to it.' She grew, grew wiser, abler, more efficient, more interested yearly. She was asked far and wide to give 'Bread Talks' to schools and clubs.

Her husband—who most sincerely loved her—grew proud of her in spite of himself. After all if breadmaking was not a woman's business, what was?

In the end there came to him an unexpected misfortune. Mr Edgers suddenly departed with the entire available funds of their business, at a time when it meant ruin.

'Gerald,' said his wife. 'Oh, my dear! Don't look like that, dear! What if he has! Let the poor wretch go and forget it. You're young enough yet to go ahead and do better than ever. And in the meantime I wish you'd help me out. My work is getting quite beyond my managing ability—I wish you'd take hold and straighten it out for me.'

He consented to look at her papers—and was surprised; pleased in spite of himself. A large and growing trade, a demand from neighboring towns, a branch already started in one, and in the city, three—there was need for careful management.

He gave her the help of his experience, his larger business grip; she joyfully shifted the 'money end' as she called it, on to his shoulders, and went on developing the 'bread end.'

In a few more years they formed a Baking Company of solid importance and assured success.

Then one day, as they sat together in the evening, discussing some little difficulty in one of the shops, rejoicing in their growing prosperity, she suddenly came around the table and ran into his arms.

'Oh, Gerry! Gerry!' she cried. 'I'm such a happy woman! We *are* partners now, for keeps!'

IF I WERE A MAN

THAT was what pretty little Mollie Mathewson always said when Gerald would not do what she wanted him to—which was seldom.

That was what she said this bright morning, with a stamp of her little high-heeled slipper, just because he had made a fuss about that bill, the long one with the 'account rendered,' which she had forgotten to give him the first time and been afraid to the second—and now he had taken it from the postman himself.

Mollie was 'true to type.' She was a beautiful instance of what is reverentially called 'a true woman.' Little, of course—no true woman may be big. Pretty, of course—no true woman could possibly be plain. Whimsical, capricious, charming, changeable, devoted to pretty clothes and always 'wearing them well,' as the esoteric phrase has it. (This does not refer to the clothes—they do not wear well in the least; but to some special grace of putting them on and carrying them about, granted to but few, it appears.)

She was also a loving wife and a devoted mother; possessed of 'the social gift' and the love of 'society' that goes with it, and, with all these was fond and proud of her home and managed it as capably as—well, as most women do.

If ever there was a true woman it was Mollie Mathewson, yet she was wishing heart and soul she was a man.

And all of a sudden she was!

She was Gerald, walking down the path so erect and square-shouldered, in a hurry for his morning train, as usual, and, it must be confessed, in something of a temper.

Her own words were ringing in her ears—not only the 'last word,' but several that had gone before, and she was holding her lips tight shut, not to say something she would be sorry for. But instead of acquiescence in the position taken by that angry little figure on the veranda, what she felt was a sort of superior pride,

Physical Culture (July 1914), 31–4.

a sympathy as with weakness, a feeling that 'I must be gentle with her,' in spite of the temper.

A man! Really a man; with only enough subconscious memory of herself remaining to make her recognize the differences.

At first there was a funny sense of size and weight and extra thickness, the feet and hands seemed strangely large, and her long, straight, free legs swung forward at a gait that made her feel as if on stilts.

This presently passed, and in its place, growing all day, wherever she went, came a new and delightful feeling of being *the right size*.

Everything fitted now. Her back snugly against the seat-back, her feet comfortably on the floor. Her feet? . . . His feet! She studied them carefully. Never before, since her early school days, had she felt such freedom and comfort as to feet—they were firm and solid on the ground when she walked; quick, springy, safe—as when, moved by an unrecognizable impulse, she had run after, caught, and swung aboard the car.

Another impulse fished in a convenient pocket for change—instantly, automatically, bringing forth a nickel for the conductor and a penny for the newsboy.

These pockets came as a revelation. Of course she had known they were there, had counted them, made fun of them, mended them, even envied them; but she never had dreamed of how it *felt* to have pockets.

Behind her newspaper she let her consciousness, that odd mingled consciousness, rove from pocket to pocket, realizing the armored assurance of having all those things at hand, instantly get-at-able, ready to meet emergencies. The cigar case gave her a warm feeling of comfort—it was full; the firmly held fountain-pen, safe unless she stood on her head; the keys, pencils, letters, documents, notebook, checkbook, bill folder—all at once, with a deep rushing sense of power and pride, she felt what she had never felt before in all her life—the possession of money, of her own earned money—hers to give or to withhold; not to beg for, tease for, wheedle for—hers.

That bill—why if it had come to her—to him, that is, he would have paid it as a matter of course, and never mentioned it—to her.

Then, being he, sitting there so easily and firmly with his money in his pockets, she wakened to his life-long consciousness about money. Boyhood—its desires and dreams, ambitions. Young manhood—working tremendously for the wherewithal to make a home—for her. The present years with all their net of cares and hopes and dangers; the present moment, when he needed every cent for special plans of great importance, and this bill, long overdue and demanding payment, meant an amount of inconvenience wholly unnecessary if it had been given him when it first came; also, the man's keen dislike of that 'account rendered.'

'Women have no business sense!' she found herself saying, 'and all that money just for hats—idiotic, useless, ugly things!'

With that she began to see the hats of the women in the car as she had never seen hats before. The men's seemed normal, dignified, becoming, with enough variety for personal taste, and with distinction in style and in age, such as she had never noticed before. But the women's——

With the eyes of a man and the brain of a man; with the memory of a whole lifetime of free action wherein the hat, close-fitting on cropped hair, had been no handicap; she now perceived the hats of women.

Their massed fluffed hair was at once attractive and foolish, and on that hair, at every angle, in all colors, tipped, twisted, tortured into every crooked shape, made of any substance chance might offer, perched these formless objects. Then, on their formlessness the trimmings—these squirts of stiff feathers, these violent outstanding bows of glistening ribbon, these swaying, projecting masses of plumage which tormented the faces of bystanders.

Never in all her life had she imagined that this idolized millinery could look, to those who paid for it, like the decorations of an insane monkey.

And yet, when there came into the car a little woman, as foolish as any, but pretty and sweet-looking, up rose Gerald Mathewson and gave her his seat; and, later, when there came in a handsome red-cheeked girl, whose hat was wilder, more violent in color and eccentric in shape than any other; when she stood near by and her soft curling plumes swept his cheek once and again, he felt a sense of sudden pleasure at the intimate tickling touch—and she, deep down within, felt such a wave of shame as might well drown a thousand hats forever.

When he took his train, his seat in the smoking car, she had a new surprise. All about him were the other men, commuters too, and many of them friends of his.

To her, they would have been distinguished as 'Mary Wade's husband'—'the man Belle Grant is engaged to'—'that rich Mr Shopworth'—or 'that pleasant Mr Beale.' And they would all have lifted their hats to her, bowed, made polite conversation if near enough—especially Mr Beale.

Now came the feeling of open-eyed acquaintance, of knowing men—as they were. The mere amount of this knowledge was a surprise to her; the whole background of talk from boyhood up, the gossip of barber-shop and club, the conversation of morning and evening hours on trains, the knowledge of political affiliation, of business standing and prospects, of character—in a light she had never known before.

They came and talked to Gerald, one and another. He seemed quite popular. And as they talked, with this new memory and new understanding, an understanding which seemed to include all these men's minds, there poured in on the submerged consciousness beneath a new, a startling knowledge—what men really think of women.

Good average American men were there; married men for the most part, and happy—as happiness goes in general. In the minds of each and all there seemed to be a two-story department, quite apart from the rest of their ideas, a separate place where they kept their thoughts and feelings about women.

In the upper half were the tenderest emotions, the most exquisite ideals, the sweetest memories, all lovely sentiments as to 'home' and 'mother,' all delicate admiring adjectives, a sort of sanctuary, where a veiled statue, blindly adored, shared place with beloved yet commonplace experiences.

In the lower half—here that buried consciousness woke to keen distress—they kept quite another assortment of ideas. Here, even in this clean-minded husband of hers, was the memory of stories told at men's dinners, of worse ones overheard in street or car, of base traditions, coarse epithets, gross experiences—known, though not shared.

And all these in the department 'woman,' while in the rest of the mind—here was new knowledge indeed.

The world opened before her. Not the world she had been reared in; where Home had covered all the map, almost, and the rest had been 'foreign,' or 'unexplored country;' but the world as it was, man's world, as made, lived in, and seen, by men.

It was dizzying. To see the houses that fled so fast across the car window, in terms of builders' bills, or of some technical insight into materials and methods; to see a passing village with lamentable knowledge of who 'owned it'—and of how its Boss was rapidly aspiring to State power, or of how that kind of paving was a failure; to see shops, not as mere exhibitions of desirable objects, but as business ventures, many mere sinking ships, some promising a profitable voyage—this new world bewildered her.

She—as Gerald—had already forgotten about that bill, over which she—as Mollie—was still crying at home. Gerald was 'talking business' with this man, 'talking politics' with that; and now sympathizing with the carefully withheld troubles of a neighbor.

Mollie had always sympathized with the neighbor's wife before.

She began to struggle violently, with this large dominant masculine consciousness. She remembered with sudden clearness things she had read—lectures she had heard; and resented with increasing intensity this serene masculine preoccupation with the male point of view.

Mr Miles, the little fussy man who lived on the other side of the street, was talking now. He had a large complacent wife; Mollie had never liked her much, but had always thought him rather nice—he was so punctilious in small courtesies.

And here he was talking to Gerald—such talk!

'Had to come in here,' he said. 'Gave my seat to a dame who was bound to have it. There's nothing they won't get when they make up their minds to it—eh?'

'No fear!' said the big man in the next seat, 'they haven't much mind to make up, you know—and if they do, they'll change it.'

'The real danger,' began the Revd Alfred Smythe, the new Episcopal clergyman, a thin, nervous, tall man, with a face several centuries behind the times, 'is that they will overstep the limits of their God-appointed sphere.'

'Their natural limits ought to hold 'em, I think,' said cheerful Dr Jones. 'You can't get around physiology, I tell you.'

'I've never seen any limits, myself, not to what they want, anyhow;' said Mr Miles, 'merely a rich husband and a fine house and no end of bonnets and dresses, and the latest thing in motors, and a few diamonds—and so on. Keeps us pretty busy.'

There was a tired gray man across the aisle. He had a very nice wife, always beautifully dressed, and three unmarried daughters, also beautifully dressed—Mollie knew them. She knew he worked hard too, and looked at him now a little anxiously.

But he smiled cheerfully.

'Do you good, Miles,' he said. 'What else would a man work for? A good woman is about the best thing on earth.'

'And a bad one's the worst, that's sure,' responded Miles.

'She's a pretty weak sister, viewed professionally,' Dr Jones averred with solemnity, and the Revd Alfred Smythe added: 'She brought evil into the world.'

Gerald Mathewson sat up straight. Something was stirring in him which he did not recognize—yet could not resist.

'Seems to me we all talk like Noah,' he suggested drily. 'Or the ancient Hindu scriptures. Women have their limitations, but so do we, God knows. Haven't we known girls in school and college just as smart as we were?'

'They cannot play our games,' coldly replied the clergyman.

Gerald measured his meager proportions with a practiced eye.

'I never was particularly good at football myself,' he modestly admitted, 'but I've known women who could outlast a man in all-round endurance. Besides—life isn't spent in athletics!'

This was sadly true. They all looked down the aisle where a heavy ill-dressed man with a bad complexion sat alone. He had held the top of the columns once, with headlines and photographs. Now he earned less than any of them.

'It's time we woke up,' pursued Gerald, still inwardly urged to unfamiliar speech. 'Women are pretty much *people*, seems to me. I know they dress like fools—but who's to blame for that? We invent all those idiotic hats of theirs, and design their crazy fashions, and, what's more, if a woman is courageous enough to wear common sense clothes—and shoes—which of us wants to dance with her?

'Yes, we blame them for grafting on us, but are we willing to let our wives work? We are not. It hurts our pride, that's all. We are always criticizing them for making mercenary marriages, but what do we call a girl who marries a chump with no money? Just a poor fool, that's all. And they know it.

'As for those physical limitations, Dr Jones, I guess our side of the house has some responsibility there, too—eh?

'And for Mother Eve—I wasn't there and can't deny the story, but I will say this, if she brought evil into the world we men have had the lion's share of keeping it going ever since—how about that?'

They drew into the city, and all day long in his business, Gerald was vaguely conscious of new views, strange feelings, and the submerged Mollie learned and learned.

MR PEEBLES'S HEART

HE was lying on the sofa in the homely, bare little sitting room; an uncomfortable stiff sofa, too short, too sharply upcurved at the end, but still a sofa, whereon one could, at a pinch, sleep.

Thereon Mr Peebles slept, this hot still afternoon; slept uneasily, snoring a little, and twitching now and then, as one in some obscure distress.

Mrs Peebles had creaked down the front stairs and gone off on some superior errands of her own; with a good palm-leaf fan for a weapon, a silk umbrella for a defense.

'Why don't you come too, Joan?' she had urged her sister, as she dressed herself for departure.

'Why should I, Emma? It's much more comfortable at home. I'll keep Arthur company when he wakes up.'

'Oh, Arthur! He'll go back to the store as soon as he's had his nap. And I'm sure Mrs Older's paper'll be real interesting. If you're going to live here you ought to take an interest in the club, seems to me.'

'I'm going to live here as a doctor—not as a lady of leisure, Em. You go on—I'm contented.'

So Mrs Emma Peebles sat in the circle of the Ellsworth Ladies' Home Club, and improved her mind, while Dr J. R. Bascom softly descended to the sitting room in search of a book she had been reading.

There was Mr Peebles, still uneasily asleep. She sat down quietly in a cane-seated rocker by the window and watched him awhile; first professionally, then with a deeper human interest.

Baldish, grayish, stoutish, with a face that wore a friendly smile for customers, and showed grave, set lines that deepened about the corners of his mouth when there was no one to serve; very ordinary in dress, in carriage, in appearance was Arthur Peebles at fifty. He was not 'the slave of love' of the Arab tale, but the slave of duty.

If ever a man had done his duty—as he saw it—he had done his, always.

His duty—as he saw it—was carrying women. First his mother, a comfortable competent person, who had run the farm after her husband's death, and added to their income by Summer boarders until Arthur was old enough to 'support her.' Then she sold the old place and moved into the village to 'make a home for Arthur,' who incidentally provided a hired girl to perform the manual labor of that process.

He worked in the store. She sat on the piazza and chatted with her neighbors.

He took care of his mother until he was nearly thirty, when she left him finally; and then he installed another woman to make a home for him—also with the help of the hired girl. A pretty, careless, clinging little person he married, who had long made mute appeal to his strength and carefulness, and she had continued to cling uninterruptedly to this day.

Incidentally a sister had clung until she married, another until she died; and his children—two daughters, had clung also. Both the daughters were married in due time, with sturdy young husbands to cling to in their turn; and now there remained only his wife to carry, a lighter load than he had ever known—at least numerically.

But either he was tired, very tired, or Mrs Peebles' tendrils had grown tougher, tighter, more tenacious, with age. He did not complain of it. Never had it occurred to him in all these years that there was any other thing for a man to do than to carry whatsoever women came within range of lawful relationship.

Had Dr Joan been—shall we say—carriageable—he would have cheerfully added her to the list, for he liked her extremely. She was different from any woman he had ever known, different from her sister as day from night, and, in lesser degree, from all the female inhabitants of Ellsworth.

She had left home at an early age, against her mother's will, absolutely ran away; but when the whole countryside rocked with gossip and sought for the guilty man—it appeared that she had merely gone to college. She worked her way through, learning more, far more, than was taught in the curriculum; became a trained nurse, studied medicine, and had long since made good in her profession. There were even rumors that she must be 'pretty well fixed' and about to 'retire'; but others held that she must have failed, really or she never would have come back home to settle.

Whatever the reason, she was there, a welcome visitor; a source of real pride to her sister, and of indefinable satisfaction to her brother-in-law. In her friendly atmosphere he felt a stirring of long unused powers; he remembered funny stories, and how to tell them; he felt a revival of interests he had thought quite outlived, early interests in the big world's movements.

'Of all unimpressive, unattractive, *good* little men—' she was thinking, as she watched, when one of his arms dropped off the slippery side of the sofa, the hand thumped on the floor, and he awoke and sat up hastily with an air of one caught off duty.

'Don't sit up as suddenly as that, Arthur, it's bad for your heart.'

'Nothing the matter with my heart, is there?' he asked with his ready smile.

'I don't know—haven't examined it. Now—sit still—you know there's nobody in the store this afternoon—and if there is, Jake can attend to 'em.'

'Where's Emma?'

'Oh, Emma's gone to her "club" or something—wanted me to go, but I'd rather talk with you.'

He looked pleased but incredulous, having a high opinion of that club, and a low one of himself.

'Look here,' she pursued suddenly, after he had made himself comfortable with a drink from the swinging ice-pitcher, and another big cane rocker, 'what would you like to do if you could?'

'Travel!' said Mr Peebles, with equal suddenness. He saw her astonishment. 'Yes, travel! I've always wanted to—since I was a kid. No use! We never could, you see. And now—even if we could—Emma hates it.' He sighed resignedly

'Do you like to keep store?' she asked sharply.

'*Like* it?' He smiled at her cheerfully, bravely, but with a queer blank hopeless background underneath. He shook his head gravely. 'No, I do not, Joan. Not a little bit. But what of that?'

They were still for a little, and then she put another question. 'What would you have chosen—for a profession—if you had been free to choose?'

His answer amazed her threefold; from its character, its sharp promptness, its deep feeling. It was in one word—'Music!'

'Music!' she repeated. 'Music! Why I didn't know you played—or cared about it.'

'When I was a youngster,' he told her, his eyes looking far off through the vine-shaded window, 'father brought home a guitar—and said it was for the one that learned to play it first. He meant the girls of course. As a matter of fact I learned it first—but I didn't get it. That's all the music I ever had,' he added. 'And there's not much to listen to here, unless you count what's in church. I'd have a Victrola—but—' he laughed a little shame-facedly, 'Emma says if I bring one into the house she'll smash it. She says they're worse than cats. Tastes differ you know, Joan.'

Again he smiled at her, a droll smile, a little pinched at the corners. 'Well—I must be getting back to business.'

She let him go, and turned her attention to her own business, with some seriousness.

'Emma,' she proposed, a day or two later. 'How would you like it if I should board here—live here, I mean, right along.'

'I should hope you would,' her sister replied. 'It would look nice to have you practising in this town and not live with me—all the sister I've got.'

'Do you think Arthur would like it?'

'Of course he would! Besides—even if he didn't—you're *my* sister—and this is my house. He put it in my name, long ago.'

'I see,' said Joan, 'I see.'

Then after a little—'Emma—are you contented?'

'Contented? Why, of course I am. It would be a sin not to be. The girls are well married—I'm happy about them both. This is a real comfortable house, and it runs itself—my Matilda is a jewel if ever there was one. And she don't mind company—likes to do for 'em. Yes—I've nothing to worry about.'

'Your health's good—that I can see,' her sister remarked, regarding with approval her clear complexion and bright eyes.

'Yes—I've nothing to complain about—that I know of,' Emma admitted, but among her causes for thankfulness she did not even mention Arthur, nor seem to think of him till Dr Joan seriously inquired her opinion as to his state of health.

'His health? Arthur's? Why he's always well. Never had a sick day in his life—except now and then he's had a kind of a break-down,' she added as an afterthought.

Dr Joan Bascom made acquaintances in the little town, both professional and social. She entered upon her practise, taking it over from the failing hands of old Dr Braithwaite—her first friend, and feeling very much at home in the old place. Her sister's house furnished two comfortable rooms downstairs, and a large bedroom above. 'There's plenty of room now the girls are gone,' they both assured her.

Then, safely ensconced and established, Dr Joan began a secret campaign to alienate the affections of her brother-in-law. Not for herself—oh no! If ever in earlier years she had felt the need of some one to cling to, it was long, long ago. What she sought was to free him from the tentacles—without re-entanglement.

She bought a noble gramophone with a set of first-class records, told her sister smilingly that she didn't have to listen, and Emma would sit sulkily in the back room on the other side of the house, while her husband and sister enjoyed the music. She grew used to it in time, she said, and drew nearer, sitting on the porch perhaps; but Arthur had his long denied pleasure in peace.

It seemed to stir him strangely. He would rise and walk, a new fire in his eyes, a new firmness about the patient mouth, and Dr Joan fed the fire with talk and books and pictures with study of maps and sailing lists and accounts of economical tours.

'I don't see what you two find so interesting in all that stuff about music and those composers,' Emma would say. 'I never did care for foreign parts—musicians are all foreigners, anyway.'

Arthur never quarrelled with her; he only grew quiet and lost that interested sparkle of the eye when she discussed the subject.

Then one day, Mrs Peebles being once more at her club, content and yet aspiring, Dr Joan made bold attack upon her brother-in-law's principles.

'Arthur,' she said. 'Have you confidence in me as a physician?'

'I have,' he said briskly. 'Rather consult you than any doctor I ever saw.'

'Will you let me prescribe for you if I tell you you need it?'

'I sure will.'

'Will you take the prescription?'

'Of course I'll take it—no matter how it tastes.'

'Very well. I prescribe two years in Europe.'

He stared at her, startled.

'I mean it. You're in a more serious condition than you think. I want you to cut clear—and travel. For two years.'

He still stared at her. 'But Emma—'

'Never mind about Emma. She owns the house. She's got enough money to clothe herself—and I'm paying enough board to keep everything going. Emma don't need you.'

'But the store—'

'Sell the store.'

'Sell it! That's easy said. Who'll buy it?'

'I will. Yes—I mean it. You give me easy terms and I'll take the store off your hands. It ought to be worth seven or eight thousand dollars, oughtn't it—stock and all?'

He assented, dumbly.

'Well, I'll buy it. You can live abroad for two years, on a couple of thousand, or twenty-five hundred—a man of your tastes. You know those accounts we've read—it can be done easily. Then you'll have five thousand or so to come back to— and can invest it in something better than that shop. Will you do it—?'

He was full of protests, of impossibilities.

She met them firmly. 'Nonsense! You can too. She doesn't need you, at all—she may later. No—the girls don't need you— and they may later. Now is your time—*now*. They say the Japanese sow their wild oats after they're fifty—suppose you do! You can't be so *very* wild on that much money, but you can spend a year in Germany—learn the language—go to the op-era—take walking trips in the Tyrol—in Switzerland; see England, Scotland, Ireland, France, Belgium, Denmark—you can do a lot in two years.'

He stared at her fascinated.

'Why not? Why not be your own man for once in your life—do what *you* want to—not what other people want you to?'

He murmured something as to 'duty'—but she took him up sharply.

'If ever a man on earth has done his duty, Arthur Peebles, you have. You've taken care of your mother while she was perfectly able to take care of herself; of your sisters, long after they were; and of a wholly able-bodied wife. At present she does not need you the least bit in the world.'

'Now that's pretty strong,' he protested. 'Emma'd miss me—I know she'd miss me—'

Dr Bascom looked at him affectionately. 'There couldn't a better thing happen to Emma—or to you, for that matter—than to have her miss you, real hard.'

'I know she'd never consent to my going,' he insisted, wistfully.

'That's the advantage of my interference,' she replied serenely. 'You surely have a right to choose your doctor, and your doctor is seriously concerned about your health and orders foreign travel—rest—change—and music.'

'But Emma—'

'Now, Arthur Peebles, forget Emma for awhile—I'll take care of her. And look here—let me tell you another thing—a change like this will do her good.'

He stared at her, puzzled.

'I mean it. Having you away will give her a chance to stand up. Your letters—about those places—will interest her. She may want to go, sometime. Try it.'

He wavered at this. Those who too patiently serve as props sometimes underrate the possibilities of the vine.

'Don't discuss it with her—that will make endless trouble. Fix up the papers for my taking over the store—I'll draw you a check, and you get the next boat for England, and make your plans from there. Here's a banking address that will take care of your letters and checks—'

The thing was done! Done before Emma had time to protest. Done, and she left gasping to upbraid her sister.

Joan was kind, patient, firm as adamant.

'But how it *looks*, Joan—what will people think of me! To be left deserted—like this!'

'People will think according to what we tell them and to how you behave, Emma Peebles. If you simply say that Arthur was far from well and I advised him to take a foreign trip—and if you forget yourself for once, and show a little natural feeling for him—you'll find no trouble at all.'

For her own sake the selfish woman, made more so by her husband's unselfishness, accepted the position. Yes—Arthur had gone abroad for his health—Dr Bascom was much worried about him—chance of a complete breakdown, she said. Wasn't it pretty sudden? Yes—the doctor hurried him off. He was in England—going to take a walking trip—she did not know when he'd be back. The store? He'd sold it.

Dr Bascom engaged a competent manager who ran that store successfully, more so than had the unenterprising Mr Peebles. She made it a good paying business, which he ultimately bought back and found no longer a burden.

But Emma was the principal charge. With talk, with books, with Arthur's letters followed carefully on maps, with trips to see the girls, trips in which travelling lost its terrors, with the care of the house, and the boarder or two they took 'for company,' she so ploughed and harrowed that long fallow field of Emma's mind that at last it began to show signs of fruitfulness.

Arthur went away leaving a stout, dull woman who clung to him as if he was a necessary vehicle or beast of burden—and thought scarcely more of his constant service.

He returned younger, stronger, thinner, an alert vigorous man, with a mind enlarged, refreshed, and stimulated. He had found himself.

And he found her, also, most agreeably changed; having developed not merely tentacles, but feet of her own to stand on.

When next the thirst for travel seized him she thought she'd go too, and proved unexpectedly pleasant as a companion.

But neither of them could ever wring from Dr Bascom any definite diagnosis of Mr Peebles' threatening disease. 'A dangerous enlargement of the heart' was all she would commit herself to, and when he denied any such trouble now, she gravely wagged her head and said 'it had responded to treatment.'

MRS MERRILL'S DUTIES

GRACE LEROY, in college, was quite the most important member of the class. She had what her professors proudly pointed out as the rarest thing among women—a scientific mind. The arts had no charms for her; she had no wish to teach, no leaning toward that branch of investigation and alleviation in social pathology we are so apt to call 'social service.'

Her strength was in genuine research work, and, back of that, greatest gift of all, she showed high promise in 'the scientific imagination,' the creative synthesizing ability which gives new discoveries to the world.

In addition to these natural advantages a merciful misfortune saved her from the widespread silvery quicksand which so often engulfs the girl graduate. Instead of going home to decorate the drawing-room and help her mother receive, she was obliged to go to work at once, owing to paternal business difficulties.

Her special teacher, old Dr Welsch, succeeded in getting a laboratory position for her; and for three years she worked side by side with a great chemist and physicist, Dr Hammerton, his most valued assistant.

She was very happy.

Happy, of course, to be useful to her family at once, instead of an added burden. Happy in her sense of independence and a real place in the world; happy in the feeling of personal power and legitimate pride of achievement. Happiest of all in the brightening dawn of great ideas, big glittering hopes of a discovery that should lighten humanity's burdens. Hardly did she dare to hope for it, yet it did seem almost possible at times. Being of a truly religious nature she prayed earnestly over this; to be good enough to deserve the honor; to keep humble and not overestimate her powers; to be helped to do the Great Work.

Then Life rolled swiftly along and swept her off her feet.

Her father recovered his money and her mother lost her health. For a time there seemed absolute need of her at home.

Forerunner, 6:3 (March 1915), 1–5.

'I must not neglect plain duty,' said the girl, and resigned her position.

There was a year of managing the household, with the care of younger brothers and sisters; a year of travel with the frail mother, drifting slowly from place to place, from physician to physician, always hoping, and always being disappointed.

Then came the grief of losing her, after they had grown so close, so deeply, tenderly intimate.

'Whatever happens,' said Grace to herself, 'I shall always be glad of these two years. No outside work could justify me in neglecting this primal duty.'

What did happen next was her father's turning to her for comfort. She alone could in any degree take her mother's place to him. He could not bear to think of her as leaving the guidance of the family. His dependence was touching.

Grace accepted the new duty bravely.

There was the year of deep mourning, both in symbolic garments and observances and in the real sorrow; and she found herself learning to know her father better than she ever had, and learning how to somewhat make up to him for the companionship he had lost. There was the need of mothering the younger ones, of managing the big house.

Then came the next sister's debut, and the cares and responsibilities involved. Another sister was growing up, and the young brother called for sympathetic guidance. There seemed no end to it.

She bowed her head and faced her duty.

'Nothing can be right,' she said, 'which would take me away from these intimate claims.'

Everyone agreed with her in this.

Her father was understanding and tender in his thoughtfulness.

'I know what a sacrifice you are making, daughter, in giving up your chemistry, but what could I do without you! . . .' You are so much like your mother . . .'

As time passed she did speak once or twice of a housekeeper, that she might have some free hours during the day-time, but he was so hurt at the idea that she gave it up.

Then something happened that proved with absurd ease the

fallacy of the fond conclusion that nothing could be right which would take her away. Hugh Merrill took her away, and that was accepted by everyone as perfectly right.

She had known him a long time, but had hardly dared let herself think of marrying him—she was so indispensable at home. But when his patience and his ardor combined finally swept her off her feet; when her father said: 'Why, of course, my child! Hugh is a splendid fellow! We shall miss you—but do you think I would stand in the way of your happiness!'—she consented. She raised objections about the housekeeping, but her father promptly met them by installing a widowed sister, Aunt Adelaide, who had always been a favorite with them all.

She managed the home quite as well, and the children really better, than had Grace; and she and her brother played cribbage and backgammon in the evenings with pleasant reversion to their youthful comradeship—he seemed to grow younger for having her there.

Grace was so happy, so relieved by the sudden change from being the mainstay of four other people and a big house to being considered and cared for in every way by a strong resourceful affectionate man, that she did not philosophize at all at the easy dispensibility of the indispensable.

With Hugh she rested; regained her youth, bloomed like a flower. There was a long delightful journey; a pleasant homecoming; the setting up of her very own establishment; the cordial welcome from her many friends.

In all this she never lost sight of her inner hope of the Great Work.

Hugh had profound faith in her. They talked of it on their long honeymoon, in full accord. She should have her laboratory, she should work away at her leisure, she would do wonderful things—he was sure of it.

But that first year was so full of other things, so crowded with invitations, so crowded with careful consideration of clothes and menus and servants, the duties of a hostess, or a guest—that the big room upstairs was not yet a laboratory.

An unexpected illness with its convalescence took another long period; she needed rest, a change. Another year went by.

Grace was about thirty now.

Then the babies came—little Hugh and Arnold—splendid boys. A happier, prouder mother one would not wish to see. She thanked God with all her heart; she felt the deep and tender oneness with her husband that comes of parentage, with reverent joy.

To the task of education she now devoted her warmly loving heart, her clear strong mind. It was noble work. She neglected nothing. This duty was imperative. No low-grade nursemaid should, through ignorance, do some irremediable injury to opening baby minds.

With the help of a fully competent assistant, expensive, but worth all she cost, Mrs Merrill brought up those boys herself, and the result should have satisfied even the most exacting educator. Hearty, well-grown, unaffected, with clear minds and beautiful manners, they grew up to sturdy boyhood, taking high places when they went to school; loved by their teachers, comrades and friends, and everyone said: 'What a lovely mother she is!'

She did not admit to anyone that even in this period of lovely mothering, even with the home happiness, the wife happiness, the pleasant social position, there was still an aching want inside. She wanted her laboratory, her research, her work. All her years of education, from the first chemistry lessons at fourteen to the giving up of her position at twenty-four, had made her a chemist, and nature had made her a discoverer.

She had not read much during these years; it hurt her—made her feel an exile. She had shut the door on all that side of her life, and patiently, gladly fulfilled the duties of the other side, neglecting nothing.

Not till ten more years had passed did she draw a long breath and say: 'Now I will have my laboratory!'

She had it. There was the big room, all this time a nursery; now at last fitted up with all the mysterious implements and supplies of her chosen profession.

The boys were at school—her husband at his business—now she could concentrate on the Great Work.

And then Mrs Merrill began to realize 'the defects of her qualities.'

There is such a thing as being too good.

We all know that little one-handed tool combination which carries in its inside screw-driver, gouge and chisel, awl and file— a marvellously handy thing to have in the house. Yes—but did you ever see a carpenter use one? The real workman, for real work, must have real tools, of which the value is, not that they will all fit one hollow and feeble handle, but that each will do what it is meant for, well.

We have seen in Grace Leroy Merrill the strength of mind and character, Christian submission, filial duty, wifely love, motherly efficiency. She had other qualities also, all pleasant ones. She was a pre-eminently attractive woman, more than pretty—charming. She was sweet and cordial in manner, quick and witty, a pleasure to talk with for either man or woman. Add to these the possession of special talent for dress, and a gentle friendliness that could not bear to hurt anyone, and we begin to feel 'this is too much. No person has a right to be so faultless, so universally efficient and attractive.'

Social psychology is a bit complicated. We need qualities, not only valuable for personal, but for social relation. In the growing complexity of a highly specialized organization the law of organic specialization calls for a varying degree of sacrifice in personal fulfillment. It is quite possible, indeed it is usual, to find individuals whose numerous good qualities really stand in the way of their best service to society. The best tools are not those of the greatest 'all round' variety of usefulness.

When the boys were grown up enough to be off her mind for many hours a day; when the house fairly ran itself in the hands of well-trained servants; when, at last, the laboratory was installed and the way seemed open; Mrs Merrill found herself fairly bogged in her own popularity. She had so many friends; they were so unfailingly anxious to have her at their dinners, their dances, their continuous card parties; they came to her so confidingly, so frequently—and she could never bear to hurt their feelings.

There were, to be sure, mornings. One is not required to play bridge in the morning, or dance, or go to the theatre. But even the daily ordering for a household takes some time, and besides the meals there are the supplies in clothing, linen, china; and the spring and fall extras of putting things away with mothballs, having rugs cleaned and so on—and so on.

Then—clothes; her own clothes. The time to think about them; the time to discuss them; the time to buy them; the time to stand up and be fitted—to plan and struggle with the dressmaker—a great deal of time—and no sooner is the feat accomplished than—presto!—it must be done all over.

Day after day she mounted the stairs to her long looked-for work-room, with an hour—or two—or three—before her. Day after day she was called down again; friends at the telephone, friends at the door; friends who were full of cheerful apology and hopes that they did not disturb her; and tradesmen who were void of either.

'If only I could get something *done*!' she said, as she sat staring at her retorts. 'If once I could really accomplish a piece of good work, that should command public acknowledgement— then they would understand. Then I could withdraw from all this——'

For she found that her hours were too few, and too broken, to allow of that concentration of mind without which no great work is possible.

But she was a strong woman, a patient woman, and possessed of a rich fund of perseverance. With long waiting, with careful use of summer months when her too devoted friends were out of town, she managed in another five years, to really accomplish something. From her little laboratory, working alone and under all distractions, she finally sent out a new formula; not for an explosive of deadly power, but for a safe and simple sedative, something which induced natural sleep, with no ill results.

It was no patented secret. She gave it to the world with the true scientific spirit, and her joy was like that of motherhood. She had at last achieved! She had done something—something of real service to thousands upon thousands. And back of this first little hill, so long in winning, mountain upon mountain, range on range, rose hopefully tempting before her.

She was stronger now. She had gotten back into the lines of study, of persistent work. Her whole mind stirred and freshened with new ideas, high purposes. She planned for further research, along different lines. Two Great Ones tempted her; a cheap combustible fluid; and that biggest prize of all—the mastering of atomic energy.

And now, now that she had really made this useful discovery, which was widely recognized among those who knew of such matters, she could begin to protect herself from these many outside calls!

What did happen?

She found herself quite lionized for a season—name in the papers, pictures, interviews, and a whole series of dinners and receptions where she was wearied beyond measure by the well-meant comments on her work.

Free? Respected? Let alone?

Her hundreds of friends, who had known her so long and so well, as a charming girl, a devoted daughter, an irreproachable wife, a most unusually successful mother, were only the more cordial now.

'Have you heard about Grace Merrill? Isn't it wonderful! She always had ability—I've always said so.'

'Such a service to the world! A new anesthetic!'

'Oh, it's not an anesthetic—not really.'

'Like the Twilight Sleep, I imagine.'

'It's splendid of her anyway. I've asked her to dinner Thursday, to meet Professor Andrews—he's an authority on dietetics, you know, and Dr North and his wife—they are such interesting people!'

Forty-six! Still beautiful, still charming, still exquisitely gowned. Still a happy wife and mother, with Something Done—at last.

And yet—

Her next younger sister, who had lost her husband and was greatly out of health, now wanted to come and live with her; their father had followed his wife some years back and the old home was broken up.

That meant being tied up at home again. And as to the social engagements, she was more hopelessly popular than ever.

Then one day there came to see her Dr Hammerton. His

brush of hair was quite white, but thick and erect as ever. His keen black eyes sparkled portentously under thick white eyebrows.

'What's this you've been doing, Child? Show me your shop.'

She showed him, feeling very girlish again in the presence of her early master. He looked the place over in silence, told her he had read about her new product, sat on the edge of a table and made her take a chair.

'Now tell me about it!' he said.

She told him—all about it. He listened, nodding agreeably as she recounted the steps.

'Mother? Yes. Father? Yes—for awhile at least. Husband? Yes. Boys? Of course—and you've done well. But what's the matter now?'

She told him that too—urging her hope of forcing some acknowledgment by her proven ability.

He threw back his big head and laughed.

'You've got the best head of any woman I ever saw,' he said; 'you've done what not one woman in a thousand does—kept a living Self able to survive family relations. You've proven, now, that you are still in the ring. You ought to do—twenty—maybe thirty years of worthwhile work. Forty-six? I was forty-eight when you left me, have done my best work since then, am seventy now, and am still going strong. You've spent twenty-two years in worthwhile woman-work that's *done*—now you have at least as much again to do human work. I daresay you'll do better because of all this daughtering and mothering—women are queer things. Anyhow you've plenty of time. But you must get to work.

'Now, see here—if you let all these childish flub-dubs prevent you from doing what God made you for—you're a Criminal Fool!'

Grace gave a little gasp.

'I mean it. You know it. It's all nonsense, empty nonsense. As for your sister—let her go to a sanitarium—she can afford it, or live with her other sister—or brother. You've earned your freedom.

'As to clothes and parties—Quit!'

She looked at him.

'Yes, I know. You're still pretty and attractive, but *what of it?* Suppose Spencer or Darwin had wasted their time as parlor ornaments—supposing they could have—would they have had a right to?'

She caught at the names. 'You think I could do something— Great?' she asked. 'You think I am—big enough—to try?'

He stood up. She rose and faced him.

'I think you are great, to have done what you have—a task no man could face. I think you will be greater—perhaps one of the big World Helpers.' Then his eyes shot fire—and he thundered: 'How Dare you hinder the World's Work by wasting your time with these idle women? It is Treason—High Treason—to Humanity.'

'What can I do?' she asked at last.

'That's a foolish question, child. Use your brain—you've got plenty. Learn to assert yourself and stand up to it, that's all. Tell your sister you can't. Disconnect the telephone. Hire some stony-faced menial to answer the door and say: "Mrs Merrill is engaged. She left orders not to be disturbed."

'Decide on how many evenings you can afford to lose sleep, and decline to go out on all others. It's simple enough.

'But you've got to *do it*. You've got to plan it and stand by it. It takes Courage—and it takes Strength.'

'But if it is my duty—' said Grace Merrill.

The old man smiled and left her. 'Once that woman sees a Duty!' he said to himself.

GIRLS AND LAND

IF DACIA BOONE'S father had lived he would have been a rich man, a very rich man, and a power in politics also—for good or ill. He was of the same stamp as Mark Hanna, a born organizer, an accumulator and efficient handler of money. His widow was deeply convinced of this, and expressed her opinion with explicit firmness, more rather than less as the years advanced.

She expressed it to Dacia and her older sisters from infancy up; to all her friends, relatives and associates; and, unfortunately, to Mr Ordway, her second husband. He was, as she would plaintively explain, a far nicer man to live with than Her First; but he had no gift for making money—which was entirely true. He managed to feed and clothe her three Boone daughters, and the later brood of little Ordways, also to give them a chance at an education, but that appeared to be his limit.

They moved from place to place, in search of better fortune, urged always by the uneasy mother. She seemed to feel that if he could only find his proper place and work he would do well, but as a matter of fact he did fairly well in each attempt, and never any better.

When Dacia was twenty the family had a homestead in the state of Washington, a big fertile place, lacking only a good road to the nearest station to be a profitable fruit ranch. Of this ranch they had hopes, high, but distant. For the rest they lived in a small house on one of Seattle's many hills, and Mr Ordway worked at what jobs he could get,—as a foreman, manager, small contractor. He had experience enough for a dozen; he could handle men, he was honest and efficient; but blind to the various side issues wherein other men made money.

The two older girls were married, and using what powers they had to spur their husbands on toward high financial achievements; but as for Dacia—she worked in a store. Her mother had opposed it, naturally; but the girl was quietly persistent, and usually got her way.

Forerunner, 6:5 (May 1915), 1–5.

'Oh, what's the use, mother!' she said. 'I shan't marry—I'm too homely, you know that.'

'It's not your looks, my dear child,' Mrs Ordway would mournfully reply. 'There's plenty of homelier girls than you are—much homelier—that marry. But it is the way you act—you somehow don't try to be—attractive.'

Dacia smiled her wide, good-natured smile. 'No, I don't, and what's more, I won't. So what between lack of beauty and lack of attractiveness—'

'And lack of money!' her mother broke in. 'If your father had only lived!'

'I don't believe I could have loved him any better than I do the father I've got,' said the girl loyally. As a matter of fact, for all her frequent references to the departed, the only salient point his widow ever mentioned was that capacity of his for making money.

Dacia went to work, trying several trades, and was in a good position as saleswoman—she flatly refused to say 'saleslady'—by the time she was twenty.

She was homely. A strong, square, dark face, determined and good-natured, but in no way beautiful; rather a heavy figure, but sturdy and active; a quiet girl with a close mouth.

'You certainly are the image of your father!' her mother would say; adding with vain pathos: 'If only you had been a man!'

Dacia had no quarrel with being a woman. She had had her woman's experience, too; a deep passionate, wild love for the man who had quite overlooked her and married one of her sisters. They had gone back to Massachusetts to live—for which the lonely girl was deeply thankful. Also she was thankful that no one knew what she had felt, how she had suffered. It was her first great trial in keeping still, and had developed that natural instinct into a settled habit. But though she said little, she thought much; and made plans with a breadth, a length, a daring, that would have made her father proud indeed—had she been a boy.

She saved her money too, steadily laying up a little nest egg for clear purposes of her own. To Mr Ordway she gave a partial confidence.

'Daddy,' said she, 'what do you really think would be the best way to develop our ranch—if we had the money.'

He had ample views on the subject. There were apples, of course; berries—all kinds of fruit. There was market garden ground, flat and rich where the valley spread out a little; the fruit trees grew best on the slopes. There was timber in plenty—if only they had that road to the station! There was power too—a nice little waterfall—all on their land.

'It'll be worth a lot by and by,' he asserted. 'And if only I could raise the capital—but what's the use of talkin'!'

'Lots of use, Daddy dear, if you talk to the right person—such as me! Now tell me something else—who *ought* to build that road?'

'Why, there is a kind of a road—it's laid out all right, as you know—it just needs to be made into a good one. I suppose the town ought to do it, or the county—I don't rightly know.'

'If they furnished the labor, could you manage it, Daddy? Could you build a real good road down to Barville? And how much do you think it would cost?'

'Oh, as to labor—it would take—' he scribbled a little, with a flat carpenter's pencil, and showed her the estimate. ' 'Twould take that many men, at least,' his blunt forefinger pointing, 'and that long. To pay them—that much; to feed them—that much more—to say nothing of shelter. Are you proposing to go into the road-making business next week, my dear?'

She grinned and shook her head. 'Not next week, Daddy. But I like to know. And you are so practical! If you had the men—and the County let you—you could build that road and be a public benefactor—couldn't you?'

'I could indeed. There's good road metal there too; a stone crusher could be run by that waterfall—or we'd burn the wood for it. Just advance me a hundred thousand dollars or so out of your wages, and I'll do it! But *what's* the use of talkin'!' he repeated.

'Lots of use,' she answered again, 'if I talk to the right person—such as you!'

Then she said no more on that subject, though he joked her about it when they were alone, and devoted herself to another branch of tactics. She frequented the YWCA, the Social Settlement, one or two churches, and after some months of quiet inquiry found the woman she wanted, a woman with a high enthusiasm for Working Girls' Clubs.

Dacia was interested, became very friendly, said she could get together quite a number, she thought. She brought to this woman the kind of help she needed, earnest capable girls who saw the value of the work, and inside of two years there were established a whole chain of 'R & P Clubs,' self-supporting, and very popular.

R & P? Rest and Pleasure, of course.

With a first group of one hundred girls, paying 25 cents a week, they were sure of $100.00 a month for their rent and furnishing. The same number, paying 20 cents a day for lunch, found to their surprise that half of it fed them, and the remaining half, $60.00 a week, paid for the extra fuel and service, with $10.00 left for profit. When two hundred came to the same place for lunch they laid up $50.00 a week for their sinking fund.

Their big rooms were open in the evening for reading and dancing, for club and class work; and their various young gentleman friends who came to see them there and paid a modest five cents for light refreshment, found it the cheapest good time in the city—and the pleasantest.

The idea spread; Tacoma took it up, and Portland, Bellingham, Everett and Spokane; the larger cities had more than one group.

Meanwhile Dacia went to her father with another modest proposition.

'Daddy,' she urged. 'I've found a nice Swede who is a good carpenter and cabinet maker. He and his wife want a place in the country. Would you be willing to have him cut some of your timber and put up a camp for us—for our clubs, that is—for a Vacation Place?'

'Who's going to pay him?' he asked.

'Oh, I'll pay him, all right; I've got a Fund. But I want you really to sell him a little piece of the property—will you? Just a couple of acres or so, where the garden land is good, and let him pay for it in labor. You can make him agree to sell back to you if he wants to leave.'

This being done, and Dacia allowed to dictate the 'labor,' she set the man to work in good earnest, with some assistants, and soon had camping accommodations for a hundred.

Dacia's Fund, which she had been saving out of her salary for three years, amounted to $500.00, and served to buy the necessary bedding and other supplies. For further gain, she counted as future asset, a Vacation Fund the Clubs had been saving. There were three now in Seattle, comprising well over four hundred working women, and these had been urged to set aside 25 cents a week for a fortnight's vacation. For this $12.50 of a year's easy saving they were to have transportation and board for two weeks in the hills.

Mrs Olsen, sturdy and industrious, had not been loitering while her husband sawed wood. She had fed him and his assistants; had established a hennery, and a vegetable garden. A few young sheep were kept within safe bounds by a movable wire fence, a device which seemed to Dacia too obvious to avoid, where there were two men to unroll and fasten it to the trees with a quick tap of the hammer, and to reel it up and move it when desired. There were two good cows, also a litter of cheerful young pigs, who basked and grew fat on the little farm.

When it was time for the first detachment of Vacationers, Dacia's fund was all spent, but that hundred times $12.50 was in the savings deposit account of the R & P Clubs, and the girls paid their board with pride and satisfaction. Of the Seattle group of four hundred members, over three hundred had subscribed to this vacation fund; and they came, in self-elected groups, two weeks at a time, all summer long. $3,750.00 they paid in, and when the summer was over Dacia sat down with her father to estimate results of the thirteen weeks.

It had cost $2.40 each to get them there and back with their baggage. To feed them, using the animals on the place and the garden, was not above $2.00 a week. This left $2,430.00. To Mrs Olsen and the sturdy flaxen-braided damsel she had to help her, Dacia paid cash,—$10.00 a week, including the girl's board, but this was only $130.00. Then Dacia paid herself back the $500.00 she had invested, allowed $300.00 for refitting, and had a clear $1,500.00 for her further plans.

Dacia smiled and put it in the bank. She was twenty-two now. That winter she rented a pleasant hall; supplied it with refreshments from the lunch room; had dancing classes established under decent and reasonable management; sublet it for part of the time, and added steadily to her little fund.

Another summer's vacation income, with greater patronage and small additional expense, left her, at twenty-three, with quite a little sum. She had all together her first saving of $500.00, additional for a year $200.00 (she earned $15.00 a week, boarded for $7.00, dress and incidentals, $3.00 and saved $4.00), the first year's $1,500.00, the winter's additional earning from her rented hall, amounting to $800.00, and the second year's increased income of $1,800.00—in all $4,800.00.

'Daddy,' said she, 'let's you and me go into the road business. Can't we rent a stone-crusher? How many horses would it need? Don't you think the county will help?'

Mr Ordway went up to the ranch with her and looked over the plant. There were the rough but usable sleeping and eating accommodations, and a small saw and planing mill. There were the Olsens, extremely pleased with themselves. The good wife had earned not only her wages but about half of the board money, paid in for milk, meat, eggs and vegetables. This had gone promptly back to Dacia in payment for their stock, and also enabled them to lay in groceries for the winter. Fuel was plenty and Mr Olsen's two years' work had already covered most of their purchase money.

'But how about labor, Miss Promoter?' asked Mr Ordway. 'Do you realize what it means to feed and pay the force of men we'd need?'

'And how about The Unemployed?' she answered promptly. 'Some of them are good workmen—and you know how to pick and manage them. If they are sure of shelter and food and steady work, even at moderate pay—don't you think you could get 'em to come?'

Mr Ordway consulted with local officials and other owners of homesteads and timber land in the neighborhood. Everyone wanted the road. Here was some capital offered, waterpower, a competent manager and accommodations for the men. And here was 'The Problem of The Unemployed' looming ahead for the winter. This would remove a little of that difficulty.

So the County was induced to help.

'It's only a drop in the bucket,' said Dacia, 'but if County Canomish can do it, why can't the others? There's Power enough—there's Material enough—there's Brains enough—and there's Labor enough. And a little capital goes a good way, seems to me.'

By spring they had a good hard road, opening up much valuable land and adding much to the prosperity of the whole region; and Dacia had just enough money left, from another winter's earnings and saving, to fumigate and refit her camp.

But that year everything was easier on account of the road, and the greater popularity of the place kept it fuller, and longer open. Five hundred girls and women, in different parties, came up; and Dacia invested one dollar from each $12.50 in improving and beautifying the place, still clearing over $2,500.

She was twenty-four now, and very happy. So was Mr Ordway. He was able to dispose of some of his lumber and start planting the fruit ranch which his heart desired. Mrs Ordway viewed it all with grudging admiration.

'Yes—it's very nice,' she admitted to her daughter. 'Very nice, indeed, but I can't help thinking what your father would have done with a chance like this. But then, he was a man of Financial Genius! If only you had been a boy, Dacia! And if he had only lived to help you!'

'But my second father is helping me,' said Dacia. 'And I'm perfectly willing to be a girl—rather glad I am one, in fact.'

Then she consulted further with Mr Ordway. 'Daddy—can you make furniture out of the kind of wood you've got there?'

'Why, yes—I *could*, I suppose. I never thought of it—plain kitchen sort of furniture. There's not much hard wood.'

'But there's some. And you can set out more, can't you?'

'Set out—! Plant hardwood trees! Child, you're crazy. Hardwood timber doesn't grow up like lettuce.'

'How long does it take to be—cuttable?'

'Oh—thirty years at least, I should say.'

'Well—let's plant some. It will be valuable when I'm fifty-five or so—and your own children will be younger—they may be glad of it. But meantime I want to propose that you start a little Grand Rapids right by our waterfall there. Can't the mill be turned into a furniture factory? Nice cheap plain furniture—

painted or stained—and sold to the folks out here that can't pay the freight on Eastern stuff.'

'Hm!' Mr Ordway considered. He got out his pencil. He made some estimates. 'There's that young Pedersen,' he said, 'the Olsen's cousin—he's a good designer—you've seen what he's made for them?'

Dacia had seen it, and had thought about it quite carefully, but she made no admissions.

'Do you think he'd be useful?'

'I'm pretty sure he would,' said Mr Ordway. 'Dacia, child, you surely have a business head—why there's no real furniture factory on this coast. We might—we might do pretty well, I think.'

Olaf Pedersen thought so too.

'Your wood is much like the wood of our country,' he said. 'And we make furniture. I have no capital, but I will design and work, gladly.'

They began cautiously, with a small workshop, a moderate investment in machinery, and Dacia's big connection of people of small incomes, as advertising ground. She herself had so much faith in the enterprise that she gave up her position and became 'the office force' for the undertaking.

Next year they established the firm of Ordway, Boone & Pedersen. The modesty of their methods was such that they encountered practically no opposition until it was too late to crush them.

'A pleased customer is the best advertisement.' And there were several hundred pleased customers spreading the good news. Furniture that was solid and strong; that was simple, novel and pretty; that was amazingly cheap; that was made right there in their own state—it really pleased the people, and they supported the business.

Even the railroads, finding that their freight payment was as good as others, and that their trade was steadily growing, ceased to be antagonistic.

Mr Ordway settled down to steady work that had a future.

'Dacia,' said he. 'I'm mighty glad that, well, that I inherited you. You see, I can work and I'm honest, but you've got the brains. You can push.'

'It's Olaf, too, Daddy—it's mostly Olaf—he puts the novelty and beauty into it.'

'Yes, it's Olaf too. You are both good partners. I shall leave the business to you when I go.'

And he did,—to two who were partners of a closer sort long before then; and Boone & Pedersen developed a furniture industry which was of immense service to the whole coast.

DR CLAIR'S PLACE

'You must count your mercies,' said her friendly adviser. 'There's no cloud so dark but it has a silver lining, you know,— count your mercies.'

She looked at her with dull eyes that had known no hope for many years. 'Perhaps you will count them for me: Health— utterly broken and gone since I was twenty-four. Youth gone too—I am thirty-eight. Beauty—I never had it. Happiness— buried in shame and bitterness these fourteen years. Mother-hood—had and lost. Usefulness—I am too weak even to support myself. I have no money. I have no friends. I have no home. I have no work. I have no hope in life.' Then a dim glow of resolution flickered in those dull eyes. 'And what is more I don't propose to bear it much longer.'

It is astonishing what people will say to strangers on the cars. These two sat on the seat in front of me, and I had heard every syllable of their acquaintance, from the 'Going far?' of the friendly adviser to this confidence as to proposed suicide. The offerer of cheerful commonplaces left before long, and I took her place, or rather the back-turned seat facing it, and studied the Despairing One.

Not a bad looking woman, but so sunk in internal misery that her expression was that of one who had been in prison for a life-time. Her eyes had that burned out look, as hopeless as a cinder heap; her voice a dreary grating sound. The muscles of her face seemed to sag downward. She looked at the other passengers as if they were gray ghosts and she another. She looked at the rushing stretches we sped past as if the window were ground glass. She looked at me as if I were invisible.

'This,' said I to myself, 'is a case for Dr Clair.'

It was not difficult to make her acquaintance. There was no more protective tissues about her than about a skeleton. I think she would have showed the utter wreck of her life to any who asked to look, and not have realized their scrutiny. In fact it was not so much that she exhibited her misery, as that she was nothing but misery—whoever, saw her, saw it.

I was a 'graduate patient' of Dr Clair, as it happened; and had the usual enthusiasms of the class. Also I had learned some rudiments of the method, as one must who has profited by it. By the merest touch of interest and considerate attention I had the 'symptoms'—more than were needed; by a few indicated 'cases I had known' I touched that spring of special pride in special misery which seems to be co-existent with life; and then I had an account which would have been more than enough for Dr Clair to work on.

Then I appealed to that queer mingling of this pride and of the deep instinct of social service common to all humanity, which Dr Clair had pointed out to me, and asked her—

'If you had an obscure and important physical disease you'd be glad to leave your body to be of service to science, wouldn't you?' She would—anyone would, of course.

'You can't leave your mind for an autopsy very well, but there's one thing you can do—if you will; and that is, give this clear and prolonged self-study you have made, to a doctor I know who is profoundly interested in neurasthenia—melancholia—all that kind of thing. I really think you'd be a valuable—what shall I say—exhibit.'

She gave a little muscular smile, a mere widening of the lips, the heavy gloom of her eyes unaltered.

'I have only money enough to go where I am going,' she said. 'I have just one thing to do there—that ought to be done before I—leave.'

There was no air of tragedy about her. She was merely dead, or practically so.

'Dr Clair's is not far from there, as it happens, and I know her well enough to be sure she'd be glad to have you come. You won't mind if I give you the fare up there—purely as a scientific experiment? There are others who may profit by it, you see.'

She took the money, looking at it as if she hardly knew what it was, saying dully: 'All right—I'll go.' And, after a pause, as if she had half forgotten it, 'Thank you.'

And some time later she added: 'My name is Octavia Welch.'

Dr Willy Clair—she was Southern, and really named Willy—was first an eager successful young teacher, very young. Then she spent a year or two working with atypical children. Then, profoundly interested, she plunged into the study of medicine and became as eager and successful a doctor as she had been a teacher. She specialized in psychopathic work, developed methods of her own, and with the initial aid of some of her numerous 'GPs' established a sanatorium in Southern California. There are plenty of such for 'lungers,' but this was of quite another sort.

She married, in the course of her full and rich career, one of her patients, a young man who was brought to her by his mother—a despairing ruin. It took five years to make him over, but it was done, and then they were married. He worshipped her; and she said he was the real mainstay of the business—and he was, as far as the business part of it went.

Dr Clair was about forty when I sent Octavia Welch up there. She had been married some six years, and had, among her other assets, two splendid children. But other women have husbands and children, also splendid—no one else had a psycho-sanatorium. She didn't call it that; the name on the stationery was just 'The Hills.'

On the southern face of the Sierra Madres she had bought a high-lying bit of mesa-land and steep-sided arroyo, and gradually added to it both above and below, until it was now quite a large extent of land. Also she had her own water; had built a solid little reservoir in her deepest canyon; had sunk an artesian well far up in the hills behind, ran a windmill to keep the water up, and used the overflow for power as well as for irrigation. That had made the whole place such garden land as only Southern California knows. From year to year, the fame of the place increased, and its income also, she built and improved; and now it was the most wonderful combination of peaceful, silent wilderness and blossoming fertility.

The business end of it was very simply managed. On one of the steep flat-topped mesas, the one nearest the town that lay so pleasantly in the valley below, she had built a comfortable, solid little Center surrounded by small tent-houses. Here she took ordinary patients, and provided them not only with good medical advice but with good beds and good food, and further with both work and play.

'The trouble with Sanatoriums,' said Dr Clair to me—we were friends since the teaching period, and when I broke down at my teaching I came to her and was mended—'is that the sick folks have nothing to do but sit about and think of themselves and their "cases." Now I let the relatives come too; some well ones are a resource; and I have one or more regularly engaged persons whose business it is to keep them busy—and amused.'

She did. She had for the weakest ones just chairs and hammocks; but these were moved from day to day so that the patient had new views. There was an excellent library, and all manner of magazines and papers. There were picture-puzzles too, with little rimmed trays to set them up in—they could be carried here and there, but not easily lost. Then there were all manner of easy things to learn to do; basket-work, spinning, weaving, knitting, embroidery; it cost very little to the patients and kept them occupied. For those who were able there was gardening and building—always some new little place going up, or a walk or something to make. Her people enjoyed life every day. All this was not compulsory, of course, but they mostly liked it.

In the evenings there was music, and dancing too, for those who were up to it; cards and so on, at the Center; while the others went off to their quiet little separate rooms. Everyone of them had a stove in it; they were as dry and warm as need be—which is more than you can say of most California places.

People wanted to come and board—well people, I mean—and from year to year she ran up more cheap comfortable little shacks, each with its plumbing, electric lights and heating—she had water-power, you see—and a sort of cafeteria place where they could eat together or buy food and take to their homes. I tell you it was popular. Mr Wolsey (that's her husband, but she kept on as Dr Clair) ran all this part of it, and ran it well. He had been a hotel man.

All this was only a foundation for her real work with the psychopathic cases. But it was a good foundation, and it paid in more ways than one. She not only had the usual string of Grateful Patients, but another group of friends among those boarders.

And there's one thing she did which is well worth the notice of other people who are trying to help humanity—or to make money—in the same way.

You know how a hotel will have a string of 'rules and regulations' strung up in every room? She had that—and more. She had a 'Plain Talk With Boarders' leaflet, which was freely distributed—a most amusing and useful document. I haven't one here to quote directly, but it ran like this:

You come here of your own choice, for your own health and pleasure, freely; and are free to go when dissatisfied. The comfort and happiness of such a place depends not only on the natural resources, on the quality of the accommodations, food, service and entertainment, but on the behavior of the guests.

Each visitor is requested to put in a complaint at the office, not only of fault in the management, but of objectionable conduct on the part of patrons.

Even without such complaint any visitor who is deemed detrimental in character or behavior will be requested to leave.

She did it too. She made the place so attractive, so *comfortable*, in every way so desirable, that there was usually a waiting list; and if one of these fault-finding old women, or noisy, disagreeable young men, or desperately flirtatious persons got in, Dr Clair would have it out with them.

'I am sorry to announce that you have been black-balled by seven of your fellow guests. I have investigated the complaints and find them well founded. We herewith return your board from date (that was always paid in advance) and shall require your room tomorrow.'

People didn't like to own to a thing like that—not and tell the truth. They did tell all manner of lies about the place, of course; but she didn't mind—there were far more people to tell the truth. I can tell you a boarding-place that is as beautiful, as healthful, as exquisitely clean and comfortable, and as reasonable as hers in price, is pretty popular. Then, from year to year, she enlarged and developed her plan till she had, I believe, the only place in the world where a sick soul could go and be sure of help.

Here's what Octavia Welch wrote about it. She showed it to me years later:

I was dead—worse than dead—buried—decayed—gone to foul dirt. In my body I still walked heavily—but out of accumulated despair I had slowly gathered about enough courage to drop that burden. Then I met the Friend on the train who sent me to Dr Clair. . . .

I sent the post-card, and was met at the train, by a motor. We went up and up—even I could see how lovely the country was—up into the clear air, close to those shaggy, steep dry mountains.

We passed from ordinary streets with pretty homes through a region of pleasant groups of big and little houses which the driver said was the 'boarding section,' through a higher place where he said there were 'lungers and such,' on to 'Dr Clair's Place.'

The Place was apparently just out of doors. I did not dream then of all the cunningly contrived walks and seats and shelters, the fruits and flowers just where they were wanted, the marvellous mixture of natural beauty and ingenious loving-kindness, which make this place the wonder it is. All I saw was a big beautiful wide house, flower-hung, clean and quiet, and this nice woman, who received me in her office, just like any doctor, and said:

'I'm glad to see you, Mrs Welch. I have the card announcing your coming, and you can be of very great service to me, if you are willing. Please understand—I do not undertake to cure you; I do not criticize in the least your purpose to leave an unbearable world. That I think is the last human right—to cut short unbearable and useless pain. But if you are willing to let me study you awhile and experiment on you a little—it won't hurt, I assure you—'

Sitting limp and heavy, I looked at her, the old slow tears rolling down as usual. 'You can do anything you want to,' I said. 'Even hurt—what's a little more pain?—if it's any use.'

She made a thorough physical examination, blood-test and all. Then she let me tell her all I wanted to about myself, asking occasional questions, making notes, setting it all down on a sort of chart. 'That's enough to show me the way for a start,' she said. 'Tell me—do you dread anaesthetics?'

'No,' said I, 'so that you give me enough.'

'Enough to begin with,' she said cheerfully. 'May I show you your room?'

It was the prettiest room I had ever seen, as fair and shining as the inside of a shell.

'You are to have the bath treatment first,' she said, 'then a sleep—then food—I mean to keep you very busy for a while.'

So I was put through an elaborate course of bathing, shampoo, and massage, and finally put to bed, in that quiet fragrant rosy room, so physically comfortable that even my corroding grief and shame were forgotten, and I slept.

It was late next day when I woke. Someone had been watching all the time, and at any sign of waking a gentle anaesthetic was given, quite unknown to me. My special attendant, a sweet-faced young giantess from Sweden, brought me a tray of breakfast and flowers, and asked if I liked music.

'It is here by your bed,' she said. 'Here is the card—you ask for what you like, and just regulate the sound as you please.'

There was a light movable telephone, with a little megaphone attached to the receiver, and a long list of records. I had only to order what I chose, and listen to it as close or as far off as I desired. Between certain hours there was a sort of 'table d'hôte' to which we could listen or not as we liked, and these other hours wherein we called for favorites. I found it very restful. There were books and magazines, if I chose, and a rose-draped balcony with a hammock where I could sit or lie, taking my music there if I preferred. I was bathed and oiled and rubbed and fed; I slept better than I had for years, and more than I knew at the time, for when the restless misery came up they promptly put me to sleep and kept me there.

Dr Clair came in twice a day, with notebook and pencil, asking me many careful questions; not as a physician to a patient, but as an inquiring scientific searcher for valuable truths. She told me about other cases, somewhat similar to my own, consulted me in a way, as to this or that bit of analysis she had made; and again and again as to certain points in my own case. Insensibly under her handling this grew more and more objective, more as if it were someone else who was suffering, and not myself.

'I want you to keep a record, if you will,' she said, 'when the worst paroxysms come, the overwhelming waves of despair, or that slow tidal ebb of misery—here's a little chart by your bed. When you feel the worst will you be so good as to try either of these three things, and note the result. The Music, as you have used it, noting the effect of the different airs. The Color—we have not introduced you to the color treatment yet—see here—'

She put in my hand a little card of buttons, as it were, with wire attachments. I pressed one; the room was darkened, save for the tiny glow by which I saw the color list. Then, playing on the others, I could fill the room with any lovely hue I chose, and see them driving, mingling, changing as I played.

'There,' she said, 'I would much like to have you make a study of these effects and note it for me. Then—don't laugh!—I want you to try tastes, also. Have you never noticed the close connection between a pleasant flavor and a state of mind?'

For this experiment I had a numbered set of little sweetmeats, each delicious and all beneficial, which I was to deliberately use when my misery was acute or wearing. Still further, she had a list of odors for similar use.

This bedroom and balcony treatment lasted a month, and at the end of that time I was so much stronger physically that Dr Clair said, if I could stand it, she wanted to use certain physical tests on me. I almost hated to admit how much better I felt, but told her I would do anything she said. Then I was sent out with my attending maiden up the canyon to a certain halfway house. There I spent another month of physical enlargement. Part of it was slowly graduated mountain climbing; part was bathing and swimming in a long narrow pool. I grew gradually to feel the delight of mere ascent, so that every hilltop called me, and the joy of plain physical exhaustion and utter rest. To come down from a day on the mountain, to dip deep in that pure water and be rubbed by my ever careful masseuse; to eat heartily of the plain but delicious food, and sleep—out of doors now, on a pine needle bed—that was new life.

My misery and pain and shame seemed to fade into a remote past, as a wholesome rampart of bodily health grew up between me and it.

Then came the People.

This was her Secret. She had People there who were better than Music and Color and Fragrance and Sweetness,—People who lived up there with work and interests of their own, some teachers, some writers, some makers of various things, but all Associates in her wonderful cures.

It was the People who did it. First she made my body as strong as might be, and rebuilt my worn-out nerves with sleep—sleep—sleep. Then I had the right Contact, Soul to Soul.

And now? Why now I am still under forty; I have a little cottage up here in these heavenly hills; I am a well woman; I earn my living by knitting and teaching it to others. And out of the waste and wreck of my life—which is of small consequence to me, I can myself serve to help new-comers. I am an Associate—even I! And I am Happy!

A SURPLUS WOMAN

HER father was killed in the war. He was a doctor, executed by a well-directed shell that destroyed a hospital; a most efficient shell—some of those wounded might have recovered.

Her brother was killed in the war. He was a non-combatant on principle, a stretcher-bearer, picked off by a well-aimed bullet; a most efficient bullet—why encourage the work of salvage?

Her lover was killed in the war. He was a soldier pure and simple, who expected to be killed and was not disappointed. He had not, however, expected to be burned alive, not having been educated in those methods of warfare.

Moreover most of the young men she knew were killed in the war; and hundreds of thousands of young men she did not know. As there had already been a large majority of surplus women in her country, even before the wholesale destruction of a whole generation of masculine youth, the result was as plain as an example in simple arithmetic; there were now over a million women who could not marry—and she was one of them.

Her younger sister, who was very pretty and as frisky as a healthy kitten, tossed her gay curls and said she wouldn't give up! She'd wait for some of these nice young boys who were growing so fast and not give them a chance to wait for the still younger girls also growing.

'No single blessedness for me!' said Miss Betty.

Her older sister, who was a widow, but not permanently discouraged, also declined to give up, though she did not say so. She shook her head slowly under its flowing veil of crepe and said that loneliness was cruelly hard for a woman. And there were still many men who had been too old to go to the war—this was vaguely in her mind. 'A woman's place is the home,' said Mrs Watson.

We should not overlook one remaining male relative, Uncle Percy. The girls had always called him Uncle, because he was more than old enough to be one, but he was really only a cousin.

Forerunner, 7:5 (May 1916), 1–6.

As he possessed a most exalted sense of duty, both his own duty and those of other persons, he had come to visit them after Dr Page's death, in order to lend some masculine dignity to the distressed family. This visit continued and repeated itself until Uncle Percy became quite a fixture. At first it had been of some assistance to Mrs Page, and quite possibly she accepted his presence as another of her 'duties'; he certainly interpreted it as his.

Betty did not mind him at all; rather coquetted with the old gentleman indeed, and he made quite a pet of her.

Mrs Watson declared him invaluable—he used to divide his visits with her, before Mr Peters assumed headship of that household.

But Susan found him wearing and irritating in the extreme because of his ceaseless emission of advice. Sometimes it was a heavy rain, sometimes a cloudburst, but always a depressing drizzle. She did not enjoy advice.

Susan Page was not pretty, not frisky, not clinging, not 'domestic.' She had expected to knock about the world with her soldier-man, and while not herself of a belligerent disposition, she greatly admired the fine organization and high purpose of the army.

As long as the war lasted she had worked hard enough to keep down her pain. There was nursing at the front, where she had learned much not merely in the exacting labors of her calling, but in the patience and strength of the sufferers all about her. The sum of that suffering was so great that her own part of it could not monopolize her.

Being sent home to recover from a serious illness, her convalescent interest and returning strength were devoted to the constructive activities of the country; the careful organizations which were handling the civil problems of the time,—the sick and wounded, the refugees, the cripples, the blind, the deaf and dumb, the widows and orphans of soldiers. In all this flood of misery and loss she could not presume to overestimate her own.

'It's not just my sorrow,' she told herself. 'It is *our* sorrow. It is on us all. Why should I pick out mine to fuss over?'

And she did not fuss; she worked.

Having a natural taste for large organized activities, and the vivid experience of her hospital work, as well as the civil undertakings which followed, she had been a most useful helper through all that terrible time of stress and service.

Now it was over. The war was ended; the nation breathed again. The helpless were cared for and the half-helpless placed where they could do something for themselves. The men not killed or wounded came back, and took the places saved for them, the places which in their absence had been filled by women. All the wheels began to turn again, slowly and creakingly at first, as the great country turned from its old task of warfare to the new task of reconstruction.

Susan Page was dispossessed of the place she had held, as were so many others. She now became one of a larger army than that which had been slain; one of more than a million surplus women.

Susan's grandmother was Irish, a woman of wit and resource, with that streak of genius so frequent among her people. Her mother was Scotch, a stern sense of duty harnessing her unusual statesmanlike abilities to the routine of a mercilessly well-managed household. A strain of Welsh blood was in Susan's veins also; the touch of mystic devotion, the dream of music and beauty. She was an excellent representative of Great Britain; and what she had she held.

Now, twenty-eight, with all her personal life in ruins, the family fortune gone, her mother and grandmother still to be cared for, she faced the years before her.

Betty was provided for; for Mrs Watson was now Mrs Peters, and had her home in London, where she said Betty would have more advantages. So Betty went to live with her, thankfully, and waited for her schoolboy.

Susan had no illusions. As a girl she was not misled by baseless hopes, and now—with such grim facts behind her, she was not likely to delude herself.

'Twenty-eight,' said Susan. 'Mother is fifty-two, strong and eager as ever. Grandmother is seventy-five, and both vigorous and cheerful. I probably have forty or fifty years to live, anyhow. What is the best thing to do?'

In the matter of what was to be done, both by Susan and her countless fellow sufferers, Uncle Percy had much to say.

'It is a lamentable misfortune to the country,' quoth he, solemnly to Mrs Page, who listened with her self-contained patient unsmiling air; and to Susan, who was not so patient nor so easily able to control herself. 'It is an unmitigated disaster—this vast mass of helpless women turned loose upon our hands. This is one of the most cruel consequences of war, an economic injury quite outside the pain of bereavement.'

He looked at the widowed, son-less mother, the pre-widowed girl, with solemn sympathy, but neither of them seemed grateful.

'Here are a million bread-winners gone, a million producers of wealth, and we are left with many more than that number of dependent females, consumers only; denied their natural place and power; merely adding to the expenses of the nation. You, my dear Margaret,' he had a deep respect and some affection for Mrs Page, 'are fortunately provided for, though but narrowly, and your daughters shall not suffer while I live.' Uncle Percy was not rich; but he had enough money to keep him living in idleness as a gentleman should. He certainly was not a producer.

He seemed to expect some response from Susan, so she said: 'Thank you, Uncle Percy,' and soon went to her own room, where she did much clear and careful thinking.

Presently, with a dry smile, she determined to 'call a meeting.'

'That's the way they begin,' she told herself. 'I'll get Eleanore to do it.'

The meeting was not a large one. There was Lady Eleanore, now the sole survivor of the Wardours of Wardour Hall. She was a neighbor, and a close friend since early girlhood. Gertrude Murray, the tall dark sturdy girl from Manchester, and Joan Whyte from Devon were friends she had made while nursing, and while working in London. Little Mrs Bates from the village was a plump rosy woman, bubbling over with energy, who had proved her executive force in the crowding activities of local relief work. Lady Eleanore had an immense respect for her, though Mr Bates had kept a shop—before the war took him; and his wife had kept it since, or tried to.

The five women gathered in the big shadowy drawing-room of The Hall. All had been brought out by the war, out from their previous limitations, aspirations, and contentments. Everyone of them was larger and stronger, abler, more open to idea and to action, because of that cataclysmic experience. They had been democratized by it, not merely in theory, but in the practise of associate labor. Lady Eleanore, eager and devoted, had been in the hospital work for a while, till sent home with her invalided husband; she had learned to know Gertrude and Joan, one at the front, one in the equally necessary civic work; and to honor their courage and ability. As for Susan, she had worked with them all; she loved them all; she knew them all; and felt sure of her ground.

They had their tea, chatting a little of what Mrs Carson could do, of Maud Westcote's search for employment, and the needs of Molly Masters, and the Simpson girls, till Lady Eleanore said:

'Now, Susan, this is all your doings. You will have to make us a speech to begin with.'

Susan looked around her with her guarded earnest little smile, studying each strong kind face in its different grade of power.

'My speech will be mostly questions,' she said. 'I want a real discussion, a definite long-distance planning as to what "we-all" are to do.'

'"We-all"?' Lady Eleanor looked at her inquiringly.

'It's an expression they have in The States,' Susan said. 'I read in a story. "We-all" and "you-all"—I think it very expressive. What I mean by "we-all" is all we women of England who are dispossessed, now, at one time—more than a million of us.'

'It is a very grave question,' agreed Lady Eleanore.

'They can go back to the land—some of them,' urged Joan Whyte. She had been one active in managing the farm-laboring women movement during the war, and believed in it.

'Not by millions, Joan,' protested Miss Murray. 'The men have something to say, and the land on this island is a bit limited. But there are all the trades—some women have proved their abilities—it's a matter of competition, I suppose.'

Mrs Bates shook her head firmly. 'That's all very well for those who have the ability, but how about those who haven't? Just plain working-women, widows and girls, by hundreds of thousands, who have no trade at all—and the men all back now taking up every place there is. Not that I blame 'em,' she added hastily. 'We've no call to support 'em in idleness.'

'There are many of us interested in this problem, Susan, as of course you know,' Lady Eleanore gently suggested. 'It is proposed that we secure a grant from the government to establish schools, technical schools, I mean, and to devise means of employment for as many as possible.'

Susan smiled a little more warmly. 'Yes, I know. But—do we need it?'

They looked at her, waiting, and she began to speak, eagerly.

'You know what they say about us—call us "surplus women", say we are "denied our natural functions", and have become "an economic burden on the state", call the men "producers", and us "consumers". And then here's this talk about a "grant" for us, about government aid and so on. It is like—why it is like the way they talked about the suddenly enfranchised negroes in the States.'

'Well——' Lady Eleanore narrowed her fine eyes with an air of judicial consideration. 'There are points in common, Susan.'

'Perhaps—but there are points of difference also. What I have to suggest is this: Everyone of us women, given suitable occupation, is able to produce more than she consumes, even now. Very well; now if we can do three things: A, develop our opportunities; B, increase our efficiency; and, C, decrease our expenses—then we should become not only an independent class of citizens, but a productive class—a positive benefit to the community.'

'That's all true enough,' agreed Gertrude Murray, 'but what miracle is going to do all this?'

'No miracle at all,' answered Susan calmly. 'Just the laws of nature! What we ought to realize first is that this is not a personal matter; it is a social phenomenon. It is sudden and of course, transient, but the practical fact is that we constitute an enormous body of women who must be celibates.'

'Unless——' commented Gertrude grimly.

'Oh, yes, I know the "unlesses". But we women of England are not going to accept polygamy, much less prostitution. No— we are a vast mass of enforced celibates. We know perfectly well that the way to bear it is to fill our lives with work that is loved and honored, big satisfying work which not only tires us and feeds us, but fills our hearts.'

'We can't all be reformers—even if we earn our living by it,' urged Joan.

'Of course not—nor do we wish to be. But here is what I have in mind: a simple form of organization, with some straightforward name like the Women's Economic Alliance, which shall have for its purpose those three things I spoke of: to develop the opportunity, to increase the efficiency, and to decrease the expenses of women.'

'Go on,' they said, as she looked around for comment.

'Of course I have only a sketch of it in mind,' she continued; 'but it would be something like this. A headquarters in town, of course; in the very best hands; women known and trusted by everybody. There would be at first a mass of secretarial and research work to do; no less than listing and classifying all the women who wished to join; sending in name, address, capacity, preferred occupation, and one shilling.'

'Some mightn't have it,' suggested Joan.

'We'd begin with those who had—there would be plenty, and that would carry expenses from the start.

'The first duty of this organization would be to open a national employment agency for women, with branch after branch till every town and village had its "WEA" office. Then all those who wanted to employ women could have an authoritative place of reference, and the workers too. That would be to take the best advantage of existing conditions.

'Second comes the educational work; to be developed as fast as our funds increased. It could begin with small local classes—you see how this works, locally, don't you? Say that we here, with Lady Eleanore to head it, proceeded to take a little economic census of women, classify it, and send it in to headquarters; then we could open evening classes for such of our girls as had no trade whatever, and not only give them such special instruction as we could, but general education too, lectures, cinema pictures, legitimate helpfulness. In time we'd have a high grade vocational college, with branches everywhere, with a traveling library, with a special corps of lectures and teachers—we would deliberately plan to lift the standard of efficiency among all our women.'

'What's to make them come in?' questioned Gertrude.

'Economic advantage of course. Prompt and reliable employment service. The help of solidarity. Every year would build up the value of our "WEA" recommendation.'

'"WE Alliance",' said Gertrude, '"WE All"—there's your "we-all"!'

'All right—go on—how are you going to decrease living expenses?'

'By the simplest of economic devices; the same old easy method of organization. The reason we never could do it before was because of the concentric force of the family circle. Now, because we women have lost our chance of having any family circle, we are—by virtue of our misfortune—able to combine.'

A steady courage shone on each face. Every one of them had lost that chance—and they knew how many more were with them.

'Don't you see,' urged Susan. 'It's no fault of ours. We haven't *wanted* to be celibates. The men are—gone, that's all. And it leaves us in the same class as the bees and ants everybody's always quoting. We can't be mothers, but can be——Co-Mothers, Sisters, Co-Workers for the common good.'

'I thought all this was for our own advantage,' said Gertrude.

'It has to be, primarily. What we have to do first is to take ourselves off the shoulders of our men; to show that we are not mere consumers, but producers also. See, now. Each of us women, to live, has to pay for food, clothing, shelter, service. Now this organization will establish, one after another, residence groups, which will at the same time furnish employment to some of our members and living accommodations to others.

'Take the one field of laundry work; in a given village there is just so much of this work to be done. A "WEA Laundry" is opened, meeting the needs of the town, regularly employing as many laundresses as are needed, and doing the work of all WEA members at cost price. A "WEA Bakery and Cook-Shop", "WEA Sewing and Mending rooms"—millinery—dressmaking—all *organized*, all furnishing steady employment on the one hand and reduced rates to members on the other. It is good economics—not a new device.'

'And living accommodations?'

'Yes—in the big towns we will open Club-houses; not "Homes," you know, but agreeable club-houses for working women of different grades and at different rates, but—all WEA.

Then our producing groups play into the hands of all our living groups——'

Joan Whyte sat up suddenly. 'I see!' she said. 'We have women on the land—small farmers—market gardeners—fruit-raisers—jam-makers—poultry, eggs, butter——'

'Exactly,' said Susan. 'Little by little we "consumers" become producers. We learn to raise our own food—as cheaply as we can, with good conditions and wages for the workers.'

'I see, too,' said Gertrude. 'We work productively, and not competitively; for pure human advantage—not to scrape profits off each other. It's good business.'

'Of course I'm looking way ahead—and it is a splendid picture. You see any woman could join. Rich women could, to profit by the employment bureau, and the reliable products—no sweat-shops, no starving laborers—no exploitation; and poor women would be enormously advantaged by the wide labor exchange, the reduced living expenses, and the educational features. There need not be any more of these helpless "unskilled" girls—after a few years.

'But immediately, and locally, we can begin just where we live, starting one WEA branch after another——'

'They are not branches, Susan,' suggested Lady Eleanore, 'they are roots, separate plants that "run" like strawberries. Also the Central Bureau can begin at once. I'll write to Maud Russell—and Constance Howard—the registration and employment part can start at once. All we need to begin with is a little money for initial advertising—there'll be no trouble about that.'

'I can reach every girl in the village, with no expense whatever,' suggested Mrs Bates, 'and so can others in their villages. All it needs is somebody to go around and talk about it. You can do that, Miss Page, I'm sure.'

'I can try,' said Susan.

In ordinary times a plan like this would have had a hard time in reaching the consciousness of the people; a harder time in rousing action. But this period was one of wide social upheaval, of hearts exalted, of eyes opened to large issues. Moreover these 'Surplus Women' were an immediate problem, by some considered an immediate menace.

The Central Bureau was opened at once, under the most

reliable management, and its appeal for registration promptly and widely answered. The existing field of employment was soon filled—and then the Alliance set to work on its growing task of education, organization, and industrial development.

As an immediate meeting of a public need its usefulness was undeniable.

As an educational influence it became a power with no visible limits.

And then, from year to year, its income growing from steadily enlarging membership and from its widening industrial enterprise, it became a power in wealth as well as in enlightment and organization, a band of protection and defense, a basis of safety, a source of hope and a steady inspiration to all those women, no longer a 'surplus' but a benefit to the whole nation.

'It is against nature,' said Uncle Percy. 'Women cannot work together.'

'See us do it,' replied Susan cheerfully.

JOAN'S DEFENDER

JOAN'S mother was a poor defense. Her maternal instinct did not present that unbroken front of sterling courage, that measureless reserve of patience, that unfailing wisdom which we are taught to expect of it. Rather a broken reed was Mrs Marsden, broken in spirit even before her health gave way, and her feeble nerves were unable to stand the strain of adjudicating the constant difficulties between Joan and Gerald.

'Mother! Mo-o-ther!' would rise a protesting wail from the little girl. 'Gerald's pulling my hair!'

'Cry baby!' her brother would promptly retort. 'Tell tale! Run to mother—do!'

Joan did—there was no one else to run to—but she got small comfort.

'One of you is as much to blame as the other,' the invalid would proclaim. And if this did not seem to help much: 'If he teases you, go into another room!'

Whether Mrs Marsden supposed that her daughter was a movable body and her son a fixed star as it were, did not appear, but there was small comfort to be got from her.

'If you can't play nicely together you must be separated. If I hear anything more from you I'll send you to your room—now be quiet!'

So Joan sulked, helplessly, submitted to much that was painful and more that was contumelious, and made little remonstrance. There was, of course, a last court of appeal, or rather a last threat—that of telling father.

'I'll tell father! I'll tell father! Then you'll be sorry!' her tormentor would chant, jumping nimbly about just out of reach, if she had succeeded in any overt act of vengeance.

'I shall have to tell your father!' was the last resource of the mother on the sofa.

If father was told, no matter by whom, the result was always the same—he whipped them both. Not so violently, to be sure, and Joan secretly believed less violently in Gerald's case than in hers, but it was an ignominious and unsatisfying punishment which both avoided.

'Can't you manage to keep two children in order?' he would demand of his wife. 'My mother managed eleven—and did the work of the house too.'

'I wish I could, Bert, dear,' she would meekly reply. 'I do try—but they are so wearying. Gerald is too rough, I'm afraid. Joan is always complaining.'

'I should think she was!' Mr Marsden agreed irritably. 'Trust a woman for that!'

And Joan, though but nine years old, felt that life was not worth living, being utterly unjust. She was a rather large-boned, meager child, with a whiney voice, and a habit of crying, 'Now stop!' whenever Gerald touched her. Her hair was long, fine and curly, a great trouble to her as well as to her mother. Both were generally on edge for the day, before those curls were all in order, and their principal use appeared to be as handles for Gerald, who was always pulling them. He was a year and a half older than Joan, but not much bigger, and of a somewhat puny build.

Their father, a burly, loud-voiced man, heavy of foot and of hand, looked at them both with ill-concealed disapproval, and did not hesitate to attribute the general deficiencies of his family wholly to their feeble mother and her 'side of the house.'

'I'm sure I was strong as a girl, Bert—you remember how I used to play tennis, and I could dance all night.'

'Oh I remember,' he would answer. 'Blaming your poor health on me, I suppose—that seems to be the way nowadays. I don't notice that other women give out just because they're married and have two children—*two!*' he repeated scornfully, as if Mrs Marsden's product were wholly negligible. 'And one of them a girl!'

'Girls are no good!' Gerald quickly seconded. 'Girls can't fight or climb or do anything. And they're always hollering. Huh! I wouldn't be a girl—!' Words failed him.

Such was their case, as it says so often in the *Arabian Nights*, and then something pleasant happened. Uncle Arthur came for a little visit, and Joan liked him. He was mother's brother, not father's. He was big, like father, but gentle and pleasant, and he had such a nice voice, jolly but not loud.

Uncle Arthur was a western man, with a ranch, and a large family of his own. He had begun life as a physician, but weak lungs drove him into the open. No one would ever think of him now as ever having been an invalid.

He stayed for a week or so, having some business to settle which dragged on for more days than had been counted on, and gave careful attention to the whole family.

Joan was not old enough, nor Mrs Marsden acute enough, to note the gradual disappearance of topic after topic from the conversation between Uncle Arthur and his host. But Mr Marsden's idea of argument was volume of sound, speed in repetition, and a visible scorn for those who disagreed with him, and as Arthur Warren did not excel in these methods he sought for subjects of agreement. Not finding any, he contented himself with telling stories, or listening—for which there was large opportunity.

He bought sweetmeats for the children, and observed that Gerald got three-quarters, if not more; brought them presents, and found that if Gerald did not enjoy playing with Joan's toys, he did enjoy breaking them.

He sounded Gerald, as man to man, in regard to these habits, but that loyal son, who believed his father to be a type of all that was worthy, and who secretly had assumed the attitude of scorn adopted by that parent toward his visitor, although civil enough, was little moved by anything his uncle might say.

Dr Warren was not at all severe with him. He believed in giving a child the benefit of every doubt, and especially the benefit of time.

'How can the youngster help being a pig?' he asked himself, sitting quite silent and watching Gerald play ball with a book just given to Joan, who cried 'Now sto-op!' and tried to get it away from him.

'Madge Warren Marsden!' he began very seriously, when the children were quarreling mildly in the garden, and the house was quiet: 'Do you think you're doing right by Joan—let alone Gerald? Is there no way that boy can be made to treat his sister decently?'

'Of course you take her part—I knew you would,' she answered fretfully. 'You always were partial to girls—having so many of your own, I suppose. But you've no idea how irritating Joan is, and Gerald is extremely sensitive—she gets on his nerves. As for *my* nerves! I have none left! Of course those children ought to be separated. By and by when we can afford it, we mean to send Gerald to a good school; he's a very bright boy—you must have noticed that?'

'Oh yes, he's bright enough,' her brother agreed. 'And so is Joan, for that matter. But look here, Madge—this thing is pretty hard on you, isn't it—having these two irreconcilables to manage all the time?'

The ready tears rose and ran over. 'Oh Arthur, it's awful! I do my best—but I never was good with children—and with my nerves—*you* know, being a doctor.'

He did know, rather more than she gave him credit for. She had responded to his interest with interminable details as to her symptoms and sensations, and while he sat patiently listening he had made a diagnosis which was fairly accurate. Nothing in particular was the matter with his sister except the fretful temper she was born with, idle habits, and the effects of an overbearing husband.

The temper he could not alter, the habits he could not change, nor the husband either, so he gave her up—she was out of his reach.

But Joan was a different proposition. Joan had his mother's eyes, his mother's smile—when she did smile; and though thin and nervous, she had no serious physical disability as yet.

'Joan worries you even more than Gerald, doesn't she?' he ventured. 'It's often so with mothers.'

'How well you understand, Arthur. Yes, indeed, I feel as if I knew just what to do with my boy, but Joan is a puzzle. She is so—unresponsive.'

'Seems to me you would be much stronger if you were less worried over the children.'

'Of course—but what can I do? It is my duty and I hope I can hold out.'

'For the children's sake you ought to be stronger, Madge. See here, suppose you lend me Joan for a long visit. It would be no trouble at all to us—we have eight, you know, and all outdoors for them to romp in. I think it would do the child good.'

The mother looked uncertain. 'It's a long way to let her go——' she said.

'And it would do Gerald good, I verily believe,' her brother continued. 'I've often heard you say that she irritates him.'

He could not bring himself to advance this opinion, but he could quote it.

'She does indeed, Arthur. I think Gerald would give almost no trouble if he was alone.'

'And you are of some importance,' he continued cheerfully. 'How about that? Let me borrow Joan for a year—you'll be another woman when you get rested.'

There was a good deal of discussion, and sturdy opposition from Mr Marsden, who considered the feelings of a father quite outraged by the proposal; but as Dr Warren did not push it, and as his wife suggested that in one way it would be an advantage— they could save toward Gerald's schooling—adding that her brother meant to pay all expenses, including tickets—he finally consented.

Joan was unaccountably reluctant. She clung to her mother, who said, 'There! There!' and kissed her with much emotion. 'It's only a visit, dearie—you'll be back to mother bye and bye!'

She kissed her father, who told her to be a good girl and mind her uncle and aunt. She would have kissed Gerald, but he said: 'Oh shucks!' and drew away from her.

It was a silently snivelling little girl who sat by the window, with Uncle Arthur reading the paper beside her, a little girl who felt as if nobody loved her in the whole wide world. He put a big arm around her and drew her to him. She snuggled up with a long sigh of relief. He took her in his lap, held her close, and told her interesting things about the flying landscape. She nestled close to him, and then, starting up suddenly to look at something, her hair caught on his buttons and pulled sharply.

She cried, as was her habit, while he disentangled it.

'How'd you like to have it cut off?' he asked.

'*I'd* like it—but mother won't let me. She says it's my only beauty. And father won't let me either—says I want to be a tom-boy.'

'Well, I'm in loco parentis now,' said Uncle Arthur, 'and I'll let you. Furthermore, I'll do it forthwith, before it gets tangled up to-night.'

He produced a pair of sharp little scissors, and a pocket-comb, and in a few minutes the small head looked like one of Sir Joshua Reynold's cherubs.

'You see I know how,' he explained, as he snipped cautiously, 'because I cut my own youngsters' on the ranch. I think you look prettier short than long,' he told her, and she found the little mirror between the windows quite a comfort.

Before the end of that long journey the child was more quietly happy with her uncle than she had ever been with either father or mother, and as for Gerald—the doctor's wise smile deepened.

'Irritated *him*, did she?' he murmured to himself. 'The little skate! Why, I can just see her *heal* now she's escaped.'

A big, high-lying California ranch, broad, restful sweeps of mesa and plain, purple hills rising behind. Flowers beyond dreams of heaven, fruit of every kind in gorgeous abundance. A cheerful Chinese cook and houseboy, who did their work well and seemed to enjoy it. The uncle she already loved, and an aunt who took her to her motherly heart at once.

Then the cousins—here was terror. And four of them boys— four! But which four? There they all were in a row, giggling happily, standing up to be counted, and to be introduced to their new cousin. All had short hair. All had bare feet. All had denim knicker-bockers. And all had been racing and tumbling and turning somersaults on the cushiony Bermuda grass as Joan and her uncle drove up.

The biggest one was a girl, tall Hilda, and the baby was a girl, a darling dimpled thing, and two of the middle ones. But the four boys were quite as friendly as Hilda, and seeing that their visitor was strangely shy, Jack promptly proposed to show her his Belgian hares, and Harvey to exhibit his Angora goats, and the whole of them trooped off hilariously.

'What a forlorn child!' said Aunt Belle. 'I'm glad you brought her, dear. Ours will do her good.'

'I knew you'd mother her, Blessing,' he said with a grateful kiss. 'And if ever a poor kid needed mothering, it's that one. You see, my sister has married a noisy pig of a man—and doesn't seem to mind it much. But she's become an invalid—one of these sofa women; I don't know as she'll ever get over it. And the other child's rather a mean cuss, I'm afraid. They love him the best. So I thought we'd educate Joan a bit.'

Joan's education was largely physical. A few weeks of free play, and then a few moments every day of the well-planned exercises Dr Warren had invented for his children. There were two ponies to ride; there were hills to climb; there was work to do in the well-irrigated garden. There were games, and I am obliged to confess, fights. Every one of those children was taught what we used to grandiloquently call 'the noble art of self-defense'; not only the skilled management of their hands, with swift 'foot-work,' but the subtler methods of jiu-jitsu.

'I took the course on purpose,' the father explained to his friends, 'and the kids take to it like ducks to water.'

To her own great surprise, and her uncle's delight, Joan showed marked aptitude in her new studies. In the hours of definite instruction, from books or in nature study and labora-tory work, she was happy and successful, but the rapture with which she learned to use her body was fine to see.

The lower reservoir made a good-sized swimming pool, and there she learned to float and dive. The big barn had a little simple apparatus for gymnastics in the rainy season, and the jolly companionship of all those bouncing cousins was an education in itself.

Dr Warren gave her special care, watched her food, saw to it that she was early put to bed on the wide sleeping porch, and trained her as carefully as if she had some tremendous contest before her. He trained her mind as well as her body. Those children were taught to reason, as well as to remember; taught to think for themselves, and to see through fallacious arguments. In body and mind she grew strong.

At first she whimpered a good deal when things hurt her, but finding that the other children did not, and that, though patient with her, they evidently disliked her doing it, she learned to take her share of the casualties of vigorous childhood without complaint.

At the end of the year Dr Warren wrote to his brother-in-law that it was not convenient for him to furnish the return ticket, or to take the trip himself, but if they could spare the child a while longer he would bring her back as agreed—that she was doing finely in all ways.

It was nearly two years when Joan Marsden, aged eleven, returned to her own home, a very different looking child from the one who left it so mournfully. She was much taller, larger, with a clear color, a light, firm step, a ready smile.

She greeted her father with no shadow of timidity, and rushed to her mother so eagerly as well-nigh to upset her.

'Why, child!' said the mother. 'Where's your beautiful hair? Arthur—how could you?'

'It is much better for her health,' he solemnly assured her. 'You see how much stronger she looks. Better keep it short till she's fourteen or fifteen.'

Gerald looked at his sister with mixed emotions. He had not grown as much. She was certainly as big as he was now. With her curls gone she was not so easy to hurt. However, there were other places. As an only child his disposition had not improved, and it was not long before that disposition led him to derisive remarks and then to personal annoyance, which increased as days passed.

She met him cheerfully. She met him patiently. She gave him fair warning. She sought to avoid his attacks, and withdrew herself to the far side of the garage, but he followed her.

'It's not fair, Gerald, and you know it,' said Joan. 'If you hurt me again I shall have to do something to you.'

'Oh you will, will you?' he jeered, much encouraged by her withdrawal, much amused by her threat. 'Let's see you do it—smarty! 'Fraid cat!' and he struck her again, a blow neatly planted, where the deltoid meets the biceps and the bone is near the surface.

Joan did not say, 'Now *stop*!' She did not whine, '*Please* don't!' She did not cry. She simply knocked him down.

And when he got up and rushed at her, furious, meaning to reduce this rebellious sister to her proper place, Joan set her teeth and gave him a clean thrashing.

'Will you give up?'

He did. He was glad to.

'Will you promise to behave? To let me alone?'

He promised.

She let him up, and even brushed off his dusty clothes.

'If you're mean to me any more, I'll do it again,' she said calmly. 'And if you want to tell mother—or father—or anybody—that I licked you, you may.'

But Gerald did not want to.

APPENDIX A

IMPRESS 'STORY STUDIES'

Story Studies: Rudyard Kipling

The author chosen for study in the issue of October 6th was Rudyard Kipling.

None of our younger writers have made a more distinctive impression upon literature than has this Anglo-Indian.

The first and clearest impression given by his work is that of strength. Here is a voice to which you do not have to listen with strained ears as you do to the dull monotone of some of our realists, the irregular screams and gasps of some of our romanticists, and the receding whispers of those who seek in ever-weakening faintness to touch the languid palate of the age.

Kipling is strong with the wholesome natural power that appeals to children, that would have appealed to early peoples who knew no literature but the epic, and that still appeals to the submerged reader of this century. He simply says what he has to say with the fierce brevity of the French, yet constantly modifies that fierceness with the gentlest and most musical phrases, so that the ear is never wearied, even with a monotony of freshness.

Besides this first essential quality are many more beyond the limits of these paragraphs, which aim to show merely what points of our author's style were brought out in last week's story.

The name is easily Kiplingesque, as in 'The Rescue of Pluffles,' 'The Madness of Private Ortheris,' etc. The initial stanza, from some ballad that never was written, and more in the body of the tale—always begging his pardon for verses in mere burlesque—these points are also easily recognizable.

Then the nature of the story itself, a thing of minor importance treated with all the gravity of a great theme; and the cheerful reference to characters unknown save by that passing mention, yet so handled as to live vividly before you. This is one of Kipling's marked distinctions. The very familiarity of his

touch, and the lightness of his allusion, carries with it by impli-
cation a full and friendly acquaintance with the persons concerned. The pseudonym of 'The Galoot,' the little fling at a
foreign phraseology in an italicized 'yahoo,' the putting of
periods where commas ought to grow, and the occasional bracing
snap of a far-fetched comparison—these are the salient points on
which is based 'The Misleading of Pendleton Oaks.'

It is interesting to remark, in this connection, that there is a far
better example of the same thing in the October *Overland*, by
Frank Norris—'Outward and Visible Signs.'

Merely as a title this is good, and the subtitle, 'After Strange
Gods,' makes it better. Then the Oriental coloring and contrast,
using only the Chinese charmer instead of the Hindu, is more
broadly and recognizably Kipling than a mere society story.
The style is perfect. A closer and more scholarly study it would
be hard to find. The very beginning—'This is not my story'—
strikes the Kipling note unerringly; and it does not
cease to ring till the closing paragraph: 'This is the story as my
friend, Kew Wen Lung, the *gong toi* told it to me. Personally, I
do not believe very much of it; however, you may have it for
what it is worth.' The plot, action and treatment are admirably
rendered; and some touches are simply inimitable in their perfect expression of the very spirit and body of Kipling's work. Mr
Norris offers no prize for guessing the model of his study, however, and has indeed omitted to indicate in any way that it is an
imitation.

This, to return to our author's manner, is sometimes called by
another name.

Impress (13 October 1894), 2.

Story Studies: Mary E. Wilkins

She whose brief and simple tales so well bring up to us the
piteous starved lives of the New England villages and outlying
farms, Miss Mary E. Wilkins, was the subject of study in our last
week's story. Miss Wilkins' style looks very easy at first, easy to

adopt and handle. Some country dialect, a strain of pathos, clear local color, and bits of vivid personal description, vivid, yet very delicate and simple; these seem at first sight to be Miss Wilkins. But there is much more in her. Under the dialect and color, under the pathos and the description, in the very least and briefest of these stories, lies a whole human life. Sometimes several, always some one. And this life is revealed not by direct narration, but by subtle side and rear touches; by what seems almost a chance phrase, yet which reveals years of tragedy in its casual mention.

The sum of her work is a patient melancholy, broken by occasional light gleams of hope. Two notes of grief are sounded oftenest,—failure to marry, and failure to pay the mortgage. Also there is the frequent spectre of family intolerance and oppression.

'A Day's Berryin'' in THE IMPRESS of October 13th has the New England *locale* very strongly, and the New England dialect. The pathos is there, too, but, as is Miss Wilkins' way, it is only hinted at and shown by inference. The characteristic touch in personal description is not fully given, but the suggestion of buried lives—of the patient martyrdom that makes no sign and bears the pang without the palm—this is clearly shown in the pictures of three at least of these scant characters.

Impress (20 October 1894), 5.

Story Studies: Nathaniel Hawthorne

Nathaniel Hawthorne, so widely known and honored as one of the distinctive glories of American literature, was the model chosen for the study in THE IMPRESS of October 27th.

Not the greatest and deepest characteristics of so great and deep a writer could be rendered in this brief story. Indeed its brevity was one of the essential difficulties in this case, the style of Hawthorne being comparatively diffuse. But the superficial qualities are fairly represented, notably the general air of gloom and quiet with which his writings are infused.

This sombre hush is entered upon with the first sentence, and well maintained, with the careful touches of light in the scarlet flowered bean vines and bright cheeked sister which do but enhance the prevailing depression. The slow but elegant diction is also followed with some accuracy; and the old New England background is, of course, easily put in. But the most Hawthornesque feature is in the character of the story itself: the tone of sadness and hint of supernaturalism, the family strain of pride and unforgiven injury long past, and the sudden dark catastrophe which brings it to an end.

To be more fully like our author would have required more space, more room for filling in the background with those delicate touches which so clearly bring out the scenery and personages involved, yet keep so well the dark, cool tone of the picture. In some authors the most essential distinction is in a certain long-windedness. Scott, for instance, would be impossible to treat in these limits save in an extract. But Hawthorne has enough of shorter tales to make this pass unmistakably.

Impress (3 November 1894), 4.

Story Studies: George Eliot

In the eighth of our series of studies in literature, George Eliot is represented. The fragment of a chapter, which was all that it was possible to give in her own marked style, hints at a deep, strong character growing up under conditions of difficulty in one sense and of great freedom and power in another.

The general scheme of color, of quiet English village life some fifty or sixty years ago, the subdued, even tone of the treatment, and the flowing elaboration of a clear but somewhat heavy style, these are all George Eliot; but there is necessarily lacking in this brief attempt that sweeping breadth of vision, deep insight, and wide scholarship which make the author of 'Romola' so great a power in literature.

It is interesting to compare the diction of this noted author, still so much a standard, with the increasing brevity and fluency of our modern writers. We seek to express an idea with the least expense of words, strengthening it by skillful harmonies and contrasts,—by 'value' rather than elaborate richness of color and form.

The old school, for all its heavy ornament and rich coloring, seems dull when compared with the ringing tones, the sudden surprises and soft gradations of color in the work of to-day.

Impress (1 December 1894), 5.

Story Studies: Louisa May Alcott

Every girl in America ought to be able to recognize the author given in 'Five Girls.' There might well have been a moment's hesitation between one and another of our young girls' favorites. Mrs A. D. T. Whitney might well have had a thought, and some few others; but none of them all has the breezy swing and warm cheerfulness of our old favorite Louisa M. Alcott.

In this little sketch, the points of composition kept in view are these: the dealing with earnest, gay, young people as characters; the whole-souled indifference to detail; the broad humanitarian trend, the insistence on happy family life, and on freedom and progress. In style, the little trick of three adjectives together, the general swift ease of handling, and the strongly personal trait of finishing a sentence in conversation with the act of the person speaking: as, '"Indeed we will!" said Kate, and rushed out of the room.' Or, '"O girls, they've come! They've come!" and pretty Susan fairly flew down stairs to meet them, while Rob pranced madly after.'

Impress (8 December 1894), 5.

Story Studies: Edgar Allan Poe

No reader and lover of Poe can fail to recognize something of his spirit in the mingled beauty and horror of 'The Unwatched Door.' The horror of Poe has a deeper hold on the reader than that of any lesser master of the same theme, because it is so closely allied to beauty. No crude brutality can give the convulsive thrill that at once drives you from and draws you toward the cause of sensation, as does this poetic, rhythmic touch which commands the attention and holds you in shuddering fascination. When the element of horror is allowed to verge on loathing, it no longer horrifies—it merely disgusts and repels.

Poe delights, while he harrows your feelings; it is an 'ecstacy of woe,' and you fairly enjoy your pain. The fantastic poise of his imagination is well given in this instance—the strange unreal setting with its deep chords of color and tone; the haunting melody of phrase and heavy clinging richness of expression pervading it all. It is an atmosphere like the tuberose and heliotrope odors of a funeral, and adds to the effect of horror with most subtle art of literature.

Impress (15 December 1894), 5.

Story Studies: Henry James

Our twelfth example of literary style, 'One Way Out,' falls a little short of the standard of excellence desired to be maintained in these studies; perhaps because the author represented is so finished in his mastery of the art of wordsmanship as to render imitation an inefficacious flattery.

The conception is like, very like, to those subtle modernities of thought, feeling and action, so keenly perceived and so exquisitely portrayed by Henry James; but the style lacks the inimitable firmness in delicacy, the 'iron-hand-in-the-velvet-glove' effect, which distinguishes this author.

If close comparison is made, much of resemblance, will be found, especially in the limitless finesse of the conception. That the young medical student should be brought to realize the family fate, about to be concentrated by his marriage with his cousin; that, being a modern man, he should see the danger, and long to save her from the probable injury so entailed, and therefore prepare to give her up,—this is easily conceivable; but that he should so arrange for their disunion as to have the proposition come from her, and come from such cause as left no sting behind—this is a piece of ingenuity quite worthy of Mr James himself. Nevertheless, the execution is unequal and lacking in the deliberate finish of this master.

Impress (5 January 1895), 5.

Story Studies: Mark Twain

'An Unpatented Process,' in No. 15 of THE IMPRESS, was after the manner of our most noted American humorist, Mark Twain. Several guessers have confounded it with the more recent work of Stockton; but it has not that faint, undefinable absurdity which marks Stockton's touch. There is a sturdy reasonableness in the matter of the tale, and a gentle suggestive, irresistible humor in the treatment, which, while characteristic in the large sense of American humor as a whole, finds its most typical exponent in Mark Twain.

The young girl's special sensitiveness to social minutiae—objecting to a belated bridegroom; the numerous emotions of the attendant friends at the departure; the change in character being laid to a hypothetical change at nurse; and, perhaps most distinctive of all, the look in Nettie's eyes 'like Paracelsus or Archimedes or any of those absorbed experimentalists'—these are Twain's unmistakably.

Impress (26 January 1895), 3.

Story Studies: Edward Bellamy

'A Cabinet Meeting' in our last issue will be easily identified by almost every reader as after Edward Bellamy. It is not easy to give the exact personality in literary style in a case where the original has so little of this quality. 'Looking Backward' was a book of the age in its thought, but as literature it had little distinctive merit. So, in this presentation, no attempt is made at technique, but there is given the largeness of thought, the daring imagination, the careful, practical planning of detail, and the immense human love, which mark Bellamy's work.

To those who care only for style and nothing for idea, Mr Bellamy's books seem careless. But let any one follow for a moment the thought processes involved in some of these bald sentences, and they will see power enough, though it be not that of the literary artist. Writing has other uses beyond that of giving pleasure by its artistic excellence, and a man who can sway the thought of the age, as Mr Bellamy has swayed it, is no mean author. It is hoped that the conception involved in 'A Cabinet Meeting' is not unworthy of the writer represented.

Impress (12 January 1895), 3.

APPENDIX B

'WHY I WROTE "THE YELLOW WALLPAPER"?'

Many and many a reader has asked that. When the story first came out, in the *New England Magazine* about 1891, a Boston physician made protest in *The Transcript*. Such a story ought not to be written, he said; it was enough to drive anyone mad to read it.

Another physician, in Kansas I think, wrote to say that it was the best description of incipient insanity he had ever seen, and—begging my pardon—had I been there?

Now the story of the story is this:

For many years I suffered from a severe and continuous nervous breakdown tending to melancholia—and beyond. During about the third year of this trouble I went, in devout faith and some faint stir of hope, to a noted specialist in nervous diseases, the best known in the country. This wise man put me to bed and applied the rest cure, to which a still good physique responded so promptly that he concluded there was nothing much the matter with me, and sent me home with solemn advice to 'live as domestic a life as far as possible,' to 'have but two hours' intellectual life a day,' and 'never to touch pen, brush or pencil again, as long as I lived.' This was in 1887.

I went home and obeyed those directions for some three months, and came so near the border line of utter mental ruin that I could see over.

Then, using the remnants of intelligence that remained, and helped by a wise friend, I cast the noted specialist's advice to the winds and went to work again—work, the normal life of every human being; work, in which is joy and growth and service, without which one is a pauper and a parasite; ultimately recovering some measure of power.

Being naturally moved to rejoicing by this narrow escape, I wrote *The Yellow Wallpaper*, with its embellishments and additions to carry out the ideal (I never had hallucinations or objections to my mural decorations) and sent a copy to the physician who so nearly drove me mad. He never acknowledged it.

The little book is valued by alienists and as a good specimen of one kind of literature. It has to my knowledge saved one woman from a similar fate—so terrifying her family that they let her out into normal activity and she recovered.

But the best result is this. Many years later I was told that the great specialist had admitted to friends of his that he had altered his treatment of neurasthenia since reading *The Yellow Wallpaper*.

It was not intended to drive people crazy, but to save people from being driven crazy, and it worked.

Forerunner, 4 (October 1913), 271.

THE WORLD'S CLASSICS

A Select List

HANS ANDERSEN: Fairy Tales
Translated by L. W. Kingsland
Introduction by Naomi Lewis
Illustrated by Vilhelm Pedersen and Lorenz Frølich

LUDOVICO ARIOSTO: Orlando Furioso
Translated by Guido Waldman

ARISTOTLE: The Nicomachean Ethics
Translated by David Ross

JANE AUSTEN: Emma
Edited by James Kinsley and David Lodge

HONORÉ DE BALZAC: Père Goriot
Translated and Edited by A. J. Krailsheimer

CHARLES BAUDELAIRE: The Flowers of Evil
Translated by James McGowan
Introduction by Jonathan Culler

R. D. BLACKMORE: Lorna Doone
Edited by Sally Shuttleworth

MARY ELIZABETH BRADDON: Lady Audley's Secret
Edited by David Skilton

CHARLOTTE BRONTË: Jane Eyre
Edited by Margaret Smith

EMILY BRONTË: Wuthering Heights
Edited by Ian Jack

GEORG BÜCHNER:
Danton's Death, Leonce and Lena, Woyzeck
Translated by Victor Price

CHARLES DICKENS: Christmas Books
Edited by Ruth Glancy

Oliver Twist
Edited by Kathleen Tillotson

FEDOR DOSTOEVSKY: Crime and Punishment
Translated by Jessie Coulson
Introduction by John Jones

ARTHUR CONAN DOYLE:
Sherlock Holmes: Selected Stories
Introduction by S. C. Roberts

THEODORE DREISER: Jennie Gerhardt
Edited by Lee Clark Mitchell

ALEXANDRE DUMAS *fils*:
La Dame aux Camélias
Translated by David Coward

MARIA EDGEWORTH: Castle Rackrent
Edited by George Watson

GEORGE ELIOT: Daniel Deronda
Edited by Graham Handley

Felix Holt, The Radical
Edited by Fred C. Thompson

Selected Critical Writings
Edited by Rosemary Ashton

GUSTAVE FLAUBERT: Madame Bovary
Translated by Gerard Hopkins
Introduction by Terence Cave

A Sentimental Education
Translated by Douglas Parmée

ELIZABETH GASKELL: Cousin Phillis and Other Tales
Edited by Angus Easson

THOMAS HUGHES: Tom Brown's Schooldays
Edited by Andrew Sanders

HENRIK IBSEN: An Enemy of the People, The Wild Duck,
Rosmersholm
Edited and Translated by James McFarlane

Four Major Plays
Translated by James McFarlane and Jens Arup
Introduction by James McFarlane

HENRY JAMES: The Ambassadors
Edited by Christopher Butler

The Bostonians
Edited by R. D. Gooder

The Spoils of Poynton
Edited by Bernard Richards

M. R. JAMES: Casting the Runes and Other Ghost Stories
Edited by Michael Cox

JOCELIN OF BRAKELOND:
Chronicle of the Abbey of Bury St. Edmunds
Translated by Diana Greenway and Jane Sayers

GWYN JONES (Transl.):
Eirik the Red and Other Icelandic Sagas

BEN JONSON: Five Plays
Edited by G. A. Wilkes

JUVENAL: The Satires
Translated by Niall Rudd
Notes and Introduction by William Barr

RUDYARD KIPLING: Stalky & Co.
Edited by Isobel Quigly

MADAME DE LAFAYETTE: The Princesse de Clèves
Translated and Edited by Terence Cave

MOLIÈRE: Don Juan and Other Plays
Translated by George Graveley and Ian Maclean

GEORGE MOORE: Esther Waters
Edited by David Skilton

E. NESBIT: The Railway Children
Edited by Dennis Butts

ORIENTAL TALES
Edited by Robert L. Mack

OVID: Metamorphoses
Translated by A. D. Melville
Introduction and Notes by E. J. Kenney

EDGAR ALLAN POE: Selected Tales
Edited by Julian Symons

JEAN RACINE: Britannicus, Phaedra, Athaliah
Translated by C. H. Sisson

ANN RADCLIFFE: The Italian
Edited by Frederick Garber

THE MARQUIS DE SADE:
The Misfortune of Virtue and Other Early Tales
Translated and Edited by David Coward

PAUL SALZMAN (Ed.):
An Anthology of Elizabethan Prose Fiction

OLIVE SCHREINER: The Story of an African Farm
Edited by Joseph Bristow

SIR WALTER SCOTT: The Heart of Midlothian
Edited by Claire Lamont

MARY SHELLEY: Frankenstein
Edited by M. K. Joseph

ÉMILE ZOLA:
The Attack on the Mill and Other Stories
Translated by Douglas Parmée

Nana
Translated and Edited by Douglas Parmée

A complete list of Oxford Paperbacks, including The World's Classics, OPUS, Past Masters, Oxford Authors, Oxford Shakespeare, and Oxford Paperback Reference, is available in the UK from the Arts and Reference Publicity Department (BH), Oxford University Press, Walton Street, Oxford OX2 6DP.

In the USA, complete lists are available from the Paperbacks Marketing Manager, Oxford University Press, 200 Madison Avenue, New York, NY 10016.

Oxford Paperbacks are available from all good bookshops. In case of difficulty, customers in the UK can order direct from Oxford University Press Bookshop, Freepost, 116 High Street, Oxford, OX1 4BR, enclosing full payment. Please add 10 per cent of published price for postage and packing.